THE SOMETHING MORE

HK JACOBS

To everyone who has learned to accept the love they can't imagine
they deserve

CHAPTER ONE

AUTUMN, NOW

I possess the world's most potent olfactory bulb. So potent in fact that the mere whiff of something familiar sends me hurtling into the past, the scent grappling for a memory like an extended hook. And when it catches, a moment of my life unwinds like a movie reel in my brain.

Most of the time it's a good moment. Like when the smell of antiseptic with a tinge of sweat reminds me of the first surgery I ever performed. Or the whiff of lilacs and freshly mown grass reminds me of my mother.

Sometimes it's a bad moment like when I inhale the particularly potent odor of tequila, and I immediately taste dirt in my mouth. And rarely a certain smell coaxes open *the* moment. A moment so blissfully life-altering, so precious and wondrous that, at the time, I failed to appreciate how truly rare it was. The best moment of my entire life. And a moment that I have tried most ardently to forget ever happened.

Which is why, when I found myself perusing a quaint bookstore in central New Jersey at the behest of my best friend, I scanned shelves like I was on a mission and tried to take tiny breaths.

I had always been told that olfactory cognition was a gift. Hardly. I sipped the air like I was sampling wine. Trying to ignore the fresh paper and ink. The light coating of dust on leather. The wooden floor creaking under hesitant footsteps. Dust motes dancing in the sunlight. The memory of warm breath on my neck that I felt in my toes...

"Quinn, what am I looking for?" I vaguely heard Sid's rich tenor through my sensory fog. "Quinn?" The sharpness of her tone was a welcome needle that popped any chance of memories resurfacing.

"Maybe something like this?" I flashed her the first book that caught my eye. A glossy paperback with a pink cover. A cartoonish couple sat facing one another on a park bench. A saucy tabby cat perched between them.

Sid wrinkled her nose, her freckles coalescing into a single brown splash of contrasting color on her otherwise smooth complexion. "Not that one."

I read the title. *The Purrfect Couple.* Wincing, I put it back, flipping it over. "Too soon. I'm sorry, Sid."

She sliced through the air with her hand without meeting my eyes. "Argh. I'm over it."

She wasn't. Not in the slightest but, at the moment, I wasn't ready to challenge my former college roommate with master's degrees in psychology and education. "You must have some idea what kind of book you're looking for."

"Something..." she mused, fingering the ends of her newly wound locks as she browsed.

"I might need more to go on than 'something,'" I said, my lips twitching up in a grin.

Sid tossed her head back and examined the shelf towering above her five-foot frame. "Something captivating," she declared. "Transportive. Something smart but sexy."

"You've just described every woman in history's fantasy."

"Fantasy books or fantasy lovers?" she said with a hint of the devilry I knew she possessed. It had been a while since she'd shown that side. But I had known it would resurface. That my spirit animal of a best friend would be okay. Despite loving Derrik. Then marrying Derrik. Then having her heart broken by Derrik.

"Both," I said smugly.

Sid cut her eyes in my direction. "Is that what Gavin is? Your greatest fantasy?"

I halfheartedly rolled tired eyes that were still recovering from my one in the morning emergent gastric foreign body removal. "Gavin is nice and...steady."

"Oooh." Sid shimmied her shoulders to a rhythm only she could hear.

"Not everyone wants a fantasy, Sid," I muttered.

"Says the pragmatist."

"Sometimes reality is more appealing."

"And sometimes it's not." Sid concentrated on the shelf at eye level, lips curled and brows furrowed.

I knew better than to argue with her when her fantasy turned reality turned nightmare had come crashing down less than a month ago. Derrik was lucky I hadn't used my surgical instruments to cut his brakes. I squeezed Sid's shoulder as I brushed past her, sidling between two imposing bookcases.

My eyes roved over the artfully hung wooden signs on the walls. Art. Literature. Cooking and Travel. I paused near a rickety square table piled high with used paperbacks. Behind me, spines cracked, and pages ruffled. A warm feeling sank into the depths of my chest. Something serene and uncomfortably familiar.

I cleared my throat. "Where is your retreat again?"

"Kiawah Island."

"That should be nice."

"It would be much nicer if you hadn't backed out."

My stomach tightened as I replied, "You won't miss me." I bent my neck to study the disorganized pile on the table in front of me.

"Probably not," Sid snarked, and she elbowed me in the ribs. The top of her head appeared next to my shoulder as she began sifting through tattered paperbacks alongside me. "But you'll be missing meditation and organic meals and yoga on the beach—"

"You know I hate yoga," I interrupted.

"And apparently time off."

"Not time off…just time off right now. Mitch is up my ass during show season."

"And every other season."

"What can I say? Mitch appreciates my attentiveness." My lips formed something closer to a smile than a frown as I thought of the wiry horse trainer who was the human equivalent of rambutan. Spiky on the outside and mush on the inside.

"And your ass," Sid grunted.

"No way. It's not like that. He's more like a disgruntled uncle."

Sid raised a brow before slowly drawling, "Anyway…just promise you'll come next year, okay?"

"Of course." I flashed her my best smile. But deep down, I knew that I would disappoint her again. My lower thigh banged against the edge of the table and a paperback slid off the top of a pile, landing face up. I pointed to it and nudged Sid with my hip. "What about that one?"

Without even stopping to read the title, Sid answered, "That's the one we're reading for book club this month."

"Oh yeah," I mused, studying the cover—a couple holding hands amidst the backdrop of a mangled Paris circa 1940.

"You're coming right?" Sid was as serious about her book club as I was about proper hoof care.

"Yes." I nodded emphatically as I pushed the book back into the pile. "Absolutely. What night is it again?"

"Thursday," she answered with pursed lips. "How do you like the book so far?"

"It's...captivating," I said unconvincingly.

Sid snorted in disgust. We both knew I hadn't read a word.

"I'm sorry," I groaned. "I'll read it this week. Between cases if I have to."

"Mmhmm," she answered absentmindedly, her attention now laser focused on the next table over and its geometric stacks of this month's bestsellers.

As I organized the chaos of the used books table, I mentally sent myself through my weekly gauntlet of clinic appointments, meetings with potential clients, scheduled surgeries, and the bane of my existence—documentation. I had a complicated tendon repair coming up. And an osteotomy on a yearling. Not to mention a trip or twelve out to Mitch Jenkins to check on the mares about to drop foals.

Life as an equine vet always sounded glamorous when I said it out loud. *Nice to meet you. I'm Dr. Quinn McClain, and I perform lifesaving surgery on sleek show horses that cost more than my house.*

In reality, my chosen career was more dirty cracked fingernails and long nights under lights that were never quite bright enough. Cold damp mornings and crappy coffee and hard collisions with a snout to the side of my head if I wasn't paying attention when I plunged a needle into a fat neck vein. Days were long. Nights were longer. And mornings came way too early. But I loved it. It was literally coded into my genetics to love it.

"How's your dad these days?" Sid asked, her voice trailing

off as she put down the volume in her hand only to pick up the one next to it.

How did she always know where my mind was heading? "He's good. Busy with the clinic like always." I turned my head the other direction so she wouldn't see the frown tugging on my mouth. I hadn't heard from my dad in months. And from Aunt Jackie...even longer. They had curated the core of who I was yet had somehow shrunk into the tiniest corner of my life.

The small Texas town where I grew up and they still lived might as well have been in another universe. Emails and the occasional text messages were sent of course. But pared down to only the most essential information. *I'm fine. Busy. Good.* And it had taken a decade and a mountain of sheer will, but I *was* fine and busy and good.

A rare stab of guilt pierced my chest so thoroughly that I grabbed the nearest steady object. The placard announcing twenty percent off along with the neat pile of books next to it went clattering to the floor. I sighed, my knees cracking as I bent down to retrieve the paperbacks, their pages splayed out like wings. Above me, Sid let out a low hum followed by a hissing sound.

"Yesssss."

"Did you find *the something?*" I asked, restacking a copy of *Wuthering Heights* on top of *The Count of Monte Cristo*. When she didn't reply, I glanced up to find her edging toward me as she thumbed through a thick volume wrapped in a glossy black cover. One that sparkled when it was bathed in the sunlight filtering through the nearest window. Her eyes greedily skimmed over the words, the pages held reverently in her hands before she flipped to the back cover.

My knees cracked again when I stood up from the floor, a full head and shoulders above Sid's neat part.

"Yes," she repeated, the word a statement and a question.

An emotion flitted over her face, a muscle twitching in her cheek. "I feel like I've heard of this author, but I can't remember where." Sid shrugged as she handed me the book.

I weighed it in my hands. Perfectly heavy and portable at the same time. The single word title was embossed and backlit by the glow of a full moon. *Lune.*

The sight of it jerked a scene from the recesses of memory. The smell of wildflowers at night. The hum of cicadas and the gentle ripple of water against a shore of sharply hewn rock. A finger tracing the skin under the hem of my sweatshirt...

I narrowed my gaze on the author's name. A novel by J William. Heart pounding, I flipped the book over to examine the back cover. The edges of my vision blurred until I could only make out individual words rather than sentences. A row of stars followed by "riveting masterpiece" and "outstanding achievement."

I forced myself to study the square photograph in black and white at the bottom. It was tasteful. Classic. Just like him. Dark hair neatly combed rather than tousled. Piercing eyes that I knew were ice blue behind rimmed glasses. A set jaw that had only become more angular with time. No sign of the dimple that appeared in his left check when he was amused.

I traced the name printed in classic font under the photograph. J William. Not the name I had known him by. I handed the book back to Sid like it might explode in my hand.

"Quinn?"

I heard Sid say my name through the aftershock of my worlds colliding. The current one where I was a confident, witty, wildly successful East Coast veterinarian and the other one. The one I had left behind. "Yeah?" My voice cracked, earning an arched brow from Sid.

"I said what do you think?"

"About the book?"

"No about the geopolitics of British colonialism." Her hands went to her hips. "Yes, about the book."

I swallowed hard as I watched a spider scurry across the shelf above Sid's head. I focused on where my feet met the ground just like Brené Brown had taught me and ignored the panic in my chest. "It's perfect," I said with a wide, forced smile. And it was. Undeniably. Irrevocably. Perfect. I immediately hated the sight of it.

"It's exactly what I was looking for." Sid hugged the book to her chest, bright toothy smile stretching between her rounded cheeks, before making a beeline for the checkout counter.

I followed behind her, weaving through the maze of Cherry Hill Books until I pushed through the glass door and staggered onto the sidewalk.

I closed my eyes, tilting my face toward the welcome appearance of a mid-afternoon sun. Hoping. Praying that the waning autumn light was enough to burn holes through the picture in my mind. The fading curled photograph of a desolate country road, a boy leaning against his car. A boy who was beautiful and lost in every way possible.

CHAPTER TWO

SUMMER, THEN

"Quinn!" My one syllable name stretched into many as my dad's baritone voice with a purposeful brogue reached me down the sterile hallway. He was third generation Scottish and did not speak with a placeable accent unless he was about to give me a hard time.

I glanced toward his office, the door swung wide, his broad frame filling the doorjamb. In one hand he held a mug of coffee, his typical afternoon brew from the shop down the street, and in the other he twirled a set of keys. During this one second of distraction, the feisty tomcat I was holding raked his claws down the soft inner surface of my arm.

"Ouch," I yelped and shook him into the belly of the open cage pinned between my knees.

"You all right, Quinnie?" In two strides my dad was standing next to me in the low-lit alcove near the rear door of the clinic.

"I'm reconsidering taking the rabies vaccine this year," I grumbled, latching the cage with more force than was necessary. I surveyed the damage. Two angry linear scratches ran from my elbow to my wrist.

9

My dad clucked his tongue, his voice lowering to that of a conspiratorial whisper. "Why don't you ever want to play Monopoly with a cat?"

Oh good grief. I wasn't going to give in this time and ask. If my dad excelled at anything, it was telling the best horrible jokes. That and making sure every stray cat within a hundred-mile radius was properly divested of its sex organs. He regarded me silently, the unsaid punchline making his lips quiver in anticipation. *You know you want to know,* they silently commanded me. And I did. I always did.

I pressed my teeth into my lip to stifle a reply, but it came out anyway. "Okay, why?"

"Because they tend to be cheetahs."

Outwardly, I rolled my eyes and groaned like a proper teenager while inside I giggled like a seven-year-old. Dad chuckled, the bald patch on his head glowing like a homing beacon. When the moment passed, his face transitioned into the professional one of my summer employer. "When you are finished reveling at my wit, I need you to take those cats we neutered and drop them off at Mrs. Abbott's."

I glanced down at the dastardly calico in the cage. "She won't mind?"

"Nah. She said she would take on a few barn cats as long as they came without testicles."

"Dad," I groaned, ducking my head and grinding my teeth together. I should have been relieved that my dad was so cavalier with medical terminology that made most adults cringe. A set of keys sailed through the air. I fumbled but caught them before they hit the ground.

"Good catch."

"One of my many talents."

My dad winked. "See you at the house for dinner. Don't be late. It's Tuesday."

My jaw dropped in mock horror. "Never!"

His face faltered for a moment, his steel gray eyes softening. "You look like your mother when you make that face." He pulled a bouquet from behind his back, a cluster of delicate purple buds. "Drop these off for her, okay?"

My mood sobered a notch, and I cleared my throat. "Sure thing, Dad." Taking the flowers in one hand and the cat in the other, I exited through the rear door of the building into the Texas heat.

The air above the pavement shimmered as I schlepped out to the parking lot and the monstrosity of a pickup truck we owned. By the time I lowered the tailgate and slid the cages inside, the first trickles of sweat lazed down the middle of my back. It was barely June and already the air around me was a thick blanket of heat and swarming insects. Our small busybody town was smackdab between two limestone rivers that, during rainy season, filled up the creek beds with silvery green ribbons of trickling water. Beautiful to look at and excellent for mosquito breeding.

The leather steering wheel of my dad's pickup truck seared my hands as I pulled myself into the cab. A fine layer of road dust coated the interior and its contents, a roll of industrial-grade paper towels and the worn leather bag my dad didn't go anywhere without. When I was little, it had reminded me of the one in Mary Poppins, spelled to be bottomless and magically required to provide him with anything he needed.

When I got older and brave enough to root around inside it myself, I found a leather roll of shiny instruments, a headlight, sterile towels, and a neat box of tiny glass vials. When he had caught me snooping, instead of admonishment, I had been bathed in praise. "One day this will all be yours, Quinnie," he had told me. As an eighteen-year-old on the cusp of her professional dreams, I couldn't wait for that day.

I glanced back over my shoulder at the plastic mounds

nestled together in the truck bed before massaging the engine to a low growl. As I pulled out of the parking lot, the blinker acted as a steadying heartbeat as I turned toward town and the cemetery that lay just beyond it.

Linzberg was a small dot on the map about forty miles northwest of the gigantic dot of San Antonio. It had started as a well curated mecca of German antique shops and Polish bakeries until a family from California had moved here in the eighties and realized that the soil was ideal for growing grapes. Grapes that would be made into wine. And wine that would become the flame for the moths that would descend on our sleepy little village and turn it into a tourist attraction.

Despite taking the long route and winding through the main thoroughfare of kitschy shops and mom-and-pop restaurants, the drive through town took exactly seven minutes. I slowed to a crawl, monitoring the hordes of pedestrians milling about every street corner.

Every summer was the same—couples sipping wine as they window shopped and gaggles of ladies on a weekend trip strolling about in elaborate hats and custom leather-tooled cowboy boots. I exhaled with relief once I made it over the bridge bordering the town's edge and entered the massive iron gate beyond it.

Once off the main road, I maneuvered along a gravel path, winding past the twisted mesquite trees. I kept going until I reached the back corner, where jutting gray stones were separated by huge swaths of green.

When I switched the engine off, the quiet heat suffused through the truck and covered me like a blanket. A lone bee whizzed past my open window, carrying with it the scent of honeysuckle. I spotted the familiar heart-shaped headstone in the same spot it had been for the last thirteen years and slid out of the truck, flowers in hand.

"Hi, Mama." I knelt in the stubby grass and plucked the shriveled corpses of the flowers I had brought a few weeks ago from the vase next to her name. I replaced them with the fresh bouquet, the petals like drops of starlight. Lilacs had been her favorite, and my dad made sure that, even in death, everyone knew he carried the biggest torch for her.

I had definitely been a love child—the product of a third-generation Scottish veterinarian and the daughter of Polish immigrants who had landed here at the end of World War II. The result of a passionate summer affair when my father, in between semesters at college, had taken a job as a handyman for my grandparents' rundown homestead.

Their lovely artist daughter had finished high school and had yet to decide her course in life. And one night the sky had been too full of stars and her smile had been too perfect. My dad had sought her out as she had gazed at the moon at the end of a long pier that extended over the river behind her house. Love at first sight.

I had always loved that story. And when my dad told it, he made sure to mention that it was actually love at first moonlight. That when my mom was growing up, she made sure to go outside to bask underneath every full moon—a habit she maintained after they got married and lived in a tiny apartment in Philadelphia.

When I was a baby, she would rock me to sleep by the window, staring at the sliver of a moon she could see from the third-story brownstone on Walnut Street. It was a nice image.

A desperate yowling brought me back to reality and I popped up from the ground in time to see a scraggly orange tabby lurking behind a headstone. We regarded one other for a moment before he scampered underneath the wheels of the truck. By the time I covered the distance, the cages inside the bed rattled with activity—despondent howls and claws scratching over unforgiving plastic walls.

The orange tomcat gave me a scathing look and I gave him one right back. "You're on my list for next month's neuter-fest, Tom," I muttered. Pinning his ears back at the sound of my voice, he slunk in the opposite direction.

"Go on. Get outta here."

I startled at the rough voice that reminded me of sandpaper on stone. Mr. Solomon, the cemetery caretaker laughed deeply as his voice sent the cat into a loping run. I waved to the figure in a long-sleeved pearl snap shirt across a row of tight green hedges. He tipped the brim of his trucker hat in my direction.

"Hot out today, darlin'. You make sure you're drinkin' plenty of water," he instructed as I climbed back into the truck.

"I will if you will," I called back through the driver's side window before pulling onto the gravel path. As a reply, I heard the rev of a buzzing motor and watched bits of grass swirl through the air as I drove past him.

By the time I reached the turnoff that led to Mrs. Abbott's place, sweat pooled between my thighs and dripped onto the leather seat. The wind rippling through the open window did nothing to unpaste the T-shirt from my soaking skin. So much for the power of convection.

"We have a two fifty A/C," my dad had told me last week when our truck air conditioner had broken. When my face had soured, he had added, "Two windows down and fifty miles an hour." And then he had walked away, his shoulders shaking as he bellowed with laughter.

The sun beat down on the arm I had casually thrown across the window frame, and I fanned my fingers in the breeze. Thank goodness I had inherited my mom's tendency to turn brown instead of my dad's tendency to look like a boiled lobster.

When I rounded the next curve, painfully slowly thanks to the scrabbling cargo in the back, I noticed a sky-blue convertible pulled off onto the shoulder on the opposite side of the road. A figure leaned back onto the hood, squinting into the sun like it might give him the answers to everything he ever wanted to know.

I stomped on the brakes a little too eagerly, fishtailing to a stop on the narrow shoulder. When I picked up my arm to shield my eyes from the glare, I noticed the layer of grime covering it. I swiped it quickly on the hem of my shirt.

"Are you lost?" I shouted from the driver's seat, my voice an octave higher than normal. A layer of dust mixed with sweat coated my tongue when I licked my lips.

The figure in front of me, a willowy shape in a black T-shirt and jeans, one hand propped on the hood of a vintage automobile, didn't answer. Instead, he held up a palm in greeting. He was sleek and trim. Like an exotic panther misplaced from the jungle and stranded in the middle of this dusty country road. The waves flopped over on his forehead were so dark they seemed to absorb the sunlight. I had never seen anyone like him. Not anyone from around here anyway. He was definitely lost.

I sighed heavily, slipping out of the truck, glancing east then west along the two-lane road before crossing it. The landscape between the town and the green jewels of hills in the distance was mostly patches of poorly tended grass separated by piles of rock. Desolate. Quiet. But it had a wildness about it if you knew where to look. The only other sign of life today was a solitary crow perched on a fencepost. He cocked his head at me, staring with a beady, knowing eye.

"Shoo," I said, flicking my fingers at him as I strode past. He didn't budge.

When I got closer, I noticed that the guy in the road was nearly my age. Maybe exactly my age. I recognized the similarly innocent stance and youthful roundness to his chin as he rubbed it. His hips barely held up the jeans that ended at the ankle above a pair of canvas low tops. A tan arm extended toward me in greeting then paused awkwardly when I failed to take the outstretched fingers. I wiggled my fingers in the air between us.

"Sorry," I said. "My hand has been places today that you probably don't want to touch."

His dark brows shot up in surprise as his eyelids peeled back. A pair of ice blue eyes regarded me with a combination of shock and amusement. I wiped my hand down the side of my jeans.

"I've been handling animals all day," I clarified.

He rocked back on his heels, folding his arms across a chest that was thin but defined. "What sort of animals?" A smiled played on his lips.

"All kinds." I smirked as the tension eased between us. "Dogs, cats, goats, a ferret." His eyes widened with the mention of each one. "My dad's the vet in town," I added quickly.

He nodded in understanding, a shallow dimple appearing near the left corner of his mouth. "And you live around here?"

"Unfortunately." As I studied his face, a smile split my lips and stretched past my cheekbones nearly to the angle of my jaw. I tried to stop it from spreading but the light in his eyes, the full lips and singular dimple. The way his hair cast his face in shadow. His features did something unexpectedly visceral to me.

"I'm Will," he said, fingers twitching at his side.

"I'm Quinn." My neck was beginning to cramp from looking up at him, rare for me at my above average height, but I couldn't seem to stop. I studied the dark curl plastered to his forehead and a short gash on his chin where he had cut himself.

"Enchanted to meet you," he said.

I watched his throat bob—up and down—and up and down a second time. I imagined words bobbing in the sea of his throat. An insane curiosity suddenly consumed me. I wanted to know exactly what he was thinking but not saying, what thoughts and feelings and memories filled his head. My mind was a tidal wave of the questions I wanted to ask him. The first one came out unintentionally harsh.

"What are you doing all the way out here on the side of the road?" I finally tore my eyes away, embarrassed by my own ogling.

I found a cedar tree to study in the distance and shoved my hands into the back pockets of my jeans. A rare breeze lifted the tuft of my blonde braid. In my peripheral vision, I watched him run a hand through his own hair, the tousled ends springing in a variety of directions before he patted the hood of the car next to him.

"I thought I might take a drive today and have a look around. My grandfather told me there was a place to swim...a natural pool of sorts. And it's unbearably hot so...I thought I might try to find it." His words lingered with the hint of an accent I couldn't place. Maybe British or South African? I never claimed to be able to tell the difference.

"And you got lost trying to find it?"

"I believe I did." When I looked over at him, a sheepishness rouged the edge of his cheekbones. "Would you happen to know how to find this place?"

"I'm going to need some...details." I had no idea what he was talking about. And that intrigued me to my bones.

A gleam of mischief sparked behind the gold flecks in his eyes. "It's the one about this deep." He dragged the edge of his hand across his chest. "And blue. Turquoise blue to be exact. With water so clear you can see the bottom."

I nodded, half my face quirked up in a smile. "Uh huh. Go on."

"And it's filled with magical creatures that were trapped there when a dark force took over the land. The legend says" —he paused for dramatic effect, stepping close enough to me that his towering frame blocked out the midday sun—"that only the most beautiful, most courageous maiden of all time can vanquish the dark and set them free."

My body shivered as the fabric of his T-shirt grazed my forearm, even as my eyes narrowed in disbelief. For a moment I was that maiden, hidden in shadow but ready to forfeit my life to save and protect those magical creatures in Will's fantasy world. My heart swelled and I stepped back, kicking a spray of dust onto his shoe as I did so.

"You're ridiculous," I said, but I kept smiling. He merely shrugged.

"Did you grow up here?" he asked, settling his lower half back onto the hood of his car.

I nodded. "Yep." He looked at me with what I interpreted as sympathy, so I added, "But I'm leaving for college at the end of the summer."

He shifted his body, every movement practiced and graceful. Like the black cat that lived behind the clinic. "So, you just finished high school? I did as well."

"Oh," I breathed. He seemed older somehow. Worldly. Mature and cultured in a way that I knew I would never be. "Are you going to college?"

He nodded his head, a flash of something imperceptible in his eyes before he spoke. "Yes, but I'm taking a gap year."

Gap year? I had never heard of such a thing. "What will you do?" I asked, cocking my head.

The skin around his eyes tightened and a shadow

dimmed the glimmer in his eyes. His lips parted several seconds before he spoke. "Hang out. Maybe have a bit of fun."

I nearly scoffed out loud. "In Nowheresville?"

His lips twisted into a smile. Full decadent lips that glistened once he ran his tongue across them. "I suppose so."

A fluttering trilled inside my chest. I held my breath to quiet it. "Do you have family here?"

"Yes. You actually might know them." He pointed to the sun now hanging low in the sky like a ripe orange. "They live just over that hill."

Only one property lay in that direction. "You're related to the people that own Deremer Vineyards?"

He ducked his head shyly, a dark wave flopping over onto his forehead. "They're my grandparents."

I let out a low whistle. Deremer Vineyards was the nicest, most lucrative property in our entire tri-county area. Although we didn't run in the same circle as Mr. and Mrs. Deremer, I had seen them at town events over the past few years. Mrs. Deremer was tall and willowy and always wearing long sleeves, no matter how sweltering it was outside. "Wow. Do you get free wine?"

"Not really." His eyes lit up again, sparking with mischief.

My eyelids widened in mock horror. "You steal it?"

"Not at all." He laughed with a sound that was deep and unfiltered. "Sometimes they have these events." He gestured toward the back edge of their property. "Which means that a lot of people with very deep pockets drink a lot of wine in the name of something or other charity."

"And?"

"And no one notices if I swipe a glass or two from the bar."

"I've never had wine," I mused.

"Some of it's really good...the rest tastes like cough syrup."

It was my turn to laugh. It bubbled over my lips like something cool and effervescent. "You're funny."

"Not usually." He pressed his lips together to keep from smiling, his eyes softening. "Well then, are you going to help me or not?"

The words hung between us. I had to stop the word yes from rolling off my tongue. "With what exactly?" I eyed the ground critically, wrinkling my nose as I avoided noticing the way his shirt clung with sweat to his mid-section.

"Finding the magic pool."

When I glanced up, he was looking at me as if he already knew my answer.

CHAPTER THREE

AUTUMN, NOW

"Yes!" The word felt aberrant. Foreign. My stomach cramped with a tinge of betrayal. I ignored it.

Instead, I focused on the contrast between the pale, trembling hands in front of me and the black as night velvet box they held. Time slowed for a millisecond before accelerating into an arc, tugging me along with its gravity. I heard the click of the box open a moment before the chandelier lights of the restaurant reflected off the contents.

"I didn't ask yet," Gavin said slowly, the cuff of his powder blue shirt extending past his jacket as he removed the ring from the box.

"Oh." My smile faltered, my nerves quivering as a quartet of violins erupted into song behind me. "Did I jump the gun?"

"I had a speech prepared," he said, lips twisting up as he took the ring out of its box and slipped it onto my finger.

It barely made it over my knuckle, scraping off a layer of skin as it settled around the base of my fourth finger. My heart rate spiked chaotically. This thing was so tight it was never ever coming off. Even if I wanted it to. Which I never would, of course.

The box snapped closed, and Gavin scooted it to the edge of the table. He slid his hand under mine, smooth white fingers like marble that contrasted with my tan, callused ones.

I watched his thumb trace a linear scar on the back of my hand. I didn't even remember how or when I had gotten it. Probably last month when a horse shoved me into a barbed wire fence.

I tilted my hand under the flickering candlelight and caught myself smiling as the shadows overpowered the checkerboard of imperfections on my hand. The story of my life was written in scars.

Somewhere behind me a champagne bottle exploded with a *pop* and a *whoosh*. Gavin released my hand to motion the waiter over. I blinked. Slowly. Methodically. Feeling every drag of my sparkling eyelid through what I expected to be a thin film of tears.

Instead, I got hung up somewhere on the grit in my eyes which forced me into an awkward squint. I peeled them open again by sheer force of will. I was on the verge of arguably the most significant life moment I had experienced since birth. About to clinch the penultimate trophy of adult single women everywhere and I couldn't muster one crystalline tear.

Instead, while a duet of violins serenaded our table, I stared at the suffused overhead lighting refracting through the faceted diamond on my finger, mesmerized by the spectrum of colors contained in a speck of pressurized carbon. It was as large and round as a marble, as big as the fake one I had popped out of a toy turnstile at the grocery store one time. That one had only cost me a quarter. I couldn't imagine what this one had cost. Three month's salary like the magazines suggested? Surely not.

"Congratulations." The white jacketed man with a shock of hair to match tilted a green bottle until a stream of liquid gold filled my glass. His smile played underneath a bushy mustache. The violins crescendoed as Gavin lifted his glass to me.

"To us," he said in a voice that covered me in a smooth splash of cool water. His smile stretched so big that it pushed the rims of his glasses onto his nasal bridge.

"To us." I mimicked his movement, stretching my cheeks until they burned with effort. He eyed me as he took a methodical sip of champagne.

"Do you like the ring?" When his throat bobbed, my heart constricted inside my chest. I tightened my fingers around the stem of my glass.

"It's perfect," I said, finding the edge of my glass with my hastily painted lips. The bubbles coaxed my tongue to relax, and my face followed. This was it. A dream realized. I settled into it like I would a woolen sweater in the winter's chill. It felt good. It felt right. "How long have you been planning this?" I asked with a coy smirk.

Gavin ran a hand through his combed shock of sandy hair that always flicked upward toward the end of the day. He shrugged sheepishly. "Six months, give or take."

"Six months!" As my eyes widened, I took in the details of the man sitting across from me. The matching suit and tie and gleaming wristwatch. The clean-shaven face that most of the time appeared thoughtful and observant. The straight posture and reed-like arms. Gavin had always reminded me of a gangly teenage horse that hadn't quite figured out the length of his extremities.

"You didn't suspect anything?"

I shook my head before downing the rest of my champagne. "Not at all. I thought we were going out tonight to celebrate your promotion."

Gavin's eyes tightened. "I'm not sure that being promoted to chief actuary warrants dinner at Gadot's." He glanced over his shoulder to the panoramic view of the New York City skyline. The top of the Empire state building gave us a knowing wink.

"Of course, it does," I said, my head swelling like a balloon as the champagne fizzed through my bloodstream. "But this is much better."

He looked wary as he massaged his palm with his thumb, one of his many habits. Something he did when he was nervous or tired. Or both. "I love you, Quinn," he said matter-of-factly. I barely heard him over the buzzing din in my head.

Winking playfully, I responded with, "I know you do."

"I'm serious." His voice wavered as he clutched my fingers, bending them so the ring was on full display. "I want us to have a life together. I want you to let me make you happy."

Something wistful in his expression sobered me. The last of the champagne bubbles popped into nonexistence. My heart pounded slowly, purposefully against the undersurface of my sternum. *Boom.*

The sound reverberated inside my ears and traveled somewhere deep into the interior of my brain. Somewhere where the hardened edges had been sanded smooth by the bottle of wine we had drunk during dinner. I hadn't had wine that good in years. Not since moving to the East Coast. And not since...*him.*

My mind slammed shut on the past before it became a deluge of images and whispered words. Over the years, blocking out everything from that night had become easier. *It had not been real.* Acknowledging that was the only reason I was about to get the rest of what I wanted. I peeled my tongue from the roof of my mouth to speak.

"I want that too." I twisted my other hand into the hem of my dress to simulate my grip on reality. Not fantasy. Not the dream of a girl who had barely been an adult. I was a woman who could have everything she ever wanted. And it was all right here.

THE NEXT MORNING, I rolled out of bed, careful not to disturb the rising and falling form under crisp white sheets next to me. I hunted around for my keys, my eyes flicking past the neat array of items on the bedside table. Phone in its charger, glasses in their leather case, a hardback copy of *Investing with Principle*, the edge of a bookmark extruding through the middle.

Gavin had been in the apartment on Fifty-second Street for the better part of three years. Seven hundred and ten square feet of meticulousness—the only way a person could survive living somewhere where pancakes could be flipped from the only toilet seat.

I didn't mind spending a night or two here but any more than that filled me with a restless desire to claw my hands down the wall. I should have been more grateful to the apartment with beige walls and gray carpet. It was the reason Gavin and I had met when he was just another wanderlust soul contemplating light fixtures in a hardware store in the Cherry Hill shopping center.

"I like that one," I had said and sidled up next to him as I pointed at an ornate brass sconce that looked like it belonged in a sixteenth-century castle. His brown eyes had clouded in confusion, but he had smiled politely, the corners of his mouth lifting when he had noticed my mischievous grin.

"I'm not sure it's my style," he had said dryly.

"Too bad. It really makes a statement."

"What kind of statement?"

I had sighed dramatically. "That you're an old soul with taste."

To his credit, he had ducked his head shyly, eyes flicking over my mouth. "I'm more of a modern day computer nerd who lives in a high rise and takes the subway to work."

"Oh," I had said smugly. "Are you a nerd who likes sushi?"

It turned out he had hated sushi, but he had really liked me.

And now, two years and ten months later, we were engaged.

I tugged on a pair of yoga pants and an oversized sweatshirt, swiping my grown-out bangs behind my ear to steal a glance at the man snoring lightly in the bed, his hair still combed perfectly over a smooth forehead. Part of me hoped he rolled over and bid me a dream-infused goodbye. But the other part was glad he didn't. The silence hugged me like a cocoon, and I was grateful for it.

I scooped my bag up from the floor and fished around the bottom until I felt the familiar shape of my keys, the hand that closed around them newly heavy and foreign. As I lifted them out, careful to avoid the unwanted jangle, a watery trickle of sunlight danced off my ring. It was real. This was real. An unexpected hope began to bloom. Maybe the part of me that had always lived in the past—lived in the what if— could finally stop haunting me like a ghost.

I would live for the moments that might not be the best but would be good enough. My life was good enough. Gavin was...good enough. And most importantly, he was real. Things had turned out just fine. My life...our life...would keep ticking predictably along.

Something inside me jolted awake. *One last time,* it whispered. I didn't have the energy to fight it this morning. I opened the door to that perfect moment and let it all rush back to me.

I remembered every detail. How I had wanted to live and die in the same breath. How my world had shifted with the quarter turn of a kaleidoscope, colors falling into a pattern so brilliant that I nearly combusted. The soft tendrils of hair on my cheek. Moonlight on bare skin. Murmured promises that were meant to be kept. The wine that tasted like fallen starlight. The most perfect crush of lips to mine.

And most of all the feeling of wholly belonging to someone else. And, for a moment, believing I deserved to be loved like that. God, it had been beautiful...

My thoughts shifted to last night with Gavin. We had walked home, my arm wound through his, our steps slightly off kilter from too much champagne. As the streetlights had bathed us in a celebratory glow, a nagging thought had trailed me like a shadow. I had said yes to something that could never compare to what I had let go.

Sighing, I twisted the heavy bauble on my ring finger so that it sat perfectly straight. One day a perfect moment would happen that would make me forget to remember the other one. But not last night. Without looking back, I reached for the doorknob and quietly slipped into the carpeted hall.

BY NOON my ringed left hand was halfway inside a mare's rectum while my phone jangled in my back pocket. I grunted with effort, a crown of sweat beading on my forehead. My nostrils flared, sucking in the sweet smell of fresh hay and horse.

"Want me to get that for you?" said a voice so rough and gritty that it reminded me of high-grade sandpaper.

"No thanks." I grimaced as I flexed my fingers inside the long sleeve of latex that protected my arm, gently but purposefully fanning the ultrasound probe as I stared at a screen of undulating shades of gray. The phone paused then resumed an incessant cadence of ringing.

Mitch Jenkins crossed his arms and arched a brow. "How 'bout now?"

I rolled my eyes at the weathered horse trainer and blew a strand of hair out of my mouth. "Be my guest, you pervert," I grunted. He chuckled as he reached a tentative hand toward the phone jutting from my back pocket.

"Dr. McClain," I announced tersely, "You're on speaker phone."

"Quinn, it's me," rang a familiar voice. A voice that sounded like rum and sunshine.

"Hello, Sid." My expression softened considerably at the sound of my best friend.

"What time are you getting here tonight? Can you stop by the store and grab some of that cheese shaped like a cupcake?" Her words came at me like the staccato of gunfire.

The rest of Sid's instructions were drowned out by my own ragged breath as my eyes lasered toward the undeniable floating sac inside the mare's pelvis. For a moment, I forgot about everything except for the thrill of what was inside it. By next spring, this amalgam of tissue and bone would enter the world as a wobbly foal.

"You forgot, didn't you?" The ire in Sidney's voice tugged me back to reality.

"Of course, I forgot," I answered, half exasperated. "But I'll make it up to you in cheese." I grinned even though she couldn't see my face and tugged my arm out of the slippery darkness and into the waning autumn sunlight. Mitch's eyebrows rose like a singular bushy gray caterpillar, and he mouthed "Well?" I cocked a smug brow.

"Be on time and I might forgive you." Her words sounded authoritatively cross, but I knew her well enough to know she was fighting the urge to laugh.

"You got it, Sid. See you tonight."

"Seven o'clock, Quinn." She clicked her tongue rhythmically. "Don't be late."

I discarded the glove into the straw and grabbed the phone from Mitch. "Wouldn't dream of it," I teased into a blank screen. Pressing end, I tossed the phone into the mouth-like opening of my backpack.

"Well?" Mitch barked as I absentmindedly rubbed the mare's ebony haunches. The veins in his neck had risen to the surface as thick fleshy cords.

"Congratulations," I said brightly. "You're going to be a father."

As I watched him pump his fist into the air, I tightened my eyes and force-filled my head with images of church pews and white tulle, finally letting myself relax into life's newest happiness.

CHAPTER FOUR

AUTUMN, NOW

"You know 'book club'"—I made dramatic air quotes with my index fingers— "is actually code for 'let's get together to drink wine and complain about our lives.'"

Sid looked up from where she was chopping a pile of peppers into strips. "Entire friendships are forged from reading books and drinking wine...and complaining."

I exhaled dramatically and began arranging finger-length veggies around a porcelain bowl of hummus. Sid was my closest friend. Ever since freshman year of college when the Princeton housing office had decided to pair a second-generation Jamaican from New York with a small-town Texas girl.

"Reading is good for you," she added, nudging me playfully with an elbow.

I scrunched my face into a scowl.

"Oh, come on, it hasn't been too bad this year."

"If I read one more historical romance novel, I'm going to hurl."

Sid's eyes crinkled and narrowed. "Everyone wants a happy ending, Quinn."

The words socked me in the gut, and I watched her return to chopping cucumbers with measured precision. After several minutes, Sid's interminable quiet had me scooting around the island to give her shoulders a squeeze. "I'm really sorry about Derrik," I murmured. It had been nearly two months since her marriage had gone up in proverbial flames, and I was still considering cutting the brakes of a certain someone's BMW 5 series.

She shrugged, her face molded into a mask of placid. "It's fine. I just never thought I would turn into one of *those* women."

"What women?" I tilted my head so that my blonde strands meshed with her neat row of braids.

"The ones who use wine and book clubs and carbs"—she gestured to the loaf of bread waiting to be sliced— "to distract me from my own sad reality."

"You are the strongest, most badass woman I know. Like" —I searched my vocabulary for a stellar comparison—"a combination of Oprah and Angelina Jolie."

She side-eyed me, her brown orbs cutting across my face like a blade. "You've always been terrible at compliments."

Heat rushed into my cheeks as I pressed on. "And you've always been terrible at feeling sorry for yourself."

Her face cracked with a twisted smile before she swiped a tear the corner of her eye. "True." She buried her hands into a dish towel, one I had bought her in Mexico that read, "When life gives you lemons, ask for tequila."

"So, what's your happy ending? Gavin?" she asked pointedly. The arch in her brow was so fierce it nearly punctured me.

My face flooded with all the emotions I had been keeping on a tight leash.

"You broke up with him, didn't you?" she accused, wrinkling her nose.

"No," I sputtered. "He asked me to marry him."

Sid's face transitioned from admonishment to shock. "Really?" She rapped me on the arm with a wooden spoon. "When were you going to tell me?"

I rubbed my stinging elbow. "Definitely not in the middle of us talking about your divorce."

"Did you say yes?"

The question took me off guard, like the world heaved upward and threw off my balance. "Did you think I would say no?"

Sid chewed on her lip for a moment before speaking. "Actually...yeah."

"What? Why?" I reeled in my arms to my chest and crossed them.

"I'm sorry." She gestured with her spoon-wielding hand. "I've known you for over ten years and..." She paused as if to cushion her next words. "I never thought that Gavin was your person."

"Well, he is," I replied hastily.

She gave me a look that said it all. *'Really, Quinn? Because I've seen you in love and this is...not...it.'* She didn't have to say the words. I saw them flash across her face like subtitles in a foreign film.

"We've been together for almost three years. That has to mean something." I stepped away from her, keeping my arms crossed.

Sid reached over and clasped my elbow. "It does. And I'm sorry. Just ignore me. It's probably the wine and the book we read this month for book club. It put my head in the clouds."

I gave her a blank stare.

"You didn't read the book," she accused.

"Not all of it." *Or any of it.* I tugged at the neckline of my T-shirt. Why did Sid always make me feel like I was sitting across from a high school principal? Probably because she was one.

She glanced around the counter then pointed at a stack of books. "It's over there," she said, turning her attention to something bubbling on the stove. "And you have fifteen minutes until everyone else gets here."

I flashed her a bright, sarcastic smile. "Yes ma'am."

"You should actually read this one." Sid winked at me playfully. "It might even light up your dim romance bulb."

"Never." I snorted lightly as I scooped up the books stacked neatly on the counter's edge.

A wistful look crossed her face, and for a moment, the tired lines around her eyes relaxed. "Never say never. It gives new meaning to the word *unrequited*."

Unrequited. The absolute last word I needed in my vocabulary. I surveyed this month's book club choice like it was a pariah. Flipping it over, I quickly skimmed the back cover, scowling as I read. "Let me guess—Stacey picked this one."

"I picked it," she said defensively, reaching for a spatula to loosen a row of feta-and-onion- filled tarts.

"Hmm," I said with an arched brow. "I would have expected something more esoteric from someone with two master's degrees from Princeton."

Her lips thinned and her eyes hardened into what I called her "take no shit" principal look. "Historical romance as a genre is highly underrated."

"Who knew?" I teased, as I began methodically sorting through the books on her counter and laying them in a row. When I reached the bottom of the pile, I found the shiny hardback I had helped her choose last weekend.

This time I was able to absorb the details of the cover. The outline of a scaled dragon silhouetted by shafts of moonlight that cascaded into a turquoise pool. A woman with pointed ears and a longbow stood on the shore, her golden hair fanning out behind her. I traced the title with a charged fingertip. Bold and classy in its sans serif font. *Lune.* I still couldn't believe *he* wrote this. My heart thudded painfully against my sternum as I turned the book over in my hands.

I slid my thumb over the glossy square image in black and white at the bottom. Seeing it for the second time was mildly more tolerable. I stared at him. He stared back with eyes that were the perfect combination of amused and thoughtful. Like he saw everything and reveled in laughing at his own wit.

I read the caption under the photograph. *J William*—I wondered when he had dropped his last name—*has a doctorate in English literature from Berkeley, where he is currently a professor of creative writing. Lune is his debut novel.* And then nothing else. No personal details. No mention of hobbies or children or a wife. But he had gone to California and stayed for some reason.

A burgeoning emotion rose into the back of my throat. Longing? No. It was relief. Relief that we were separated by an entire continental United States. I inhaled a calming breath, which was a mistake, because along with it came the heady scent of fresh paper and a slip of a memory.

"What are you writing?" I had asked, thrilled when my fingers grazed the inside of his wrist and his eyes had snapped to mine.

"Something not worth reading." The edge of his lips had lifted in amusement.

"You won't know until you actually let someone read it." I had smiled up at him, squinting against the midday sun, from where I was supine on our favorite flat stretch of rock.

"Maybe someday I will." The breath carrying his words had caressed my ear, every nerve ending sparking with possibility...

The book thumped to the floor, and I nearly leaped out of my skin. I stared at it like it was a living thing that might grow claws and fangs and bite my toes off at any given moment. Gingerly, I picked it up by the cover, letting it hang in front of me like a carcass.

"Quinn." I heard my name through the sound of rushing water. "Quinn!" Sid shouted a second time.

"Yes?" I answered absentmindedly.

"Can you answer the door?" Sid asked from somewhere down the hallway. When had she left the kitchen?

Following the incessant clanging of a bell, I wobbled to the front door and twisted the knob. Four sets of eyes regarded me with minimal interest as they filed through, their personalities undergoing a mystical shift as they crossed the threshold. Frowns transitioned to smirks, light sparked behind dull eyes, and jackets with remnants of the day's sandwich making and dish scrubbing were discarded. A wool peacoat was flung in my direction, and I caught the sleeve with one hand.

"Oh my God, I love your new furniture." The voice came from Carly, the curly redhead sporting a baby bump under a pale blue sweater. The rest of the group murmured their agreement.

Stacey, dressed in a floor length crinkle skirt, flounced to the head of the pack and wrapped an arm around Carly. "I don't care if spikes were coming out of this couch, I would sit down and love every second of it." They both collapsed dramatically onto the floral upholstery.

"What are we drinking, ladies?" Sid called as she appeared from the kitchen, brandishing two bottles.

"Leave that prosecco right here," Stacey piped as she pointed to an empty spot on the glass end table next to the couch.

Sid disappeared for a moment only to return with a tray

of flutes brimming with fizzing liquid. After taking a glass, I settled into an armless velvet chair and surveyed the room. I knew Stacey and Carly from previous book club meetings. The other two women looked familiar but in the current jumbled state of my brain, I couldn't come up with their names. They could have been paper dolls from a catalog for athleisure wear, with their ankle-length Lycra blend pants and oversized sweatshirts.

Sweatshirt One took a slim yellow pepper from Sid's tray and began munching on it. Loudly. The sound grated on my nerves.

"So, what's new with everyone?" Stacey asked as she reached over Carly's engorged lap for the prosecco bottle.

Carly rubbed a hand along her flank as she rested her head on the couch cushion. "Nothing exciting," she moaned. "Unless you count growing a baby."

"That's exciting," I quipped, feeling jumpy and nervous. Like my sentences were sparks shooting out of my mouth.

"It was exciting the first three times. Now, not so much." Stacey shrugged her shoulders as Sweatshirts One and Two glared at her in horror.

"No, she's right." Carly flitted a hand toward Stacey. "I've become a breeding machine. A regular broodmare."

My ears perked up at the comparison. "Broodmares are known for their..." I paused as the adjective I was going to use completely snuffed out like a candle in the damn wind. What was I going to say? Ample hips? Receptive uterus? I cleared my throat before croaking out, "Fortitude."

I plastered on my best smile as the rest of the room frowned and shifted their eyes to the platters of food filling the coffee table. *Mother above.* A film of sweat developed between my palms and my wine glass. Crunching filled the silent void.

"What's up with you, Sid? How's the D word?" Stacey asked behind a mouthful of pretzel.

Sid carelessly rolled her eyes, but I saw the tautness knit her shoulders together like a bowstring.

"You can say it out loud, you know," Carly said. "It's not a bad word."

"I know it's not," Stacey volleyed back. "I've been there. It sucks." She turned to Sidney, her bob whisking over her shoulders as she twisted. "I'm sorry, Sid. How's the divorce?" She enunciated divorce with every oral muscle she possessed.

"It...sucks," Sid said through tight lips that lifted in a forced smile.

Stacey threw up her hands. "See?"

Sweatshirts One and Two flitted their eyes back and forth across the room like they were monitoring a tennis match. Stacey topped off her wineglass, an effervescent glop of prosecco foam landing on the glass surface of the coffee table. "It's not so bad after the first couple of years," she continued.

"We'll see," Sid murmured, settling onto the spare couch cushion with a glass of red wine.

"By this time next year, you'll be dating and who knows? Maybe having hot car sex in the high school parking lot."

Sid pinched the bridge of her nose. "I don't think that's going to happen."

Next to Stacey, Carly pursed her lips as she reached inside an enormous yellow tote bag. "Sure, it will, Sid, but until then"—she pulled out the intended quarry from the bottom of her bag— "you can read stuff like this."

A copy of *Lune* landed on the table in front of me, burning its perfectly embossed letters into my retinas. A mixture of giggles and sighs cascaded across the room. My own emotions simmered near the surface, undulating beneath my skin like a serpent. A long-forgotten chasm of longing. And hatred. And regret. And hatred of my regret.

Stacey pushed back from the table and tucked an ankle under her knee, the sumptuous gold fabric of the sofa gilding her like a frame. "I read that one in like two days."

The twins on the couch nodded and smiled secretively. Carly pushed up from her position on the sofa and grunted. Everyone tensed for a moment before she relaxed into a throw pillow. "I had to lock myself in the bathroom to finish it," she admitted. "But it was worth every second." Her eyes fluttered upward, her mouth forming a perfect 'o.'

"When he says..." Stacey crooned, her expression nearly feral.

"I know," Carly screeched, "and that part by the river where—"

"Don't ruin it for me," Sid interrupted. "I haven't read it yet."

My eyes rounded in shock, my brain begging them to please, please ruin it.

"Where can I find a man exactly like Dagen?" whined Sweatshirt One.

"Men like that don't exist," Stacey chastised her. "That's why people love these kinds of books."

Carly giggled on the couch. "I felt bad for my husband, Brad. He kept asking me why I was so pissed off after reading this book."

"Why were you?" I asked, genuinely curious.

"I wasn't mad at the book. I was pissed at him for all the ways he's not like Dagen."

"And for all the things you want done to you that Dagen does to—"

A timer dinged in the background. Sid sprinted to the kitchen. I heard the creak of an oven door followed by a decadent aroma. I welcomed the distraction and siphoned up the smell like it was oxygen. Like it could cleanse my blood of the horrifying adrenaline thrumming through my veins.

I would never—could never—read this book. But I could imagine what was in there. Hell, I had spent the better part of my twenties imagining what was inside his head. And now here it was. Splayed open in front of me like a platter of forbidden fruit.

While everyone was distracted by the platter Sid carried into the room, I craned my neck to steal a final glance at the back cover. My eyes roved the page, devouring the words like the book club ladies were devouring Sid's goat cheese tarts.

In the land of the Fae...the last princess of Eriton...a chance encounter with a human who saves her life and falls in love with her before a terrible secret tears them apart. Can two lost stars find their way back to each other as a looming war threatens to destroy everything?

What in the actual hell?

I read it again, surprise electrifying my skin. Surprise that morphed into anger. I bit the inside of my cheek hard enough to make it pucker.

"Sid, you make the best snacks!" Carly grinned, a glistening streak of oil brightening her upper lip.

"Thanks." Sid picked up an empty plate then surveyed the half-eaten dishes without choosing anything. "I have a lot more time on my hands these days."

Stacey dolloped hummus next to a pile of pepper strips. "You should come to yoga with me. It's Saturdays in the park and we get brunch after."

"Thanks." Sid chewed her lip and finally took a triangle of pita bread smeared with feta and garlic. "I'll think about it."

"Don't think about it. Just do it. You gotta get out there. Not to meet a man necessarily but for you. For your own wellness."

While Stacey rambled on, I watched Sid begin shrinking into herself, her brown skin slackening like a raisin in the sun. My beautiful, spirited friend with her stylish hair and multitude of suede heels had become a bleating goat in the middle of a pack of unintentionally vicious lionesses. My heart stuttered at her pleading expression.

"I got engaged." The words flew from my parted lips and four pairs of eyes lasered to my face instead of Sid's. I willfully schooled my expression into one of wonder and awe. A face that a girl should have when he finally puts a ring on it. The face of a bride-to-be who would soon be floating down the aisle dressed like a pastry on her wedding day.

A torrent of questions erupted. "To Gavin?" "Didn't you guys break up?"

"We never actually broke up," I clarified.

"How did he do it?" Sweatshirt One asked. She had moved to the edge of her cushion, pressing her knees together in anticipation.

"We went out to dinner." When her smile faltered, I continued. "To that place in New York that rotates." I made a circle in the air with my index finger for emphasis.

"Oh." Sweatshirt One scooted back onto the loveseat and took another bite of tart.

Carly squealed, "Can we see the ring?"

Sid looked at me expectantly as I held out my left hand. But unlike the other night, the lamplight found only bare skin.

"He didn't get you a ring." Sweatshirt Two wrinkled her nose in disgust.

"He did," I stuttered. "I had to take it off for work, and I guess I left it on my desk." I frowned as I tried to remember exactly where.

The littered top of my wooden desk in the corner office I shared with my partner was plastered with framed photos and copies of *Equine Vet Monthly* we had yet to read. Earlier today I had operated on a Thoroughbred jumper. A sleek machine of a horse with a ligamentous injury to his back leg. I knew I had taken it off before surgery.

"Who takes off their engagement ring?" Stacey bellowed from the hallway where she was stepping into the guest bathroom.

"I had to take it off," I yelped, hoping she could hear me through a layer of drywall. "I can't wear it into surgery."

My breath caught as I remembered sitting at my desk in a panic, realizing the ring was a half size too small for my finger. It had taken a sizable scoop of lubricant to scrape it over my knuckle before scrubbing in. A visible shroud of guilt settled over my shoulders.

"Have you guys set a date yet?" asked Sid, eyeing me curiously as she tapped her index finger on the surface of her wine glass.

I shook my head. "No and it won't be anytime soon. Gavin just got promoted at his job and I can't leave my practice so..."

My words halted as I absorbed the nonplussed expressions around me. Some throat clearing. A few changes in position. This had to be the worst engagement story in history.

When Stacey emerged from the bathroom moments later, I nearly rejoiced at the distraction. "Who wants more wine?" she asked, and I immediately held up my glass.

CHAPTER FIVE

SUMMER, THEN

"Yes," I said after a beat of silence, the word coming out a little too breathy. A little too eager. Will's eyes flared and I cleared my throat. "I guess I can help you find this hidden pool of magic and wonder."

"Okay then." Will dipped his chin, a pleased expression softening the hard line of his jaw.

At the time, I didn't recognize what it was, but this one simple exchange solidified the start of something between us. A common thread we would tug on from time to time over an entire summer. When he smiled down at me, I was mesmerized by the sun forming a cosmic halo around his head. It was dazzling. Too dazzling. I chewed on my lower lip and forced myself to take a step back.

"I can't today but maybe soon." I quickly checked over my shoulder at the dusty hood of my dad's truck as the unmistakable sound of faint scratching met my ears.

Will's brows furrowed, his expression morphing into bewilderment. "What's in the back of your truck?"

"Why don't you see for yourself?" I backed away and pivoted on my heel. He followed and when we peered over the tailgate, a symphony of hisses ensued. Will barked in surprise.

"What in the world are you doing with all those cats?" he asked, reaching out an index finger to stroke a tuft of fur sticking through the wire mesh.

"I wouldn't do that," I warned him. The cat whipped around, opening its maw to showcase an impressive set of teeth.

Will jerked his finger into his chest. "Noted," he mumbled.

"My dad spends his weekends spaying and neutering feral cats," I explained, patting the nearest cage with a resounding thump.

"Wow...that's simply...what a way to give back?" Will's face was a combination of disbelief and contained humor.

I cut my eyes to the ground. "Anyway...I'm helping him out this summer. Sometimes he even lets me do part of the operation."

He dropped his head into a mocking bow. "Pardon me then. I couldn't possibly deter you from such a noble pursuit." His lips quivered enough that I burst out laughing and was grateful when he did as well.

"I'm around tomorrow," I added quickly once our laughter subsided. "If you still need help by then." Without giving him a chance to respond, I hopped in the truck and waved through the open window as I pulled onto the asphalt, leaving him in the road, hands in his pockets, a promise in his eyes.

SEVERAL DAYS PASSED where I searched for the curious round headlights of Will's vintage car on every street corner. Being trapped inside the clinic was worse. I practically jumped out of my skin every time the bell on the front door jingled.

Three tortuous days later, about the time I was losing hope...and patience, I spied his car sandwiched between two pickup trucks in the parking lot. My stomach flipped and flopped, mimicking the erratic movements of the goat I was wrangling from the outdoor pen into the backdoor surgical suite.

"Calm down," I hissed into his furry lop of an ear. Tightening my hold on the lead rope, I delivered a solid whack to his haunches as he stared me down with his rectangular-shaped pupils. I paused to put my hands on my hips and glare right back. "If you didn't eat everything in sight, you wouldn't be in this mess." I ground my teeth with frustration.

"Quinnie?"

"I'm right outside, Dad," I shouted at the pea-green door labeled "surgery" in white stenciled letters.

The door creaked open on rusted hinges revealing my father in green scrubs and a surgical cap brandishing a metal syringe. "Someone's asking for you in the front."

"Oh?" I feigned innocence, praying the adrenaline spike in my bloodstream didn't show on my face.

I watched my dad teeter between thoughts for a moment, his eyes shifting to me then to the goat I had in a headlock then toward the parking lot. His face remained undecipherable, my knees nearly buckling in the time it took him to make a decision. "Why don't I take Ray here and you can see what he wants."

My face flooded with excitement. I could tell by the way my dad looked at me, his brows rising nearly to the brim of his surgical cap. With a swift transfer of Ray's lead rope to his open palm, I dashed around the side of the building before he changed his mind.

When I skidded around the corner, Will was sitting on the chrome bumper of his sky-blue car, a book splayed across his lap.

"Hi." The word croaked from my throat like I was a bull-frog in summer.

"Hi there," he said smoothly, closing the volume nestled in his lap. He was dressed similar to the first time I had seen him in dark jeans and an even darker T-shirt.

"Still lost?" I asked, shielding my eyes from the sun's interminable glare.

"That depends." He crossed a pair of sinewy arms across his chest.

"On what exactly?" Every step I took toward him lifted the corner of my mouth higher on my cheek.

"It depends on you knowing how to get to a movie theater." Will uncrossed his ankles and stood up. At his full height, I realized my forehead would barely graze his chin.

"I might." I smirked and shoved my hands into my back pockets.

He crossed his arms, cocking his head expectantly.

"Follow this road to the highway then take a left." I pointed toward the sliver of asphalt that ran in front of the clinic. "The only movie theater near Linzberg is about twenty miles down the road on the right. You can't miss it." A part of my stomach flipped with anticipation. I suddenly felt every chafing inch of my jeans.

"I think I might. Miss it, that is," he said solemnly, eyes widening into discs of aquamarine.

"Seriously?" I taunted while my insides busily performed backflips. He lowered his chin, pulling his book into his abdomen. An abdomen that was probably as rock hard as the outer cover of the book he was clutching.

"Would you allow me a confession?" He reached up to rub the back of his neck.

I snorted, the most unladylike noise possible escaping my nose. Was this nineteenth century England and was I Elizabeth Bennett? "Please," I said, holding in a laugh. "Confess away."

"I have a terrible sense of direction."

"I can draw you a map," I teased, not daring to move an inch as he closed some of the distance between us.

"And I'm sure it would be...helpful. But I was hoping for a tour guide instead," he said, his arm making a sweeping gesture toward the driver's seat of his car.

By the time we arrived at the ramshackle four-plex on the outskirts of San Antonio, a heavy cover of clouds filled the sky. Will had let me drive his fancy convertible and was content to ponder the sun-crisped landscape for most of the way there. We had left the top down and a thick layer of dust coated my arms by the time we eased into the parking lot. I not so casually slid my forearms across my jeans before opening the door.

Only one couple stood ahead of us at the ticket booth. They huddled together and could have been mistaken for teenagers except for their sagging skin and snow-white hair. Did people actually fall in love and stay that way for decades? It seemed as unlikely as vampires or self-driving cars. I frowned into the backs of their polyester button-downs.

"What do you care to see?" Will asked, tapping his chin thoughtfully with his index finger.

"Anything is fine," I mumbled. "It's been forever since I saw a movie in the theater." As I scanned the marquee, I nearly danced on my toes when I found the listing I was hoping for. Will's attention landed on my face, and I tried, and failed, to shift my expression into neutral.

He shook his head from side to side. "Anything is *not* fine. There's something you want to see. What is it?"

I bit my bottom lip.

"The vampire one? The one where the girl—"

"No!" I barked, narrowing my eyes, truly horrified. "I was

actually thinking that one." I pointed at the poster next to the ticket window.

He had the nerve to cast me a disbelieving look. "Two for *Iron Man*," he said loudly then smirked.

"Was that really necessary?" I hissed.

"We couldn't have anyone thinking you would see a movie about a girl falling in love with a vampire anti-hero."

I rolled my eyes as I followed him into the building. There was no one around who cared about my movie choices.

A grand total of five people, including us, reclined in tattered cloth seats while we waited for the movie to start. The overhead lights were blinding and the screen completely blank. When I shifted position, my seat squawked in protest. The pungent odor of burned popcorn lingered in the air.

"We're here early," I said apologetically.

"And I'm so glad we are." Will brushed a hand through his windblown hair and twisted toward me. "One additional confession," he started, his lips mulling over every syllable, "I love being inside the movie theater."

"Why?" I asked, my curiosity piqued.

"Because it's total freedom. There's nothing to do besides wait. No one interrupting your thoughts. Similar to being on an airplane."

I had never even been on an airplane, so I nodded along, flitting my eyes to the rip in the upholstery of the seat in front of me. Had I ever felt like that? Total freedom? I wasn't sure I knew what that even meant. My life had always been fun...but free? More like purposeful with a side of work ethic heaped with responsibility and a healthy fear of failure.

"So that's two for me." He settled back in his seat and eyed me expectantly.

"Two what?"

"Confessions. Now you owe me two."

I suddenly forgot every mildly interesting thing about myself. "Like what?" My voice bordered on a squawk.

"Anything." The tip of his tongue slid over his bottom lip.

I fidgeted and clenched my hands into fists.

"Maybe start with your name," he offered. "Your full name."

"Quinn Elizabeth McClain."

"Elizabeth?"

I lightly punched his bicep, my tension becoming kinetic energy. "Tell me yours."

"Jacob William Deremer." The name rolled off his tongue like sweet honey in my ear. It was a beautiful name. The surname that also belonged to the most prominent winery in Linzberg, lest I forget. A memory floated to the surface. A childhood memory. I snatched at it like a leaf in a stream.

"I visited your house once when I was little. I think your grandma had a terrier named..." I paused, the memory dissipating into watercolor.

"Nelson!" Will barked a surprised laugh. "Do you remember what you were doing there?"

I shook my head. "No, I only remember playing on the floor with a brown and white dog...and there was a fountain. You have a fountain in the middle of your living room."

Will cocked his head to the side. "Entryway to be exact but yes, we have a fountain."

"You're such a snob," I teased.

"Only when necessary," he fired back, his smile widening as he playfully tapped me on the nose. "You owe me one more."

"Fine." My mouth opened but no words came out. My mind was literally as blank as the movie screen. A white canvas of nothingness. A colorless void. I begged him for help with my eyes.

"How about"—he paused to rub his chin—"the best moment of your life?"

I blinked and the only image that came to mind was seeing him for the first time, leaning against the hood of his car on the side of a dusty country road. My tongue took its time unfurling in my mouth. "I don't think it's happened yet."

He nodded speculatively, his eyes alight with the resonance of understanding. "How about the worst?"

I averted my eyes when the question left his lips. And for a moment, I wanted to tell him. I wanted to tell him about the horrible day that I could barely remember. I wanted to tell him how I was haunted by what I knew...and even more by what I didn't. But I couldn't do it. My thoughts staggered around my head like a sick herd of cattle.

"I don't know," I answered weakly. "Probably the time my dad caught me sneaking out of the house."

This took him by surprise. He flashed his eyes to mine, the blinding lights of the theater glinting off the flecks of gold. "Where were you going?"

I settled back into my seat, grateful that he was distracted from the flood of emotions churning under my skin. Smirking, I recalled the details of that night. I had been eleven. "It was Halloween," I started. "And a full moon. And a clear beautiful night where you could see every single star."

His face had gone slack with wonderment as he waited in perfect silence. I took this as encouragement to continue. "I didn't plan on sneaking out, but I could see the night sky from my window, and I just wanted to be out there...to experience it...to be a part of something wild and beautiful." I heard him clear his throat. "I'm kind of obsessed with the moon."

"So, you're a lady of the night then?" he asked, his tone light and teasing.

A blush bloomed on my cheeks. "No," I sputtered. "I'm not like that."

"Like what?" he asked softly. "A beautiful girl who loves the night sky?"

My heart caught in my throat at the word *beautiful,* and I immediately brought my fingertips to the jagged white pencil-thin scar running from my temple down to my jaw. "I don't know about that."

"Maybe you could show me sometime?" he said. "How the moon looks in the Texas sky?"

My heart fluttered inside my chest like a trapped bird, and I pressed my thighs together. "Maybe." A whispered word that I hoped would become a promise. He peered into my face like he ached to see behind it. Like he ached to see me. I wondered whether anyone had ever looked at me like that before. Or ever would again.

It was my turn to clear my throat. The lights began to dim, and I panicked. I wasn't ready for this game to be over. "Where did you grow up?" I whispered. "I know it wasn't around here."

"Here and there," he said enigmatically.

"That's not an answer."

He blew a breath out of his nose like a colt. "London mostly. And most recently New York."

I whistled low and steady. "That explains a lot."

"What exactly does it explain?" he asked, at a pitch so low I barely heard it.

Dramatic clips of a high-speed car chase with a thumping bass beat in the background flashed across the screen. I leaned over and dared to place my lips within a hairsbreadth of his ear. A tendril of his hair tickled the end of my nose as I said, "Your complete failure to understand the geography of the Texas hill country." He stiffened as my warm breath clouded the shell of his ear. I slid back over to my seat.

A minute later he leaned over and whispered, "That's what you're for."

CHAPTER SIX

AUTUMN, NOW

"No, I can't do it Thursday. I have to leave early that day." I drummed my fingers on the only vacant space on my desk and tucked my phone into my shoulder.

Across from me, the office door opened with a squeal. Patricia, my surgical assistant, poked her head of corkscrew gray curls through the opening, wedging the door open with her hips. She pointed at her wristwatch, her eyes, the color of packed earth, hardening when she noticed I was on the phone.

Patricia was a stickler for our schedule. I shrugged dramatically and mouthed "Mitch," and she responded with a death glare. The grizzled trainer and my middle-aged Polish surgical technician had never quite warmed to one another.

"Friday morning, Mitch. It's the best I can do." I held the phone away from my ear as a stream of expletives erupted from the other end of the line. "I'll be there before the sun rises," I promised brightly then pressed end before he could launch into another tirade.

Patricia glared at me, her hands perched on either hip,

expanding her frame so that it took up the entire doorway. "What'd that old buzzard want?"

"He's taking the barn to a show this weekend and needs me to check out the horses."

Patricia snorted, her nose flaring out like a disgruntled mare. "He always needs something."

The corner of my mouth quivered with the beginnings of a smile. "Well, he does run a forty-five-horse barn on the biggest farm in Central Jersey."

"Then you would think he could do a few things on his own by now. Instead of calling you every time a horse farts wrong."

A bark of laughter escaped my lips and I tried to smother it with a cough. "It's job security. And if any of his riders make it to Paris next summer..." I trailed off as Patricia's phone rang and she fished it out of her labcoat pocket.

Mitch had tantalized me with a halfhearted offer to take me along to oversee the horses that would be competing in the Salon du Cheval. My entire body vibrated when I thought of it. I glanced at the glossy new copy of *Equine Vet Monthly* on my desk. This time next year, I could be on the cover. The coveted personal veterinarian for the world's most elite Thoroughbreds.

When my wistful gaze met with Patricia's prune-shaped mouth, she shoved her phone into her pocket and barked, "Your nine o'clock case is here Dr. McClain." She forced an accent into my last name, like I was fresh from the highlands of Scotland. I pushed back from my desk and followed her out the door. It was always a good day when Patricia was giving me shit.

While I scrubbed my hands at the sink, exfoliating a proper layer of epidermis, I followed the movements of my team around the room. It took no fewer than eight of us to prepare a thousand pounds of horse for surgery.

Two of the technicians guided the mare, hobbled and strung up to the ceiling, along the I-beam toward a thickly padded platform. Her chestnut body seemed to float through the air, mane streaming behind her until her head was tilted to the side and her body followed in a heap.

The smell of antiseptic clouded the room as Patricia prepped the mare's shaved foreleg, the burnt orange droplets raining down onto the floor. Prepping for surgery was a dance I had performed a thousand times yet still thrilled me. I dried my hands on a blue surgical towel before shoving them through the arms of a sterile gown. Behind me, someone began playing nineties rock music over the speakers.

I surveyed the room, my domain of utter badassery, and said, "Shall we get started?"

THE SUN WAS past its apex by the time I stepped outside, reaching skyward and feeling the coils of tension unfurl in my back. A gust of wind whipped around my shoulders, tearing a few golden tendrils from my sloppy ponytail. I drew in a slow breath and then another.

The advent of fall on the East Coast was a magical time. Some people considered spring the season of renewal—the time of budding growth and twitterpated animals procreating to their heart's content. Not me. For me it was autumn.

It was the shedding of leaves until the trees dared to be stark naked. It was the scent of ripe fruit—apples as red as candy and pumpkins as big as my head. It was the way the wind sang the earth to sleep under an ebony blanket of stars. I even welcomed Halloween with its kitschy parties and streets filled with kids riding a sugar high.

This year Gavin was coming for the weekend so we could

hand out candy from the front porch of my two-bedroom bungalow house in Haddonfield. Maybe this year I could even convince him to wear a costume. I chuckled to myself. He might look cute as a nerdy superhero.

"You did good work in there."

I turned around. My boss and mentor, crisp as always in a set of navy-blue scrubs and white leather trainers, trudged up the path behind me.

"Thanks." I grinned and folded my arms across my chest. "It took me a while to get the second plate in."

He nodded, a shock of white hair rippling in the rising breeze. "The post-op films looked good. Exactly what I would have done for that kind of injury."

"I hope it heals okay." I toed a line in the dirt as my mind relived the last three hours of handiwork I had performed on a shattered foreleg.

"Who does she belong to?" Steve asked.

"Andy Kerrigan."

He let out a low whistle. "Surprised he hasn't shown up yet to see how it went."

"I know." I chewed the inside of my lip until it was painful. "He makes Mitch Jenkins seem like a fuzzy bunny." About that time my phone rang. Before I pulled it out of my back pocket, I knew who it would be. "Andy," I said brightly. "How are you?" A rich accent met my ears, thick enough that I had to concentrate on the vowels between the heavy consonants.

Steve mouthed "good luck" and strolled past me toward the building that housed the aquatherapy center. My gut clenched and I wrapped my sweaty fingers even tighter around the phone. "She's doing fine. Everything went exactly as expected."

"When will she be ready?" he growled in a low voice.

"Two weeks give or take. We need to make sure the bones

set and get her started on a rehab program." I willed confidence in my voice and widened my stance for a man that was nothing but a voice on the other end of the line.

"I'll expect you to oversee her recovery...personally." The r's continued to roll inside my head long after he was finished speaking.

"Consider it done."

"Good," he said, followed by a click as he ended the call.

By the time Thursday came, I buzzed with energy. The temperature had dropped another ten degrees overnight and the penned horses behind the clinic were snorting puffs of sublimated vapor into the air when I approached holding my morning coffee. I bustled through rounds, peering underneath bellies and grasping outstretched forelegs to examine a row of stitches, leaving notes for the techs who would show up later to change bandages. Today was purely administrative, a time to catch up on charting and order supplies. To return emails and make phone calls to potential clients.

As far as the equine surgery world, Steve and I weren't the only game in town. But I thought we were the best one. When my boss had bought into this practice nearly thirty years ago, he was fresh out of vet school. And ten years into his career, when his partner had retired, Steve Hauserman had been in the market for a fresh face to carry the Central Jersey Equine Surgical Center into the future.

We were introduced at an alumni dinner when I was finishing up my surgical residency at the University of Pennsylvania. Two rounds of bourbon and a game of pool later, I had a job interview. Later, I asked Steve how he knew I was the right fit for the practice. He said that anyone with that much hand-eye coordination after drinking half a bottle of bourbon was meant to be an exceptional surgeon. Since that moment, I had spent every day trying to prove him right.

In the end, our partnership was melded together by a

shared belief in providing excellent care to the horses first and their owners second. We navigated the teetering balance of handling the high-dollar investments in our surgical skills because we were exact opposites. I softened his rough edges, and he challenged me to operate on the inoperable.

Where he was quiet and obsessive, I was vocal and had a knack for customer service. He laid a foundation where I could grow as I pleased and mentored me into someone who was now asked for by the best trainers around. I'd never dreamed a small-town girl from the Texas hill country would end up as a premiere veterinarian on the East Coast. Yet here I was.

I strolled into the office, my coffee having long ago faded to lukewarm, and slipped into the tattered fabric chair behind my desk. Patricia poked her head into the doorway wearing a pointed black hat with a crow balanced on the brim.

"What are you doing for Halloween?" she asked.

I smiled as I dumped the coffee into the trash bin. "Gavin's coming in on the train and we're going to hand out candy and watch a scary movie."

"Ooh," she said sarcastically. "I hope you're at least going to wear a costume." She waggled thick black brows that had been filled in with a pencil.

"Gavin's not...into all that." I waved my hand in the air before cracking open the lid of my laptop.

Patricia grunted and tossed a thick folder onto the chaos of my desk. "Are you?"

"Am I what?" I absentmindedly began scanning the slew of emails in my inbox.

"What keeps those wheels greased, Quinn? Come on. Give me something to gossip about."

Without looking up, I blew out a breath. "Patricia, get out of my office you cougar."

"I'll see you after my lunchbreak," she said without missing a beat. "And I'll expect an answer."

When the door banged shut, I sagged in relief, clicking open the first email in my queue. Mitch Jenkins reminding me to show up at his place tomorrow. Like I could forget. The next one was a request from a pharmaceutical company to participate in a research trial. Four or five emails down the list I found one from David McClain, DVM.

Quinn,
Even though you're too famous and important to think about us simple country folk, it
wouldn't kill you to come visit every now and again.
love,
(your patient and not getting any younger)
Dad

I sighed and tried to conjure the image of my father reclined on the porch swing of our ranch-style home with the wrap-around porch. And couldn't. When was the last time I had been home? The summer after vet school maybe? And that had been a quick visit to pack up some boxes of books before I moved to Philadelphia for my equine surgery residency. That was six years ago. The realization smacked me in the face. It wasn't that I didn't love where I had grown up, but I had made a promise to myself. A promise that was easier to keep if I stayed away.

My eyes flitted away from my computer and landed on the folder Patricia had tossed onto my desk. I read the name plastered on the tab. Kerrigan Farms. Was this another referral? My gut twisted with anticipation. Visions of torn tendons and stress fractures from young horses who were pushed to perform beyond their maturity level appeared in the spot where my computer screen should be. I rubbed my thumb over the knife-like edge of the folder before opening it and beginning to read.

By the time I coasted into the train station that evening it was already a quarter after five. I spied Gavin's silhouette, briefcase in hand, and I gave a perfunctory honk. He looked up, eyes smiling behind black-rimmed glasses, and raised a hand in greeting. He was nothing if not efficient. No wasted motion. A stillness about him that stabilized my chaos. That was probably why things between us worked so well.

"How was your day?" he asked, climbing onto the running boards of my Toyota and then into the passenger seat.

I gunned the engine and pulled out of the parking lot before answering. "Finer than most. How about yours?" I side-eyed him when I stopped at a traffic light. He was still in work clothes. Thick wool trousers and a crisp button-down. He must have taken off his tie while riding the train.

"Brutal enough that I felt justified taking tomorrow off so I could spend a long weekend with you."

"Oh yeah? What did you have in mind?" I accelerated through the next light without slowing down.

"Sleeping in." He leaned over and slid his fingers along my knee. "Making breakfast together. Maybe discussing some wedding plans?"

My insides stilled, frozen like the hands of an ornery clock. I beat back the instinct to panic. "Yeah, that sounds great," I babbled. "Except for the part about sleeping in. I have to be at Mitch's place before dawn to clear some jumpers for a show this weekend and also the part about breakfast because my fridge is down to beer and a bag of apples."

"Takeout it is then." His fingers left my knee, but his posture seemed content as he settled into the seat.

Chastising myself, I twisted the knob on the radio to drown out my own guilt.

We had barely made it into my 1920's bungalow home on a quiet street in Haddonfield before the hesitant knocking started. I sent Gavin inside to change and ended up spending the next hour camped out in my foyer handing out sugar to what seemed like every kid in my neighborhood.

"Trick or treat!" echoed down the hallway as I scrambled to dump another bag of candy into a plastic cauldron. When I wrenched open the door, two Elsas and a Mulan greeted me with sugar-coated smiles and cheeks rosy from the biting wind.

"I can't believe it," I exclaimed, the girls regarding me with wide eyes. "Three Disney princesses have come to my house on Halloween."

"We're not really princesses," said Mulan as she swept dark bangs out of her eyes.

"I beg your pardon," I said, dropping a handful of candy into each bag. "I know what princesses look like and you three are definitely the real deal." They responded by giggling their thank yous and running across my lawn to the next house over.

"Was that the last of them?" Gavin called from the living room.

"Better be. I'm almost out of candy," I lamented and flipped off my porch light. The fuzzy blur of the television drew me to the sofa, and I plopped down next to my favorite version of Gavin, dressed down in joggers and a white T-shirt, hair damp from his shower, a glop of foam behind one ear from shaving. I leaned over and inhaled the scent of him, right above his collarbone. No matter the time of day, he always smelled like dryer sheets.

"Hold on," I yelped and scrabbled over the back of the couch toward my bedroom.

"I'm starting the movie," he called as I frantically threw my closet open and began rifling through a long-forgotten container on the floor. When I found a vintage leather mini-dress and fishnet stockings, I shimmied out of my jeans and put them on.

"What do you think?" I paused in the doorway for dramatic effect before gliding over to the couch and planting my thighs on either side of Gavin's lap. His eyes widened behind his lenses, pupils dilating to the size of grapes. I parted my lips to reveal a pair of pointy canines. He laughed nervously and patted the seat cushion next to him. He shifted so that I slid off his lap, an arm curling me into his side.

"Were the vampire teeth too much?" I asked, my words coming out garbled.

His lips found my temple and planted a featherlight kiss there. "Possibly," he said slowly as he worked his jaw.

"I know"—I spit the teeth into my hand—"that costumes really don't do it for you."

"No, they do. But I guess I prefer a little something less...lady of the night."

"Like what?" I asked, brightening my face to dim the hurt. "So that I know for next time."

"Cheerleader?"

"Noted," I said and snuggled into his side, intentionally lasering my focus on the television.

On the screen, a gnarled zombie keeled over when he was run through with a sword. Part of me died right along with it.

CHAPTER SEVEN

SUMMER, THEN

The night of the movie with Will, a maelstrom of rain greeted me when I got home and continued into the next morning and the morning after that. I couldn't have cared less about the weather. I floated through my days thinking about Will. I cleaned cages and dissected our conversations. I held frightened animals who needed vaccines and wondered when I would see him again. The memory of him driving me home with painful care as storm clouds gathered above us played like a loop in my head.

"Should I close the roof?" he had asked, and I had shaken my head. Something about him unleashed a recklessness inside me. And potentially getting caught in the rain with no roof over my head was the wildest, most irresponsible choice I could make at that moment.

His amused smile had been affirmation enough of my choice. We had driven in easy silence, the radio playing low enough in the background that I couldn't make out the words.

Nature had refused to cooperate with my vision of Will and me caught in a drenching downpour and needing to rely on each other's body heat to stay warm. She had waited until I was out of the car and just shy of the porch steps for the raindrops to fall in a deluge on top of my head.

"Quinnie," my dad boomed as I passed his office, effectively extracting me from my daydream. With the door wide open, I could see that he was crouched over his desk making notes in a pile of cream-colored folders. Patient charts. I looked at the stack and inwardly groaned. I was certain I would be filing those later today.

"What can I do for you, Dr. McClain?" I smirked and grabbed the two sides of the doorjamb. He hated when I called him that.

Steepling his fingers under his chin, he studied me, mouth holding in a smile even as his dimples deepened. "What do you have planned for the rest of the day?"

I narrowed my eyes. He knew what I had planned. I twirled the end of my braid around my fingers, the strands more like spun gold than wheat since summer had started. "That depends."

My dad pushed back from his desk and barked a laugh at my impudence. "On what exactly?"

"On what you're about to ask me to do."

He nodded and rubbed his jaw with his forefinger.

My insides clenched as I waited for him to speak. He loved being the center of attention, keeping me teetering on the edge until the moment he made his big reveal. I always thought he had done it on purpose. To make my childhood seem more magical than it was. To make even the regular seem extraordinary. A bicycle that was a surrogate for a race-horse. A plastic ring from a quarter turnstile machine that turned me into a princess from a long-lost land. I knew he did it to balance out the pain and grief we had experienced...and I loved him for it.

"Take a guess." Light and mischief twinkled behind his blue-gray eyes.

"You want me to take your car on a road trip?"

My dad owned a black 1977 vintage Camaro that he loved only slightly less than me. He snorted and flipped closed the chart he had been working on. "Guess again."

Screwing my face up in concentration, I said, "You decided to let me spend my summer having fun like a normal teenager instead of working?"

"Even better," he said, dimples deepening into caverns on either side of his face. "I have a job that you're going to love."

"Please tell me it doesn't involve more cats."

Chuckling, he removed a sheet of lined paper from his drawer and began scrawling a name and an address. "Here." He shoved the paper to the ravaged edge of his wooden desk.

"What's this?" I picked it up, studying the unfamiliar name. "Selma Vanderhal. Who is that?"

"Some well-to-do from Rhode Island. She bought a little piece of land right off River Road and thought it would be a nice place for a few horses."

"What does that have to do with me?"

"Her mare is about to foal—probably tonight—and she's nervous. She doesn't want to be by herself in case things don't go right."

"And you want to put me on midwife duty?"

"Yes ma'am. It isn't every day you get to witness a miracle."

I shoved the paper into my back pocket. "Dad, please," I scoffed. "I know what goes on during birth. There's a lot of pain...and liquid...and then plop—a baby drops into the world."

"But you've never actually seen it happen."

"No, but..." I paused my argument. It was true. I hadn't actually witnessed a baby anything born. The closest I had

64

come was finding our Golden Retriever licking her newborn litter one morning when I was twelve.

My dad gave me a double thumbs up. "Then tonight's your lucky night." He stood up at his desk, stretching to his full six-foot height. "Give me a call if you need anything."

Lucky night, indeed. Selma Vanderhal lived on the same stretch of road as Deremer Vineyards. I plugged her address into my GPS, and my eyes nearly bugged out of their sockets when I realized the route would take me right by the giant wrought iron gate with the D in perfect script on the front. My hands trembled as I flipped open my cell phone and began painfully scribing a message that I then erased over and over again.

> Will, I was wondering...

Delete.

> Will, if you aren't doing anything...

Delete.

"Oh, to hell with it," I muttered and then typed with renewed vigor.

> If you want to see a horse born, meet me at your front gate in ten minutes.

Snapping the phone closed, I tossed it on the passenger side of the pickup and cranked the engine.

When I sped down River Road toward my destination, dust billowing behind me, I refused to slow down enough to check behind the Deremers' front gate. He was probably busy. After all, it was a Friday evening, and he didn't look like the type of guy who spent many of those at home.

As I trundled past the gate, the driver's side tire landing in a pothole that I felt in my teeth, I checked my rearview mirror. And there he was. Will with his arm awkwardly lofted into the stratosphere. I allowed myself a moment to smile broadly before chucking the gearshift into reverse.

"I thought you weren't going to stop." He was chuckling as he gracefully cleared the running board and landed like a cat in the seat beside me. And when he winked at me, closing his lid over an eye that sparkled with amusement, the air whooshed out of my chest.

"I didn't think you'd actually be there," I confessed.

"What?" He pressed on the dashboard with both hands for emphasis. "And miss out on the miracle of birth?"

"Well, it's not for everyone."

He pondered that for a moment, and I watched facets of his mind turning over. "Don't you think that if you have the chance to experience something extraordinary, no matter what it is, you should do it?" His words floated into my ears, melodic and visceral. My body tightened and liquefied at the same time.

The air in the truck crackled with electricity, thick heady tension that I wanted to tug on. Anything to bring him closer to me.

A honk erupted behind me, splitting my chest into shards. I stuck my hand out the window and motioned them to go around me. Will secured himself into the seatbelt before extending his arm out the window to hold on to the truck frame. Shaking my head, I gunned the engine.

In the year that Selma Vanderhal had owned her river-front property, it had transformed from dilapidated buildings and overgrown thornbushes into a manicured estate. A row of white fence line ran the length of a concrete driveway that ended at a stucco two-story with a tiled roof.

Behind the house, a turquoise pool sparkled in the rays of a descending sun. And even farther still, past a small crop of mesquite trees, an A-frame barn, its doors thrown open in welcome, glinted in the sunlight.

Will and I poked our heads into the dim interior, dust motes dancing like wayward fairies above our heads. "Hello?" I called. "Mrs. Vanderhal?"

A petite woman in chestnut brown riding breeches and tall English boots emerged from one of the open stalls. She strode toward us, arms outstretched in her long-sleeved button-down.

"You must be Quinn." The crow's feet around her eyes crinkled as she grabbed both my hands and stood on tip toe to plant a kiss on both of my cheeks. "Your father speaks very highly of you."

I stood paralyzed for a second, both from absorbing the compliment as well as the overt affection from a complete stranger. "Thank you," I said, struggling to get the words out. Her attention turned to Will, passing over him with an assessing eye.

He smoothly extended a hand and flashed her a smile that dazzled. "I'm Will Deremer."

Tilting her head in thought, she asked, "Like the wine?"

He bowed his head in response. "My grandparents own the vineyard a bit farther down the road."

"I must make it there one day. I hear the grounds are breathtaking."

Will cleared his throat. "They are and I'll have my grandmother give you a call to arrange a tour."

Her milky irises lit up in response and she clasped her hands to her chest like a schoolgirl. "Ooh! That would be lovely."

My curiosity piqued. I had always wondered what was behind that massive iron gate and stone walls. I couldn't even see the house from the road. Not to mention the landscape.

Like I had mentioned to Will, I had been there once...a long time ago...and I didn't remember much.

I noticed Mrs. Vanderhal slide her gaze from Will to me in a question. "Will is going to help me with the...birthing process." I flashed her a smile that I hoped rivaled Will's and gestured down the main corridor of the barn. "Can we see the mare?"

Mrs. Vanderhal's pregnant mare was none other than Rainbow Chaser, the winner of the Kentucky Oaks five years ago and second in the Breeder's Cup before she was retired from racing. I recognized her immediately by the white arch on her forehead in stark contrast to the deep coppery color of her coat. I wondered if my dad knew how high dollar this horse was...and if he should be here instead of me. The mare shifted her weight back and forth in the straw then made a half circle before pinning her ears back and baring her teeth.

"Is this her first foal?" I asked surveying the stall for a safe place where Will and I could settle in for the evening.

"Yes. And she has been like this all afternoon. I assumed she would have delivered by now."

Quietly, I crept over to her haunches and placed a steady hand on her quivering musculature. She lifted a hoof but didn't lash out at me. "Horses usually prefer privacy. It's why most babies are born in the middle of the night," I explained. "Typically, as soon as we stop watching them."

"Does everything look normal?" Mrs. Vanderhal asked with a note of concern.

I gave her the most reassuring look I knew how at age eighteen. "Absolutely."

"Well then, I'll leave you to it. If you need anything, run up to the house and ring the doorbell."

I nodded, waving confidently as she disappeared out of the mouth of the barn. The sun had started to set, its final rays filtering through the barn like candlelight.

Will remained motionless inside the doorway of the stall, hands thrust in his pockets as he followed the movements of the mare around the enclosed space. I squatted down into the corner, as far into the shadows as I could go, and began fluffing the straw into a shapeless pile. Once I settled onto the pile, reclining my back against the woodgrain, I patted the ground next to me. "We'll sit over here and hopefully she'll forget all about us."

Will covered the width of the stall in two strides and folded himself into a cross-legged position next to me. "Are all horses like this when they have a baby?"

I shook my head. "I don't think so. She seems...agitated. But it's her first one so she has no idea what to expect."

Will shifted his position, the outside of his thigh brushing mine. "That makes sense. I wonder if people are like that."

I shrugged as a blush crept up my neck. "I wouldn't know," I said. "I've never seen a human baby born."

"Would you want to?" he asked, completely transfixed by the mare who had flopped onto her side, her overly large belly heaving with effort.

"I don't know...maybe if it was my own?" The blush continued from my neck into my jawline.

"So, you want to have children?"

"Yeah...maybe...someday." I grabbed a handful of straw to distract myself from the twisting in my gut. "You ask a lot of questions."

His eyes cut to mine, guileless and sincere. Kind eyes that held only the best of intentions. "I find myself wanting to know a lot of things."

"Like what?" My chest filled up with breath.

"Like..." He began tracing circles in the dirt with his index finger. Beautiful, perfect circles that would have made Archimedes proud. "What do you want to do after college?"

I exhaled, strong and true. That was an easy one. I tilted

my head toward the mare who had launched herself into a sitting position and was sniffing underneath her own belly.

"You want to get pregnant?"

With my palm, I smacked him in the chest and then tried not to concentrate on how solid it was beneath my fingers. How warm. "No! I want to be a vet."

"A vet for horses?"

"Yes, an equine vet."

"Very cool."

"How about you?"

"I don't know yet...but I think maybe a writer."

"Like a journalist?"

"No...like books or screenplays."

"So, you want to be the next JRR Tolkien?"

"Something like that." His eyes flared with intensity underneath hooded lids, and he became quiet, drawing into himself. Into a world that I couldn't see or experience. I desperately wanted to know where he had gone.

Swallowing past the congestion in my throat, I asked, "So where are you going to college? After your gap year, I mean."

"California. I got into Berkley."

My eyelids drew upward in surprise. "You didn't want to start this year?"

I watched his breath stall in his chest. "I...couldn't."

"Why not?"

"My mom. She got sick last year. Breast cancer."

My heartrate spiked into a thunderous gallop. "Where is she now?"

"She...died...which is why I'm spending the summer with my grandparents. And taking some time off from school."

My stomach lurched as I stared at his bowed head, the curled tufts of his wayward hair framing his face. I picked up the hand in my lap to place it—where? On his cheek? I tucked it back into my lap. "I'm so sorry." The words sounded weak and watery. Flimsy for the degree of emotion that churned through me.

He exhaled through his nose while I floundered to say something profound. Something life changing. But what could I say? What had anyone ever said to me that had made losing my mom even a little easier?

A few beats of silence passed while Will gripped his knees, his knuckles tense. "How about you?" he asked. We both relaxed into the shifting subject matter.

"College?"

He nodded.

"Princeton."

It was his turn to gape in surprise. I was relieved to see the shadows disappear from his face.

"What?" I shrugged innocently. "You didn't think a small-town girl could get into an Ivy League school?"

His cheeks pinked in embarrassment. "No, I wasn't thinking that I only meant...it's so beautiful around here. Why would you want to be so far away?" His face shone with wistfulness and mystery.

"If you had grown up here, you would know it for what it really is—a boring wasteland." I chuckled thinking of all the summers I had spent combing the hills behind our house for something interesting. Anything interesting.

He grew quiet, furrowing his brows in thought. "I wish I had...grown up here, that is."

"Why is that?"

His expression softened into a mixture of regret and amusement, a smile contained inside the contours of his mouth. A mouth that I willfully tore my eyes from when the mare heaved a breath and settled on her side once more.

"She's getting close," I whispered as Will dared a look at her haunches and the protruding bluish bulge.

"Is that...?"

"Yep," I replied, pushing back on my heels until I was flush with the side of the stall. Will followed suit and settled in next to me. Close enough that I could feel his breath skate over the top of my head. I settled into his warmth like a hug. A tuft of his hair tickled my ear when he leaned down to whisper, "What do we do now?"

A shiver started behind my neck and skittered all the way to my toes. "We just wait."

Time passed slowly then quickly then slowly again as we sat in utter silence. The blue blob emerged a few inches at a time, enough that I could identify a hoof then the slice of a muzzle. We eventually reclined into the corner of the stall, a quiet comfort descending as we watched. And waited.

"How long should it take?" Will asked, his words in my ear as soft as a summer breeze.

"Not long now," I answered. His face was close enough that if I turned my head, I would be within a millimeter of his mouth. Too close for someone I barely knew. And it thrilled me.

A grunt from the mare centered my resolve, and before my next breath, a gush of fluid then a membranous lump slid out onto the straw. A black muzzle poked free followed by two hooves. And suddenly we were staring at a foal, wet and gleaming, her eyes bright and wondrous as they saw the world for the first time.

Her body writhed as she cast off the excess membranes and made her first attempt at standing. Bits of straw clung to her fur as she rose then fell then rose again on spindly splayed-out legs that shook from effort. Didn't we all come into the world like this? Awkward and unsteady until we finally learned to stand on our own.

Will's body was taut beside me, barely moving each time he inhaled. A warmth seeped into my arm, and I realized he had grabbed my hand. Smiling at the weighty, heady feel of it, I didn't dare take my eyes off the horses.

CHAPTER EIGHT

AUTUMN, NOW

The partial moon was still high, cushioned against a sumptuous black night sky when I edged out of bed. The wood floor groaned underneath my bare feet, and I paused briefly as the form next to me flopped from his back to his side. Gavin was measured in everything he did, except for sleep. I thought it was perhaps the only time he truly let go. His face was slack, mouth half open and slanted downward as he blew out a light snore.

Despite my failed seduction as a sexy vampiress, we had made love last night. Slowly but effectively inside the chill of my bedroom. It was still too warm for heater weather and probably too cold without it, but body heat was free. Unlike heating a one-hundred-year-old home that was as drafty as an airplane hangar.

I dressed in the dark, pulling my typical field outfit from the bottom drawer of my dresser. Jeans, long-sleeved T-shirt, and an old vet school sweatshirt that would be filthy by the time the sun rose. My engagement ring winked at me from the top of the dresser where it sat next to my keys and a ticket stub from a Patty Griffin concert last year.

A wave of unexpected guilt washed over me. I glanced back at Gavin, now on his belly stretched over the full width of my queen-sized bed. I shoved the ring over my fourth knuckle and soundlessly pulled the door closed behind me.

When I skidded into the driveway of Brookwood Farms, Mitch Jenkins was already waiting for me at the gate, arms folded across his wiry chest, a newsboy cap pulled low over his eyebrows. I rolled down my window, a gust of cold wind snaking into the warm cab of my truck.

"Is this early enough for you?" I teased. He grumbled something I couldn't understand, and I motioned my head for him to join me in the truck. I drove at a snail's pace down the serpentine gravel road, past the neat line of white fencing and the outcropping of storage buildings that housed mowing equipment. When the stable loomed ahead of me, I pulled over and parked under a towering oak tree, its branches still filled with the warm golds and honey browns of fall.

"How many do you have for me this morning?"

He tipped the brim of his hat to massage the furrows on his forehead. "Twelve...give or take."

"Twelve!" I gasped. "You're taking twelve horses to the Pemberly show?"

"That's what I said, didn't I?"

"What time are you leaving?"

"We need to be loaded up to go right after breakfast. Eight at the latest."

My eyes widened. Three hours to examine and clear twelve horses. That was one horse every fifteen minutes. And that was without breaks and excluding any issues that might come up.

"And you couldn't get Steve or one of the other vets around here to come over yesterday?" I barked. "You thought you'd drag my ass out of bed before dawn to make me do the impossible?"

He snorted, warm breath condensing on the windshield next to him. "Well, I wouldn't bother with you if you weren't the best."

I regarded him through a side eye, revealing nothing on my face. Definitely not the pride blooming there. Wrenching open the door of the truck, I hopped onto the ground.

"Flattery is for those who are insecure. I'll take coffee instead." I winked, long and slow, before sauntering into the barn and surveying the endless double row of stalls with perky heads already thrust over the half doors. "Okay kids, who wants to be first?"

Two hours passed in a flurry of warm horse breath and dancing hooves and switch-like tails landing on every crevice of my face. Despite the frigid temperature, sweat collected on my hairline and between my toes stuffed into wool-lined waterproof boots. I was grateful that I'd been negligent at the hair salon the past few months. My blonde layers had grown out past my shoulders, long enough to be twisted into a bun at the nape of my neck.

I ran a hand down another slim foreleg, pressing and kneading as I went, searching for any areas of abnormal warmth or swelling. Hoping I wouldn't find an aberrant angle or detect a light pop when the horse shifted its weight.

"You know, I could go faster if you didn't follow behind me like a stalker."

Mitch jangled his keys and edged up to the cross ties on either side of the filly's head. I struggled up from a squat, my back clenching in protest.

"Can I unhook this one?" Mitch said gruffly.

"Sure, but isn't she a little young? Why are you taking her all the way to Pemberly?"

He stroked the young mare's head, his fingers light as a

feather on the pristine white star on her forehead. "This one is...special." He grunted out the last word like it was in another language. Mitch began whispering in her ear as he unhooked the crossties. The mare blew breath onto his face like a would-be lover.

My chest tightened at the display of intimacy. No matter that it was between human and equine. Mitch might be rough around the edges on his best day but he had the gift...and he knew how to use it to his advantage. I imagined that was why there had never been a Mrs. Jenkins. Who would want to be a wife to a man with a harem of mistresses?

I cleared my throat as her hooves clopped away from me down the thoroughfare. "She's fine by the way," I called and turned my attention to the next stall.

It was fifteen after eight by the time eleven of the twelve horses were loaded onto sleek silver trailers and began their four-hundred-mile trek to one of the most prestigious horse shows on the East Coast. I sighed and dumped my untouched coffee onto a bush. Dirt was caked under my fingernails, thick and resilient. I followed the streaks upward to my engagement ring, its shine now dulled by layers of dust and sweat. Frowning, I used the edge of my sweater to wipe it clean.

If only it were that easy to uncover the sparkle in everything. I was the polar opposite of this diamond. All my sparkle was on the outside to hide the grit and angst underneath—the dirty parts of me that no one needed to see. Not even the person who wanted to spend his life with me.

As if I had somehow broadcast my distress through the atmosphere, my phone buzzed in my pocket. When I dug it out of my jeans, a picture of Gavin from New Year's last year lit up the screen.

"Good morning," he said brightly.

I smiled when I heard the hiss of bacon in the background. "Are you making breakfast?"

"Now what kind of boyfriend...excuse me, fiancé, would I be if I didn't make you breakfast?"

I smiled wider, imagining him in my kitchen in a white undershirt, hair still mussed from sleep, as he flipped pancakes.

"Good point," I laughed into the phone and stamped my tingling feet a few times. "I'll be home in the next—" My words were interrupted by a steady vibration in my ear. I glanced at the caller. Andrew Kerrigan. Shit. A thousand reasons rushed through my brain as to why he would be calling me on my day off. None of them were good.

Gavin's voice rose and fell but the roaring in my ears drowned it out. I interrupted him mid-sentence. "I have to take this. Let me call you back." I switched over before he even responded. "Mr. Kerrigan. What can I do for you?"

"I have a problem," he said gruffly before silence ensued.

Was I supposed to know what he meant? Yesterday before I had left work, I had checked on his mare, and she was recovering well. I smashed the phone into my ear. "If this is about the mare I operated on–"

"It's not."

Oh. I breathed a tender sigh of relief. I heard voices in the background. Panicked voices. As my heart rate slowed, I eased my grip on the phone and brushed a limp strand of hair out of my eye. "Tell me what you need."

I heard a door slam closed before he spoke again, still terse but softer than before. "Pharoah's Mistress is ready to foal...and something is not right."

My eyebrows shot up. That mare was the top line of his stock. And she was carrying the product of her mating with Shadow Dancer, a horse who had barely missed winning the Triple Crown.

"Don't you have a vet there?"

"Yes, but..." I waited several seconds for him to elaborate. "I want to see what you think."

Wow. The most successful racehorse breeder in the Northeast was requesting my opinion. My ego expanded way beyond my skull. "I'll be right there." I hung up before either of us could change our minds.

My aging Toyota groaned with distaste when I massaged the accelerator around a bend in the road, and I fumbled with the phone enough to redial Gavin. He answered on the second ring. "Pancakes are ready, and I'm about to start on the eggs."

"Don't bother," I said, and it came out harsher than I meant it. "Damn it. I missed my turn," I grumbled.

"Is everything okay?"

"Yes...I mean no." I whipped the truck around in an illegal U-turn. "I have to go over to Kerrigan's. There's a problem with one of the horses and he needs my help." I heard the clank of metal on metal as Gavin whisked eggs.

"He needs you on your day off?"

"I'm sorry," I babbled as I frantically searched for the turnoff to Kerrigan farms. "I'll make it up to you I promise."

"No need. I'll see you when you get here."

My chest loosened a notch as I careened into the driveway and began making the long jaunt to the two-story barn in the distance. "See you soon," I shouted over the rumble of my engine and pressed end before Gavin could respond. I knew he understood. And he wouldn't even resent me for it later. The best and worst thing about Gavin—he could make it with or without me.

When I jogged into the barn, the smell hit me in the face like a phantom gust of wind. Antiseptic mixed with something metallic that could only be blood. The end stall door had been thrown wide open. A semicircle crowd gathered at the doorway. All men of varying sizes and shapes with arms crossed over their chests. Mr. Kerrigan stood closest to the thin, reedy man I recognized from last month's cover of my *Equine Vet Monthly*. Stewart Jameson.

I breezed between the two men and turned to offer a greeting. "Dr. Jameson," I said giving him a professional nod and watched the surprise flare in his chestnut eyes. "Mr. Kerrigan." I thrust my hand out in greeting and he gave me a half-hearted shake between chubby golden-brown fingers. Neither of them spoke as tension radiated between them. This was going to be interesting. "What can I do for you?"

Before either of them answered, the ground shuddered under my feet, and I whipped around to peer into the recesses of the cavernous stall behind me. A black shape rose and fell, grunting and straining, her legs going stiff and then relaxing. She hurled her head upward as she tried to rise but couldn't and then flopped it onto the floor with a crunch.

The smell of blood was unmistakable. When I looked closer I could see it, splotches of reddish brown drying on the mare's legs, the undersurface of her dark belly, the straw beneath her hindquarters.

"The foal will not come."

I turned around and Andrew Kerrigan glared at me through eyes that were chips of granite. Like it was somehow my fault. I knew better but still, it punched me in the gut.

Stewart unfolded his arms to gesticulate in the air. "The foal is wedged inside the birth canal, otherwise known as dystocia." He enunciated the last word as he finally made eye contact with me.

Stifling a retort, I schooled my face into neutrality. "How long has she been in stage two labor?"

"Too long."

"How many minutes exactly?" I asked evenly, daring them

not to answer me. The wrinkled face of the legendary vet hardened into a mask of stubbornness.

"Forty-five minutes by my count. And as I have told Mr. Kerrigan here"—he tilted his head toward the man with thinning black hair and a hawkish nose—"she's out of time. Let me explain to you, honey, that when the foal is nearly dead, we don't..."

I didn't wait for him to finish his sentence before I slung my pack off my shoulders and lowered myself to the ground to crawl toward the horse's hind end.

"Is there anything that can be done?" Andrew said and for the first time in any of our interactions, I heard notes of fear in his voice. His fear severed the leash I had been keeping on my inner badass.

"I need towels—clean ones. Diluted bleach if you have it and someone to hold her legs. I need someone strong...like Incredible Hulk strong." As I scrambled through the wet straw, blood and amniotic fluid soaking through the knees of my jeans, I noticed Stewart Jameson fling his hands upward.

"I don't want any part of this," he grumbled and spun on his heel before stalking off.

Good riddance. Everything I had asked for appeared next to me in a matter of moments. A pile of pristine white towels that had barely seen the outside of a department store. A pail of warm water that smelled familiarly sterile. I dunked my hands inside.

"Andrew," I called, not bothering with formality at this point. "Unzip my pack and toss me the plastic baggie inside." I smiled to myself as the rotund man bent down without complaint and did as I requested. Out of the sealed plastic bag, I removed a hefty syringe, the silver tip glinting in the overhead lighting when I ripped off the cap.

My hands, still damp from the bucket, steadied on the

mare's neck as I palpated the groove where her internal jugular pulsated. She didn't even flinch when I pricked through her thick hide and emptied the syringe into her vein.

"What did you give her?" Andrew fidgeted nervously behind me, his steel-toed boots acting as mirrors.

"Ketamine," I said, shifting my attention to her other end, the one that groaned and heaved every couple of minutes. "It will relax her so that I can get the baby out."

Two stable hands dressed in overalls with baseball caps pulled low over their eyes appeared in the awning of the stall door. They looked no older than twenty and barely bigger than a track jockey. I stifled a sigh and pointed to the mare's glistening legs. "Each of you take a leg and pull it up and toward the head."

They shuffled inside as a unit and didn't hesitate to do exactly as I had asked. "Okay, boys, brace yourselves." There was no time for donning latex. I had removed my top layers down to my undershirt and pushed both of my bare arms into the mare's vagina up to my elbows. Loosing a breath, I planted my feet in the hard earth underneath the straw and pushed.

Less than an hour later, I sat gasping in the corner of the mare's stall. Sweat ran in rivulets down my face, my chest, my abdomen. My head lolled against my shoulder as a shout rippled through the expanding crowd outside the stall. One of my eyelids cracked open against the grime slathered on my face. In front of me, a baby horse struggled to its feet, swaying and wobbling until it gained a precarious foothold in the dirt. A claim to this earth. This life.

A singular tear stung the corner of my eye and cascaded down my cheek. I tried to remember the last time I had really cried. Probably the summer I had been devastated. Over *him*. Among other things. Ironically, I had been in a barn then too. I stood up and brushed my hands over the back pockets of my jeans, the only place on my legs that wasn't soaked with some kind of fluid. At least this shedding of tears was worth it.

As quiet as a wraith, I edged around the newly born foal as he received a thorough sniffing by his weary mother. Soon this spindly-legged creature would take his first steps. It was better for humans not to crowd the miracle as it took place. When I exited the stall, Andrew Kerrigan clamped a meaty hand on my shoulder. I met his unreadable face with one of my own.

"That was..." He floundered and averted his eyes as he struggled for words. I had never seen him this shaken. "You were everything I expected."

"I know." I winked and flounced right past him toward my truck.

The compliment was nice, but it wasn't what emptied adrenaline into my bloodstream during the drive back to my house. It wasn't his words that made me feel alive. It wasn't even the sight of that mare and her foal and the life that almost wasn't. It was a memory dredged up from the depths of my brain by the raw edge of my own vulnerability. A memory I hadn't let myself think about in a very long time. Another barn. Another horse. A time when I still possessed the giddy delusion of being enamored with someone. I had been an idiot back then. Maybe I still was.

When I crunched into the driveway of the clinic, I still vibrated with emotion. It welled up from somewhere deep inside my bones, ebbing and flowing through my bloodstream. I hopped out of the truck and slipped inside the back entrance.

This part of the building was quiet. No scurrying technicians or stamping hooves. A light odor traipsed through the air. The smell of disinfectant and preserved tissue. This was the place where samples were kept and spun through delicate machines or sliced up and mounted on tiny glass plates for viewing under a microscope.

Although I preferred the hustle of the surgical suites, the quietude of the lab was a balm to my jittery nerves. Plus, the showers with the best water pressure were right outside the pathology suite.

I ducked through the heavy metal door into a brightly lit room with aging white tiles covering the floor and three of the walls. Catching a glimpse of myself in the mirror, I chuckled. I looked hideous.

The only bright spots on my entire body were the silvery tint to my eyes and the ring on my finger. I reached over to yank it off. Even with a coating of birth fluid and sweat, it wouldn't budge. Flicking my eyes to the shower, I sighed. At least I wouldn't lose it down the drain.

Showering felt like shedding an entire layer of skin. I watched as the grime mixed with soapsuds sluiced down the drain. I hoped some of the sullied parts of my heart were down there too. Seeing Will's face again, even in two dimensions and plastered on a book jacket, had awoken a part of my brain I thought I had excised.

I glanced again at the ring on my finger, now shinier than it had been in days. Gavin was a good guy. Too good really. Definitely too good for me. Too good for someone who maintained such a stubborn grip on the past.

When I stepped out of the shower, I forced a hard look in the mirror. *No more,* I mouthed at my toweled reflection distorted by a sheen of fog. "No more." I said it out loud this time. My new mantra.

My phone buzzed on the counter, clattering over the porcelain tiles. I turned off the water and ignored it. It vibrated again. I tried to close my ears to the sound, but my mind was already navigating the possibilities. Kerrigan? Mitch? Gavin maybe? Drying off my hand, I reached for it and swiped past a number I didn't recognize. "Hello. Dr. McClain speaking."

A brief staticky silence and then, "Are you Quinn McClain?" The voice sounded official, terse even.

"I am." My stomach tightened, holding in my exhale.

"I'm calling about your father."

CHAPTER NINE

SUMMER, THEN

"What did the mama horse say to her foal?" My dad was bent over a stack of charts on his desk scribbling notes.

I plopped down in a heap on the upholstered chair in the corner of his office. "I give up," I said, my words distorted by a jaw-splitting yawn.

"It's pasture bedtime," he said brusquely without looking up.

"Very funny," I said, stifling another yawn.

He removed his reading glasses and sharpened his focus on me. The sun had barely cracked the horizon. A singular golden ray of light pierced the window above his desk, scattering as it entered the dimly lit room. "You just finish up?"

"Yeah." I scrubbed a hand down my face. "I stuck around to make sure the baby stood up and was able to feed."

"Good girl," he said warmly, and my heart swelled at the pride in his voice. "Everything turn out okay last night?"

I nodded, trying out my best clenched-jaw professional face. A whisp of graying hair flopped over my dad's forehead when he bent down to continue scribbling. "Mrs. Vanderhal

said you brought an assistant with you last night." He
smirked when he said 'assistant.'

My eyes, which were drifting closed, snapped open and I
gripped the arms of my chair as I straightened my posture.
Damn it. Could nothing happen in this town without
everyone finding out?

"He's just a friend," I said evenly.

"Does your 'just a friend' have a name?"

"Will," I said, trying to hide how much I loved saying his
name. How it rolled off my tongue like the most decadent
chocolate.

"Will," my dad repeated flatly as if evaluating my new
friend's intentions. Will's formidableness as an adversary.

"Will," I said again, this time with less emotion and
watched my dad's thick brows furrow.

He put down his pen and steepled his fingers under his
chin. His signature pose for imparting wisdom. "Quinnie," he
started, using my childhood nickname. I used to love it.
Because it rhymed with whinny, like the sound a horse made.
These days it made me bristle. "We haven't talked about this
in a while..."

This meant sex. And no, we had never discussed it again.
Not since I was twelve and sobbing in the bathroom over my
first period, my dad gently explaining through the bathroom
door how natural this was and what it meant. He had been
two years too late.

I interrupted him before he could continue whatever
horribly embarrassing comment he had planned next. "Aunt
Jackie covered it, Dad. Multiple times over the last few
years."

"Oh," he grunted. And then we sat in heavy awkward
silence while he seemed to be at a loss for what to say next.
I waited on needles of anticipation for a bad joke to come
out of his mouth. Instead, he continued with, "We've been

really lucky to have her around while you were growing up."

"I know," I said softly. Jackie, my dad's sister, had put her entire life on hold to help raise me.

"I know she's not your mom but..."

"She did everything right, Dad. You both did." And nothing was truer. Every holiday had been postcard perfect. Every birthday a week-long celebration culminating in a store-bought cake and a house filled with balloons.

As a child, I had been practically suffocated by love and attention. Not spoiled necessarily but always made to feel important. Special. Cared for.

As I had grown older and more realistic, I wondered if one day this bubble of love wouldn't actually hold up in the real world. That I would never be able to recreate it. Or love someone else like my family had loved me. But inside a tiny glowing part of me held on to the belief that this kind of love was the real kind...and I would find it again.

In his worn leather office chair, my dad teetered on serious, which always gave me a case of nerves. I readjusted myself in my chair, predicting that the conversation was shifting from the uncomfortable topic of sex to one that was even harder. My mother. I swallowed the growing lump in my throat. I didn't want to cry today.

"We're real proud of you, Quinnie. *She* would have been proud of you."

And because I was still an immature teenager, I changed the subject. "It's not like I have time for any fun this summer anyway, Dad." I crossed my arms for emphasis.

A smirk appeared beneath his bushy mustache. "Just the way I like it," he teased.

"Can I not work today? Or this weekend?" I added hurriedly.

"Hmm." He fiddled with the end of his mustache. "You might've earned a short vacation."

I scowled at him, brushing the tangled mess of my hair over my shoulder. "Come on, Dad."

"Answer this question correctly and I'll set you free for a few days."

"Hit me," I said.

He screwed up his face in concentration, mustache quivering under his straight nose. "Who was the last horse to win the Triple Crown?"

"Affirmed in 1978...and before that Secretariat in 1973." I stuck out my hands for the truck keys. He reached in his desk drawer and handed them over.

"You're going to have to come up with something better next time." I grinned over my shoulder as I flounced out of his office.

By the time I stumbled into the doorway of our two-story home with its creaking floors and lemon smell, my fatigue had quietly ruined the grand plans I had devised while driving home. At the kitchen table, Aunt Jackie was balancing her checkbook and writing out bills. I leaned down to hug her from behind. She always smelled like floral perfume with a light note of hairspray.

"I thought you'd be up at the clinic." She closed the vinyl flap of her checkbook and clasped my forearm.

"Dad gave me a few days off." I unwrapped my arms from her shoulders to sit at the opposite end of the table.

"You hungry? Can I make you something?"

"Starving and yes, please."

She smiled and pushed up from the table. "Grilled cheese?" she called over her shoulder as she opened the cabinet for a pan.

My stomach grumbled its answer. "That would be great."

"Bacon?"

My stomach grumbled again. "Yes, please." For a few minutes I listened to the harmonizing lull of pan scraping.

"David said you delivered your first foal last night."

I fingered the edge of the floral tablecloth and shrugged. "I didn't really do anything."

"Of course, you did," my aunt insisted. "I'm sure it all went well because of you."

"The mare did it all," I yawned. "I was cheering from the sidelines and praying nothing went wrong." She slid a plate in front of me and I stuffed a corner of sandwich into my mouth.

"I find myself doing the same thing most of the time." Her blue-gray eyes, several shades lighter than mine and my dad's, twinkled with affection.

"What are you ever going to do without me?" I teased, my words garbled around a mouthful of sandwich.

She sighed dramatically. "I'm sure I'll figure out something."

I swallowed. "You make the best grilled cheese. How am I going to live without it?" I frowned down at my plate.

"I'm sure *you'll* figure out something," she said, smoothing my hair before picking up a pen to jot a list on a scrap of paper.

I chewed thoughtfully. "Will you stay in Linzberg when I leave for college?"

She paused, her pen poised above the table. "You say that like you're never coming home again."

"I'm sure I'll be home all the time. So much that you'll be begging for me to go back to Princeton."

"I doubt that."

"And when I'm done with vet school, I'm sure Dad will convince me to join the practice and live out his dream of badgering me for life." I smiled until I caught the groove develop above my aunt's neatly plucked brows.

Jackie put down her pen, flattening her manicured hands on the table. "He doesn't expect you to come back here, you know. We want you to do whatever you want, live wherever you want...as long as you're happy. As long as you have the life you want."

"What about you?"

"What about me?"

"Did you ever want to live anywhere else?" I searched her face as I chewed.

"No." Her mouth said one thing, but her eyes never lied.

"Yes, you did! Where did you want to live?"

"Rockville," she answered with a secretive smile.

"Rockville! There's nothing there but...grass." Something in her expression changed with a wistful upturn of her mouth. A faraway look in her eyes. I had never seen my aunt look twice at a man, but at that moment, I was certain this was what lost love looked like. "What was his name?"

She startled, sending the pen rolling off the table and hitting the floor with a high-pitched thump. Her lips pursed then parted for a full two seconds before anything came out. "Jeremy."

"Jeremy?" I cocked a brow. "You were in love with him?"

"Once upon a time."

"What was it like?"

"Why are you asking?" Jackie's eyes were twin laser beams to my face. The heat rose in my cheeks.

"I don't know," I stammered. "I've never been in love, and I'm...curious."

She sat back in her chair, satisfied with that answer. "It was...he was...something else."

"What happened?" I asked then internally cringed. Of course, I knew what had happened. My mom had died, and she had moved here to raise me.

"It didn't work out." She blinked her eyes and pressed her

lips closed as if there was nothing more to say. "I have the life I want...and so does he."

As I sat there, chewing thoughtfully, I wondered if she was telling me the truth.

When I climbed into bed later that morning, my mother stared at me from her perch on the top of my purple dresser. In the picture, her hair was down, the shorter layers blowing across her face, her mouth shaped in an 'oh' of pleasant protest.

Probably directed at my dad for aiming the camera when she wasn't ready. She was leaning against the doorframe of a silver sedan, bathed in watery autumn sunshine, a shopping bag draped from one arm. I loved this photograph. Even more because it was the last one that had ever been taken of her.

I had never known what inspired my dad to take it. Something he felt in the wind. Something that threatened to destroy our happy life like it was no more than a sandcastle. And once a vicious wind scattered sand, the beach never looked the same again.

CHAPTER TEN

AUTUMN, NOW

Too quickly yet somehow not quick enough, I was exiting a taxi along a semi-circular driveway filled with cars. The air, heavy with dust and humidity, settled into my lungs as I drew a ragged breath. Past the sliding glass doors and shiny lobby. Past the surly woman at the information desk. I took the elevator to the fourth floor and when the doors opened, I was running. Somewhere in the depths of my memory, I was five years old, running down a hospital hallway, blood dribbling down my chin.

"Excuse me." A shrill voice cut into my consciousness like a knife. "Excuse me," the woman in lavender scrubs repeated.

I skidded to a stop, my boots squeaking on the polished linoleum floor. Running a hand through the limp shag of my hair, I panted, "I'm looking for the ICU. My father was admitted here yesterday."

She directed me with a sagging brown arm toward a circular desk. "You'll need to check in there." I didn't waste a second to thank her.

The desk was empty as I shoved my midsection into its formidable shape, willing someone to appear behind it. I still wore my threadbare scrubs from the clinic and my paddock boots, having hastily changed and driven straight to the airport without even stopping at my house. It had been too far out of the way anyway, and I would have missed the last direct flight from Newark to San Antonio.

In the scramble to my truck and harried drive to the airport, I hadn't gleaned much from the surgical resident who had called me. Only that my dad had fallen from a twenty-five-foot ladder and had been transferred from our small town emergency room to the trauma center at University Hospital, where he was now in the intensive care unit.

Gavin had remained silent on the phone as I had waited in line at the American Airlines ticket counter and babbled the news through twin streams of snot that ran from my nose. He had wanted to come. But I had said no. And I didn't have time to ask myself why.

My impatience grew until even the tips of my fingers twitched with agitation. In a moment of complete insanity, I reached over the desk and plucked the receiver of a phone from its base.

"Ma'am! Ma'am, you can't do that," drawled a scratchy voice.

I proffered the phone like a bartering tool. "Can you tell me where my father is?"

The man with graying hair, a stethoscope slung across his shoulders, shuffled toward me. "And who might your father be?" He reached out with a gentle sunspotted hand and took the phone, the dial tone filling the void between us.

"David McClain."

"David McClain," the man repeated, returning the phone to its receiver and flicking his eyes toward the whiteboard behind him, a chaotic list of scribbled room numbers and initials and diagnoses. "Come with me," he commanded and my heart plummeted into my feet.

He didn't look back to make sure I followed as he rounded the desk and angled into the first hallway to the left. I nearly collided into his back as he stopped outside a glass door with the curtain drawn.

"He's in here," he clipped. "Visiting hours end at seven."

I charged through the door, drawing back the curtain, forcing my eyes wide to absorb every terrible detail. For the first time in my life, my six-foot hulking man of a father looked frail. His jaw hung slack, a rhonchorous noise occurring every time he took a breath. A violaceous hue bloomed under his eyes and his nose was crooked to the right with a spot of dried blood at the entrance.

Tubes crisscrossed over his body like webbing, a few clear ones and one that was deeply crimson. A blood transfusion. Amid the beeps and shrieks of the bedside monitor, I heard a gentle bubbling, like a babbling brook from a bedtime story.

I peered at the floor. A chest tube was connected to suction tubing, a steady stream of blood dumping from my father's right chest into the collection chamber. I started to cry again, fat droplets raining down my cheeks and dripping off my chin.

When I approached the bed, he stirred and tried to lift his head. I took one of his hands in both of mine. His huge hands and sturdy fingers that could operate on a kitten and fix my bike in the same day. They felt rough and familiar. I pressed my lips to his calloused palm and his eyes fluttered open.

"Dad?" I breathed. I watched him assess the details of my face with jerky eye movements. He coughed violently while moving his lips. "What was that, Dad?" I leaned closer so that my ear was near his mouth. He smelled like a hospital, stale and metallic.

"What do you call...a cow...with no legs?" he asked in a hoarse whisper.

"What?" I straightened and slowly released my grip on his

hands. One edge of my dad's peeling lips twitched as he cleared his throat.

"I said," he answered in a slightly louder whisper, "what do you call a cow with no legs?"

"Seriously, Dad?" I pressed the heels of my hands into my eyes as I contemplated whether to laugh or devolve into another bout of crying.

"Ground beef," he wheezed then laughed gingerly, his chest barely rising and falling. A thin stream of blood gushed through his chest tube with the motion.

"That's the worst joke I've ever heard." I sniffed before allowing myself one quick burst of much needed laughter. I raked my eyes over every inch of him under rumpled white sheets before asking, "What happened?"

He sighed and patted the edge of the bed. I knelt to the floor instead, the cool hardness a necessary adjunct for what I was feeling on the inside. The need to ask forgiveness. To repent for being the prodigal daughter. I might as well have been kneeling at an altar. But it had been so long since I had prayed. I didn't think I knew how anymore.

"Tell me what happened," I repeated and ran my bare forearm across my sodden nose. His eyes bore into me. The same ones that reflected back at me from the mirror each morning. Eyes that were gray like the sky right before a summer rain. Steely yet soft.

"I fell," he said, lips tightening over a set of too-white teeth. Teeth that had been replaced after a cow had kicked him in the mouth when I was a teenager.

"What were you doing at the top of a ladder?" I asked, my voice laced with irritation.

"Trying to figure out where the damn roof was leaking."

"When did the roof start leaking? And why didn't you call someone instead of climbing up there yourself?" I knew my voice was rising. I couldn't stop its momentum.

"Because I'm not too old to take care of my own house." His eyebrows rose in a challenge. Pride from a man who had established a thriving vet practice while raising a daughter by himself. Pride in his resourcefulness. His independence. Traits that he had imbued into me. Something in my chest eased, the sharp edge of grief dulled by the fact that, although injured, my dad was surprisingly intact.

"You're lucky to be alive, Dad."

He tried to lift a hand to swat at my arm but failed and redirected it to the slim white button hanging from a cable in his bed. He pressed it once. My eyes swept the room once more and this time noticed the contraption hanging from the end of the bed.

"Is that traction? Did you break your leg too?"

He nodded slowly, his face slackening with the opiate that now dripped into his bloodstream. His eyes shuddered closed. "Femur, collarbone, a few ribs I didn't need..." His speech slurred as he drifted into oblivion. For a moment, I wished I could join him. I slid my hands underneath his instead.

"*Visiting hours are now over.*" The smooth voice purred through the speakers over my head. Carefully, I wiggled my fingers until they pulled free, realizing for the first time how my dad and I shared the exact same knuckles. I pressed mine into my teeth to stifle a groan as I pushed to my feet, swaying as I did so. When was the last time I had eaten? I didn't remember. Stumbling past the carefully strung curtain, I headed out of the ICU.

Somehow, I staggered to the waiting room. A room of peeling paint and vinyl chairs and a single window facing west with a view of nothing but ebony sky. A moonless abyss. A starless night. The glow of headlights on the distant highway blinked at me in mockery. *We are headed home,* they seemed to say. *To our houses and our families and a bowl of something warm and delicious.* My stomach grumbled in response.

I trudged over to the vending machine before realizing it only accepted coins. Sighing in despair, I plucked a foam cup from a stack and poured thick, black liquid into it from a cracked pot. I took a tentative sip. It tasted like a forgotten sock but at least it was warm. My belly clenched then calmed in response.

Because I was alone, I tottered over to the window and pressed my forehead against the glass. It was warm compared to the clamminess that had spread across my exposed skin. Even my reflection showcased the pallor of my cheeks, the purple shadows under my eyes. I watched while a storm brewed in the distance, and minutes later the sky let loose with streaming droplets of rain.

It had been raining *that* day too. A flash of lightning lit up the sky and for a moment all I could see was the bent fender of a silver sedan, red taillights winking in the downpour. I traced the scar that cleaved my face from my temple to my jaw. I wondered what my mom would have said if she had known Dad had fallen off the roof. In her calm quiet way, she would have used words that both scolded and soothed at the same time. At least, that was what I imagined her voice had been like. I didn't actually remember.

I'd realized long ago that I was nothing like her. Everyone had always said so. I was awkward next to her grace. Brash and sometimes intimidating rather than meek. More like my father. Even though she had been gone for years, my chest still ached from time to time when I least expected it. When I stared too long in the mirror. When I couldn't find the right shoes to go with a pair of jeans. When I was in my car and "Baby Blue" came on the radio. When I had a question, and I knew that she would know the answer. If only I could ask her.

Behind me, the door to the waiting room swung open, the knob hitting the wall with a *thunk*. I turned away from the rain-streaked window to see a familiar head poking through the opening.

"Aunt Jackie?"

My bleary eyes adjusted to the face I knew well. To the large blue eyes, a force of nature swirling behind them. The perfectly arched brows and laugh lines that stretched and deepened with every movement of her mouth. The faded brown hair with new golden highlights coursing through the roots. She closed the distance between us in the span of two heartbeats.

"I'm so glad you made it." Arms—soft and warm and clad within the confines of a denim jacket—were thrown around my waist. She pulled back to critically regard my rumpled scrubs and tear-stained grime on my face. Her nose wrinkled. "Did you see him yet?"

I nodded, the ball in my throat growing larger. "When did you get here?" Jackie lived two hours away in a small town west of Austin. A place she shared with three Australian Shepherds, two alpacas and a cadre of stray cats. A place I still had not visited. The last time I had seen her was over three years ago. She had been in Virginia Beach for a dog show, and I had driven down to meet her for lunch.

"This morning," she grunted, heaving a large tote bag off her shoulders. "Once David got out of surgery, I drove over to the house to pick up a few things." I glanced at the bag and sure enough it was filled to the brim with toiletries and pajama bottoms. I recognized the waffle weave blanket from the chair in his bedroom folded neatly on the top. "How about you?"

"Just now." My knees wobbled as I spoke, my muscles fading in protest.

With a sharp glance, my aunt cupped my elbow to direct

me into a hard plastic chair. She was the only person in this world who had ever been able to manhandle me. "Sit down before you collapse." Her glare stopped my words when I opened my mouth to protest. "I'm dropping off these things at the nurses' station. I'll be right back." Whipping around, her gold earrings twinkling in the fluorescent lighting, she headed toward the glass door.

"What then?" I called after her.

Without even pausing a beat to turn around, she said, "I'm taking you home."

CHAPTER ELEVEN

AUTUMN, NOW

"It's been so long since you were here, I'm surprised you remember what it looks like."

The cream brick two-story with forest green shutters stared at me accusingly. My temper flared. "Like I would forget what my house looked like, Aunt Jackie." I ran a hand through my grown-out bangs and came away with a layer of grime. My left hand was still smoothing back my hair when it was suddenly jerked in the opposite direction.

"And when," Jackie said accusingly, "were you going to tell me about this?" Her bony fingers, thin apart from the giant knuckles that characterized our gene pool, yanked my wrist closer to her face.

She squinted dramatically, examining the glinting metal and diamond on my fourth finger from every angle. My engagement ring looked strangely foreign in the dim overhead light of her sleek white sedan. "When did this happen, Quinn?"

I tried to pull my hand out of her death grip and failed. "A few weeks ago. I was going to tell you."

A golden brow arched over a critical blue eye, the corner

twitching a few times while she tilted my hand back and forth. "Well, Gavin certainly has good taste." Her posture tensed and she finally released my hand. "It *was* Gavin, right?"

I clutched my hands in my lap and tried to twist the ring around my knuckle. It didn't budge. "Of course it was Gavin." It sounded sharper than I'd meant it to. "I mean...we've been together for a few years. It made sense as the next step."

"That sounds...practical."

My mouth turned down into a frown. "Do you have something against Gavin?"

"I'm not sure. I've never actually met him." Her voice was cool but her look shot daggers into my chest.

"Well...you will," I stammered. "And you'll love him."

"I'm sure I will, Quinn." She tucked a limp strand of hair behind my ear. "We're happy as long as you're happy."

"I am." My voice was strained by exhaustion, but at least the words were true. Emphatically true. So true that I considered tattooing them on my forehead. *I...am...happy.*

My aunt pursed her lips but said nothing. Instead, she swung open her car door, squeezing my hand on her way out of the car. "Let's get you inside and feed you."

In the years since I had moved away to college and then to vet school, my childhood home had remained the same. Like a time capsule of the life of Quinn McClain. The same cognac leather couch where I had sprawled out to do my homework while watching reruns of *Friends*. The same chintzy curtains that ruffled with the breezing in and out of the seasons. The same notes of vanilla and lemon wood polish.

The same row of framed photographs as a timeline through my precocious phase then my awkward phase then into womanhood like a butterfly exiting its chrysalis. In one photograph, I was gangly and angular, all elbows and knees, jutting hip bones and pointy chin. In the next, I had mounds and curves and trendy layers that accentuated my neckline.

When I stepped through the doorway, habitually reaching toward the side wall to flip on the light, I immediately knew everything had changed. The smell of plaster and fresh paint permeated the air. My feet scuffed along a hardwood floor instead of sinking into a woolen rug.

I flipped the switch and blinked against the beacon of light flooding our living room. I looked upward first. A chandelier had been hung from the exposed beams of our peaked ceiling. A massive iron monstrosity with lightbulbs that looked like real candles.

The cozy worn couch and mismatched chairs had been replaced by a sleek sectional. I tiptoed forward cautiously, my feet creaking on the hardwood, until I reached a towering bookshelf. Trinkets and stacks of books and framed photographs filled the shelves, arranged with artistry and thoughtfulness. My childhood self stared back at me and something in my gut twisted.

"When did Dad redecorate the house?" I asked when I heard my aunt shuffling her shoes off at the front door.

"About a month ago."

Behind me the floor creaked merrily as she walked toward me. I frowned. "He never said anything."

My aunt reached out and straightened a stack of books. "He wanted to surprise you next time you came home."

I examined the room one more time. Masterfully perfect and tasteful. Completely unlike the rambling chaos where I had grown up. "It doesn't even look like home anymore." I knew I sounded petulant, and I didn't care.

"David wanted this place spruced up and I offered to help."

"You did all of this?" I stared at her wide-eyed.

"He helped...a little." Her thin lips twitched into a grin and suddenly she looked twenty years younger. My vibrant, ask-forgiveness-rather-than-permission aunt. I supposed that was where I had inherited that part of my personality. "What can I fix you to eat?"

If Aunt Jackie excelled at anything, it was mothering. A wave of guilt settled into my bones. She had been too busy raising me to have children of her own.

"I'm tired. I think I just want to shower and go to bed."

Narrowing her eyes, she swished past me into the kitchen where granite countertops had replaced our soapstone ones. "If you change your mind, I'm making grilled cheese."

I wouldn't change my mind. Not if my life depended on it. Trudging up the stairs, I paused at the top to survey her petite frame opening a sleek stainless-steel refrigerator. Probably one that wouldn't even hold our magnet collection.

At the end of the hall, I twisted the knob to my old bedroom, holding my breath as the hinges squealed in welcome. My face relaxed into a grin. At least some things hadn't changed. Other than my bed now pushed against the wall to make room for a row of cardboard boxes, everything was exactly as I had left it.

The wall was a montage of posters of famous racehorses and a bulletin board of movie ticket stubs and old birthday cards and a few snapshots from high school. There was even one from college when Sid and I had gone to a fraternity party dressed as Thelma and Louise.

I moved to the dresser I had painted purple one summer when I was bored. Two framed photos adorned the top. One of my dad and me at my vet school graduation. I had a ridiculous smile in my deep blue regalia and had shot the camera a thumbs up while he pulled me into a hug. I remembered every second of that moment—his pride leaching through the arm he had thrown over my shoulders and me thinking, *I finally made it.* I could take care of myself. I could have my own life. And he could have his.

I swept the tips of my fingers over the second glass frame and came away with a layer of dust. I wondered what she would look like now. Older but probably more beautiful. A familiar gnawing ache unfurled deep inside me. I didn't have the strength to close it back up.

My phone jangled inside my bag, shooting sparks through my nerve endings. I fished it out and swiped clumsily. "Hey."

"Hi there," said a quiet voice. Measured. Almost timid.

"Gavin," I started, tripping over my own tongue. "Thanks for...thanks for calling."

"How's your dad?"

I swallowed past the dry desert that had become my throat. "He's in the ICU with a lot of injuries but hopefully no permanent damage."

"Good." He paused, an uncertain silence growing between us. "That's good news, right?"

"Yeah, it is."

"Are you okay?"

"Yeah, of course." The lies spewed off my tongue too easily. But how could I ever explain my mountain of guilt with a peak that was now another thousand feet higher? I couldn't. Or more accurately, I didn't want to.

"So, how long are you planning to stay?"

The question was like a splash of freezing water on my face. "I haven't gotten that far but not long."

"Do you think you'll be home for Thanksgiving? My parents are coming into the city this year and they were asking..." He trailed off and I paused a beat to swallow my annoyance.

The question was innocent, but it irked me. Even after a few years of being together, I had only seen Gavin's parents a handful of times. They lived in upstate New York and rarely made it to Manhattan. And it wasn't like I could predict when Mitch Jenkins' horses were going to get injured or go into labor. But now that we were engaged, it was probably time to know the people I would be sharing holidays with. The thought sobered me for some reason. My forehead wrinkled into the bridge of my nose. "I should be home by then."

I heard him release a breath. "Okay that's great because my mother wants to meet with you about the wedding."

Meet with me? Like this was a war council or a courtroom case. "Sounds good," I said through clenched teeth. As his voice rose and fell in steady waves, I mostly tuned out, my eyes drifting over the lavender bedspread and the peeking edge of a flowered sheet, imagining myself sandwiched between layers of bedding softened by a countless number of cycles in our washing machine. "Gavin," I interrupted. "I'll call you tomorrow, okay?"

I heard him reply faintly and then the next thing I knew, my entire body was horizontal.

THE NEXT SEVERAL days passed in a predictable blur. I woke well before dawn, my internal clock permanently accustomed to the East Coast time zone. Before my eyes had even adjusted, I picked up my phone to scroll through a barrage of text messages and emails. Mostly work related. Today there was one from Sid. *Quinn, call me later.* I sighed and began typing a reply to Mitch Jenkins about his deworming schedule.

After a monster coffee, Jackie and I would make the hour and a half trek into the city so we could arrive at the hospital in time for bedside rounds. A cluster of white coats over green scrubs wearing stained white trainers would shuffle over to my father's door every morning.

The most exhausted-appearing one—a ginger-haired man-child with delicate hands—would recite a series of numbers and acronyms while the rest of them scrolled through their phones and nodded along. I could keep up with most of it. It wasn't that different from caring for an injured horse. More numbers. More medications. More imaging studies. But essentially a slew of broken bones that would heal over time.

A familiar word made my ears perk. "I'm sorry. Can you repeat that last part again?"

The redhead sighed and stuffed a stack of papers in his pocket without making eye contact. "I said we should transfer him to the floor and then to a rehab facility next week."

Rehab facility? Visions of horses on pulleys being plunged into swimming pools flashed through my mind. "Is he ready for that?" My stare bounced from the redhead to a man around my height with gray along his temples. I realized my own bias but didn't care. I hated when trainers overlooked me for my taller, more distinguished, and much grayer partner.

The older physician looked down at me and smiled gently. I had the overwhelming feeling of being six years old again and about to be told which school bus to ride home. "He's ready," he said. "The femur fracture is healing nicely. He has a long road ahead, but I imagine he'll do well with inpatient physical therapy." He moved one foot behind the other in preparation to shuffle away and my pulse skyrocketed.

Now that Dr. Gray Hair had opened the door for conversation, there was no way I was going to let him get away that easily. "You know he's a veterinarian, right? The only one in our entire area."

The lines smoothed around the older physician's face as he regarded me. "That's good to know." He stared at me through a set of round lenses as if he were seeing me for the first time. "What kind of veterinarian?"

"The old-school kind," I replied and received a twitch of his mouth in response. "The country kind who spays a cat, pulls a calf, and does a house call for a goat with mastitis before lunchtime."

"I see." He took off his glasses, cleaning the lenses on the lapel of his white coat. "He'll be able to go back to work." My spine slumped in relief. "After a few months of therapy."

I straightened, my mouth opening in shock. "Months?" I croaked. "How many months exactly?"

"Hopefully after the first of the year but maybe longer."

First of the year. The news sank like a stone into the pit of my stomach. Clunk. Next to me Jackie tightened the grip on her purse strap. The scrubs filtered past us like a river of green around our stationary inertia. We were the rocks in the way of their daily progress. When they had all filed out, we were alone, standing on the threshold of a glass-enclosed room, watching the rise and fall of my dad's midsection under stark white sheets to the tempo of beeping.

As soon as the sun rose, sending slanting shafts of light across the hospital floor, Jackie and I silently clustered around the edge of the hospital bed to watch my dad devour a plate of scrambled eggs. The scrape of his fork on the empty plate might as well have been along my nerve endings. His color was better today, his cheeks now a shade darker than his bedsheets.

From the waist up, he almost looked normal again. Most of the tubes had been removed from his chest and face, the scrapes heavily scabbed over and the bruises greenish-yellow instead of purple. Only his leg still told the tale of his ordeal. It jutted awkwardly from his pelvis, the external fixator device encasing it in some method of medieval torture. I briefly wondered if anyone had ever tried to use something like this on a horse.

As soon as he was done eating, Jackie swooped in and slid his tray off the table. "I'll take this over to the nurses' station," she said and was out of the room before I could blink.

When Dad and I were alone, the air between us suddenly seemed suffocating, the sun too bright through the east-facing window, the smells too potent and sterile. Dad leaned back into the lumpy foam mattress, completely unperturbed. His eyes slid to half-mast, and his hands settled on the soft round lump of his abdomen. I exhaled forcefully through my nose. "Dad?"

"Mmhmm?" His lids stayed nearly closed.

I steeled myself, finding solace in wrapping my fingers around the curve of his wrist and feeling the steady thump of his pulse. "I talked to the doctors this morning." My voice trailed off in a desperate plea. Maybe he already knew. He didn't answer but his eyes opened a fraction more. Barely enough for me to see the glint of gray iris behind his lids. "I have some good news. They think you're ready to leave the ICU today."

"Fantastic," he murmured, his voice back to the steadiness I knew so well.

"It seems...quick. Do you feel ready?" I bit the corner of my lip.

"They must have realized what I am."

"What are you?"

"A god among men."

I stifled a snort and some of the tension inside my abdomen loosened. His unshaven chin quivered as he showed a rim of pearl white teeth. My grip on his wrist tightened. "They also said that when you leave the hospital..." I steadied my breathing while my heart took off at a frantic gallop. "You would need to go to a rehab facility." I paused to choke out the rest of the words. "For a few months."

His eyelids flew open at this news and I couldn't read anything from the steely flint of his gaze. Anger? Sadness? Guilt? I could feel my face scrunched up into a twisted pretzel of an expression. And then he relaxed, the skin around his mouth softening as his lips parted to whistle a breath. "I know."

I recoiled back into my chair. "You know?"

"I only pretend to sleep during rounds."

"Oh, geez Louise, dad." I palmed my face with my own hands.

"Next I'm sure you're going to ask what my plans are for the clinic and all my patients."

My dad. Always five steps ahead of me. If this were a game of chess, my queen would be toast. "What *are* you going to do about the clinic?"

"I've had some time to think about that. You want to know what I came up with?" He waggled his eyebrows at me, and I did not want to know. Not in the slightest.

CHAPTER TWELVE

SUMMER, THEN

I smelled terrible. Bending my neck to rub my face with the neckline of my scrub top gave me a thorough whiff of sweat and manure-infused dirt. The shovel handle was slick between my palms. I rested my forehead on it for a moment while a pair of oddly shaped eyeballs criticized me from the corner.

"Don't even start with me, Ray."

He bleated a reply that sounded suspiciously like an insult.

"Someone has to clean up your disgusting living quarters." I flung a hand in his direction, and he trotted toward me expecting a treat. I gave him a guilty pat on the head instead. "Sorry friend. You're on a strict diet." I bent down to run my fingers over the rectangle of belly devoid of hair, held together by a neat row of stitches.

Ray was a frequent flyer, a grumpy goat belonging to the Royce family that ingested something tragic every few months. This time, it had been Mr. Royce's size twelve loafer. I skittered my fingers over Ray's side, and he sidestepped away, tossing his head in protest.

For the hundredth time that afternoon I wished I was in the passenger seat of Will's convertible flying down a twisty backroad. The wind whipping hair into my face. Cringing at our combined voices belting twangy country music at the tops of our lungs.

Or like yesterday when we'd waited out a thunderstorm, listening to the rain beat a melody on the windshield. In our quest to find Will's elusive swimming hole, we had combed half the county over the last two weeks.

Every afternoon since the foal was born, I had found him waiting for me in the clinic parking lot, leaning against the hood of his car, usually a book in one hand. And from the minute I slid into his passenger seat until I crawled into bed that night, something inside me came alive. Something I couldn't quite define. But I knew I liked it. Liked who I was when I was with him.

One day last week, Will had brought a streaky black and white copy of a topographical map he had pilfered from the county archives.

"Unfortunately, there's no icon for 'magic swimming hole' on this particular map," I had teased.

Will emitted a light snort as he gazed into the distance, eyes glued to a jutting pink monstrosity dotted with sage brush and yellow flowers. He squinted against the orange ball of a setting sun. "You are absolutely no help."

"That's me," I said, "completely useless."

"I wouldn't go that far," he chided.

"What exactly am I good for then?" My heart had sped up. A fishing expedition to find out what Will thought of me. To attain some type of reassurance that I was special.

He rubbed his chin thoughtfully before brandishing his index finger. "You never travel without proper snacks." We both glanced at the plastic wrappers littering the floorboard of his car.

"Just confess already," I said with faux exasperation. "You love Moon Pies too."

His lips curved in a soft smile. My favorite one, where the left dimple on his cheek deepened and beckoned. The liquid turquoise portion of his eyes softened while the gold flecks glinted like a vein of metal inside a rock.

"Fine," he said, his British accent a touch heavier than usual. He pulled another one out of the box and examined the yellow disk of sugar and marshmallow sealed in plastic. "What is it about you that is so enchanting?"

He had slid his gaze to me, a half-amused, half-contemplative look on his face. On the outside I had shot him a mocking grin, while I on the inside, I was exploding with sparks.

Now, in the corner of the pen, Ray ran his teeth along the metal railing. The sound prickled the back of my neck, and I dropped the shovel into the dirt. Sighing, I glared at it without picking it up. I knew my dad had purposefully stacked my work schedule lately. Which made me think he didn't altogether approve of my outings with Will. But it wasn't like he had anything to worry about unless he didn't approve of a few longing looks and accidental finger brushes.

"*Mi hija.*" A throaty voice bounced off the exposed beams of the building. "You in here, *mi hija?*" Sonia, one of the assistant technicians, poked her head over the gate.

"Where else would I be?" I grumbled at the moon-shaped face and dark, close-cropped curls. Her lips, painted berry red, upturned into the beginnings of a smile. Sonia had been with us since I was in middle school. Though, at least once every few years, she threatened to leave and pursue a new career.

Once it was cosmetology school. Once it was to open a food truck. And last year, she started her own business selling shirts bedazzled with uplifting messages. But apparently the women of Linzberg could wear only so many V-necks with "blessed" spelled out in pink rhinestones.

Sonia's deep-set cola-colored eyes regarded me with a mixture of warmth and enthusiasm, which usually contradicted her attempts at professionalism. "Your *papi* needs you for an important job, *mi hija*."

"More important than shoveling Ray's manure?" I nudged a pile of droppings with my boot for emphasis.

Sonia wrinkled her nose. "You're feisty today, *mi hija*."

"Sorry, Sonia," I said as guilt needled my chest. "Don't pay any attention to me. I'm just tired of being stuck in here."

"What a blessing then," she said serenely, "because your *papi* needs you to go over to Mrs. Everett's house and remove the stitches from her little dog."

"Wasn't she supposed to bring her in for a follow-up appointment today?"

Sonia heaved a sigh, her cleavage swelling until I could read what was spelled out in crystals on her scrub top. *Give grace.* "She called and said her husband wasn't home and she couldn't get Daisy in the car by herself."

"Don't you think Daisy Mae is a strange name for a Great Dane?"

"At this point, *mi hija*, I've heard it all and I don't judge."

"Just like your shirt says." I winked at her before I vaulted over the railing and left her muttering to herself in Spanish.

The drive to Mrs. Everett's single-story bungalow was long enough that the wind blowing through the open truck window dried the sweat under my armpits and loosened some of the dirt caked along the back of my neck.

When I pulled through the gates of the Stone Oak Country Club, I rumbled past the spray of a fountain then took my first left down a row of stucco homes with identical wooden garage doors. The one I was looking for happened to be directly across from a gargantuan resort-style pool.

I parked on the street across from Mrs. Everett's perfectly manicured lawn and took a longing look at the undulating waves of cool water and the bobbing heads of swimmers. A diving board creaked followed by a fantastic splash. I imagined the cool spray hitting the exposed V of my chest.

A group of teenage girls gathered near the water's edge, flashing smiles and tossing their hair. I watched them like a scientist observing a flock of brightly colored birds.

I had never been one of them. And I didn't mind. Not one bit. I existed between echelons. Not cool enough to be in the inner circle but liked well enough to be invited to parties and fist bumped in the hallways of Linzberg High School.

I recognized one of the girls. Mary Alice. She was a year below me in school. Olive-skinned with dark curls and toned legs. A cheerleader and member of the cross-country team.

When I waved from the sidewalk, she slid her eyes away from the glistening human pulling himself out of the water and smiled brightly at me with a perfect row of teeth. I barely saw her motion me over.

My gaze snagged on the shoulders and chest that I hadn't realized were quite so defined. The ones belonging to the boy exiting the water. He ran a hand through his hair, a depthless black now that it was wet.

The girls surrounded him like a preening charm of finches, squealing when the droplets from Will's hair landed on their sun-kissed skin. Mary Alice waved at me again. I took a mechanical step toward them, my stomach winding itself into an intricate knot. And similar to the first time I had met Will, the kaleidoscope of my universe shifted as I watched Mary Alice casually curl her fingers around his bicep.

By the time I crossed the narrow swath of emerald green grass and the peach sandstone of the pool coping, my face was the epitome of pleasant neutrality. Not the bitter jealousy coating me from the inside. I halted shy of Mary Alice's fuchsia toenails.

"Hey Quinn," she said, doeish brown eyes wide under a set of fluttering lashes. "I haven't seen you all summer."

She was so casual and perky and completely oblivious to the acid building on my tongue. It took a herculean effort for me to avoid looking over her head at Will.

"I've been...busy," I hedged, "working."

Mary Alice twisted around to her friends. "This girl is so smart. She's going to be this town's next veterinarian just like her dad."

"We'll see," I said.

"Dr. McClain is so nice," she gushed. "He totally saved our dog's life last year after she got hit by the mail truck."

"That's my dad." I emitted a tense laugh as the girls looked on with feigned interest. Will cleared his throat.

"Oh Quinn!" Mary Alice tugged Will forward by his forearm. "This is Will. He's new in town."

"Hello, Will," I said evenly. Tension radiated between us like summer heat off the asphalt.

"Quinn," he said smoothly. Too smoothly. His unreadable expression fueled my growing irritation.

"You guys know each other?" Mary Alice blinked several times in succession. I couldn't help but notice the disappointment in her tone.

"We've met," I said quickly. It was subtle but I watched Will draw back at the bite in my words. Something inside me faltered. I didn't have any right to be irritated or angry or God forbid...jealous. He wasn't mine. It didn't matter that I wanted to be his. The back of my throat began to close at this realization.

"Then you should join us, Quinn," Mary Alice said in a considerably brighter voice. "After...whatever it is you're doing today."

"Removing stitches," I said matter-of-factly. "And although I typically wear my bikini under all this"—I gestured to my sodden work clothes—"I didn't today."

The cluster of girls stared at me, like a herd of blinking fawns, until Mary Alice burst the tension bubble with her laughter. I caught Will looking at her with simple amusement. My heart wrung itself out in my chest.

"You're funny, Quinn," Mary Alice said.

I mustered my brightest smile. "Nice to see you, Mary Alice. Enjoy the pool." As I turned to leave, I caught her subtle head tilt toward Will, a fog of adoration in her eyes. I swore he mirrored the look right back to her.

"Quinn...Quinn, wait up!"

I willed the swift gait of my dusty paddock boots to slow and counted to three before turning around. Will jogged toward me in bare feet, a dry T-shirt thrown over his swim trunks. He stopped a foot shy of me, close enough that water droplets from his hair landed on the tip of my nose. After running through an array of possible responses, I decided on, "What's up?" and mentally congratulated myself on how casual I sounded.

"Are you quite all right?" I simultaneously loved and hated his British accent.

"Me?" I pointed at my sternum. "Absolutely. I mean I have to hold down a dog that outweighs me by a good thirty pounds and remove her stitches but other than that, I'm great."

"Oh," he said, brow furrowing. "Would you like some help?"

"No. I don't need help," I said hastily. "And anyway, you seem...occupied." I shifted one step away from him.

"Yeah." He reached up to brush the hair out of his eyes. "I only just met them today, but Mary Alice seems like a sweetheart."

"She is...the sweetest," I stuttered, forcing my lips into a wide smile. "Cupcakes and candy corns have nothing on her."

The furrow in his brow deepened, his mouth set in a puzzled line. "All right then if you're sure you don't need me..."

"I don't." Sarcasm dripped off me like a melting ice cream cone followed by a shard of guilt. By Will's expression, he knew exactly what I was doing but was too polite to call me out on it.

His tongue darted over his bottom lip. A tell, I had discovered, for when he was nervous about something. "They invited me to a barbecue tonight."

Was this a question? A statement? An invitation to insert myself in his plans?

"You should go." I nodded my head up and down like an ornery goat. My lips saying one thing while my heart screamed the opposite. "I'll see you around," I tossed over my shoulder, covering the few yards to Mrs. Everett's front walk before Will could reply.

Not until I was shrouded in the safety of her front porch awning did I turn around to see Will striding back the way he had come.

I watched like the masochist I was as Mary Alice motioned him over to where the girls had lined up for the diving board. I supposed Will had found what he was looking for this summer. A magical swimming pool filled with wondrous creatures.

CHAPTER THIRTEEN

AUTUMN, NOW

"What's going on?" Jackie asked as soon as I slid into the passenger seat of her sleek white sedan.

A strange combination of relief and contempt filled me as I stared at the phone in my hands. When she revved the engine, my thumbs began moving assuredly and swiftly before I could change my mind. Swipe. Type. Send. First to my boss, Steve. Then to Sid. And Gavin. I hesitated before hitting send on the final text to Mitch Jenkins.

"I must be insane," I muttered. Jackie daggered me with her eyes as she sped down the ribbon of highway. When I was finished, I turned my phone over in my lap to avoid reading any of the replies. Every few seconds, a buzzing sensation skated across my jiggling thigh.

"Well?" Jackie's eyes were so wide her fine lines had all but disappeared.

A sigh rushed out my chest. I could smell the anxiety on my breath. "Dad's worried about the clinic." My aunt nodded, her eyes brightening as they trained on the giant tanker truck in front of us. "About what's going to happen to it while he's recovering." I bit my lip. "I mean it's going to be months before he can work again."

"I know."

"And there's not another vet clinic in the entire county." The buzzing on my knee grew incessant, stoking my anxiety.

"What are folks in this town going to do without him?" Jackie lamented, a giant smile stretching to her tasseled earrings.

"Exactly." I threw out my hands in emphasis before pausing on the precipice of my next words. "He needs someone to run the vet clinic. Just until he recovers."

My aunt's hands gripped the steering wheel as she changed lanes. "And?" she barked.

I tensed my abdomen against the swerve of the car. "I said I would do it."

A giant squeal pierced my eardrums before I finished exhaling. One of her hands shot to my knee and squeezed. I couldn't believe the sound that left my throat. A combination laugh and snort and scream all rolled into one unholy sound that I hadn't made since I was little.

"I'm callin' Randy tonight," she said matter-of-factly. "To let him know not to expect me back for a while." Randy was her handyman/gardener and the only one she trusted to care for her menagerie while she was out of town.

"Jackie," I protested, squirming away from the hand still clutching my knee. "You don't have to stay here. I'm a grown woman now." I arched a brow for emphasis. "Perfectly capable of taking care of myself and my dad and the clinic."

She gave a breathy scoff and recaptured the steering wheel before we veered completely off the road. "I know but to me you'll always be—"

"Don't even say it. Don't finish that sentence," I threatened. She grunted and pressed down on the accelerator, the low-slung car skating across the cement highway.

I dared to flip my phone over and read the barrage of messages lighting up my screen like Times Square. My insides like the coils of a snake as I swiped Steve's name first.

> Take all the time you need.

> Are you sure?

> I managed here once without you. I can do it again.

Well, that was easy.

> Glad to know how essential I am.

Steve followed up with a picture of Mitch Jenkins wearing a headband of reindeer antlers at last year's Christmas party.

I laughed, the edge of my tension dissipating. Mitch had responded to my news with an image of himself shrugging his shoulders. When had he even learned to make an avatar? The thought was thoroughly disturbing. I chewed the inside of my cheek with new tenacity.

> Don't worry. I'll be back in a few months.

Three dots flashed before my eyes but no words. I bit down hard with my incisors and added,

> In plenty of time to be ready for Paris.

Paris. My heart almost burst at the thought of it. An entire week of sleek Thoroughbreds prancing through arenas, taking jumps at light speed. I could almost feel the weighty badge around my neck. Official event veterinarian. I would stride along, riders and spectators parting like the sea in front of me as I arrived at the side of an injured mare and ran my hands along her foreleg. The crowd would hold their breath while I examined every ligament and crevice then sigh in relief when I hoisted myself to a stand and proclaimed it as nothing more than a mild strain. My phone dinged me into reality.

Mitch had replied, followed by a yellow emoji with a wicked smile.

> We'll see.

Bastard. He knew how bad I wanted to be there this year. I scrolled through the rest of my messages as Jackie wound us closer and closer to home. Sid wished me luck and said she would be thinking of my dad. Gavin hadn't replied yet. I checked my watch. He was predictable if anything and right about now he would be tidying up his glass-topped desk and logging off his computer. His dependency on technology was as tragic as my dependency on gas-powered vehicles and pre-packaged snacks. My brow furrowed as my phone regarded me in silence.

"You want to stop for a bite?"

I jerked my head up. Somewhere between my typing and fretting, we had made it to Linzberg and were cruising down Main Street.

"Sure," I said, feeling the lightness of a few less burdens. I rolled back my shoulders and slid my phone into my pocket. "How about the café?"

My aunt smiled her approval. "Just what I was thinking." We paused at a stoplight, and I watched nostalgia wash over her face. "We used to go there every year for your birthday."

I remembered every single one of those. Even what I ordered each time. "Yeah," I mused, my mind on a journey it hadn't taken in some time, traveling backward, further and further into the recesses of memory. The cozy booths lined in leather so worn it was nearly bare in patches. The gingham tablecloths with a tin pail of shiny utensils in the center. And always a single blooming flower in a bottle-green vase. But more than anything I remembered the warmth, the hum of voices, the sizzle of frying and the decadence of the very air we breathed.

"Do they still have peach cobbler on the menu?" I asked and my aunt shrugged.

"I haven't been here in years. Probably not since you left for college."

My lips turned down at that thought. She jerked into a parking spot, the only one left in the entire lot, bits of shale puffing from her front tire. "I hope they do," I mumbled, grabbing the handle and hauling myself out the passenger door.

"It'll be about a twenty-minute wait," drawled the hostess, a pencil tucked behind one ear with piercings all the way up her pinna. Little rhinestones that caught the fading sunlight like tiny stars. My aunt cocked her head to the side in impatience.

"I can get y'all a glass of wine on the house while you wait." The right words to soften the blow of having to wait on dinner. We both smiled in unison. The hostess used her tattooed forearm to gesture to a well-loved wooden bench.

I took two steps on the heels of my aunt before my phone jangled. My hand hesitated, hovering over my pocket for a few seconds before reaching in. I knew who it would be. "I need to take this. Be right back." I flashed her a wry smile and caught the frown lines on her forehead before I skirted to the corner of the faded red brick building.

"Hi, Gavin," I whispered, my voice hushed and silky with enough warmth to soften what I was about to say.

"Hello, Quinn," he said, each syllable perfectly measured. There was no background noise. Not even the whir of a computer or the sizzling of something on the stove.

"Where are you?" I asked, plugging my index finger into the cavern of my ear to block out the strum of a guitar that floated up from an outdoor patio.

"I was about to leave work when I got your message."

I winced. And cringed. And possibly screwed my face up into a rightful cowardly expression. "Yeah," I started. "It looks like Dad's recovery is going to take a while...which I'm not complaining about. The recovery part I mean." I stumbled over my words.

"It's fine," Gavin interrupted. "You do whatever you need to do."

I allowed myself the tiniest sigh of relief. "I didn't plan on this." But I had known I would say yes. When my father's steel gray eyes had cemented with mine earlier, I knew what he was going to ask. Saying yes was the least I could do.

His entire life had been spent building this practice, becoming so well known that it was not uncommon for someone to drive hours to bring their animals to him. And he had done it all while raising me as a single parent. He could have been world famous—or taught at an academic vet school—or traveled the racing circuit. One time, I had even found an old crumpled up letter in his desk from the San Diego Zoo asking him to come for an interview.

Yet he had stayed in our one pony town. Spaying pets and barreling down dusty roads to examine a colicky horse. Fixing up broken limbs and nipping off cancerous tumors. He said he loved our part of Texas. That the limestone was in his blood. That this was the place a wild girl like me should be raised. On country roads with green rolling hills. But I had always wondered if he had ever wanted more.

Gavin was silent and I had the prickling sensation that a question had been asked. I had no idea what it was.

"Sure," I murmured hesitantly. I heard him sigh with relief.

"That's great I'll let my parents know."

"Know what?"

"That we're still spending Thanksgiving with them," he said slowly, all the warmth leaching out of his voice.

Oh. My gut was twisted up in knots. How was I going to make that happen? I exhaled forcefully through my nose. Somehow, I would make it happen. I swallowed into the oblivion of my throat. "Great. I'll check on flights from here."

I barely registered the rest of our conversation, my eyes wandering around the parking lot and over to the guitarist on the patio then to Jackie, who pointed at a half-full glass of wine with a painted index finger. "I'll be right there," I mouthed. I could nearly taste the crisp hint of strawberries in the glass of rosé she held.

My gaze skipped over to a towering figure waiting in line for a table. Black sweater so soft it belied the rock-hard midsection I could tell was underneath. Black jeans hugging narrow hips. Richly dark hair that was thick and perfectly tousled. My heart slammed against my sternum. I dropped my phone into the dirt. His smooth fingers curled around a proffered glass of wine and swirled it around...and around. An undulating sea of deepest crimson.

I knew what I would see when he turned around. I knew the asymmetrical dimple in his left cheek when he smiled. I knew the straight nose and obscenely full lips. Those lips that were now cushioning the rim of his wine glass. His throat bobbing in a lovely way, like a cork in a stream, as he swallowed.

For a solid decade, I had played out this scenario over and over in my head. The day I would see his face again. I had

had years to plan my reaction. To construct every scenario. I had lain in my bed at night rehearsing my response down to the exact arch of my brow. Would it be cutting words and disdain? Or my personal favorite, utterly ignoring his existence.

I could easily pretend that I hadn't spent the better part of my twenties pining over him. I would be as cold as icebox lunchmeat. As statuesque as a runway model. Aloof. Emotionless.

As he turned toward me, the fading autumn sun cast a golden glow on the stretch of dirt separating us. I studied every minuscule movement. The twitch of his hand before he smoothed his hair. The tilt of his hips as he paused midstep. The droplets of wine staining the ground as his glass tipped. And when I saw his eyes go from casual to shocked, I hardened my gaze into a glare and ignored the caged butterflies all flapping in unison inside my stomach.

I ignored the parting of his lips and the widening of his eyes that were as liquid blue as a lagoon. Instead, I schooled my face into something neutral bordering on disgust, crossing my arms when he approached me. Slow and unhurried. Graceful. Like a puma. If he was a puma then I was a lioness. I stretched my spine to my full height when he stopped in front of me.

"Quinn?"

My name on his lips sounded exquisite. For the briefest of moments, I let my insides liquefy before flash freezing them into obedience. *What now?* I hastily scrolled through my scenarios. It was too late for refusing to acknowledge his existence. I was right in front of him. Staring stupidly into his crystal blue eyes.

"Hello, Will," I said. Even I was impressed with how cool and detached I sounded.

"What are you doing here?" he asked. He sounded like he

was in pain, his voice rougher yet with that same soothing quality that I had once felt all the way to my toes.

I honed my agitation like a blade and narrowed my eyes. I hoped he was in pain after what he had done. He deserved to be. *What was I doing here?* This was still my town, and he was the outsider. "What are *you* doing here?" Perfect. Now I had lowered myself to an annoying parrot.

He glanced across the street, almost sheepishly, and said, "A book signing. Among other things."

Of course he was. His face was suddenly replaced by the glossy square image I had seen on the back of his book. "At Weatherby's?"

He nodded and ran a hand through his tousled hair.

"I would have thought best-selling authors had better places to be than small town independent bookshops." It was a low blow, but worth it as I watched his eyebrows lift in surprise and he retreated a step.

A weary resolve slid into his eyes as he regarded me. And for a moment he looked desperate and almost...sad. By the time I blinked, it was gone, his face as serene and smooth as a lake in winter.

"I was in town, so I thought, why not?" He took another sip of wine.

"Since when do you come in town?" I dug my nails into the skin of my forearm.

"Since my grandparents both passed, and I inherited the house and the vineyard."

Oh. My lips parted as my jaw fell open. "I'm sorry. I...didn't know."

"It's all right. It happened a while ago." His face was completely undecipherable. Tranquil even. The longer he looked at me, the more he encased me in his silence—a silence so pure and silvery that I started to forget that I hated him. "Do you live here now?" he asked smoothly.

I snapped to attention. "No. No, I don't live here." I hadn't lived here since the summer we... My mind snapped shut like a trap. "I live in New Jersey," I said forcibly. "I'm a veterinarian for very expensive horses." No need for him to think I wasn't living the life of my dreams. Which I was. I allowed myself a smug smile.

Something in his face softened. "That's...wonderful. It's what you always said you would do." He studied me, flicking his eyes over my dusty jeans and dull leather boots. Shit. Why couldn't I have worn a leather miniskirt or a strapless dress? Not that I owned either of those.

"Are you here visiting your family?"

My gut lurched at the thought of why I was here. "Not exactly." I tightened my crossed arms. "My dad had an accident. I'm here for him."

His brows furrowed in concern. I wanted to smack the sincerity off his beautiful face.

"How long are you staying?"

"Until he can go back to work. I'm taking over the vet clinic...but just temporarily," I added quickly. "How long are you planning to be here?" *In my town. Not yours.* I struggled to swallow past the cotton in my mouth.

"Not sure," he said pensively. "It depends."

It depends? My jaw dropped another few inches, and I swore his eyes lit with amusement.

"Mr. Deremer, your table is ready." The hostess practically preened as she handed Will a menu and beckoned for him to follow her.

"It was lovely seeing you, Quinn," he said before turning to head into the restaurant.

I didn't respond with anything but bewilderment. As he walked away, my lungs scrabbled for more air. *Don't turn around,* I silently begged but he did. In all his lean, geometric glory he twisted around at the middle to hold up a palm and send me a dazzling smile.

I was a solid figurine in a sea of people and music and clinking glassware. I couldn't even defy gravity enough to raise a hand in return. I stood there. Reeling. Spinning out of the safety of my own orbit while the universe around me ground to a halt.

I stared at the face I had once fallen in love with and now couldn't stand the sight of.

CHAPTER FOURTEEN

SUMMER, THEN

I didn't see Will the night of the pool incident. Or the next. By the third night, I had envisioned every possible scenario. He had lost interest in me and whatever it was we were. Or he had left town.

Maybe his grandparents were forcing him to take a class on grape crushing. Or worse, he and Mary Alice were parked on a secluded backroad with steamy breath obscuring his back windshield. Wherever he was, it was becoming painfully obvious that it was more fun than being with me. Which made my ongoing infatuation with him wholly inconvenient.

I twisted the key in the lock of the double glass front door of the clinic, muttering to myself. "This is why I've never—"

"Never what?"

I froze, dropping the keys onto the cement then slowly crouching to retrieve them. Will's face appeared next to mine at eye level.

"Hi." The keys clanked together as I fumbled them into my bag.

"Hi," he said, throat bobbing with its signature sincerity,

his ocean blue eyes trained on my face. He stood up and he offered me a hand. I took it.

Despite the overbearing heat, his fingers felt cool and solid as he tugged me to my feet. His mouth twisted into a grin, the asymmetric dimple appearing in his left cheek. "I'm interested to hear what you've never done."

"I've never done a lot of things," I said, my eyelids narrowing with a hint of coy.

"I'm going to need examples." He dropped my hand, much to my disappointment, and tucked it into his back pocket.

I shifted my gaze to the sky, forcing myself to be mesmerized by the exploding lavender hues of sunrise instead of Will's face. "Like...karaoke," I blurted awkwardly and received silent amusement in response. "Or ice fishing or finish an entire banana split by myself or wax my eyebrows or travel to a foreign country."

His interest seemed piqued by that last one. "Where would you like to go?"

I bit the inside of my cheek in thought. "It sounds cliché, but I've always wanted to see Paris."

"Why Paris?"

No one had ever asked me this question. But I had always known the answer.

"I think a part of me would come alive there." My chest clenched and I immediately thought of my mom. My beautiful artist mom and her love of photography. I hadn't inherited a speck of her talent, but I thought if I went to Paris, some seedling inside me would sprout and it would somehow make me closer to her. Maybe remember her. I could imagine wandering through an exhibit of Henri Cartier-Bresson photographs and feeling her in my very bones.

"Paris is...lovely." Will's throat cracked on the last word, and I could sense that both of us held tightly to some yet unnamed emotion we struggled to keep under the surface.

"Of course, you've already been there," I teased.

"I actually lived there," he said, "when I was little. I barely remember it though." His eyes took on a wistful look and then a corner of his mouth turned up. "Only that we...my mum and I...had a little apartment on top of a patisserie. And that I woke up every morning to the smell of fresh croissants."

"That sounds like the absolute worst," I said solemnly, my lips twitching enough to give away my sarcasm.

The skin around Will's eyes crinkled and his mouth finished stretching into a full smile. "It was. And the culture...the art...the night sky over the Seine...also the worst."

I sighed dramatically. "I'm not sure if I could handle it...the disappointment I mean."

"Then I hope you get the chance to be disappointed," he said in a low, conspiratorial voice. My insides tightened in response as our gazes held. Steel gray eyes to ocean blue. My flinty ones in contrast to his that were lush and inviting.

The way he looked at me was intoxicating. Like he wanted to devour me like the novels that were always piled in the floorboard of his car. Which made me remember the way he had also looked at Mary Alice. I tore my eyes away toward the truck and trailer full of cattle rumbling past us. "How was the barbecue?"

"It was nice," he said evenly. "I'd never had authentic barbecue before. And Mary Alice invited me for an outing to a place called Crossroads tonight."

"Oh really?" I said, the tone of my voice in an all-out war between cordial and cringeworthy. Crossroads was, for all intents and purposes, a bar. A few nights per month they allowed entrance to the seventeen and up crowd for dancing.

I had never been inside. The closest I had come was strolling down the sidewalk with my dad and Aunt Jackie, ice cream cones in our hands as guitar notes twanged through the half-open windows. "You'll have fun. It's also very...authentic."

"I've heard," he said, "but I'll have to experience it some other time."

My tongue thickened inside my mouth, but I forced my words past it. "Why is that?"

"I've got other plans," he said, then added, "I hope."

I crossed my arms over my chest to still my stupid fluttering heart and finally looked at him. "What kind of plans?"

"It's a surprise. If you agree that is."

"I don't know." I sank my teeth into my bottom lip to bring myself back to reality. To sift through each feeling in turn. Uncertainty mixed with a thrill. Disappointment in things that hadn't even happened yet. And something soft and intangible and precious. And reckless. "I would have to ask...and I have to be at the clinic early tomorrow. Mr. Abbott is showing up with a trailer full of horses that need deworming." I tamped down the warmth in my abdomen and tried to remember how ridiculous I had felt at the pool. "You should probably go meet up with Mary Alice."

Will's face visibly sagged with disappointment. His fingers twitched at his sides. "It's not like that, you know," he said.

"Like what?"

"She's a friend, Quinn. And I'm not interested in her being anything else."

"Why not?"

"I got out of something quite recently before I left New York, and I'm not keen on starting anything else right now."

"Oh." A million questions ran through my head. I didn't ask a single one.

"What about you?"

"What *about* me?"

"Do you have a...suitor?"

I burst into a throaty laugh. "Yes," I said, "in fact I'm meeting him for a promenade around the town square later."

"You're mocking me."

"I couldn't let the opportunity pass me by." I risked a smug smile.

"Seriously though. Anyone special?"

"No."

"Ever?"

I scrunched up my face in thought. "There was my junior prom date—Charlie Ryan. He was my first kiss...first awkward groping session." My face turned sour with the memory.

"What happened?"

"I wasn't the only one he was groping."

"Ah," breathed Will, "if I were the violent type I could—"

"Don't worry," I interrupted. "Me and some other girls put nails under his truck tires."

Will snorted a laugh. "Remind me not to get on your bad side."

"My bad side is reserved for"—I held up one finger—"people who are cruel to animals and"—a second finger joined the first one—"incompetent meteorologists."

"Noted," Will said with a light in his eyes that belied the seriousness of his expression.

The part of me that I had held clenched for the last few minutes relaxed considerably. He wasn't interested in Mary Alice. But he wasn't interested in me either. Which I could accept. But I needed to know one more thing...

"So," I said, exhaling a nervous breath, "are we friends?"

He looked at me with the intensity and passion of a scholar. An explorer on the verge of discovery. "No, Quinn," he said finally. "We are something more."

~

Late that afternoon when the round headlights of Will's car pulled into our driveway, I skipped all the way to the door and vaulted into the passenger seat.

"Hi," I said as Will pulled his sunglasses down his nose and eyed me.

"That was quite an entrance."

"Freedom looks good on me."

"No doubt," he replied, his eyes drifting to my lips and lingering there.

"So where are you taking me?" I asked.

"Like I said, it's a surprise." Will smiled enigmatically as we puttered down the road in the opposite direction of town.

I folded my arms across my chest as loose strands of hair blew across my lips. "It better be good."

His face, a deeper shade of olive brown now that we were in the throes of summer, smoothed into a look of placid amusement. "It will be," he rumbled.

"I'm missing enchilada night for this," I explained.

"This will be better than food."

I scoffed lightly. "You've never had my aunt's chicken enchiladas."

"Tell me more about your family," he said, his voice barely audible above the wind.

"My dad is a veterinarian. He moved here after vet school to start his practice." I prattled on with my practiced monologue before he could interject. "My Aunt Jackie lives with us too, but I think she might move away once I go to college. She wants to raise alpacas." I smiled at the thought of her petite frame dwarfed by a herd of curious, fuzzy heads.

"Will you miss her?"

I looked away from him to the frayed edges of my denim

shorts, curling my fingers around their hems, softened with wear. "I'll be leaving for college soon so..." The words hung in the air. I didn't elaborate, letting Will interpret however he wanted.

The truth was, I would miss her. But I wouldn't miss the lingering guilt that knotted up my stomach sometimes. I thought back to our conversation about the boy she once loved, a frown tugging down my mouth.

"Tell me about yours," I blurted to divert the conversation elsewhere. I immediately wished I hadn't.

The hint of a shadow that wasn't from the sun's descent settled over Will's face. "I told you about my mom," he said thoughtfully, and I nodded.

"What about your dad?"

Will shrugged. "I never met him. My mom said he was brilliant but not that interested in settling down and raising a baby."

I frowned. I couldn't imagine someone not wanting to know the person seated next to me. To be a part of his childhood. His life. My face clouded with questions. "So, your grandparents..." I started.

"Are my mom's parents. They moved here from California when I was a baby but they're originally from France."

Wow. That would explain the exotic lilt to his accent. My bottom lip had taken permanent residence between my teeth. "What did your mom do? For a living, I mean."

Will smiled and it was equally beautiful and tragic. "She was an assistant curator for various art museums."

"Which ones?"

"A few in Paris when I was small then the Courtald Gallery in London and when I was fourteen, we moved to New York so she could take her dream job at the Met."

I had so many questions. They whirred and soared inside of me. I erupted in an explicable torrent of giggles. I was going crazy, melting and reforming all at the same time.

"What?" Will eyed me quizzically, eyebrows straightening out like a mountain range over the intense turquoise lake of his eyes.

"It's just...wow. I've barely been outside of Hicksville."

"Your time will come." He smiled secretly.

"Do you miss New York?"

"Not lately," he said and my skin warmed. "And...it wasn't my kind of place."

"How so?"

"Too noisy. I like the quiet. I like the...calm."

I nodded, understanding welling up inside of me. Because I knew he didn't mean the lack of voices or screeching tires as much as the way he felt inside. I knew because I felt it too. The rolling hills and bent mesquite trees and greenish silver ribbons of river that crisscrossed our county—I had absorbed it until my existence coalesced with the sky and the calm was rooted so deep inside me that it could never not be a part of me. "Did she ever get married? Your mom?"

He shook his head, and I noticed his hands tightening on the steering wheel. "I suspect she never really wanted to." I didn't expect the tender expression that crossed his face. "She was a bit of a wild card. A free spirit. Truly enchanting." He smiled and it was sorrowful and joyful all at the same time. "She used to coax me out into the rain and throw up her hands at the sky. And then she would dance with water streaming down her face. I miss that."

An image flickered into existence inside my head. My own mother standing in our driveway, hair slicked back from her upturned face. And then as soon as it materialized, it was gone. I blinked against the burn at the outer corner of my eyelid.

The gnawing inside my gut eased the slightest bit as I

settled into an inexplicable warmth. Not from the fading summer day. Not from the radiant skin of the boy next to me. It was from the pulsing shimmery edge of his exposed vulnerability. I wanted to slide down it like my own rainbow.

I formed the words on my tongue, only to choke on them when the car took a violent swerve to the left. My hand scrabbled for a hold on the dashboard as loose bits of road slashed my cheeks. Will stomped on the brake and I noticed the looming copse of trees, the space between their trunks filled in by overgrown grasses and stubby shrubs. He looked at me, the gold specks of his eyes shining brightly.

"We have to walk from here," he informed me.

In lieu of opening the door, I swung my legs over the doorframe, my knees quaking when they met the dirt. "Holy hell," I muttered.

"What was that?" he asked.

I offered my best smirk when I rounded the sleek hood of his car. "I said next time you can leave the off roading to me city boy."

His laugh resounded off the sky. "It wasn't that bad."

"It wasn't that good either."

He took a step toward me, close enough that I could smell the delicious scent of sweat and sandalwood. "I hope risking your life will prove to be worth it." He blinked, dark lashes sweeping downward. I could nearly feel how soft they would be against my cheek. Instead of smiling, I forced my face into an amused glare.

"We'll see about that." I gestured toward the sprawling wilderness. "Lead the way."

We picked our way forward through jutting limestone rocks and gnarled tree roots. Past woody shrubs with delicate yellow blooms and a thicket of brown-tipped grass that bowed with the breeze. The air was stifling with silence. Not even a bird cawed a welcome or an insult. Nothing slithered into the underbrush or crawled back into the earth or skittered up a tree. When we had made it nearly fifty yards from the car, Will paused and I eased up beside him. A giant slab of granite higher than my head protruded from the earth.

My hands went to my hips. "What now?"

His fingers curled around my wrist and tugged my hand toward the rock, placing it on the bare surface. It was textured and warm and friendly. A giant sentry guarding the entry of something secret. Something forbidden. I trembled with anticipation despite the heat coursing through my palm. Next to me, Will struggled to rein in his elation.

I cocked a brow and said, "Nice rock."

"It's not just any rock," he crooned.

"Oh really?" Now my curiosity was definitely piqued.

"Put your ear next to it."

I jerked my hand off the rock. "To hear what exactly?"

"Just do it." His eyes sizzled with intensity as he nestled the cusp of his ear into the granite face. Without further argument, I copied his movements and ended up with my ear pressed against a particularly roughhewn section of rock.

"What am I supposed..." I started but went silent when he moved his index finger to my lips, the smooth pad brushing the seam. I stopped breathing and willed my lips to press together instead of pucker outward. I was so focused on not kissing Will's fingertip that I didn't hear it at first—the vibratory hum that rose and fell like the cicadas as dusk. My eyes widened in surprise as I jerked away from the granite. "What was that?"

"I'd rather show you than tell you." Will moved past me with purposeful grace, his hands searching along the rock face. And then suddenly his head disappeared, followed by his shoulders. If I had not seen it with my own eyes, I would not have believed it. A misaligned portion of granite cliff face that initially looked like a scooped-out alcove. But when Will disappeared behind it, I realized that a narrow tunnel existed between the two halves.

When he was no longer visible, I shoved my head into the place where I had last seen him. "Will?" I yelped, gripping the jagged edges of rock.

"I'm here," he called, his voice echoing off the granite. A hand waved at me through the slit-like gap at the other end. I glared at it.

"How did you get over there?" My voice shook as my eyes bounced from one side of the chasm to the other to the sloped bottom and the narrow shaft of fading light trickling through the top. Will's face appeared next to his hand.

"Simply squeeze through this nifty tunnel." He looked irritatingly pleased with himself.

Squeeze, my ass. I tried to remember what I had eaten for lunch and for once was grateful that I had skipped the enchilada dinner. My foot moved in slow motion, my canvas sneakers wedging into the V formed by the two halves of sloping rock. I ducked my head and wedged half my body inside and was immediately doused in a wave of panic. I started trembling.

I couldn't see Will. I couldn't see anything but pink whorls of granite, sparkling and taunting me with its inertia. I opened my mouth, willing air to enter my lungs and then blew it out again. It wasn't enough. Sweat lined my brow like a crown.

"Will," I croaked. But I knew he couldn't hear me. I squinched my eyes closed and edged farther into the crack of earth until I could feel it on my back...under my palms...brushing my knees. I stopped, paralyzed in this formidable cocoon.

Maybe I would never make it out. Maybe my dad would have to get the paramedics to extract my sagging skeleton from this very spot...

"Quinn." My name was whispered along a gentle current of air that stroked my face. "Open your eyes." I did and darted them wildly about my surroundings until they landed on Will's face. His eyes were steady. Concerned.

I licked the crackling paper of my lips, embarrassment usurping some of my panic. "I'm really...I get really...claustrophobic."

His face softened, lips parting as his gaze drifted over my wedged silhouette. Clearing his throat, he said, "It's not far."

My chin hung almost to my chest as I slumped against the formidable rock formation behind me. "What's not far?" I asked weakly.

He hesitated, the silence filling the cavern, choking the last bit of fresh air from my nostrils. "Something extraordinary."

Fingers slid into the space between my back and the waistband of my jean shorts. I jolted into perception. Will's arm snaked through the cavern like a beacon in the shadows. A lifeline to freedom from eternity as a human geode. He tugged gently at first then more insistently until my feet slid and shuffled toward him. When I was close enough, he wrapped an arm around my waist and pulled. I was a floppy doll as he dragged me through the opening and into open space and precious sky. I bent over at the waist and rested my hands on wobbling knees. Will collapsed onto the craggy limestone slab next to me, a slight tremor in his arm when he raised it to wipe his face.

With nervous adrenaline singing through my bloodstream, I surveyed the open sky above me seen through the mouth of a towering crater. And in front of me a sparkling gem of aquamarine whose song was the gentle slap of rippling waves along a limestone shore.

"You found it."

CHAPTER FIFTEEN

SUMMER, THEN

"You found it," I repeated, dumbfounded by the beauty. The absolute serenity of this place. The pool was shallow near where we had stumbled into a heap. I could see through the turquoise water all the way to the limestone bottom. And then farther into the gorge where fingers of granite jutted from the earth, the water was darker. Navy and mysterious. Magical.

"I did," he said, his voice muffled by the arm he had thrown over his face. A thought struck me—he had been worried for me.

I knelt beside him. "I'm okay," I said, my voice barely a hoarse whisper.

He cracked one eye open. "I'm glad. I didn't fancy explaining to the entire town how I let you suffocate in a cave."

I took the liberty of smacking him on the forearm. Even with the brief contact I could feel his muscles tense. "It was hardly a cave," I sputtered. "More like a..." I struggled to find an accurate descriptor as wild laughter bubbled in my chest.

He waited a beat, eyebrow arched, before finishing my comment. "Glorified crevice?"

"I was thinking more like the world's ass crack but yours sounds better." Now I was biting my lip, sucking it into my teeth to stifle the laughter. A bark erupted from Will's throat and a moment later I joined in. Inhaling and wheezing. Clutching shaking hands to my stomach as the leftover fear dissipated.

Will pushed up to a seated position, long jean-clad legs stretching endlessly from his torso. The last gales of laughter puffed from my chest and when I fully opened my eyes, I realized how close we were.

I siphoned up the details of his face. It was perfect. Smooth and unmarred. Soft skin over sculpted angles. Lush brows and thick dark lashes. And those eyes. As blue and tranquil as the pool at our feet. The breath snagged in my throat as he lifted his hand. I tensed, awkward yet wanting.

He took his index finger and ran it along my cheek, tracing the jagged white line cleaving my face into two halves. A shard inside my chest rubbed me with its edges, still sharp even after so much time.

"What happened?"

"An accident when I was five." I jerked away to focus on the pebbles strewn over the ground.

"What kind of accident?"

"One that involved a very angry...cat who was stuck under the house," I lied, checking his response with a side eye.

"Is that why you don't like small spaces?"

I shrugged my shoulders. "Maybe. I can't remember much of it. I think claustrophobia is just one of my many quirks."

"Many?" Will pushed off the ground gracefully then extended a hand. "I can't wait to hear what the others are." Those full lips split into a playful smile.

I thought about smacking his hand away. Ruining the moment and pushing him away from the edge of my vulnerability. Instead, I grabbed it, baby hummingbirds beating their wings inside my stomach when he pulled me to standing.

"Fine," I said in mock exasperation. "I'll tell if you will."

"Deal." He smirked like a cat before dropping my hand and crossing his arms over his chest.

"You first." I arched a challenging brow at him and crossed my own arms over my chest. The act grounded me. Reminded me who I was. A girl who was not special nor beautiful. A girl with big dreams from a simple town who was not yet that interesting.

Will ran a hand absentmindedly through his hair. It had grown over the last few weeks, shaggy layers in every shade of deepest coffee and inky black. "I hate grilled cheese sandwiches."

The noise that erupted from my throat was a cross between a guffaw and a screech. "How can you hate grilled cheese? That's not even American."

"Neither am I," he retorted. "Not really anyway. For the most part, I didn't grow up here."

"Well, you wouldn't hate mine. It's the only thing I can actually cook."

His eyes sparked with amusement as they skated over me. "Your turn," he said.

"I still sleep with the closet light on."

"Really?" His forehead rose in surprise, and I grimaced.

"Now you," I grumbled.

"I despise incorrect grammar," he said with a sly grin.

"Truly shocking," I deadpanned then bit my lip in thought. "I have...perfect smell memory."

"No! Really?" He shook his head, face lit up with a beautiful combination of delight and confusion. "What does that even mean?"

"It means that whatever smell I experience during an important moment...when I re-experience that smell, I can perfectly recall the memory."

"So let me understand, if you inhale the scent of...I don't know...oranges while studying for a test—"

"Not exactly," I said slowly. "But hold on." I closed my eyes and inhaled deeply. Fully. I let the bite of summer cedar and the mineral tinge of limestone and the decadent sandalwood of Will's cologne diffuse into the deepest recess of my nose.

I opened my eyes to see Will watching me, his eyes flaring with wonder and something new...something more potent and consequential. "There," I said softly. "Now I will remember this moment forever every time I smell...the things I just smelled." I chuckled awkwardly.

"How is that even possible?" Will smiled and shook his head.

I didn't say that I would always remember every moment I ever spent with him. Smell memories or no. Instead, I whispered secretively, "My dad says it's because we're Scottish."

Will chuckled. "I don't think I can top that."

"Try," I encouraged.

"All right," he said, his eyes drifting over me, past me, past everything. "When I feel melancholy or out of sorts, I imagine a...different world."

"Like a better world? No war, no crimes against humanity? Free slushies during the summertime?"

He scuffed the toe of his sneaker in the dirt, his face scrunched up in concentration. And when he lifted his head, his eyes were no longer tranquil but the brilliant blue of a flame. "Not really...more like a fantasy world with characters that I create and magic and love and war and hope and despair. All of it, really. Just with mythical beings instead of real people." He said the last part reluctantly, sheepishly.

My eyes grew to the size of dinner plates. "Wow. So that's what's going on in your head."

"Most of the time."

"I thought maybe you were just the quiet type."

"I'm not really. Only when I have things on my mind."

"What's on your mind now?"

He cocked his head to the water lapping gently near our feet. "Now that you went through all of that trauma to get here, are you up for a swim?"

The day remained blistering hot even though the last rays of sun were being siphoned up by the coming night. Every inch of my skin not covered by clothing was layered in grime and sweat. I mentally surveyed what I had on underneath my clothes. I jerked my chin into a nod. "Okay."

While Will tugged his shirt over his head, I feigned interest in my own, occasionally stealing glances at his newly bared torso and the ridges of abdominal muscles. My hands shook as I dropped my shorts to the dirt and when I looked up, Will had already waded into the water up to his knees. I shimmied out of my bluebonnet festival T-shirt and splashed after him.

When my skin met the water, it was like ice on a hot stone, sizzling and sublimating as I pushed down a shriek. Will kept going until the water was up to his waist, undulating in gentle ripples along his back.

I slowed my pace, stepping carefully along the limestone bottom, feeling the ridges and angles beneath the soles of my feet. The pressure of the rocks calmed me somehow. Grounded me. I heard a splash, and Will had disappeared into the cerulean swirl and emerged in the center of the pool. I waved, a toothy grin stretching across my face. He motioned me to join him.

"It's not so bad once you're swimming about," he called.

I realized all the nervous heat from freaking out in the crevice had quickly dissipated and my body now protested with chaotic shivering. I crossed my arms across my chest and sucked in my stomach in case Will could see the edges of my imperfections.

I took a tentative step forward and then another one, my toes gripping the slick pebbles like lifelines. The water was well past my waist now.

"Come on in, Quinn!"

His words were slow and muffled as I sucked in a breath and dove. Deeper and deeper until I was weightless. Free. The cold seized my lungs and I didn't care. I didn't need anything. Not oxygen. Not the sky. Just dark nothingness.

Not until my chest burned did I pop through the surface. Will was a good distance away floating on his back. I treaded water and watched the shadows deepen, the sky turn a brilliant purple and orangish-pink.

We dove and swam, testing the water's buoyancy and our bodies' tolerance to cold. Tethered together by some invisible strand of tension. Orbiting each other but never exploring past an invisible boundary.

I cut my eyes over to his face, his hair slicked back along his temples and caught him watching me. His gaze was liquid and soft. Curious. And despite the freezing temperature of the water, I wanted to catch fire and burn. Maybe this pool *was* magical after all.

After that day, every moment I could escape from the clinic, Will and I headed to our newfound discovery. Swimming and splashing in the shallow end. Talking or simply floating in silence. And each time we became braver. More adventurous as we explored more of the pool and each other.

One languid afternoon, we lay on our stomachs, soaking up the heat from a flat ledge of limestone jutting over the water. This time Will had coaxed me through the crevice with the promise of a box of Moon Pies he had picked up from a gas station. Beside me, he let out a lazy groan and flipped over onto his back.

"Tell me something," he yawned.

"Every time you say that I have nothing. It's like my brain literally melts."

"Best moment of your life?" He gently elbowed me in the ribs.

"It hasn't happened yet," I chided, "which is the same answer I've given you all summer."

"Just checking," he said, his voice muffled against his forearm.

Although today was coming close to perfect. The sun was a citrine jewel against an aquamarine sky spearing the lazy water with its shafts of light.

"And don't ask me anything else. My lips are sealed for eternity."

He cracked an eye open. I could see the black pupil in a turquoise sea in the space between his forearms. "Yes, I know. You're the human equivalent of Alcatraz."

I rolled my eyes and pushed up to a seated position, an uneven area digging into my backside. "What's that supposed to mean?"

Will sighed, his head rising, his eyes burrowing into mine.

"What?" I repeated.

"Don't be cross, but..."

My eyes narrowed and I instinctively crossed my arms over my chest.

"You aren't the easiest person to get to know." His eyes shifted downward and studied the pebbled ground.

I recoiled, something turbulent pulsing in my midsection. "That's crazy," I scoffed. "You know plenty about me."

His face softened in acquiescence. "True. Very true. I know you love animals and boxed snacks that come neatly wrapped in plastic." I laughed, but Will didn't. "I know you crinkle your nose right before you say something funny and that you drive like a bat escaping Hades." He suddenly pushed up to a sitting position, so close to me that our bare knees brushed. "It's not enough," he whispered, and I tasted the mint on his breath when I licked my lips. "I want to know more."

That one word. More. It made my stomach flip in the most delicious way. And suddenly I wasn't scared. Like that word uttered from *his* lips had turned a handle inside me. A door gently cracked open.

"What do you want to know?" I asked shakily.

"Worst moment of your life?" he said gently. "The real one."

My fingers instinctively pressed the linear white scar extending from underneath my jawline all the way to the corner of my left eye. I took my time clearing my throat. "When I was really little, my mom...she was in a car accident." I paused, my mind dusting off this memory, rubbing against its contours.

I waited to see how it would feel. And for some reason the pain wasn't as sharp as I remembered. More like a deep dull ache that devolved into emptiness. An abyss of grief. The edges rounded with age. I plunged in. "And she died."

Will remained absolutely still, his gaze steadying on my face, never wavering. A shock of surprise spiraled through me. I had never said the words aloud. Ever. Not even to the best of my friends. People in town whispered and murmured of course. Or babbled incessantly when they become uncomfortable. Or shied away from me altogether.

His eyes—like a calming ocean, a weightless place to land—had me wanting to open the door wider. To tell him the rest of the story. The actual story. But I hesitated. I wasn't willing to expose the glacier's worth of guilt that iced me over from the inside. Not yet.

"She was really pretty and kind," I said thickly. "At least that's what I've been told."

His long lashes fluttered, and I knew he was studying my face. I prayed he ignored the damning scar that was entirely too visible.

"Like mother like daughter?" A corner of his mouth edged up in a smile.

"Hardly," I said, casting my eyes downward. "I have her hair"—I flipped up the end of my braid for emphasis—"but otherwise, I look nothing like her. And...anyway, I would never call myself pretty." I examined the cracks in my finger-nails like a coward.

His fingers found my chin and tipped it up. "Neither would I."

"What would you call me then?" I asked, my heart rate spiking, wondering if I wanted to know the answer to that question. Or if I didn't.

"Inevitable," he said without taking his eyes from mine.

CHAPTER SIXTEEN

AUTUMN, NOW

"Was that someone you know?" Jackie did her best impression of nonchalance as she slid into the booth across from me. Her eyes darted over the menu, but I knew she was watching me. She had eyes like a hawk. And the sixth sense of a mystic.

"No. Yes...but not really...no." I cringed and focused on the typecast font listing today's specials. "They have fried shrimp tonight," I said in a feeble attempt at distraction.

"It sure looked like you knew him." This woman was like a dog with a bone.

I sighed through my nose, my hot exhale creating a tiny circle of condensation on the plastic of my menu. "I knew him once upon a time."

"He's cute," my aunt quipped without missing a beat.

"Maybe *you* should go talk to him," I snarked.

"Maybe," she said thoughtfully, " or maybe you should since he keeps staring over here."

My throat constricted, my eyes darting wildly around the restaurant. Jackie pointed a finger over my right shoulder. When I twisted in my seat, there he was, casually perched at the bar in his black cashmere sweater and with his perfectly, tousled hair. And he wasn't alone.

A leggy brunette in a pencil skirt with an upswept bun rapid fire typed on her mobile device. Her eyes drifted upward periodically to settle on Will. Of course, they did. He had the face of an Adonis.

Will, with his singular dimple and liquid blue eyes and angular hints in his facial structure, had been noticeably attractive as a teenage boy. Now that he was a man, his face was devastating. Rugged and artistic at the same time. With the same dimple in his left cheek when he smiled. Thick, disobedient hair that I wanted to run my fingers through and a set of lips that had been on nearly every square inch of my skin. My chest delivered a silent flutter as I stared.

And then I remembered that I hated him and like an angry, red splash of paint, it stained everything I saw in that moment. He sipped his drink with one hand and gesticulated with the other as his perky date continued to type and swipe and make googly eyes at him. Good for him. She was hot and cultured and graceful. I daggered them both with my glare.

Will's lips froze mid-sentence to offer me an apologetic half smile. There wasn't enough apology capital in the universe to soothe the wound that ripped open in my gut right then. I diverted my eyes to the menu and concentrated very hard on what sides came with the fried trout.

Before the sun shattered the clouds the next day, I was awake, dressed in a set of maroon scrubs and a spare set of running shoes I had found buried in the back of my closet. My knee jiggled as I bent down to tie the laces.

I mentally chastised myself. What did I have to worry about? I could do this job with my eyes closed. Backward. In three-inch heels. But deep down I knew why. There was one person on this earth I couldn't bear to disappoint.

Jackie burst through my bedroom door like a gale-force

wind, and I nearly slipped off the bed. "Want me to drop you off at the clinic on my way to the hospital?" She reached up to adjust the hoop dangling from her left ear.

I shook my head. "No, don't wait on me. I can drive Dad's truck."

"He keeps the truck at the clinic now."

My brow furrowed in confusion. "What does he drive to work?" It wasn't far—only about four miles to the edge of town where the clinic rested on two acres of prime real estate. Jackie pointed out the window to the garage my dad had transformed into his own tinkering workshop.

"He bikes?" I asked horrified.

My aunt rolled her eyes and smirked. "No, he drives that old Camaro."

"He finally fixed it?" I asked, peering into the distant garage window like I could see the vintage beauty's silhouette. This car, despite its raw sex appeal, had been a legitimate clunker for most of my life. I had never even driven it. *"It's not safe enough for teenage girls,"* my dad used to grumble.

"He got it fixed up last year," my aunt confirmed. "You still remember how to drive a stick?"

"I'll make do," I said and practically jerked the keys out of her hand before vaulting down the stairs and out the front door.

When I twisted the ignition and pulled to the end of the driveway, my heart kicked into high gear, rivaling the rumble of RPMs beneath my hands. I had waited my entire life to drive this car and it did not disappoint. It hugged the curves better than my jeans hugged my thighs. Despite the morning chill, I rolled down the windows to feel the crisp wind whip across my face, through my hair, and down my front like icy fingers. I shivered, goosebumps peppering my flesh all the way across my chest and arms. It was cleansing and heady.

A flicker ignited somewhere inside me and roared to life

as I sped down the two-lane country road into town. I felt alive. So alive that I nearly bellowed into the wind. I had missed this place...these people. My town. My family. I growled the gears into the parking lot and inserted the car into the spot my dad had been parking in for thirty years, dust puffing up around my tires. I rested my chin on the steering wheel and blinked against the sun. I was doing this. My dad finally needed me, and I would not let him down.

Variations of my name echoed around me when I pushed through the glass doors. A chorus of Quinn, Quinnie, and Dr. McClain in a myriad of accents, pitches and tones. The baritone was Roberto, our office manager, with his golden-brown skin and jet-black hair now streaked with white. He had preceded even my father at the clinic and first met me as a child. He smiled brightly as he hoisted a stack of charts in the air like a trophy, his gold incisor glinting in the fluorescent overhead lighting.

The alto was a cackling middle-aged woman in bubblegum pink scrubs. Sonia, our longtime surgical technician, held a screeching feline inside a cardboard box with evenly spaced round holes.

The soprano I didn't recognize. A creamy hand waved at me from the front desk. Full pink lips and matching pink cheeks that glowed when she smiled. A mile of caramel waves cascaded down her front, ending at the V of her scrub top.

"Hi! I'm Kody...with a K," she trilled. "I work the front desk."

I flicked my hand to indicate I had heard her. But before I could utter a single greeting in return, I was being ushered past the front desk to a familiar long hallway with a row of closed doors, behind which lay glinting metal tables and stark overhead lighting. I inhaled deeply. Antiseptic and gauze and wet fur.

"We have a whole day scheduled for you, *mi hija*," crowed Sonia. I noticed she was no longer brandishing the cat.

"I can't wait." I gave her my broadest smile and accepted the stack of charts from Roberto.

"We're so happy to see you," Sonia said. She threw a plump arm across my shoulders.

"I'm happy to be here," I said, feeling heat rising in my cheeks. Because I was. And it had been too long.

"Go to the office and get settled," Sonia sang. "We'll come get you when we need you."

And suddenly the hallway was empty except for the shuffling of sneakers on concrete floors. I shook my head, smiling as I wandered to the rear of the building near the exit to the outdoor pens. My hand paused on the doorknob to my father's office, stroking the dents and scrapes in the burnished copper.

A twinge gripped my heart as I flung it inward. It was the same space but different than I remembered it. No haphazard stacks of paper charts. In their place was a sleek computer monitor. Books were aligned on neat rows of shelving next to outdated copies of veterinary journals. Even the air felt wrong without David McClain bellowing laughter into it.

I collapsed into the overstuffed leather chair behind his desk and spun back and forth as it creaked beneath me. Closing my eyes, I let the sunlight from the dusty window on the opposite wall stream over my face. I inhaled the leather and top notes of my dad's aftershave. It reminded me of petrichor, the smell right after the rain gushes from the sky.

I both loved and hated relaxing. Drifting into the warmth and silence of this space. My mind suddenly caught by the winds of the past—like a sailboat on the ocean. What would have happened if my mom had never died? Would we have stayed in this small Texas town? What would it have been like to grow up with a mom? Someone to braid my hair and tell me to stay away from boys. Someone whom I would call every Sunday night. Someone who would have opinions about how to cut my hair and which eye cream to buy...and which flowers to use for my wedding. Would I have moved back here after vet school instead of isolating myself in the Northeast?

I had been lucky though. Jackie and my dad had given up their lives and dreams to raise me together. I had spent the first half of my life loving every minute of their undivided attention. And then the last half too riddled with guilt to appreciate it.

I had left the moment I got the chance. And once I was gone, I had thought they would get a second chance at lives they never lived because I was the constant variable. The child whose mother had died. The kid who had needed stability and warm meals and rides to school. Being a burden had become my identity and I never wanted to feel that way again.

My eyes flew open, and I ratcheted to a sitting position when I heard footsteps squeak down the hallway. Sonia's head poked through the crack in the doorway, her tightly wound curls framing her face in shades of coffee and caramel.

"You look good in that chair, *mi hija.*"

"Thanks," I managed to say. "What do we have for today?"

The lines around Sonia's heavily mascaraed eyes crinkled as she looked upward. "A few surgeries in the morning and clinic all afternoon. Are you okay with that? You look tired, *mi hija.*"

"Of course." I sat up straighter in the leather chair. "I'm ready for anything."

Sonia threw back her head and cackled. "Just like your *papi.*"

I smiled, the tension around my shoulders easing as I stood.

"Here," she said, handing me a single sheet of paper with today's schedule.

My brow furrowed. Wow. Business had really picked up around here. Two major surgeries and at least twenty appointments this afternoon. "Did you guys pull the charts for me?" I asked and Sonia tittered with another bout of laughter.

"No, *mi hija*," she answered proudly. "Everything is on the computer now." She glanced over my shoulder at the sleek machinery gracing my dad's desk. My lower lip curled.

"I'm...impressed. I never thought Dad would give up his paper charts and favorite ballpoint pens."

Sonia fingered the hem of her pink scrub top. "The world keeps moving forward. Eventually, Dr. McClain did too."

I frowned and wondered what that meant as I followed her down the hall.

It took a total of seven minutes for Roberto and the pink ladies to reacclimate me to the clinic flow. By eight o'clock I was scrubbed into a gastropexy, arms deep into the abdomen of a Great Dane.

As soon as I threw the last suture, I hustled off to extract a foreign body from the stomach of someone's pet iguana. Without breaking stride, as the afternoon hit, I bounced from clinic room to clinic room. A tabby cat who wouldn't eat. A parcel of puppies who needed vaccines. A goat with a cough that sounded excruciatingly similar to his owner's.

The day flew by in a blur of fur and claws. Whimpers and snorts. I loved the implicit chaos of scrabbling claws on metal tables. I thrived in the skill and calm I possessed in my hands. This wasn't a high-profile equestrian clinic operating on million-dollar racehorses, but I loved it all the same.

When I finally had a break between patients, I crouched

over the computer in my dad's office, shoulders burning as my fingers hammered out an operative report for Ferdinand the Great Dane. Sonia appeared halfway through my desperate attempt at charting and part of me slouched in relief. I paused to press the heels of my hands to my eyes.

"Take a break, *mi hija*. The afternoon is slowing down. Eat some lunch."

I glanced at my phone. Three o'clock. My stomach grumbled in annoyance, but what I really wanted was coffee. "Do I have time to make it to the square and back?"

Sonia already had the back door open and was shooing me out of it by the time I slung my purse over my shoulder.

The day was bright and cloudless. My eyes pinched closed when the first blinding rays struck my face, and I was reminded how much more potent the sun was in central Texas. I walked briskly down the path behind the clinic next to a row of wiry mesquites that ran along a shallow creek bed. As the crow flew, it wasn't more than half a mile to town. I could nearly smell the rich aroma of coffee before spying the stark white brick café on the southwest corner of the plaza.

One thing that had not changed in the hundred years or so of our town's existence was the grassy square in front of me. Large century trees guarded its borders and shaded almost every inch of neatly trimmed lawn. Everything important happened around this plot of dirt. Fourth of July fireworks and farmers' markets. Girl Scout cookie sales and the yearly Christmas parade and festival.

I wondered if the holidays were still a big deal. They had been the biggest deal one could imagine when I was growing up. So big, in fact, that the governor of Texas himself had visited one year.

A bell tinkled overhead when I slipped into the coffee shop on the corner. My eyes fluttered at the decadent smell of roasting beans and frothed milk. I could nearly taste the bittersweet burn traipsing down my throat. Suddenly everything seemed possible again.

"Hi there," said the ginger ponytail behind the counter. "What can I get you?"

"Almond milk latte with an extra shot, please." I fished my credit card out of my scrub pocket and slid it across the counter.

"Oh, it's no charge." She bobbed her head in a ridiculous rhythm.

"It's free?" I frowned in confusion.

"No ma'am but the guy over there said he would take care of the charge."

My eyes flew to the outdoor tables lining the sidewalk and the figure casually draped over one of the green metal chairs. "I don't know him," I said through a clenched jaw.

The petite cheerleader in front of me had the audacity to blush as her eyes skated over Will. "Well, ma'am, he insisted so..." Her eyes widened in fear. Probably as she imagined a moody, caffeine deprived woman morphing into a lunatic right before her eyes.

As I watched her practiced movements as she made my coffee, the stress from the last few weeks—and, if I was being honest, years—rose and bubbled inside me until my mouth was a cavernous volcano. And I was ready to spew. I swiped my coffee from the counter, fuming my way out the door.

I halted within a breath's distance of Will who calmly sipped a latte as he scribbled in a leather notebook. Gone was my awkwardness from the night before. The surprise at seeing him again had evaporated. Incinerated by a decade's worth of rage.

He didn't look up at me, which meant my fantastically executed glare had gone to waste. I watched his throat bob as he swallowed, and it was so familiar. For a moment it quieted the crackling in my bloodstream and my heart stuttered as I reached out to tap him on the shoulder with my index finger.

"Hello, Quinn," he said calmly.

"Why did you buy me coffee?"

"You looked like you needed it."

"What I need is none of your concern."

"My mistake."

I could have turned on my heel, making a dramatic exit as I escaped with a free coffee and a shred of dignity. But I didn't. "What I really need is not to see your face in my town," I sputtered.

"I thought you quite liked my face once upon a time." His lips curved into a cautious smile as he finally looked up at me.

"I haven't liked your face in a while."

His eyes darkened and hardened even while his lips twitched upward. "Maybe that's about to change."

I scoffed. Loudly. Unnecessarily dramatic. "It's going to take more than coffee."

"How much more?" he murmured quietly, hesitantly.

"More than your fancy author brain can even imagine."

"I can imagine quite a lot."

"Not this much."

"Is the coffee a good start?"

I was not going to assuage his guilt. He did not get to feel better. He did not get to buy me coffee and think that he could be forgiven. I plunked my cup next to him, a delicate, milky brown droplet landing on the hand that held his pen. "Hardly." Turning on my heel, I strode toward the square.

THE BEST THING about best friends was their willingness to

invest in your drama to distract themselves from their own. Sid picked up on the first ring.

"Quinn," she exclaimed. "How are you? I've been worried...like Indian auntie worried. What's going on with your dad?"

"He's okay actually. Getting better every day."

"Thank the universe. How are you holding up?"

"Not terrible." My voice wavered.

"But not good. What else is going on?"

I heard a drawer click shut in the background. "Nothing. You sound busy. I'll call you tomorrow."

"Oh no. Not on your life. I'm not busy. My night with Bob can wait."

I smashed my cheek into the phone screen. "You're dating someone?"

She chortled into the phone. "Not exactly. Bob stands for battery-operated boyfriend."

I cackled and rolled over onto my back, bedsprings creaking under my weight.

"Ha, ha," she said dryly. "Now that you are my plans for the night, I expect to be entertained."

Biting my bottom lip to stifle a laugh, I tucked the phone close to my mouth. "Okay, do you remember freshman year when we took the train to New York City on Halloween?"

CHAPTER SEVENTEEN

AUTUMN, THEN

I squinted my eyes against the glow of my laptop and focused on willing words to flow from the tips of my fingers. Writing had never been my forte. Animals. Science. Anything outside and tangible. Not my own thoughts that seemed imprisoned in my brain by some mystical force. Prevented from appearing on the screen in front of me in word format.

My roommate, Sidney, sat on the twin bed opposite mine in much the same position. Hands poised. Eyes focused. A halo atop her ebony head from the glow of the Whitman building.

"What are you working on?" she asked without taking her eyes from the screen.

"Philosophy paper," I grumbled. My least favorite subject. If pontification were a sporting event, I would lose every time. "What's the point of life changing thought without actually doing something about it?" I continued, cringing at the scrambled together sentences in my document.

"There is no point. No spoon. No reality," Sidney droned. "We are all simply the universe's unfortunate puppets."

"I think you chose the wrong major, Plato," I snickered, letting the black-and-white screen fade into a blur.

As I chewed on my lower lip, my mail icon blinked a message at me. *New message.* I abandoned my floundering over what defines a human and clicked on the bouncing envelope.

Saying hello. (it's will)

I bit the inside of my cheek to keep my smile from shattering my jaw. For a burgeoning writer, he sure knew how to be brief.

Warm breath coated my ear, a curtain of braids cascading between me and my laptop screen. "Ooh, who's Will?" Sid asked.

"Just a friend from home."

"Like a friend friend or someone you wish was more than a friend?"

"Maybe a little of both." My cheeks heated at the thought.

"How do you know him?"

"We met over the summer. He's staying with his grandparents who live in my town."

"Summer flings are the absolute best. So hot." Sid stretched out across my bed like a cat.

"It wasn't a fling...he...I mean...I never even kissed him."

"But you wanted to." She smiled knowingly.

I blushed a deep crimson, like the hothouse roses my aunt had planted in our flower beds. "Yeah," I admitted. "I wanted to."

And I had thought he was going to. A few times actually. My wicked brain jumped to the time it had almost happened. We had been sitting in my dad's vintage Camaro, knee to knee, windows down with the night unfolding around us, a rare breeze ruffling the ends of his hair.

"What's that one?" Will pointed upward at a smattering of twinkling stars.

"Cassiopeia," I answered dreamily. The night had taken on an ethereal quality. Magical even. I startled at the thought. I had definitely been spending way too much time with Will and his fantasy world. *Or not enough*, a voice had niggled me.

"What about over there?" He leaned over to where I was reclined in the driver's seat as he'd pointed out my window. The edge of his shoulder grazed my chest. I sucked in a breath then let it out slowly. *Please don't move*, I silently begged.

I sipped the air between us. It was rich with his scent. The fresh citrus and sandalwood of whatever soap he used for showering. It encased my head like a cloud of opium. My eyes drifted closed, heavy and sedate.

"That's Venus," I croaked. "You can only see her immediately after sunset."

"Venus," he mused. "Roman goddess of love and beauty."

My stupid teenage heart hammered against my sternum. He was the beautiful one. At that moment, I knew I never would find a human as beautiful as the one next to me.

"Open your eyes," he whispered.

When I did, I blinked to bring into focus the orbs staring back at me, rims of turquoise around twin black abysses. He had a question. I could tell. I willed the answer into my face. *Yes*, it shouted. *Whatever it is, please do it!*

He dipped his head, lips pressing against the bottom of my scar, close enough to the corner of my mouth that I shivered. "Can I confess something?" he whispered against the curve of my cheek.

A bang resounded off the hood of the car, and I jumped so high that my head hit the roof. "Boo," said a deep voice as my dad's face became backlit by a flashlight. When my retinas could process images again, I found Will glued to the passenger door clutching the handle.

Sid's nudge into my ribcage brought me back to the

present. "Message him back." A wicked gleam ignited in her deep brown eyes. She looked at me sternly when I hesitated over the keypad, her bony elbow digging farther into my ribs.

"What do I say?"

Sid scampered over to her own bunk, my laptop in her possession.

"Hey," I squealed. I leaped onto the pillow next to her and we bounced a few times before settling into the divot in the middle of her bed.

Hi yourself, she typed, and then added, *What's up?*

The mail icon bounced almost immediately, and my stomach clenched.

Trying to decide about asking you something...

Sid typed, *The answer is yes,* and I squeezed her calf. "You don't even know what he's asking."

She was delirious with glee next to me. Despite the nervous roiling in my stomach, I didn't have the heart to stop her. A minute passed and then another, my brain fizzing with nervous energy.

When the tiny envelope on my screen shuttered, I clenched my eyes shut. Sid read aloud, "I was hoping you would say that."

"What does that mean?" I said in a voice somewhere between a moan and a screech. This time, I slid my laptop off her bent knees and began pounding the keys. *Care to tell me what I just said yes to?*

I could imagine him grinning as he reclined against his bed pillows. I bet he had a duvet and one of those lumbar support pillows that fit perfectly against his lower back. His reply came quickly, and my eyes scanned the screen once, twice as Sid clambered over me to read it. *Visiting NYC this weekend for a friend's Halloween party. Costumes are optional but encouraged. Bring a friend if you want. I'll send you the address.*

He was flying from Texas to New York for a party? It seemed impossible. And miraculous. For a second, I realized how big his life must be...and how small mine was in comparison.

"Quinn, please tell me we are going to this party. I swear I will do your laundry for a month." Sid vibrated with excitement next to me. "What's the point of life changing thought without actually doing something about it?" she challenged.

My eyes swung from my computer screen to her, and my "yes" was lost in her high-pitched squeal.

~

"ANY IDEA where to go from here?"

The wind whipped between our legs as we climbed the concrete stairway out of the bowels of the New York subway station. Light flared in my retinas. So much light. We stood, slack-jawed with amazement and pivoted in a semicircle to take it all in. Giant billboards of some ripped guy sporting underwear. Flashing pixels of the names of Broadway shows.

And everywhere we looked—people. As thick as ants rushing out of a disturbed anthill. Old, young, middle aged. Women in stiletto booties and men in overcoats. A woman in a red dress, a droplet of colored paint in a sea of gray tones. A little girl clutching her mother's hand, her skirt fluttering around tiny legs.

The sun set in the distance, not that we could see it behind the gargantuan buildings blocking everything except for shadows. I was nothing more than a plastic figurine inside a giant snow globe.

I stepped to the edge of the street corner, my toes peeking over the sharp edge of the sidewalk and flung my arm in the air. A yellow taxi screeched to a halt in front of us. "I've always wanted to do that." I giggled as Sid practically pushed me into the backseat.

"Where to?" the balding driver barked in a harsh accent.

"Greenwich and Moore, please," I said with confidence.

"Tribeca," Sid said then made a low whistle. "Nice taste. I like this guy already."

I smiled, wondering how much my face told the story of my infatuation with Will.

By the time we clambered out of the cab in a neighborhood of brick and iron dinosaurs from the industrial era, a light mist was falling around us.

"I think it's that building across the street," I said, tugging Sid behind me. A blood-red brick facade blanketed by the grayish sheen of dusk loomed in front of us. Eerily fitting for Halloween. Arm in arm, we hustled toward a giant wooden door and a man in a navy slicker holding a clipboard. He flicked his eyes over us before mumbling, "Names please."

"Quinn McClain and"—I squeezed Sid's elbow—"guest."

After checking a box, he wrenched open the door and nodded toward a spiral staircase. "Take the stairs to the top floor."

We almost fell over one another giggling past him as he shook his head and slammed the door behind us. I took the steps in rapid succession, my boots clicking on the worn metal. I heard Sid huffing behind me as the weight of her costume slowed her to a snail's pace.

"Here, let me help you," I offered, turning mid-stride.

"Thanks." She extended a hand, and I pulled her up to the landing where a door painted a shade of light-absorbing black awaited us. I chewed my lip and shifted to my other foot as I reached for the handle.

"Nervous?"

"A little," I admitted.

"I love it when you're hot and bothered."

I emitted a breathy laugh.

"Hey—he'd be an idiot not to like you." Sid slid a protective arm around my shoulders.

I nodded, confidence thrumming in my veins and pushed open the door. Bass music thumped and bumped between the solid matter in the room. Before tonight, the wildest party I had ever seen was Casey Griffin's eighteenth birthday party. Her parents had bought us wine coolers and let us use their barn as our makeshift dance club for the night.

My eyes widened as I surveyed the room. A fully staffed bar was set up in the corner rather than the kegs and ice chests I'd been expecting. The music boomed from the opposite corner where a live DJ spun music from his laptop. But the biggest shock of all was the people. A room full of beautifully proportioned young adults in the most elaborate costumes I had ever seen. Skimpy sequined dresses and bubblegum pink wigs and feathered hats. Wings and capes and thigh high vinyl boots.

I wrapped my leather jacket around my middle as I scanned the tightly packed throng on the dance floor. I saw *him* before he saw me. Will was dressed in a quilted blue vest over a linen shirt, leather trappings around his middle like some kind of warrior displaced from the sixteenth century. He waved his arms through the air along with the rest of the crowd. I smiled watching his face, lit up and carefree, as he gracefully navigated the six-eight time of the song. He was beautiful. And for the first time I admitted to myself that I wanted him to be mine.

My expression froze, smile faltering and face shattering, as a shapely, leggy brunette dressed as a cheerleader slid her hands over his shoulders. I watched her wind them around his neck where she fingered the sweaty ends of his shaggy hair. Will sent his hands around her waist as she tossed her ponytail in rhythm to his hips. I was going to be sick.

"So, where's your guy?" Sid shouted in my ear over the music.

Unable to speak, I raised a pointed finger at Will's gyrating backside.

"Him?" Sid gripped my arm so tightly that I knew her nails were leaving a mark.

Will spun around to face us. I wanted to stop staring but I couldn't help myself. I knew any moment he would catch me watching him, but I couldn't look away.

"Damn, Quinn. The way you described him I thought...well...I never pictured that." She flicked a hand for emphasis, catching Will's attention. He homed in on us with eyes that were twin lasers of bright blue. The room, the music, the chaos—it all ceased to exist when his face broke into a wide smile.

"How did you picture him?" I hissed into Sid's ear. Her hand slid under my elbow in support as he made graceful strides in our direction.

"Nerdier. Like maybe a cute geek. Not drop your panties hot."

I bit back a laugh and shushed her, never breaking his gaze. And then he was standing right in front of me. No longer did I have to wonder if I had imagined him last summer.

"You made it," he said, reaching up to swipe a length of hair across his forehead. "I can't believe you're here."

"Me neither," I admitted. His eyes were a shade darker than I remembered. No longer the bright turquoise that rivaled a lagoon. In this dimly lit industrial-era apartment, they were mysterious and beckoning, like the sky at twilight. Beside me, Sid cleared her throat. I fluttered back to earth. "Will, this is Sid, my roommate."

Sid thrust her slim brown hand, nails painted a violent red, nearly into Will's abdomen. He grasped it with his quite larger one. "Nice to meet you," she said, showing a row of her dazzling white teeth. "Great party. Thanks for the invite."

"You're quite welcome," he said, unclasping Sid's hand. "I'm so glad you could come."

"Our other option was toilet papering the boys' dorm tonight. It was a hard choice," I quipped.

When Will smiled down at me, the dimple on his left cheek deepened into an abyss. "I imagine it was." He wiped his hands down the back of his pants. "Can I get either of you a beverage? We have cocktails or soda if you prefer."

I opened my mouth to say yes to a soda when a long tan arm snaked around Will's waist. The cheerleader. She plastered on a fake smile as she molded her body into Will's side. "I was wondering where you went." Her whining soprano grated my nerves to shreds. "Are you going to introduce us?" She tipped her head in my direction then blinked her doe eyes at a speechless Will until he threw one arm around her shoulders.

"Danielle, this is my friend Quinn and her roommate Sid. They came up from Princeton."

My heart deflated at the word friend. "Nice to meet you," I said, choking out my next words. "How do you know Will?"

She had the nerve to giggle and put a hand on his chest. A hand that said *mine. All mine and definitely not yours.*

"Danielle is a friend from high school," Will said and quietly but effectively peeled her hand from his left pectoral. I didn't miss the glower she gave him.

"I'm at NYU now," she said, thrusting her lip into a pout. "But I should have gone to Texas with this one. I hate the cold." The hand that no longer rested on Will's chest was now tousling his hair.

"I like your costume," Sid piped up.

Danielle pivoted toward Sid like a preening bird.

"Thanks. What are you supposed to be?" She cocked her head to the side, eyeing us like we were a freak show on display.

"Vampire," I said, opening my mouth wider so she could spy the elongated canines cemented to my natural teeth with denture adhesive.

Sid had helped me do a smoky eye and we had painted my lips blood red to match the lacy tank under my black leather jacket. I didn't think I looked half bad. Passable at least. And not deserving of the placating look from someone dressed for a halftime show.

"And I'm her latest victim," offered Sid, lifting her braids to show the fake puncture wounds on her neck and then spinning around in her resale shop wedding dress splashed with red paint to resemble blood.

"That's adorable." Danielle clasped her hands together on the shelf of her cleavage.

Rather than respond, Sid rolled her eyes and cocked her head toward the bar. "I'm going to need that beverage now."

I started after her before glancing back at Will, who was being tugged toward the dance floor by an insistent Danielle. He stood rooted in indecision before cupping a hand around his mouth and shouting, "I'll catch up with you in a bit, Quinn."

Time passed too quickly with too much sensory input for me to process in a single evening. Sipping and talking. Laughing and dancing. Sid and I were thrown into the mix with dozens of interesting people all clamoring to have the night of their lives. But no matter where I was in a sea of faces, I always knew where to find Will. Like two gravitational bodies, we orbited one another, traversing time and space together. But never colliding.

When I finally looked down at my phone and the time, I yanked Sid's arm as she downed the last drops of a beer. "It's time to go. The last train to Jersey leaves in forty-five minutes."

She nodded, wiping her mouth on the sleeve of her dress and instructing me with her deep-set brown eyes. "I'll grab our purses and meet you downstairs."

I searched the crowd three times over, even shimmying up to the top of a stool so I could see better. But no Will. *I guess he wouldn't be catching up with me after all.* I brushed my hands over the rear of my black jeans and planted my boots on the floor. The hurt was palpable in my chest, like the tiny barbs of a stinging nettle plant piercing my most sensitive parts. I could only blame myself. We were friends. And that was clearly all he wanted. Maybe it was all I could handle anyway.

I wrenched open the door, welcoming the quiet of the stairs, and paused to tip my head back against the exposed brick wall. Its formidableness grounded me, holding me upright against the dizzy sway of my legs, which were jelly after dancing with Sid most of the night. I ran my palm up my chest and rested it right over my sternum where an ache bloomed from the inside. My head rattled against the wall as the door next to me swung open and then closed with equal fervor.

"I thought I might be too late," Will breathed, and I peeled back my eyelids.

"Too late for what?"

"For this." He reached down and took my hand in both of his then pressed it to his chest. "A quiet moment with you."

I debated pulling back. Peeling my palm from the broad hardness underneath it. But then I felt a string of stuttering thumps that was Will's heartbeats on my fingertips. It matched the fluttering in my own chest. I left my hand where it was. Maybe he wasn't mine. But maybe he wasn't not mine either.

"The party was fun," I said, the caliber of my voice as weak and wobbly as my knees.

"I'm glad you had a good time." He tightened his grip on my hand. "I'm sorry we didn't have a chance to talk. I didn't intend to be so occupied this evening."

I focused on the soothing blue velvet of his costume. "It's okay." I bit my lip, which hurt significantly more with my fake vampire teeth. "Your girlfriend seemed very...enthusiastic."

"Girlfriend?"

"The cheerleader."

Will snorted with an unrefined sound that I had never heard him make before. I drew back against the ridges of exposed brick as he studied me intently.

"Ex-girlfriend," he said slowly.

"The something you recently got out of?" I tilted my head up to better regard his face.

His lips thinned as he nodded.

"I think the cheerleader wants back into it," I ventured.

An amused gleam backlit the blue of his eyes making him look almost otherworldly. "I thought you knew me well enough to realize my preference for vampires over cheerleaders."

His teasing tone licked up my spine. One dangerous word edged into my consciousness. *Maybe.*

He swallowed, jaw tightening then loosening again. "Danielle is...lovely, but not what I'm looking for."

"What are you looking for?" I arched a brow of cool curiosity while my insides fizzed like an uncorked bottle of champagne.

"Something more," he said quietly, almost prayerfully. And then he brought my palm to his lips, pressing into my clammy skin with the warmth of his mouth. A hot sear traveled down my arm, straight into my chest, marking my heart like a brand. I never wanted to leave these three-square feet of space ever again.

My phone buzzed in the back pocket of my jeans. And then buzzed again. "I have to go," I said. "The train..." My voice was the strength of weak tea. My senses overstimulated to the point of everything fading except for my hand, which remained firmly planted on Will's mouth.

"Okay," he said against my fingers. His eyes, a complicated mixture of adoration and disappointment, searched my face.

My phone buzzed again, and I stood on tiptoes to press my cheek along the fine stubble of his jawline. "Thank you," I whispered before turning to go.

I was a marionette walking down the stairs with stiff, jerky movements controlled by the responsible part of my brain. Not the newly awoken part. The part made of dreams and starlight and irrevocable recklessness.

CHAPTER EIGHTEEN

AUTUMN, NOW

"So, wait a second," Sid interrupted. "Will—*freshman year* Will—is the author who wrote *Lune?*"

"What are the odds?" I said sarcastically.

She blew out a breath. "I'm so glad I picked up the phone tonight."

"I might have run into him."

"No! Where?"

"In Linzberg of all places. He's here for a book signing or something."

"This book is brilliant. Not to rub it in Quinn but he just made the *New York Times* bestseller list. What is he doing in a town that's not even on the map for a book signing?"

"Keeping a promise, I guess...which is fantastically ironic," I snarked into the phone.

Sid was quiet for too long. I could imagine the exact cock of her head as she mulled over the details. "Is he still hot?"

"Sid! What is wrong with you?" I scrunched my eyes closed like it would help his face disappear from my memory.

"Is he?" she pressed.

"Yes, of course he is because the universe hates me to the nth degree."

"You were never the same after that ended," she mused.

"Thanks for reminding me." *And you're still not the same,* a voice accused inside my head.

"Remind me, what exactly happened between you guys?"

She threw out the bait, but this fish had never bitten before, and it wasn't going to start now.

"I think whatever brief thing we had just...fizzled out." I cringed at my lie. "Anyway, I'm surprised he even remembered me."

"Are you going to the book signing?" she asked.

"Of course not. Not if someone promised me my own island. I'm counting the days until it's over and he's gone and I can eject from this stupid blast from the past."

I could nearly hear the cogs ticking against one another in her brain. "You should read the book," she said thoughtfully.

"Not happening." My jaw was clenched so tight it nearly popped out of its socket.

"Everything makes so much sense now," she said, almost to herself.

"What does that even mean?"

"Read the book and we can talk about it."

"You sound like a teacher."

"That's because I am, or was, before I became a principal."

I groaned into the phone.

"Quinn, don't take this the wrong way..." I knew she was pausing to work her jaw. "But you were pretty devastated for a while. And I think it took you years to forget him. Are you sure you're up for doing it again?"

God, how had she become so insightful? I swallowed hard before I answered. "I've done it before, Sid. It won't be that hard to do it again."

～

"How's your first week going at the clinic?" Aunt Jackie eyed me over her reading glasses, which were halfway fogged from her mug of coffee.

I sipped my own coffee, now resigned to making it at home instead of stopping at the café in case Will happened to be there again. The scalding liquid soothed the ache in the back of my throat.

"Good. Really busy. I can't even imagine how Dad has run this place all these years without a partner."

Jackie absentmindedly jotted items on a grocery list. "He loves this town and its people—almost as much as he loves you. That kind of love and dedication will keep you going when everything else runs out."

"But didn't he ever want to do anything else? A bigger practice? Bigger salary?"

Jackie pursed her lips. "Once. When you were little, he got an offer in San Diego. He really thought about going but in the end, he decided to stay."

"Why?"

"He said that California wasn't the right place to raise a kid. The houses were too big, and the yards were too small. You know your dad. He likes his space."

This bothered me more than I cared to admit, like a stone that had sunk deep into the pit of my stomach and kept sinking without end. Doing things out of love always had consequences. Sometimes terrible ones. Ones that couldn't be fixed. Ones that left a permanent shroud of guilt.

I drained my coffee and stood up to leave. At least I finally had the chance to make up for some of it.

"What do you think I should cook next week?" Jackie asked as I shrugged on my field coat.

"For what?"

"Thanksgiving," she said with a flash of irritation.

Visions of a giant golden-brown turkey and a mile-high pile of mashed potatoes smacked me in the face. *Was it really next week?* I blinked at her expectant face a few times before I answered. "I actually won't be here."

Hurt flashed through her eyes. So potent that it singed my skin when she stared at me.

"I'm supposed to spend Thanksgiving with Gavin's parents in New York and with Dad in the hospital I wasn't sure we'd even be doing anything." The back of my neck grew warm as I babbled. "I thought you might want to go home and check on the alpacas. I'm sure you don't want to spend the entire day cooking for me."

Jackie pushed her cherry-red reading glasses on top of her head and glared at me. Hard. "What was the last holiday you spent here?"

"I don't know," I fumbled. "Christmas a few years ago."

"Six years ago. You haven't been back since you graduated vet school, Quinn."

Emotional heat rushed up the back of my neck. "I've been busy with work...and life."

"You never come home anymore, Quinn."

"It's not that I don't want to."

"That's what it seems like so if there's another reason, I'd love to hear it."

We were really doing this. The gritty conversation I had been avoiding since seeing Jackie in the hospital waiting room. The words were ash in my mouth, but I said them anyway.

"It's time for you and Dad to live your own lives. Stop worrying about me and taking care of me and trying to make every moment of my life perfect." My words hung in the room, thickening the air between us. I glared at her. She glared right back.

And at first, I thought it was a trick of the light fracturing in through the kitchen window, but the sparkling sheen in her eyes was undeniable. I had never seen my aunt cry. Not once. Her spine was carved from granite. I had seen her as mad as a nest of disturbed hornets and bubbling over with joy. Emotional but never overcome to the point of tears.

Instead of responding, she pushed back from the table and, without looking at me, barreled through the back door, keys in hand.

THE WAITING room of the clinic was already packed and spilling over onto the sidewalk by the time I rumbled into the parking lot. I skirted between a pug and a tabby cat having a disagreement right outside the front door and charged through the chaos into the back hallway.

"It's busy today, *mi hija,*" Sonia announced as she handed me a white paper bag. Her other hand was fanning the underside of her neck with a copy of *Texas Monthly.*

"Are you okay?" I asked, opening the bag to peer inside.

"Hot flashes," she groaned.

"That sounds...awful," I said, pausing to fish out the cream cheese kolache in the bottom of the bag and take a huge bite.

"Enjoy being young, *mi hija,*" she crooned as she trudged down the hallway, a hand fluffing the short caramel strands framing her face. "Menopause is like hell...only hotter."

I shook my head, laughing quietly, as I entered the first room of the day. A balding man stood there, nose too large for his face and fluffy tufts of white hair springing from his ear canals. My tall frame dwarfed him like he was some sort of leprechaun. He held a felt cowboy hat in one hand and extended the other in my direction. For his size, his hands were on the larger side. He gripped my hand once, flexing his forearm muscles, a quick, formidable squeeze then let go. I noticed he was alone.

"Hello, ma'am. I'm lookin' for Doc McClain if he's available. Tell him it's Calvin."

"I'm Dr. McClain," I said patiently, and his wrinkled lids popped open in surprise. "The other Dr. McClain."

His thin lips parted in a smile. "Well, I'll be." He slapped his knee for emphasis as he studied my face. "I shoulda known. You have your dad's—"

"Eyes," I finished. "I know." I glanced around the sterile room, noting the empty table, searching for a dog cowering in a corner or maybe a cage I had missed. "What can I do for you, Calvin?" I crossed my arms over my peacock-blue scrubs and tried to look as confident and formidable as my dad.

"One of my hounds is deliverin' pups soon." He twisted his hat between his hands, his forehead furrowing into neat rows. "It's her first litter and she's not takin' too well to it."

"In what way?" I asked.

"Well now, she's drinkin' water but won't eat. She's growlin' one minute and whinin' the next."

"Some dogs get really anxious the first time around. How long has she been acting like this?"

"Since yesterday evenin'."

I drummed my fingers on my elbow. "The first stage of labor can take a while. Especially with the first litter. I'm sure everything will be fine."

He didn't look convinced but dipped his head anyway. "You're the doc. You would know better than me."

Something clenched in my gut. A warning maybe? A premonition of sorts. It was enough that I snatched the prescription pad and scribbled down my phone number. "Here's my personal cell," I said, handing him the scrap of paper. "If you don't have puppies by the end of the day, give me a call."

The rest of the day passed quickly. It was Thursday, the one day a week when no elective surgical cases were scheduled. By four o'clock, our last appointment finished up, and the staff was itching to go home. I couldn't blame them. My brain and my lower back begged me to return to equine surgery where I either sat in a chair operating all day or dealt with hooved patients that towered over me. If one more cat with a bezoar tried to claw my arm off, I was seriously contemplating closing the clinic for an entire week.

Sonia poked her head through my door while I typed notes on our last customer for the day—a little girl's pet bunny with new onset seizures. Probably an infection. But the medications I had given her would keep the seizures at bay until it resolved.

"You okay if we leave for the day, *mi hija?*" Sonia asked.

"Oh, sure thing," I replied, glancing up from my laptop screen.

She paused, red lips pursed like she wanted to say more but decided on, "See you *mañana.*"

The door shut behind her and I returned to typing. Sitting in my dad's leather chair with the sun drifting lower in the sky was peaceful. A microcosm of quiet solitude that I didn't often acknowledge that I needed. The conversation from this morning played through my head.

You never come home anymore, Quinn. Jackie's words had stung but what truth didn't? I hadn't come home in years. I had wanted to. Desperately. But I had my reasons for staying away. My family had given me a perfect childhood. Me—the selfish little girl who cried for her doll until her mom turned the car around. Me—the constant reminder of a tragedy that never had to happen. Me—the reason they both sacrificed jobs and dreams and even love. How was I supposed to make up for any of it if they wouldn't let me?

I remembered the summer I had come home from college after freshman year. I had stayed out late one night. *With Will.* The light had still been on and my dad and Aunt Jackie were sitting at the table. They were speaking to each other in whispers, and I could barely make out the words. But when I had edged closer and heard what they were saying...

I had been shocked at first. Rooted in place on the mat inside the backdoor. A kaleidoscope shift of realization had made tendrils of cold acceptance slither up through my bare feet. Everything had finally made sense. There had been a reason for the guilt forever clawing at my insides. I felt guilty because I deserved to.

My phone vibrated and I jerked at the unexpected noise.

Can't wait to see you next week, honey.

I exhaled through my nose as I stared at the text. Gavin never called me anything but my given name. And shit, I needed to get a flight before everything was sold out. Instead of typing a reply, I delved into a rabbit hole of discount airline tickets. I was on the verge of purchasing the last seat on a direct flight from Austin to New York City when my phone jingled with a number I didn't recognize.

"Hello, this is Dr. Quinn McClain," I said into the receiver.

"Howdy there, Dr. McClain. I'm sorry to bother you after hours," said the whiskey-smooth voice I recognized from earlier this morning.

"It's no problem, Calvin," I said. "What's going on with your dog?"

"Well, ma'am, I can tell she's been laborin' for a while now, and I ain't seen no pups. Would you mind comin' out and takin' a look?"

For a few seconds I was puzzled, wondering why he

didn't simply load her into the truck and bring her into the clinic. But house calls sounded like the kind of service Dad would deliver and people now expected. "Of course." I looked at my watch. "Text me your address. I'm leaving the clinic right now."

With my bag slung over my shoulder, Calvin's address already programmed into my phone, I slid into the vintage Camaro like a superhero with a purpose. A purpose that would distract me from wallowing in self-psychoanalysis. The engine rumbled beneath my hands as I sped out of town toward a remote farmhouse at the western edge of the county. Classic rock blasted from the radio, and I rolled down the windows to let the crisp fall air whip across my face. I started humming along with Aerosmith's *Crazy*.

When I stopped at a T-intersection along a familiar dusty country road, I rolled to a stop, the engine shuddering before becoming silent.

"Shit," I breathed. I turned the key off then on again while pumping the clutch. Nothing but a wheezy sputter and a succession of clicks. I released a string of expletives and tried again. The car made no sound at all this time. Perfectly content to sit in silence. "You're a hunk of junk, you know that," I swore softly. "I'm sorry I ever thought you were cool."

I leaned my head forward to rest on the leather steering wheel then dialed Jackie to see if she could give me a lift to Calvin's place. No answer. She was probably still miffed at me about Thanksgiving.

I scrolled through my phone, debating whom to call next when a sleek black as night Range Rover pulled up beside me. The passenger side window slowly descended to give me a picture-perfect view of an even more perfect profile.

"Nice car," Will said smoothly.

"Shut up," I snapped, briefly wondering if he had forgotten about how much time we had spent in this car.

Windows down as the night settled around us like a blanket. Picking out constellations from the front seat to distract ourselves from the tension vibrating between us. I had been a lovesick idiot.

"Why are you stopped in the middle of the road?" He removed his sunglasses, giving me a quizzical stare.

"Car won't start," I barked, gesturing to the hood and wishing I could make another type of gesture in his direction.

"Do you need a ride?"

"No," I said abruptly right as my phone sang its impatience. *Please return to the route.* I couldn't very well do that with a deadbeat car.

"Come on," he said, leaning over to open the passenger door of his SUV. "I won't bite. Or even talk if you prefer."

I hesitated and weighed my options. Utter abhorrence for riding in a car with Will versus guilt for failing a patient. Guilt was always a more effective motivator. "Fine," I grumbled. "But no talking. Or biting. Or loud breathing even."

He smirked as I climbed in next to him. "Where are you headed?"

I consulted my phone for the map. "Calvin Hyde's place. Out past Bandera Road." He nodded and gunned the truck through the intersection. "I'm going out to see a dog though so you can just drop me off, and I'll get Jackie to pick me up later."

He screwed up his face. "I'm not dropping you off and leaving you there." We both stiffened at his choice of words.

"I hope you didn't have any plans then," I muttered and spent the rest of the drive studying the landscape.

◌

CALVIN LIVED on an expansive property in upper west Hidalgo County that backed up to the Pedernales river. The fall weather had turned everything a shade of brown and deep olive, from the scrub brush to the stubby grass to the mesquite trees with their wicked-looking thorns. We wound through at least a quarter mile of rocky terrain before arriving at a ranch-style home with a wraparound porch. The largest dog I had ever seen stood watch at the bottom of a set of stairs leading to the front door. His enormous gray head lifted in greeting.

Calvin limped down the steps to rest a hand on the top of the head that was nearly even with his waistline. The size difference made them look like an illustration in a children's book. The tiny man and his gigantic dog. He raised a hand as Will and I lumbered up the rest of the driveway. "Thanks for coming, Doc."

"It was no trouble," I said, barely needing to bend over to let the Irish Wolfhound sniff my hand. "I now see why you didn't bring Poppy to the clinic earlier." I looked over at the cherry-red Ford parked next to the house. "It must be an ordeal loading her into the truck."

He removed his cowboy hat and scratched the tuft of hair at the back of his head. "Not usually, but now that she's laborin', it's a different story."

"And is this the proud father?"

"Yep." He scratched behind the ears of the dog glued to his side and earned a satisfied whine. "This here's Killian."

"Do all of your dogs have Irish names?"

His cheeks turned rose colored as he said, "My kinfolk are all from across the pond and we been raisin' Irish Wolfhounds near fifty years."

"That's impressive," I said, kneeling on the ground to run a hand along Killian's massive front legs and chest. He leaned down and whuffed into my ear then nuzzled me with his nose.

"I do believe you got a suitor, Doc. He knows his people when he smells 'em." Calvin gave me a conspiratorial wink as I stood and brushed the dust off my knees. "If I'm not mistaken," he continued, "the McClains came from the southeast coast."

"You're probably right," I agreed, my mind already considering the potential causes for Poppy's stalled labor.

"She's Scottish, actually," said a voice behind me. Will. I had forgotten he was there. He lingered between the truck and the porch steps, arms crossed over an olive-green sweater, ebony hair whipping sideways with the wind. Like a magazine cover for *Garden and Gun*.

I squashed down a sarcastic response and instead offered, "Calvin, this is Will, my..." Luckily, my lack of an adequate descriptor was interrupted by a rumbling howl that seemed to originate beneath my feet.

"That would be my Poppy," sighed Calvin. "About an hour ago, she crawled up under the house, and nothin' I done can get her out."

As he talked, I stared at the fathomless, black opening underneath the porch until the edges of my vision blurred, and I felt myself falling through space.

CHAPTER NINETEEN

AUTUMN, NOW

"Quinn?"

I blinked into the soft glare of a dipping sun. Minuscule stars danced along my visual field like fireflies. My back had collided with something solid and warm. A viselike grip held me by the waist. In my haze, I thought I should struggle. But instead of being uncomfortable, I felt safe. Protected.

I wished whatever it was would hold me tighter. My head lolled toward my chest until I noticed my shoes, barely skimming the ground underneath my buckled knees. How was it possible I was still upright? I heard a strained voice near my ear. "She doesn't like small spaces."

My head snapped up, nearly clobbering the mouth that lingered near my ear. Will inhaled a long, slow breath. Was he smelling my hair? I pushed down at the cable-like arms and wriggled out of them, stumbling as I cursed inside my head.

"You okay, Doc?" Calvin watched me, worry limning his grayish-green eyes.

"I'm fine," I said curtly, taking down and redoing my ponytail to give my shaking hands some purpose.

"Lucky your friend was fast enough to catch you before you ate dirt." Calvin chuckled.

"He's not my friend," I muttered quietly, kneeling to unzip my bag. I pulled out a glass vial of clear liquid and began drawing it into a syringe. "If Poppy has been in labor since yesterday then I need to give her something to stimulate uterine contractions."

Calvin rubbed Killian's head as he nodded in thought.

"But I'll have to reach her, Calvin. Do you think you can get her out from under the house?"

"I done tried everything, Doc. She's way back in the corner and she's too big to be drug out."

"I would agree," I said, biting my lower lip as I surveyed the opening under the porch. If I angled my head just right, I could see two glinting orbs, belonging to a heaving, shapeless black mass.

Heat filled the space next to me as Will joined me in the dirt. "I could do it."

"Do what?" I continued organizing my supplies without looking at him.

"Crawl under there...so you wouldn't have to."

Irritation and gratitude ebbed and surged together inside me. Was this another ploy to assuage his guilt? Like the coffee incident. The frightened part of me flailed around inside my chest begging me to say yes to his offer. I clenched my nails into my fist.

"I don't think so," I answered, shaking my head. "I don't think you would fit plus I'm going to need to inject her with medication." I curled my lips into a saccharine smile. "You'd probably end up stabbing yourself."

"Don't sound so pleased with the idea," he said flatly.

I ignored him and edged closer to the mouth-like opening until I teetered on my heels at the entrance.

"You're going to need to lie down, I'm afraid," said Will, who had followed me to the opening under the porch.

"Exactly what I look forward to hearing from a man," I quipped and heard Calvin make a strangled cough behind us.

"I got you a light," he announced and flicked on a heavy-duty Maglite that he directed into the darkness. And there she was. At least fifteen feet away, curled up near a pile of bricks and God knew what else. Her tail beat twice when Calvin clicked his tongue at her, but she made no move to rise. "What's the plan, Doc?"

I straightened my shoulders before tucking the syringe deep into my scrub pocket. "I'll crawl back there and inject her with oxytocin—it's a drug that stimulates labor," I explained. "And then as the puppies are born, I'll pass them back to you."

Calvin nodded his head enthusiastically. "Cause once those pups are out, she won't have no reason to stay under there."

"She'll come out on her own," I agreed. "Calvin, can you give the light to Will and find some clean towels and a box?"

He was off in an instant, hobbling back inside the house at a surprising pace, leaving me alone with Will.

"Are you ready for this?" he asked quietly.

"Not really," I admitted, "but I don't have much of a choice, do I?" I flattened myself to the ground like a serpent and inched forward until my head and shoulders were cloaked in darkness. Bile rose into my throat, along with my afternoon latte. I swallowed forcibly and pushed forward another inch.

The ground absorbed then transmitted the impulse of my racing heart so that my chest was being pummeled from both sides. The dirt beneath me was cool and dry, the air stale from the musk of rotting vegetation and whatever had crawled under here to die in the last few decades.

Poppy made a noise between a growl and a whine when her side heaved upward then deflated. I patted my pocket to make sure the syringe of oxytocin was still there. It was a mistake to stop moving. The space suddenly felt smaller, the air heavy and suffocating. My next exhale came out as a rasp.

I was in a nightmare where I couldn't breathe or talk. I began clawing at my throat. I was going to asphyxiate in here and someone would find me in twenty years. A rotting pile of bones next to a possum corpse. My limbs flailed wildly, a primal survival instinct taking over. I didn't care about saving anyone's dog. All I wanted was someone to save me. A hand closed over my calf and squeezed.

"Quinn." His voice sounded extracorporeal as it echoed through the darkness.

"Let me go," I wheezed. "I can't—"

"You can," he said and tightened his grip. "I've got you. At any point I can pull you out." He demonstrated by curling his fingers around the back of my knee and tugging. "I won't let you go."

In some deep part of me, near the source of my unrealistic fear, lived the quiet realization that I trusted him. That I knew he wouldn't let me go.

I brushed the heel of my hand over my eyes, and it came away smeared with tears I didn't remember shedding. I brought my hand down to the dirt and dug my fingers in to push myself a few inches forward.

I was a ship and Will was my anchor. As he massaged my calf with strong, reassuring strokes, the spark of something else began to edge out the fear. From his touch, a line of heat grew up the back of my leg all the way to my lower back. I stifled a groan in the back of my throat then mentally smacked myself. Distraction. That was what he was doing.

The pressure of his fingers was exactly enough, encouraging me forward and stabilizing me at the same time.

After another two pushes, a hairy foreleg lay across my path. Poppy barely opened her eyes to this new human presence. Her exhaustion was my opportunity. I put the syringe between my teeth and pulled off the cap. The shadow of a vein taunted me for a moment before I plunged the needle inside.

The giant swollen belly in front of me shuddered and Poppy's eyes snapped open. I sent my hand to her face, very near her exposed canines and gently rubbed her snout. She nestled into my hand as her belly heaved again.

"Will...are you there?" I called but I knew he was from the hand that now encircled my ankle.

"I'm here, Quinn." His words, smooth and true as an arrow, turned something over inside my lower abdomen.

"Can you pass me a towel?" I asked shakily and reached one hand back as far as I could.

When I grasped the rough spun fabric between my fingers, I dragged it forward, as near to Poppy's backside as I could manage. The first puppy was born soon after. And once I had settled that one in the center of a towel, another one emerged. And another. And another until six wet forms lay next to me.

"I think that's it," I called behind me, my chest aching with the pressure of my exhale. "Can you reach the towel and pull them out?"

Squeaks and whimpers resounded through the tight space as the six puppies crawled and fell over each other in one wriggling mass of teeth and fur and tails. I craned my neck around to watch Calvin insert a giant pair of iron tongs into the hole, pinching the ends around the edge of the towel. The puppies slid toward the flashlight beam, and I took my first full breath in several minutes.

"I'll get you out next, Quinn," Will called right as Poppy geared up for a final heave and one additional pup slid onto the ground next to me.

"Wait, there's one more," I shouted. I picked up the unsteady female, slick with amniotic fluid, gingerly tucking her into the crevice between my shoulder and my neck. She was small. The runt of the litter. I let her settle into my body heat before I called to Will. "Okay, I'm ready."

His hands were everywhere at once. First my ankles, then my knees, then skating up the backs of my thighs to my waist where he sank his hands above the curve of my pelvis. I came out in a whoosh like I too was freshly born as I sailed through the air, Will yanking me into his kneeling frame.

My ass landed on his thighs, and he rocked backward onto the ground with a grunt. His arms curled around me, and, for the slightest second, I enjoyed their weight on my middle. A delicious heaviness that I didn't want to like. But I undeniably did.

My scrub top had become untucked, and his bare forearm rested against a strip of exposed flesh. For a moment, I could think of nothing but that spot of contact on my body.

Did skin have memories like muscles? If so, mine remembered his and what his touch did to me. It didn't care that thirteen years had passed. It forgot the decade of hurt over a broken promise. It ignored the wound that had never truly healed over. My skin heated under his arm, a deep, throbbing heat that was uncomfortable, yet I couldn't get enough of it.

Calvin chuckled and slapped his knee beside us. I realized what we must look like. A pile of limbs, covered in grime, a mewling puppy on my chest. He reached down and gingerly picked her up by the scruff and tucked her legs into the palm of his hand. "Lucky number seven and the runt o' the litter."

I smiled as she howled. She certainly didn't know she was the smallest. Nor did she care.

The first thing I did when Will and I pulled out of Calvin's driveway was crack the passenger window. I needed the crisp air in my lungs to overpower the stench that lingered in my nose from being underneath the house. And possibly the one that lingered on me.

I pressed a hand to my neck, my fingers coming away with the stickiness of afterbirth. I needed a bath. A long, hot bath. I pressed two fingers into the knotted muscles of my shoulder and winced.

Will glanced over with a worried look. He still looked pristine and crisp despite spending some time on the ground in his designer jeans. Jeans that hugged his hips in the most delicious way. I hated that I had noticed. I scooted as close to the door as I could get without falling out onto the highway. The silence between us grew until it filled up every unoccupied space in the car. And then some.

"Can I confess something?" he murmured softly. I stiffened. Not moving. Not breathing. Those words taunted my soul.

I turned my head enough to catch his profile. He was so laser focused on the highway in front of us that I couldn't read his expression. My heart pounded in anticipation of what he was about to say. Just like it always had.

Will's lips parted in a careful smile. "That's the most fun I've had in a long time."

I erupted in hoarse laughter. I was delirious and silly and disappointed and relieved all in the same breath. "Your life must really suck," I said.

He barked a laugh. "Sometimes." I watched his lips curve upward in a smile, but his eyes told a different story. They looked...haunted. And filled to the brim with regret. I flicked my gaze back to the window and the first stars peeking out from behind violaceous clouds.

"Thanks for," I stumbled over my words, "for back there." I motioned my hand in the direction of Calvin's place.

"It was my pleasure." His voice was pained yet smooth and it stabbed me right in the gut to know that he really meant it.

He still feels guilty, my brain reminded me. *That's where this is coming from.*

"Can I ask a favor in return?" He dared a quick glance at me.

I focused on the hazy outline of the moon visible behind a puffy gray cloud. "It depends on what," I said warily.

"My book signing at Weatherby's is tomorrow night." He drummed his fingers nervously on the wheel. "I want you to come."

"I didn't read the book," I said weakly.

I knew I wasn't imagining his expression this time. A wave of sadness washed over his face as he said, "I would still very much like you to come. If you don't have other plans."

Why did he care if I came to his book signing? A confused fluster churned inside me, and I hugged my arms tighter around my midsection. The truck veered off the road, and I suddenly realized we were in front of my house. The porch-light flickered on, illuminating Jackie's sleek white car in the driveway. "Oh, my dad's car!" I clapped a hand to my forehead.

Will hung his head sheepishly, a dark lock of hair flopping forward. "I texted a friend to tow the Camaro. It is, as we speak, undergoing an evaluation at PJ's Garage."

"Thanks," I stuttered. "You didn't have to do that."

"I know." He leaped out of the car, gravel crunching under his boots as he made his way to my side. The door opened and he reached toward me.

"I can get out of a car by myself. I'm not a baby." I had

degenerated to the emotional capacitance of a petulant child and I didn't care.

"You've had a rough day," he said soothingly.

I eyed him warily. "I doubt you want to touch me." I thought of my hands layered in bodily fluids, blood and dirt caked under my nails. He arched a brow then leaned over to unbuckle my seatbelt. The shell of his ear passed close enough to my lips that I could have grazed it. I held my breath until he pulled away. When he offered his hand again, I took it, grubby nails and all, and used his leverage to slide my feet to the ground.

"One last confession?" he whispered, eyes darkening, the black of his pupils nearly overtaking the blue. "I find myself wanting to touch you very much."

Shock ripped through me so thoroughly that I flattened myself against the side of the truck. He closed the distance between us, caging me in with his sinewy arms. I expected the rush of claustrophobia to hit, but, instead, something else erupted inside me. Something once buried that had somehow clawed its way out in the last few hours. Something deep and needy and flammable. Something...wrong.

"I'm engaged," I blurted.

Will froze before backing up a step, arms falling to his sides. He blinked at me, glancing between my face and my hand. "Of course, you are. I'm sorry, Quinn," he rasped. "I...you don't wear a ring so I just assumed..."

"You know what they say about assuming," I trilled, my voice high-pitched and tinny. *Fuck a duck. Where was my ring?* I cringed and stepped around the statue that he had become, rooted to one spot on my driveway. I forced my feet to keep walking. *Don't turn around,* I commanded myself. *This is weird and strange and terrifying and it's not real.*

"Quinn," he said, and my name sounded like a plea. Desperate enough that I slowed down my pace. "I'm sorry."

When I turned around to ask him for what, he was already gunning the engine of the truck.

The lights in the kitchen were off when I snuck through the back door. I discarded my shoes and tiptoed to the stairs, wondering why I was purposefully emulating a mouse. If anyone asked, I hadn't done anything wrong. But I hoped no one would ask. Especially my inquisitive aunt.

By the time I entered my bedroom and closed the door behind me, I knew why my insides were churning with guilt. Because I had felt something. An unignorable flicker. A long-buried part of myself that had reanimated. I found myself playing out an alternative ending to the night as I stripped off my clothes. Wondering what Will would have said next...or done.

My hands skimmed up and down my torso, gliding over my waist and thighs. Places he had touched earlier. Traitorous skin that had glowed underneath the heat of his hands. And traitorous me for losing my will to be pissed at him. I sucked at grudges.

After standing under a hot shower until it turned cold, I threw on a robe and strode over to my lavender dresser and the ring that lay in front of my mom's photograph. I jammed it past my swollen fourth knuckle, taking a layer of skin with it.

I flopped onto my bed and stared at the ceiling, at the glow-in-the-dark stars that had been pasted there two decades ago, and twisted the ring around my finger.

I was going to marry Gavin and it would be comfortable. Like a flannel shirt that's been washed a million times. He tolerated my unpredictable career and my absences from major life events. Every unexpected thing that happened to me went over smoothly because he was...unrufflable. Patient. And he never asked more from me than I wanted to give. I fit with someone like Gavin.

Will was too much. It would have been like trading flannel for satin. Will made me feel too much. Reveal too much. He always had. Earlier tonight the simple act of his hands on my bare skin had seared me like a brand. Invisible to everyone but me.

My calf still tingled from the way his fingers had tightened around it. And if I let myself, I could recall how they had felt on every inch of my skin as he had explored me. Learned me. Possessed me. Made me feel alive and raw and strung out and brilliant all in the same moment.

Perhaps our chemistry had burned so brightly that it had simply winked out. And that was all we had been—two freshly minted adults overtaken by a monumental yet very short-lived fling. Except what kind of fling left so much heartbreak? What kind of fling affected your life choices for your entire twenties? What kind of fling filled you with tragic awe and made you as fragile as glass and as strong as iron in the same breath? *He knew you*, my inner voice scolded me, *and he decided he didn't want you.*

A soft knock interrupted my wobbly nostalgia. "Come in," I said as Aunt Jackie slipped through the doorframe.

"I made enchiladas for dinner," she said, wrapping herself tighter inside a pink chenille robe. "They're waiting for you in the oven."

"You make the best enchiladas," I yawned, but what I really meant was 'I'm sorry for this morning.'

"I know." She smiled secretly and surveyed my bedroom. "It's chilly in here. Do you want me to bring down a quilt from the attic?"

I hadn't noticed the temperature, but, now that she mentioned it, my skin rippled with gooseflesh. "No, no. I'm fine," I reassured her.

Her forehead rose as she studied my wet hair and skin still glistening from the shower. "Busy day at the clinic?"

"Yeah, you could say that," I said, scooting to a semi-reclined position. Something must have shown on my face. A hairline crack in my defenses. In my vow to forget today ever happened. My aunt cocked an interested brow.

"Do tell," she said.

I tucked my knees under the free edge of my robe. "I had a house call—an Irish Wolfhound that wouldn't deliver." Jackie looked visibly disappointed at my lack of detail. My aunt was an adrenaline junkie, albeit usually vicariously. "It was pretty exciting," I continued. "I had to crawl under a house and everything."

"How did that go?"

"Stressful, but I managed...with some help." I bit my lip to shut myself up. Why did my mouth want to say his name so badly?

"From anybody I know?"

"No." I shook my head, hoping she wouldn't pick up on the lie. "Have you talked to Dad?"

"I went over and saw him today."

I sat up straighter and tossed my hair over my shoulder. "How did he look?"

She crossed her arms over her chest. "Like he was rode hard and put up wet."

I snorted. "Has he lost weight?"

"Yeah," she answered contemplatively, "but not his disposition or his charm. He has the rehab nurses wrapped around his finger."

"That's Dad."

The lines around her mouth deepened as she tried not to smile. "He asked me if I knew the difference between bird flu and swine flu."

"One requires tweetment and the other oinkment," I recited.

She rolled her eyes, but one side of her mouth quirked up. "Ridiculous."

"He used to tell me that one every year before my flu shot." I laughed quietly at the memory.

"They said he might be ready to come home next week."

"Really? Is he ready?"

"He's ready to be out of the hospital...and I might have promised to drive him to outpatient rehab four days a week if they discharge him."

Next week. Everything was tumbling forward at break-neck speed.

"You still planning on being gone for Thanksgiving?" Jackie regarded me carefully, her expression unreadable.

Was I? My heart squeezed with an unnamed emotion. Did I want to open the can of worms? Today had already been smothered in the unexpected. Why not add to the pile? I licked my lips nervously. "Yeah, I promised Gavin."

"What if we invite Gavin here instead?" Aunt Jackie offered, her eyes bright and expectant.

The first word screaming through my brain was 'no.' "We have plans with his parents already," I mumbled, watching as my words leached the hope from Jackie's face. "But maybe next year."

"If you change your mind," she said, voice cracking, "let me know."

When she was gone, the door tightly shut behind her, I exhaled the breath I had been holding, along with the real reason I didn't want Gavin here right now. I didn't want him anywhere near Will and the person I was in Will's proximity.

Gavin never needed to understand how much I had loved someone else...and how a part of me always would.

CHAPTER TWENTY

AUTUMN, NOW

I left the house when it was still dark the next morning, crunching down the driveway in worn leather boots and a waxed green jacket lined with flannel. Sonia pulled up in her silver Honda, and I climbed in the passenger side door. "Thanks for picking me up. Dad's car died on me yesterday."

"I heard." She clucked her tongue.

How had she heard? The gossip in this town was as virulent as chicken pox.

"I also heard you were rescued by a handsome stranger."

My eyes widened and I blinked. "He's not a stranger...and he's not really that handsome."

"If you say so, *mi hija*." She snickered as she spun the wheel to enter Main Street.

"Anyway, I'm engaged." I rubbed the diamond on my left hand protectively. Now that I had put it on again, I wasn't taking it off. I probably couldn't even if I tried.

"But I'm not," she said playfully. "Maybe you can introduce us."

I smiled in amusement. "You remind me of my assistant in our clinic in New Jersey. Total cougars, the both of you."

Sonia braked hard as she pulled into the parking lot. Despite the chill outside, she was wearing a black bedazzled T-shirt that said "blessed" tucked into her pink scrub bottoms. "Just kidding, *mi amor*. I don't need you to introduce us. I'll introduce myself when I see him tonight."

My hand paused on the door handle as my heated breath fogged up the glass pane next to my mouth. "What?"

Sonia pulled down her sunshield to check her hair in the mirror and began applying a coat of sheer lip gloss. "At the bookstore," she said loudly through wide open lips that she then smacked together twice.

"Why would he be at the bookstore?" I asked, feigning ignorance.

Sonia's face transitioned into catlike perceptiveness, her pupils dilating from the thrill of repeating gossip. "Because he's that famous author who inherited the winemaking place from his *abuelos*. But you knew that didn't you, *mi hija*?" A shaded purple lid closed over a dazzling brown orb of an eye in a conspiratorial wink.

"I don't know half of what people think I know," I grumbled.

"Oh, you do," Sonia chirped, "you just don't like to admit you do."

Releasing a low-pitched groan, I scrambled out of the car and into the building without looking back, the air nipping at my exposed cheeks and fingertips. I had to get it together. I took a cleansing breath. I glanced down at my ring sparkling in the early morning sun.

I fished out my phone and texted Gavin back. *I miss you too.* And then promised myself I would call him tonight, pushing down the uncomfortable question of why he hadn't called me. Gavin was real. Gavin was my future. And Will was...my past. Destined to be forgotten.

I straightened my shoulders and marched to the back

where we kept the white board. An eight o'clock exploratory laparotomy on a Labrador Retriever with a suspected foreign body ingestion. Piece of cake.

It turned out this monster-sized chocolate Labrador had a monster-sized appetite. The x-rays had shown a square of metal only slightly bigger than my fingertip lodged somewhere in the proximal small intestine. What it didn't show was the ladies' leather pump attached to that square of metal.

"How did this even go down your throat?" I asked the sleeping dog, her chest rising and falling in time with the ventilator. Tittering sparked in the corner where Sonia and Kody sat charting vital signs. I sighed through my nose as I worked the shoe out of the grip of the bowel wall. "Minds in the gutter, ladies?" I said primly through my mask.

Sonia howled in laughter, her backside jiggling enough that the legs of her chair shook. "Aye, no, *mi hija,*" she crooned. "We're doing our research for the book signing tonight."

I nearly stabbed my index finger with the next swipe of the scalpel. What kind of research? I trained my ears on the corner of the operating room and the soft comments and oohs as they snuck peeks on their phones between charting.

"I'm ready to close," I said sourly. Kody, two neat plaits trailing past her shoulders, jerked to a stand and shoved her phone in her pocket. "I can help you, Dr. McClain."

Of course, you can because it's your job, I snarked inside my head. With another set of hands scrubbed in, tying neat sutures in the fascia and then the skin was tedious but predictable work. It gave me plenty of time to ruminate on other things.

My mind was a sloshing stew of the past, present, and future. I never knew which one was going to bob to the surface and show itself. I had worked so hard to shove all things Will-related into an impenetrable box. But somewhere between puppies being born and moonlight confessions, the lid had cracked open, spilled contents cluttering my brain.

My limbic system flashed with images of tan skin and the smell of mint and the feel of his breath on my lips in a roiling swirl of thrill and despair and yearning. If I didn't stop myself, I would reel all the back to that night. *The* night. A night that captured my heart and held it still.

"That looks real nice, Dr. McClain."

Of course, it does. I'm an overly qualified badass equine surgeon. "Thank you, Kody." I stepped back from the metal table and stripped off my sterile gown. Sonia lumbered over and began fussing over the incision site. "If anyone needs me, I'll be in the office," I announced and faded through the pea-green double doors like a panther.

I had to congratulate myself. Work sucked me in, and I let it. Morning dribbled into lunchtime into a golden afternoon. I immersed myself in fur and hooves and lolling tongues. Sharp barks and scrabbling kitty claws. An iguana with a rash, his bumpy skin and spikes massaging my palm like a stress device.

But as the day waned, I had more time between appointments. Will's presence had followed me around like a silent specter all day and finally, when I was sore and tired and thirsty, he caught up to me.

Slumping in my dad's office chair, I oscillated between daydreaming and checking work emails. I was in the middle of a reply to Mitch Jenkins about ordering hoof protector when Sonia poked her head through the door. The caramel tips of her pixie cut had flattened out from this morning and her lipstick had faded.

"Just checking to see if you need anything, *mi hija*." Her eyes flicked around the room, landing on the perfect rectangle of sky framed by the window behind me.

"You want to leave early, don't you?" I asked dryly, leaning back in the chair and crossing my arms.

"I'm getting my nails done for tonight, and I still haven't picked my outfit," she said.

When there was work to be done, no one could do it better than Sonia. But being idle was not her forte.

"Sure." I waved my hand at her. "Get out of here. Go get pretty for a book signing."

"It's not just a book signing, *mi hija*," she said. "There's going to be a free glass of wine and photos with Mr. Deremer."

Mr. Deremer. Inside my head, I cackled like the lunatic I was. I still thought of Will as a nineteen-year-old boy with floppy hair and black Converse, scribbling in his little notebook every chance he got. Not a world-famous author. Or a vineyard owner.

I schooled my face and stared at the same sentence I had been attempting to write for the past fourteen minutes. "Have fun," I said warmly. "If anything comes up, I'm sure Kody can handle it."

"Well..." Sonia fiddled with the cross around her neck. "Kody was going to go with me to the nail salon. But it's right down the street, and I'm sure she could come back if a patient comes in."

I sighed, a funny feeling twisting in my gut as I thought of a perky, decked out Kody trouncing around Will's book signing. "No, it's fine, Sonia. I'll be fine here. By myself."

She shifted uncomfortably for a few seconds before light flared in her chestnut brown eyes. "Come with us, *mi hija*." She beckoned me with a mildly arthritic hand. "It will be fun, and you deserve a night out!" Her rotund body nearly vibrated with inspiration.

"Thanks," I told her, "But I can't." I tilted my head toward my laptop. "I have work to catch up on with my actual job."

Sonia bristled like a giant chicken fluffing up her feathers. "Life is short, *mi hija*. You've got to seize the day like they say." She flattened her palm to her chest atop the scars I knew existed underneath her blouse.

Sonia had been diagnosed with breast cancer right after I had left for college. It was the reason my dad had changed the official clinic scrubs to a sugary shade of pink.

Where Will was concerned I had done my share of seizing. And it had gotten me nowhere. As a full-fledged adult, I was no closer to understanding anything about love. Guilt and regret I knew like old playground friends. The comfortable trappings of companionship I could accept. Friendship wooed me like a worn pair of jeans. I smiled as I pictured Sid's round face and shrewd eyes.

But love? Wanting to live and die in the span of a breath? Looking into someone else's eyes and seeing the truth of yourself reflected? Feeling protected and like a protector all at the same time? Opening your universe—your pain, your joy, your utter humanity and letting someone exist there while you exist in his? I blinked through an unexpected film of tears.

Had I ever encountered love like that? Only once. With Will. And maybe I never would again. And that was okay. Because I wasn't sure I deserved it anyway. Not the kind of love in Will's fairytales, at least.

"What do you say, *mi hija*?" Sonia's deep crimson lips widened into a smile.

I shook my head and refocused my eyes on my computer screen. "Maybe another time."

The corners of her lips turned downward. "We'll be sure to take plenty of pictures then."

I nodded a curt reply and returned to typing.

No one else stopped by that afternoon. The clinic hallway was as silent as a crypt and almost as cold. At one point, I pulled a sweatshirt out of my bag and struggled into it. I had caught up on nearly all my emails. Mitch was having a grand year. Four out of his mares were pregnant and set to foal in the late spring.

I sighed in relief. I would be home in plenty of time to oversee the deliveries. And hopefully impress him enough that he would take me to Paris in June.

My phone rang and I answered it without even looking at who was calling. "Hi, this is Dr. McClain."

"Hi there, this is Calvin...Calvin Hyde." He paused and I could imagine his white mustache twitching as he quietly formulated his sentences. "You were over at my house yesterday with the new pups."

"I remember," I said. "Is everything okay?"

He paused a beat, and my insides clenched at his silence. "Oh fine...mighty fine," he exclaimed. "The mama's takin' to 'em real nice."

I whooshed out a breath and sagged into the supple folds of the leather office chair. "That's great news."

"I just called to say thank you, Doc. I bet you make your daddy real proud."

A lump stretched and grew to fill up my throat. "I hope so."

"And can you do me one favor?"

"Of course."

"Your friend...I believe Will was his name...can you deliver a message for me?"

"I can do that."

"I'd tell him myself but I'm not goin' to make it to town tonight and I know he's leavin' first thing tomorrow."

"Oh?" I tried to sound nonchalant.

"Goin' up to Los Angeles or somethin' to have some big important meetin's."

"Oh yeah, that's right." I drummed my fingers on the desk for clarity.

"Well, anyway, tell him I said good luck and I hope he comes around and sees me next time he's in town."

"I'm sure he will." We exchanged farewells through a cacophony of barking and squealing in the background. I pushed back from the desk, balancing my palms on the worn wood.

It was time to do the one thing I never had a chance to do. The one thing that would help me finally move on. It was time to say goodbye.

CHAPTER TWENTY-ONE

AUTUMN, NOW

The bookstore looked exactly as I remembered it. Neat stacks of hardbacks on angular tables. The smell of leather and dust permeating the air. A few flea market wingback chairs placed strategically by the windows. But I had never seen Weatherby's this crowded. In fact, I had never seen more than two other life forms inside the shop at one time, and that's if I didn't count the cats.

The bell tinkled when I slipped through the front door, and a gray furball immediately wound between my legs. A brightly lit space in the back of the shop had been cleared out for a long rectangular table and a mounted foam board depicting the cover of Will's book.

Behind the table sat Will in a folding chair, his face relaxed as he exchanged easy conversation with a middle-aged woman with tight ginger curls. He scribbled onto the front page of her book, and when he handed it to her, she clutched it tightly to her chest like a prized possession.

A line snaked throughout the entire shop, winding between the sagging shelves and nearly out the back door. Adult women of all ages and sizes and fashion sense.

I noticed Sonia and Kody huddled together near the cookbooks and ancient Mrs. Thurman from the library dabbing her lids with a tissue as she hobbled toward Will's table. Ms. Phipps—my high school English teacher—and Mary Alice, her belly swollen and pregnant. Wow. What was in this damn book? The seeds of curiosity sprouted in delicate green shoots as I surveyed the rest of the room.

The same tall, structured brunette from the café, tonight in a clingy sweater dress, put a hand on Will's shoulder before leaning down to whisper something into his ear. They smiled in unison—two gorgeous creatures sharing an inside joke.

Realization washed over me like a powerful wave. His girlfriend. Of course. Why would he not have a girlfriend? He was ridiculously hot and successful. And smart in a non-threatening way. And a phenomenal kisser who had probably only achieved excellence in every facet of foreplay. Blood rushed to my face so fast that my scar tingled.

Coming here was a mistake. I was suddenly desperate and irritated and sad all at once. I twisted around to exit the way that I had come but was blocked by three giggling twenty-year-olds sloshing wine on the hardwood floor.

For a moment, my insides mirrored the churning crimson liquid inside their stemless glasses. I heard my name being shouted like I was in a dream.

"Quinn!"

I ducked my head and calculated my distance to the door.

"Quinn, over here, *mi hija*." Sonia's rough-edged voice reverberated through the room. I had no choice but to turn around to where she and Kody waved and gestured with their unoccupied hands. They looked like a pair of flapping birds.

I took a slow step toward them and then another, my eyes perfectly honed on Sonia's bright fuchsia lipstick and not the catty glances and frowns being thrown my way. And definitely not at Will, whose stare was burning a hole in my skull.

"Hi, ladies," I said brightly, forcing my lips to smile. Sonia pulled me into her squishy middle for an embrace, coating me in a cloud of floral perfume.

"You came. And just in time too." She released me, holding me at arm's length to survey the rolled-up sleeves of my vet school sweatshirt and my work sneakers, little splashes of iodine on the toes. "You didn't go home to change first," she chided.

"I don't have a car," I reminded her. "I had to walk here."

Her forehead pulled so tight that all the wrinkles disappeared. "Aye, *dios mio*, I forgot."

"I think you look great, Dr. McClain," Kody sang, twisting in her faux suede mini-skirt and cream sweater to wave at someone behind me. Her chocolate hair framed her face in waves, her skin appeared flawless, her nails clean and freshly painted. I might have been a joke, but she was an insufferable kiss ass.

As we moved at a snail's pace through the line, I avoided making eye contact with Will, sneaking glances like I was stealing cookies out of a jar. Indulgent little bites of his profile. His sharp cheekbones and hair the color of bittersweet chocolate.

I watched his lips move without being able to hear his words like I was interpreting a silent film and lost myself in wondering what he was saying. What he was feeling. I knew by the tilt of his head and the faraway look in his eyes that only part of him was here tonight. The rest was conjuring a story or playing out the a scene in his next book.

When only one woman in jeans and a button-down flannel separated us from the signing table, my armpits rained anxiety. I watched Will flick his eyes over her shoulder at Kody with her pink cheeks and exposed calves. The brunette bombshell next to him snapped a picture of him signing his name inside the front cover of a book, grinning to herself as she began typing with both thumbs.

This must be what his life was like now, surrounded by beautiful, adoring women, his mind chock-full of story lines and sub-plots and characters waiting for their turn to appear on a page. A newfound sadness sank like an anchor in my stomach.

Why was I here? Couldn't I see the truth? These fantasies of him I had held onto, as tightly as these women were holding copies of his book, were mine alone. He had let me go a long time ago. His life had turned out just as it should have. As had mine.

When Will was distracted by Sonia pulling his head into her reconstructed breasts, I slipped behind a shelf of travel books and out the back door.

As I walked into the chilly night, sticking to Main Street with its few cafés and late-night wine bars, I dialed the number I knew better than any other. Gavin cleared his throat delicately before speaking. "Hello, Quinn."

"Hi." I tucked my chin closer to my chest.

"Give me a minute. I'm just now leaving the office." I heard his laptop clicking shut and the rustle of a coat being put on. "Is everything okay?"

"Yeah...it's fine. I just called to say hello."

"Hello then," he said then chuckled awkwardly to himself.

He was such a nerd. I bit the inside of my cheek. "And I wanted to ask you something."

"Okay," he said slowly. "Should I sit down on the first park bench I come to?"

"What if we get married?" I blurted.

He laughed cautiously. "I think we already are."

"No, I mean, what if we don't worry about flowers or a

cake or a guest list? What if next time we see each other, we just do it?"

"What's gotten into you, and what have you done with the Quinn McClain I know?"

"We don't have to if you—" I bit down on my thumbnail.

"I want to," he interrupted. "How about when you come to New York next week for Thanksgiving? My mom won't be thrilled, but she'll get over it. Eventually."

"Okay," I said, nearly delirious with the feeling of free fall. "We're doing this."

"I guess we are," said Gavin. "I'm getting on the train. I'll call you tomor—"

I jolted, my phone smacking the pavement, when fingers curled over my shoulder. "Jesus Christ," I screeched and whirled around, my hands flailing wildly in front of me. My palms met with the luxurious softness of cashmere and the solid human mass underneath. "Don't you know not to sneak up on people?" I chastised Will.

"I'm sorry," he said with the hint of a smirk. "I didn't mean to frighten you."

"I'm not frightened," I said sarcastically as my heart rate ticked up another notch. My fingers shook with adrenaline as I bent down to retrieve my phone. Gavin was calling back. I silenced it and shoved it in my back pocket. "Did you need something?" I asked and the words sounded as weary as I felt.

As Will assessed me, I noticed the concern churning between those flecks of gold in his eyes, and the deep purple shadows that appeared more prominent under the glow of a single streetlamp.

"You left before I got the chance to give you this."

He presented his book to me. I took it, appreciating a reason to use the arms hanging limply by my sides. Studying the cover, I traced the golden script of the title before tucking it under my arm.

"You really did it," I mused.

"As did you," he said, gesturing to my vet school alma mater on my sweatshirt.

"I did," I said. "My life is a dream come true." There was a hollow quality to my words. We regarded one another in the moonlight. His eyes, always seeing more than any human should, raked over my face so thoroughly that my blood heated.

Was he imagining what life would have been like with me? I doubted it. I was merely the road not taken. The path not chosen. The parallel universe. The *what if*. I was certain it made him feel better to see that I was happy. And I was happy. As happy as I'd ever expected to be without him.

He took a step toward me, entering the no-fly zone of my personal space. The chill was chased out of my skin by his warmth. In that moment, my mind and body warred with each other. My fingers twitched as I imagined curling them around his bicep and tugging him those last precious inches toward me until I collided with everything that was under those designer clothes.

I sent my index finger to tug the ratty neck of my sweatshirt instead. A hand encircled my wrist, my pulse beating wildly against Will's fingertips. *Hello there! We've missed you*, it said. Will's face froze into something unreadable.

"I know I shouldn't," he whispered.

"Will..." I said hoarsely and the hand on my wrist began to tremble.

Something inside both of us flared, and the next thing I knew, my face was buried in his chest. I huffed him like a drug as his heart pounded against the shell of my ear. I sent my arms around his waist, the delicious heaviness of his chin resting on my shoulder. Could I stand here forever, bathed in a magical moonlight that seemed to drive out everything wrong between us?

Frantically, I began to absorb every detail, pulling them into my chest and hoarding them for later. Because tomorrow and next month and next year and for another ten years, I wanted to remember this. To dissect and luxuriate in how it felt to be held by him one last time.

I knew that any moment it would end. Except it didn't. We stood there for a short lifetime. Long enough that Will's heart slowed into a steady, even pace that matched mine. Long enough that our body temperatures became the same.

He groaned into my hair but didn't move. "I should get back."

"I know," I said, my voice muffled against his sweater. Neither of us budged.

"One last confession?"

"Why not?" My voice was light. Tremulous.

"I don't want to let you go."

The phrase stirred something in me. A mixture of desperate longing and raw irritation. The fact was that he *had* let me go. Quite easily if I remembered correctly. I ducked underneath his arm and moved back a step, the magic bubble we had shared dissolving into nothingness.

"You probably should anyway." I hugged myself tightly, the book tucked between my arms.

"I know." He stood absolutely still for a full minute before turning to leave. "Quinn," he said, his voice strangling on my name, "promise me you'll read the book."

"Okay," I said automatically, and when he looked doubtful, I added, "I promise I'll read it and even go see the movie on opening weekend when it comes out." I smiled crookedly to hide the emotion in my face. I wasn't ready to let this end. Not yet. "Here, sign it for me," I blurted. "Something for me to remember you by."

Will took the book without diverting his eyes from my face and pulled a pen out of his back pocket. Had he had that the entire time? I supposed when you were an author, you never went anywhere without a writing instrument. He frowned, pen poised over the paper.

"I heard you're headed to California tomorrow."

He nodded absently, lost somewhere in his own head. "My publicist and I are meeting with the people at DreamWorks."

"Your publicist?"

"The woman in the bookstore with me."

"Oh," I breathed. "I thought she was your girlfriend."

He narrowed his lids. "Hardly."

"I bet she wants to be." I shrugged casually.

"I doubt it." The singular dimple appeared in his left cheek. "I think she has her sights set on someone in the crime and thriller department."

"What department are you?"

"I'm in fantasy and science fiction."

The way he said fantasy made my blood trill. He scratched a few words on the page and then scowled at them.

"For an author you sure do take a long time to write something."

He snorted lightly. "Perhaps I'm stalling because I don't want to say goodbye."

A memory jolted inside me as powerful as if I had been zapped by lightning. "I thought"—I swallowed past the lump lodged in my throat—"you didn't believe in goodbyes."

"I don't." When I met his eyes, I stared into the cobalt abyss of an ocean and realized I was on the delicate, dangerous ground of forgetting what he had done. I backed away a step.

Will's chest heaved with a sigh. "These past few days Quinn...seeing you...being near you...it's driving me mad." He gripped the cover of the book until his knuckles strained under his skin. "I can't stop thinking of you."

I smiled at him, a slow, sad, tragic smile. And repeated the words I kept telling myself. "You've forgotten me before, Will. It won't be that hard to do it again."

His eyes closed and he stiffened like I had punched him in the gut. When he opened them, he wrote a few more words inside the cover, handed me the book, and walked into the night.

CHAPTER TWENTY-TWO

AUTUMN, THEN

I *should have kissed you.*

THAT WAS the message waiting for me in my inbox after the Halloween party when I cracked open my laptop to finish my philosophy paper. Outside my dorm room window, incessant rain poured down in thick rivulets.

Sid snored softly in the twin bed across from me, one arm thrown over her face. I pulled my computer into my chest, reclining into the softness of my pillow, nestling into its center and this quiet moment of pure deliciousness.

I replied to Will's message with a single line of text.

Which time?

I hit send and bit the end of my thumbnail. It was too easy to be coy and flirtatious without having to look him in the eye. On the flip side, waiting for a two-dimensional pixelated envelope to bounce was torture. When it did, I pounced on it like a tabby on a ball of yarn.

Every time.

The rhythmic pulsing in my stomach spread to my toes. Was I still on the bed or was I hovering above it? I pressed my knees together as I typed.

Maybe someday you'll get another chance.

My inbox was populated almost immediately.

Remember what I told you at the end of last summer?

I settled into the memory, as warm and enticing as the buttery sunshine hitting the wood floors in Weatherby's book shop.

∿

"Are you going to tell me where we're going?" Will tossed a casual arm along the back of the driver's seat as I flung his car around a curve at breakneck speed.

"Nope," I replied smugly. The leather creaked under my shifting weight as I righted the car.

"Am I going to regret eating lunch?" he teased, and I whacked him on the curve of his biceps with my free hand.

"Are you implying that I'm not a good driver?" I flashed him a look of mock horror.

"No," he said, drawing out the word into multiple syllables. "I simply think you drive like someone lit you on fire."

Maybe someone did, I thought giddily. "At least I don't drive like someone roofied me first."

A warm hand exerted a delicious amount of pressure above my knee, sending me into a fit of giggles. I jabbed two fingers between Will's ribs, and he pulled his hand away laughing. Touching each other had become second nature lately. A slip of a hand on a neck or a press between the shoulder blades. Fingers wrapped around wrists or gently brushing a solid chest. Easy and comfortable. Like we had known each other more than a single summer.

A smile parted my lips when we entered town.

"Brilliant," he muttered sarcastically. "Main Street in all its afternoon glory."

"Shut it," I warned. "Or I'll drop you here and you can walk." I slipped down a side street and made a block before settling behind a neat stucco building and a wooden door painted a faded turquoise. Once we rounded the building, Will regarded the front door and the wrought iron sign hanging above it.

"Weatherby's?" His faint British accent made the name sound like a high-end boutique.

"After you." I gestured toward the door, splintered with age and sporting a round brass knob larger than my hand. A bell tinkled our arrival when we stepped into the space, the air cool and dry and feathered with the smell of paper.

"A bookstore." Will glanced around between the vintage leather furniture and shelves nearly toppling with books stacked every which way.

"It's not much but I thought you might like to see it since you want to be a writer and—"

"It's perfect," he breathed and proceeded to run his hand over a set of volumes with tattered leather covers.

He ventured forward slowly, reverently, his eyes roving over the scripted titles. Finally, he chose one off the shelf and eagerly flipped to the exact middle of the book and began scanning the page.

I wandered over, my head tilted in curiosity. "A favorite of yours?"

"Never read it actually." Will continued to devour the words in front of him.

"I'm thoroughly shocked."

He laughed silently then thumped the two halves of the book back together. "I'm deciding if I want to read it."

"And you accomplish that by reading the middle of the book?"

He shifted his eyes back to the shelves. "Yeah." He laughed softly. "The middle is what matters most."

"Not the ending?"

He shook his head, a shock of hair falling over his eyes. "Endings are all the same. He gets the girl. The villain is brought to justice. Wrongs are righted. The lost are found. The middle..." He paused, seeming to savor the words before he uttered them. It made my heart stutter. "If the middle captivates me, without knowing anything else about the book...not the beginning or the end, then I know it's for me."

For a moment, all I could manage was an indulgent stare, a longing exhale, and a brain emptied of intelligible sentences. God, he was an exquisite creature.

I was startled out of my ogling by a booming voice. "Quinn McClain!" I turned into a pair of proffered lily-white hands that pulled me into a fleeting embrace. "How's your dad?"

"He's good, Mr. Weatherby. Working too much as always."

"Good to hear. You know he and I were classmates at Texas State."

I nodded and smiled at the familiar phrase. One I had heard every time I was within earshot of Mr. Weatherby. He reached over his shoulder to rub a spot on the back of his neck.

"You must be gettin' ready to leave for school soon, Quinn."

"I am. Tomorrow actually."

Across from me, Will chewed on the inside of one cheek.

"I know you'll make your dad proud up at...where did he tell me you were goin'? Somewhere fancy in the Northeast?"

"Princeton, Mr. Weatherby."

He let out a low whistle. "Well don't forget where you're

from when you get up there with all those high falutin'
Yankies."

"I promise I won't."

Mr. Weatherby cocked his head toward Will. "And who's
your friend here?"

"This is Will." I took the liberty of tugging the book out of
Will's hands.

"Nice to meet you, son." Mr. Weatherby's petite hand was
swallowed by Will's giant one.

"Very nice to meet you, sir." Will's manners were impec-
cable when he wasn't distracted. "You have a lovely store."

"Will wants to be a writer," I interjected and Mr. Weatherby's bushy eyebrows rose as a unit.

"That right?"

A flush of color bloomed in Will's cheeks. "Someday.
That's the plan at least." Will flexed his fingers then extended
them again. I had noticed he did this when living in one
moment and existing somewhere else at the same time.

I wondered what new character he was imagining right
now. I wanted to see inside his head and live in that world. I
wanted to be part of his fantasy. I swallowed hard. And
maybe his reality too. A reality that was coming toward us
faster than I wanted it to.

I watched Mr. Weatherby gesture Will over to a stack of
volumes with fresh covers and giant block print for titles.
Will nodded, his eyes electric as he pointed at one and then
the other. It sounded like they were discussing the merits of
this summer's new releases.

"I'm more of a fan of his backlist," I heard Will say
animatedly. "There will never be another book like *Dragon's
Edge*."

Mr. Weatherby clapped Will on the shoulder. "Unless you
write one."

"It would take me a lifetime to come up with something that original."

"Better get started then." Mr. Weatherby winked at me conspiratorially. Like he could sense the same quality inside Will that I did. Something different. Something pure and purposeful. Something that made him see the world as one epic fairy tale.

"I've been working on something," Will said quietly and cast a quick glance in my direction.

My heart plummeted to my feet only to rise slowly back into my chest. For a moment, we were the only two humans in the universe. At least that was the way he made me feel. Like he saw past the guilt that anchored me to reality. That to him, maybe I could be more than a tragic dreamer.

Mr. Weatherby shook with glee as he gathered up a stack of books and began reshelving them. "You promise me, Will, that when you hit the bestseller list, you'll come back and see me in the shop."

A barking laugh, the perfect combination of rough and soothing, erupted from Will's lips. "If that ever happens," he joked, "I promise that I will."

I paused for one beautiful moment to fall in love with his face. With its earnestness as he examined book jackets. With the scrunch of his forehead over electric blue sparks for eyes. I glanced down at my watch and the inevitable end of something I couldn't stand to lose.

That day we visited the bookshop, Will had driven us back to my house slowly, looping through neighborhoods and skirting the square in the middle of town to stretch out our last hour together. When the car ground to a halt in my driveway, I felt every crunch of gravel in my bones.

Farther down the shale road, my dad strode out of our back door carrying a stack of plastic containers and lifted them into the back of our truck. My nose twitched and burned with emotion, the same as it always did when my world was about to shift. My Scottish intuition, my dad always said.

Beside me, Will's fingers played a silent beat on the steering wheel. I forced my hand to yank the door handle, separating the latch mechanism with a creaking sound that resonated through our silence.

I put one foot onto the newly visible ground and stopped. "It's time for me to go," I said, still watching my dad out of the passenger window.

"Are you...excited?" asked Will.

"Not as much as I used to be," I admitted.

"Why is that?"

"Because..." I faltered as my entire summer spun in reverse, a reel of images that all contained Will. "Because I don't want to say goodbye."

"You don't have to say it then. I don't even believe in goodbyes."

I finally turned to look at him, both of us smirking through the weight of our emotions. "What do you believe in then?"

"I believe," he said, brushing back a strand of my hair with his index finger, "that we deserve something a bit more...epic."

"Like what?"

"Like..."—he paused, his eyes softening into a sweater weather blue—"wherever we go, as long as we share a moon, we'll find each other again."

I THOUGHT about his words from the end of last summer as the rain pummeled even harder against my dorm room window. Even now, convincing myself that Will was real and not some fantasy I had conjured was difficult to believe. That this could be happening. That maybe he belonged with me. And I belonged with him. Two motherless children on the cusp of adulthood rewarded by the universe for the tragedies we had both endured.

An ecstatic tingling spread through my skin as I typed a reply.

I remember you promising to find me under the moon.

As I waited, imagining Will smiling against the backlight of his own computer, a gentle but persistent nagging developed in my stomach. Like the feeling of being on a roller-coaster at its peak, knowing that any second, it's about to plummet. And although you know exactly what's coming, for one simple second, you are thrilled to exist at the top of the world as you know it.

I chewed my lip as another email from Will popped into my inbox, hoping that whatever ride we were on would be worth the free fall at the end.

I will. I always will.

My nose burned with an emotion that I didn't dare name but was becoming more and more familiar. Dates and school assignments and flight schedules all whirled around inside my head until I had calculated and planned, to the minute, the next time I would see him again.

MY LEG JIGGLED the entire flight from Newark to San Antonio. Once on the ground, I sprinted to baggage claim like some wild pony released from its pen then bounced on my toes searching for my dad in the arrival's lane. When I spotted the dented midnight blue truck, I scrambled into the cab, luggage forgotten, and slid over the bench seat to give him the fiercest of hugs.

"Well, now," he said, patting me between the shoulder blades. "That's a greeting I haven't gotten in a while."

When I pulled back, we mirrored each other's broad smiles, our similarly steel gray eyes meeting. I thought perhaps he could see right through me. That he would realize my bubbling excitement was only partly due to being home again. That maybe the shine behind my eyes told the story of something unfurling inside me. Something I couldn't have stopped even if I had wanted to. Something that had grown and heaved and exhausted the space inside of me. And the only way to manage it was to see Will.

As I buckled my seatbelt, I felt the vibration of my suitcase landing inside the bed of the truck. I inhaled, the crispness of early winter filling my lungs with expectation.

"You pack all your books in there?" my dad asked as he gunned the engine.

"Dead body," I said solemnly.

"Good thing you told me," he deadpanned. "We'll have to make a stop before we get home."

I chuckled and twisted the dial on the radio until a country beat leaped into the air. We drove in silence as we navigated through the city to the background of a grumbling motor and the easy twang of Clint Black.

My mind wandered and meandered as easily as a country road, never lingering too long on one particular thing. My chemistry final. Will. Sid's new obsession with Korean barbecue. My aunt's Christmas tin most likely filled to the brim with star-shaped cookies. And again, Will.

A staticky silence filled the truck. "What was that, Dad?"

"I asked, how was your Thanksgiving?"

Sid and I had scrounged together a precooked turkey breast and a can of cranberry sauce that we'd split while studying for finals. "Very boring."

"And finals?"

I wrinkled my nose. "I think I did okay. My biochem final was rough."

He nodded thoughtfully as we exited the highway. "Any plans for your winter break?"

Will. Will. Will. My brain was on a repetitive cycle. I shrugged, feigning nonchalance, and watched the San Antonio cityscape fade in the rearview mirror. "Probably just...hanging out."

"With anyone in particular?"

My eyes snapped to his face. I studied it. Did he know? My lips curled into a wry smile. We lived in Linzberg. Of course, he did. "No," I said carefully, gauging his response to my obvious lie.

His jaw ticked once, twice. "So, there's absolutely no reason why Will Deremer has been to the clinic twice in the past week with his grandmother's terrier, who has absolutely nothing wrong with her?"

"I wouldn't know." I schooled my face into neutral.

My dad grunted and side-eyed me. "Are you friends with him now?"

We're something more, I wanted to say, but I had no idea what that meant. Whatever it was, I wouldn't risk jinxing it by wishing too hard. Or worse by saying it out loud. "Yeah, we're friends."

And we were. Until recently, Will had never indicated that he wanted anything else. I hadn't gone to college and pined away in my dorm room. I had even gone on a few casual dates. But the truth was, I would rather be Will's, even if we were just friends. And I had decided to stop waiting for the aberration that would send us spinning off course and let him be what he was to me—my gravity.

I stayed in silent turbulent thought, staring out the window at strip malls that morphed into subdivisions then blissful rolling hills dotted with animals. We cruised past our driveway and straight into town, parking next to a giant tinsel archway of red and white twined together.

I shielded my eyes against the glare of fading sunlight on jewel-toned ornaments and twinkling lights. *Happy holidays,* they seemed to say. *Welcome home!* Rural Texas was a far cry from the gray and brick industrialism of New Jersey, and I had missed it.

Vendors, their tented carts strung with holiday lights, had already set up along the parade route. The smell of sugared nuts and the sight of steaming hot chocolate topped with whipped cream made my stomach grumble deliciously.

The marching band was lined up in neat rows of shining instruments. I recognized my former sixth grade music teacher blowing the first bars of "Joy to the World" into a trombone.

Once we had parked the truck and were swallowed by the melee, I began scanning the crowd. Over the heads of school kids racing between flatbed trailers covered in crepe and fake snow. Between couples holding onto one another to avoid being separated by the jostling.

A waving hand caught my attention and I jolted to a new level of alertness. But the hand waving me over to a pair of striped lawn chairs wasn't Will's. Aunt Jackie smiled until the corners of her mouth nearly touched her dangling Christmas light earrings. When I reached her, she pulled me into a hug that smelled of the light floral perfume she always wore.

"We missed you," she exclaimed.

My chin rubbed the soft denim of her jacket, her arms winding around me in a viselike hold. And suddenly I couldn't breathe. Not because of the bony arms around my middle, but because, across the street, in front of a glass-front shop blowing into his cupped hands for warmth, was Will.

CHAPTER TWENTY-THREE

WINTER, THEN

I closed my eyes, the bright notes of "Jingle Bells" starting somewhere in the distance.

"Parade's about to start," I heard my dad say. I opened my eyes, entirely convinced I had imagined him. But there he was, the flickering lights casting golden shadows onto his dark hair. A tragically shy angel, living in his own head while the world spun around him. Looks were cast his way. Some curious. Some polite. Some appraising. I was positive that half the town recognized the Deremer's grandson at this point, but none of them actually knew him. Not like I did anyway.

We had emailed every day since Halloween. Sometimes more than once a day. Always a single line of text. Usually, a question or the answer to the question he had asked the day before.

This simple game had woven an intimacy between us despite our geographic distance. What's your favorite thing about college? What was the last book you read? Do you prefer animals over people? That answer had been an easy yes. What has been your biggest disappointment? What do you want for Christmas this year?

What do you miss about your mom? *Everything I can't remember*, I had typed and then written, *what about you?*

The way she listened to my stories like they were the most magnificent tales she'd ever heard.

My heart had squeezed and stuttered when I had read Will's reply. I could imagine him as a boy, thick tousled hair flopping onto his forehead as he scribbled into a notebook as his mom prepared dinner.

That was the boy who now leaned against the steel lamppost as the marching band strutted down the street. That was the boy who finally noticed me staring at him and raised a hand in greeting.

"I missed you too, Aunt Jackie," I said hurriedly as I pulled out of her embrace.

"Sit next to me and tell me everything about college." She gestured to the empty lawn chair, eyes bright with excitement and expectation.

"Okay. Sure," I replied, licking my lips in consternation as a pair of twirlers paraded past us, batons glinting in the starlight. Settling into the chair, I gripped the rickety metal frame like I might explode out of it at any moment. "The campus is huge, and classes are good."

"Uh huh." She nodded encouragement. "And your roommate? Sidney?"

The mention of my new steadfast friend who was as kind as she was adventurous made me smile. "She's great," I said. "I think we'll be friends for a long time."

My aunt leaned over to squeeze me above the knee. "Any cute boys?"

My eyes immediately cut to Will's shadowed silhouette that was sandwiched between a float filled with elves and one with bales of hay decorated to look like reindeer carrying a cowboy Santa. A smile ghosted his lips causing a thrill to bloom in my chest.

"Not really." I swallowed hard, feeling every bit of my aunt's scrutinizing gaze.

"See someone you know over there?" She turned her head to study the crowd across the street.

I pressed my lips together in a tight line. Why wouldn't I tell her? Why couldn't I say his name? It wasn't as if I really believed that doing so would destroy this thing between us. This fragile precious thing that had yet to have a beginning. A thing that I was already hoping didn't have an end.

I huffed out a breath. "Just a friend."

"She sees Will Deremer over there skulking next to the flower shop," my dad boomed over the top of my head.

"Dad," I grumbled at the same time my aunt's eyebrows lifted and she said, "Will Deremer?"

I glanced up in time to catch them exchanging a look. "He's not skulking," I said sourly as something akin to disapproval settled over my aunt's face.

My dad rubbed his temple over the spot where his sandy hair was turning gray. "I'll bet a dollar he's not here to watch the parade." The white of his teeth flashed in the dark as he chuckled.

A flush of embarrassment tickled the back of my throat. I knew Will hadn't taken his eyes off me since he had spotted me across the street. A lady in a Mrs. Claus costume waltzed by, along with a Jack Russell terrier who performed a backflip for the cookie in her outstretched hand.

Applause rippled through the crowd when a gigantic sleigh pulled by a pair of Clydesdales appeared next. Santa *ho ho hoed* his way down the street, waving his white-gloved hand and tossing candy onto the sidewalk.

When I was a little girl, I had thought the real Santa actually showed up in Linzberg every year for the Christmas parade. Not Mr. Abbott in a tightly fitting crushed velvet jumpsuit and a pasted-on beard.

Kids were spilling into the street to race after the carriage and scoop up the unclaimed peppermints and chocolates. Their freneticism spread to me and had me drumming my fingers on the arms of my chair in time to the final chorus of "Up on the Housetop" booming from a loudspeaker.

Will had long ago disappeared from view, fading into a throng of felt cowboy hats. Jackie stared straight ahead in silence, parade lights flashing across her corneas. And for once, she didn't say exactly what she was thinking.

A heavy hand landed on my shoulder. "Don't get home too late," muttered my dad, a muscle in his jaw ticking.

When I finally understood what he was implying, the roiling energy inside me exploded through the soles of my feet. I gave his forearm a quick squeeze before sprinting into the chaos of the street.

"I won't," I shouted over one shoulder.

A lifetime passed before I reached the opposite sidewalk. I paused for a breath, the chill in the air soothing the nervous heat building in the back of my throat. My nose tingled with evergreen and cinnamon, my hands suddenly clammy.

I scanned every face around me for the only one I wanted to find. Where had he gone? I made my way toward the fringes of the crowd, peering down every darkened side street for a lanky silhouette. Then the wind whistled past, carrying the whisper of my name.

"Quinn."

I didn't turn around. At the time, I wasn't sure why. Later, I would realize that I had known everything would be different once I did.

Everything we did or said from this point forward would mean something different. I wanted to savor this moment. The deliciousness of free fall at terminal velocity.

"Quinn." The voice was closer this time. The same smooth cadence and rich accent that made me think of midnight-blue velvet.

The smell of chocolate-laden steam met my nose and I turned around to find Will holding two foam cups. "I was wondering where you went," I said, smiling wide enough for my face to crack.

"I thought you might need some sugar," he said, lips quirking upward. "I doubt Southwest Airlines was able to provide you with Moon Pies during the flight."

"If only." I reached for one of the cups to give my hands something to hold, if only to keep them from trembling. I took a sip, the hot liquid searing my throat.

Will watched me intently, his throat bobbing. "You're here."

"I am." He reached toward me with his index finger to place it on the bow of my lip. It came away covered in cream. When he put it to his lips and licked it off with his tongue, my heart rate sped up to a frantic gallop. "What should we do?" I sounded breathless.

Will slipped his hand into mine, as easily as if we had been doing this for weeks...years even. "Let's take a walk."

"Where to?"

"Somewhere we can see the moon."

The night wrapped us in a shroud of darkness as we made our way past the brightly lit shops of Main Street. I gripped the searing cup in my palm, too nervous to drink it. We wound our way down a side street, past the first guitar notes being strummed at Crossroads, then veered off the pavement onto a dirt path that led into a copse of evergreens.

After a few steps, we were plunged into complete stillness and quiet except for our footsteps and the occasional scurrying of a creature in the underbrush. The trees were ghostly shapes bathed in droplets of starlight. Once the vegetation thinned, we wound down an embankment to the edge of a trickling stream.

I knew exactly where we were. I had been here countless times as a child to feed the ducks or search for arrowheads when the creek bed was dry.

But I had never been here at night. Never when the water became a conduit for dreams. Never when the moon was so bright and full of hope and promises.

I halted at the water's edge, setting my undrunk chocolate onto a flat rock. I stared up into the star-flecked dark, the sense of Will's heat at my back.

"I always find myself wondering what you're thinking," I mused.

"I'm not able to think of anything right now." He sounded rushed and breathless. Not at all like his usual purposeful self.

I bit my lip before it could stretch too widely. "You're not imagining this river leads to a forbidden island of warrior fairies?" I teased. "Or that any moment a Selkie might swim by and wave hello?"

"No," he whispered into the shell of my ear. "For once, I can't think of a fantasy better than my current reality."

His chest pressed into my back, solid and warm, as his arms wound around my middle. I knew how almost every part of his body felt, but I had never felt every part of him all at once.

Even his head drew next to mine, his nose grazing the scar running along my cheekbone. I stopped breathing as his lips brushed the corner of my mouth and tiny sparks ignited in the air that remained between us.

I turned my head, impatient for the feel of his mouth on mine. I wasn't disappointed. Those full, velvety lips that had asked me a million questions last summer, settled over mine like they belonged there. I had thought about this moment an embarrassing number of times and had expected the initial shock of it all. The explosion of my nerve endings once they brushed against Will's skin. But what I hadn't expected was the veritable calm that came next.

I moved against his mouth, wanting more. Or at least as much as he would give me. Will made a strangled noise as he shifted to stand in front of me, the slope down to the creek steep enough that we ended up exactly the same height. My hands settled on his shoulders before he pulled me in close, any space between us vanishing. His heart pounded against my sternum, and mine raced to keep up with it.

Will slid his hand along my face to cup my jaw then stroked the pad of his thumb along my lower lip before bending down to kiss me again. His lips were pillow soft and hungry. Wicked and delightful. He tasted like mint with a hint of cream. I molded my lower lip around his and sucked with the most delicate pressure.

Fire ripped through my veins as pressure built inside my lower abdomen. I rose on tiptoes to slide my hands over his broad shoulders and around his neck. Our lips were magnets —stuck to one another as we jostled for position inside a ring of uneven limestone. I parted my lips for air and sipped his exhaled breath. It filled my lungs like a drug. I was reeling. Intoxicated. Simultaneously lost and found.

A rumbling noise reverberated from Will's throat, vibrating against my mouth. Then he was kissing me deeply, his tongue caressing my palate in urgent, desperate strokes. I shoved my hands into his hair and pulled him into me, curling my fingers around thick, black as night strands with the intentions of someone wild and reckless. His hands brushed down my ribcage then lower. I shivered as he explored, feeling the weight of his grip land on the curve of my backside.

The moon slid out from behind the wisp of a cloud. I thought it might have done so just for us.

～

"HOW WAS YOUR WINTER BREAK?" Sid asked from where she was curled up with a book on her twin bed that matched mine.

I clattered through the door, my suitcase tipping over in the process. My hair buzzed around me with a staticky electricity that I was certain came from my nerves. I knew my cheeks were rose pink and my eyes bright when I answered breathlessly, "It was great."

She eyed me with look of curious anticipation and closed her book.

"How was yours?" I asked before she could undoubtedly grill me about Will.

As she spun a monologue of vacationing with her extended family in Jamaica and how her cousins had drunk too much rum on Christmas Eve and had gone streaking down the beach and how her uncle had gotten stung by a jellyfish trying to fish them out of the ocean, I listened intently. With most of my brain anyway. At least the part that had returned to Princeton. The other part was still in my tiny town of Linzberg having the best time of her life.

The Texas hill country had been unseasonably cold that year, lending a touch more authenticity to the holidays as people bustled out of shops with their scarves flapping in the wind. A bone chilling cold that everyone had complained about when they'd had to don heavy coats and mittens from the bottoms of their closets. I hadn't cared. Not in the least. Not when I had Will keeping me warm.

We had held hands while drinking cider and strolling through soon-to-be Christmas trees in the church parking lot. He had pulled me behind the tallest one and kissed me until I ran out of air and rational thought.

We had lounged in tattered velvet chairs in the book

shop, soaking in the glowing warmth of the fireplace in the corner that Mr. Weatherby now had a reason to use. We had gone on a quest to find snowflakes and talked about our dreams over warm slices of pie at the Bluebird Café and driven every back road searching for shooting stars until one night, we had found them.

"Pull over!" I had shouted over the blast of the car heater.

He had obliged, slicing through the underbrush and stopping shy of the Lost Creek Bridge. I had leaped out of the passenger seat, exiting the car before I realized a light rain had begun to fall. In that moment, I hadn't cared about anything except for the golden streaks lighting up the sky.

Will joined me, chuckling to himself, and folded me into the confines of his leather jacket. The rain picked up, and water streamed down my hair and into the neckline of my shirt.

"Are you certain you want to be doing this?" he asked.

I couldn't help thinking he meant more than standing in the freezing rain to watch a few stars implode. I met his curiously amused gaze with one of my own. One imbued with a layer of conviction. "Yes," I answered, "I do."

I watched a steady stream of droplets outline the angles of a face deep in thought. "So do I," he said, as he pressed a lifetime of promises onto my lips.

I had groaned and whimpered like an animal until he had thoroughly destroyed me with his tongue and teeth.

"So, am I your girlfriend now?" I had asked when we had paused for breath, both of us shivering as icy pellets of rain landed on our exposed skin.

"No," he said with an indulgent smile that I knew was mine. "You are my something more."

CHAPTER TWENTY-FOUR

AUTUMN, NOW

Night had settled and with it a quiet calm that dissipated my tension. I walked right past the clinic, skirting its perimeter to reach the road that ran behind it. Every crunch of my sneakers on the loose gravel took me farther from Will and closer to a future without him. A future that I was certain would not break my heart.

I was a moon ripped out of its gravitational orbit.

The wind whistled at me as I cut across the parking lot of the clinic. A barn owl hooted before it dropped out of the sky toward an unfortunate mouse in the field ahead of me.

I kept walking, fueled by the need to put distance between me and...everything behind me. Between my current life and what could have been. Every footfall was a reminder that Will had had plenty of opportunities to find me over the last thirteen years. *He* had chosen to forget *me*. Not the other way around. His nostalgia—his conflict— whatever moral crisis he was having only deepened my confusion.

I kicked an empty beer can someone had carelessly tossed

onto the road's shoulder. By this time next week, it would all be over. I would be married and Will and his flammable blue eyes and pillows for lips could die alone surrounded by books.

Headlights flashed in the distance, and I shielded my eyes as a car approached. It slowed to a crawl, the passenger window descending to frame my aunt Jackie's irritated face. "Quinn Elizabeth McClain!" I startled at my full name. "What in the world are you doing?" she asked in an exasperated tone.

"Walking home."

"Lord make me a bird," she cursed. "Stop being stubborn and get in this car."

"Impossible," I sighed but rounded the car and slid into the leather seat.

The drive home was long enough for Aunt Jackie to lecture me on the dangers of being on the road at night and short enough that I didn't have time to defend myself. We ambled into the house where a divine smell wafted from a pot on the stove. My stomach grumbled in protest as I put one foot toward the stairs.

"Don't even think about it."

I turned around to see the glow of the kitchen catching the highlights in my aunt's hair. My skin warmed with the cozy heat from the stove, the familiarity of the space drawing me in and thawing my resolve.

I tucked my layered hair behind my ears as Jackie ladled chicken chili into two bowls and sighed. I had nothing left tonight anyway. Not after seeing Will.

Jackie pointed to a bar stool. "Sit. Eat. Then tell me what's going on with you."

I plopped down and dipped a spoon in the bowl, the first bite singeing my palate. I took another one. And another one.

After a while, my mouth heated to the temperature of the soup, and I paused for the glass of iced tea that had appeared next to my bowl.

My aunt sat across from me, chin propped on her delicate hands, eyes fierce and soft at the same time. She cleared her throat, and I took that as my signal to explain myself.

I wrinkled my nose before I spoke. "I ran into someone tonight."

Her eyebrows notched up in interest.

"Someone I used to...know."

"Know how exactly?"

I shrugged before wiping my mouth with a napkin. "Someone I used to...love."

"Oh." Her brows crashed into a single furrow.

"Yeah."

"Anyone I know?" I could have sworn her throat bobbed nervously.

I shifted my eyes to the window above the kitchen sink and the half-moon I could see in the upper corner. "I don't think you would remember him."

"What happened between you two?"

What happened? I hadn't known then. I sure as hell didn't know now. I shrugged again.

"I guess, in the end, I wasn't worth it."

Fire ignited behind my aunt's blue eyes. "He must be an ass then or just plain stupid."

My lips twitched before I scraped my bowl clean. "He's neither. Unfortunately." I flicked my eyes up at her, her face settling into what looked like realization. She stood up to her full height of five feet three inches, arms crossed over her chest.

"I see."

"There's nothing to see." I willed my face into nonchalance. I was emotionless. As neutral as Switzerland. "I'm engaged," I added for emphasis.

She studied me as I shot up from the barstool and washed my bowl in the sink. Wiping my hands on my rear, I retreated to the living room and snatched up my bag.

"The hospital said we could pick up your dad next weekend," Jackie said, her expression uninterpretable in the glare of the chandelier.

"I'll be back from Gavin's on Friday," I said quickly, a twinge of guilt washing through me.

"All right then," she said before turning her back to me. Her lavender shirt collar crept up the back of her neck as her shoulders tensed. The rush of water was followed by the sound of dishes clacking against the metal sink.

My guilt swelled until somehow it became kindling for annoyance. My knuckles whitened where they gripped my bag, heavy from the weight of Will's book. "What am I supposed to do, Aunt Jackie?" I asked tersely. "Cancel my holiday plans with Gavin?"

"This has nothing to do with Gavin."

"Then what? What else could you possibly want from me?"

She whirled around, droplets of water cascading from her hands. A few of them landed on my face as she gestured at me. "For you to be happy. That's all we've ever wanted."

I dipped my chin dramatically. "Done. We're there. I have everything I've ever dreamed of." *Liar*, snarked a voice inside my head. I ignored it.

Jackie arched a brow without saying anything, lasering her gaze onto my face like she could see inside my head and was trying to sift through the chaos for a kernel of truth. "You sure about that?"

I crossed my arms. "Of course I'm sure."

Her face faltered, an additional line appearing at the corner of her downturned mouth. "I guess I always thought being home made you happy." And her. And my dad. She didn't say it aloud, but I knew what she was thinking.

It did, I wanted to cry. *You do.* Instead, I dug my toes into the hardwood floor. "What did you and Dad expect? That once I graduated vet school, I would come back here and join Dad's practice? Maybe marry a local boy and bring our kids over for enchilada night?"

My aunt's lips tightened, her back stiffening, damp hands clutching the hem of her shirt.

I looked away, focusing my anger on the cordless telephone relic that was still mounted on the wall. "I left here to live my own life so you could stop using me as an excuse to not live yours. You and Dad living your lives—that's what makes me happy."

Whirling around, I took the stairs two at a time, leaving a gulf of silence and sadness behind me.

Not until I was tucked under my floral comforter staring at the ceiling did I realize tomorrow was Saturday, and I had nowhere to be at the crack of dawn. No clinic to run. No Mitch Jenkins to tempt me out of bed before sunrise for the chance to examine a new foal.

I stretched my toes until my calves burned. I closed my eyes. The undersurfaces of my lids were gritty and dry. I dragged them open, my eyes landing on my bag in the corner, its contents half spilled on the braided rug. I saw it then. The right angle of a book corner taunting me. Tempting me.

Before I could stop myself, I held its solid weight in my hand then dove back under the covers like someone might catch me in the act.

I nestled into my pillow. The same pillow where a thirteen-year-old me had practiced kissing. The same pillow where a nineteen-year-old me had shed a million tears. And the same pillow where a thirty-two-year-old me now cracked open the spine of Will's book like I was opening a box of forbidden treasure.

Inhaling, I dizzied to a new height. It even smelled like him. Crisp paper and fresh ink. I scratched the inside cover just to see if it would bring forth the elusive spice that his skin seemed to emit.

When I turned the page, I read the dedication aloud. "To my something more." An ache spread through my fractured chest. Once upon a time, that was how he had referred to me. Who could it be now? Someone bright and bold with dark hair and creamy, unmarred skin. Someone unforgettable. Someone worthy of his love.

He had underlined each word in blue ink and signed his name below them. A stone of disappointment settled into my stomach. I had to admit I was hoping for something more...personal. A declaration. A secret clarity revealed. Some phrase that would tie up the loose end of us. Holding my breath, I flipped to the first page and began to read.

Finishing Will's novel took me days. I had spent nearly the entire weekend at the hospital watching my father sleep and devouring snatches of text while he snored peacefully.

When Monday came, I had scurried into the office between patients to read one more page. This morning I had nearly imploded when a dog hit by a car had rolled through the door, and I had to abandon Will's characters at the height of a plot twist.

And finally, hunkered down in an orange plastic chair at the airport, I flipped to the final page. I read it and re-read it, closing my eyes before quietly loosing a breath.

The story was beautiful. Ethereal yet relevant. It was the tale of a Fae queen whose kingdom had been seized by a warring clan of thugs and the human man who falls in love with her during her quest to reclaim it. In the end, she gets her kingdom, but he ransoms himself in the process and, in a cliffhanger ending, she is left to choose whether to risk the lives of her people to rescue him.

Ultimately, it was a love story. And the connection between the main characters was uncanny. Their body language. Their dialogue. Almost as if I had lived their story. And he had used our moon. Brilliant bastard.

I read the last sentence of the book again. *Wherever we go, as long as we share a moon, we'll find each other again.* With fringes of starlight rimming my visual field, I closed the book with a gentle thud, my mind reeling.

New York was frigid and wet. I shook dramatically in my thin sweater and jean jacket as I slipped into the back of a taxi.

"Lady, you bring no coat?" the cab driver asked in a harsh European accent.

"I'm wearing one." I frowned at my denim lapels.

"Is not enough."

His words sobered me. It wasn't enough. My bones rattled either with cold or realization. Maybe both. *It isn't enough*, a voice screamed inside my head, muted by my own stubborn rationale.

I clutched my carry-on to my chest. My brain must have been curdled to forget what the weather was like in the Northeast this time of year. I let my body ease into the rocking motion of the cab as we barreled downtown.

By the time I arrived at the door of Gavin's apartment on Fifty-Second Street, I was trembling like a skittish fawn.

"Is that all you brought?" Gavin looked at me skeptically

through his fogged-over black glasses as he relieved me of my weekender bag.

"Yes?" I had packed everything wearable from my dad's house minus the clinic scrubs.

"My parents want to take us out for Thanksgiving dinner."

"I thought we were eating at their house."

Gavin slung my bag over his shoulder and glanced down the street. "It wasn't practical to make the drive up there when we have to leave right after dinner."

My abdominals clenched with guilt. "I'm sorry I couldn't stay the whole time, but I have to go home Friday. My dad's coming home this weekend."

He cocked his head quizzically, his face pinched with an emotion that came and went in the span of a heartbeat. "I know. It's okay. We'll have many more holidays with my parents."

I followed him into the lobby of his apartment building, but instead of the lightness of elation, my footsteps were heavy with dread.

I thought about the first time I had met Gavin's mother and father. The woman with hair dyed blonde to hide the gray swallowed inside a cream wool coat. The man in a trim navy suit, sandy hair a few shades lighter than Gavin's and perfectly groomed into a part. Gavin had greeted them, drawing his mother in for a gesture halfway between a hug and the awkward gripping of her shoulders.

"Mom," he'd said affectionately.

"You look tired, darling," she had crooned, side-eying me as she leaned in to press her cheek to his.

"I've been busy at work," he had replied.

"Of course you have, dear." She had slid to his other side to make room for Gavin's father. They'd shaken hands and nodded at one another before all eyes had turned to me. The sweater dress I had worn had no longer seemed cute and trendy. Instead, I'd felt like a failed Old Navy ad.

"Mom, Dad this is Quinn, my girlfriend. Quinn these are my parents, Garrett and Diane."

No one had spoken for a moment as I had been scrutinized and measured. My worth evaluated. Was I good enough for their son? Even I had doubted it at that moment.

And now I would be destined to spend years of holidays with these people at a house that wasn't my home.

Gavin reached over to squeeze my shoulder. "Want to go down the street for a bite? Or I might have some leftover takeout?"

I forced a smile and shook my head. "I'm thinking I might need to just go to bed." Maybe if I was horizontal, I could stop the nausea spreading through me like I was in the middle of a bad dream.

After a fitful sleep on Gavin's couch where I had relegated myself after an hour of tossing and turning, I awoke to a watery sun trickling through the living room window and the sound of running water. "What time is it?" I croaked.

"Early," Gavin said, steam billowing up from the kitchen sink as he rinsed the coffee maker.

I touched my hair. It was tangled and coated with a layer of mixed media from the New York atmosphere. My outside was covered in grime. My inside drenched in guilt. And I was way undercaffeinated.

I had dreamed last night. Bits and pieces of memory that had flashed in and out of my consciousness like sunlight on shards of glass. Glowing brightly then darkening. In one image I had stared at my reflection in an aquamarine pool. In another, I had run my finger over a set of parted lips.

I glanced nervously at my bag, the edge of Will's book peeking from the top. My stomach churned as I pasted on a smile that wasn't altogether sincere and looked up at Gavin tidily folding a dish towel.

"What should we do today?" I asked, my voice raspy from sleeplessness.

His face broadened into a grin that pushed his glasses up the bridge of his nose. "I thought we could start with coffee, and then let's go get married."

CHAPTER TWENTY-FIVE

AUTUMN, NOW

I choked on a night's worth of saliva buildup, coughing and hacking before I managed to sputter, "Okay."

The dish towel hanging limply from Gavin's hand stilled in midair. "Unless you don't want to."

I began to struggle off the dove-gray suede couch, smoothing my hair behind my ears, watching him watch me as I floundered like a fish on a hook. Something in his face faltered and remorse nearly bowled me over.

"Of course, I want to," I stuttered, my feet hitting the thinly carpeted floor. "I'll have to move some things around, but I can fit you in." My tone was light but the smile I bore was forced.

I prayed Gavin didn't realize how hollow my words sounded. I tucked my chin over his shoulder and slid my arm around his waist so I didn't have to look him in the eyes. He let out a slow exhale and so did I. We were doing this. I was doing this. I would fling myself so far in one direction that my past would never catch up with me again.

MY SHOES SQUEAKED their newness as Gavin and I traversed Fifth Avenue. The day was layered in grays: the stalwart gray of the sidewalk under our feet, the sleek gray of the office buildings on every side of us, the soft gray of wool coats and sweaters as people scurried along with us, and the foreboding gray of the sky hovering above us.

In my newly purchased ivory colored sweater dress, I blended into the neutrality of our backdrop as we rode the wave of tourists up and down the city blocks.

A bustling excitement seemed to quicken everyone's pace even more than usual for New York City at holiday time. Gavin was the one tugging me along for once rather than the other way around. My feet in block heels protested as we cut across Central Park, my stomach grumbling from the smell of sugared cashews.

We skirted the lake just as we had on our third date. Right past the spot where Gavin had stopped so I could feed the ducks then had kissed me for the first time in front of a crowd of senior citizens out for a jaunt.

Today we didn't stop, pushed along by some force of nature that seemed to know something we didn't. The pond was empty anyway. The ducks had all flown south for the winter.

After a handful of blocks, we entered Times Square, the flashing lights chasing away the gloom that had settled over the city. This piece of New York had always been its own star.

"Do you remember that coffee shop we went to one time?" Gavin asked over the honking of a nearby taxi.

"Isn't it around here?" I scanned the street for a pink striped awning between the glitzy billboards.

I remembered that day. We had sipped terrible coffee for hours and talked about nothing while watching the billboards change. It had been easy and comfortable. And possibly the first time I had imagined myself able to be with someone else. Someone who wasn't Will.

"It was right there..." Gavin trailed off as he stopped mid-stride. I looked over to where he was pointing to a sign that read "Pita King."

"Oh," I sighed. "Too bad."

"I hope the gyros are better than that coffee was," Gavin remarked and I stifled a snort, tightening my grip on his arm.

"At least the company wasn't terrible." I locked eyes with him for what seemed like the first time in forever. The gentle caramel brown that had always reminded me of the color of a wool cardigan or maple syrup. Unwavering eyes. Dependable eyes. Eyes that would still be looking at me in fifty years. Eyes that wouldn't promise one thing and do another.

It was going to be okay. This was what life would be with Gavin. It wasn't cosmic or mind-bending. But it was enough. I smiled at him. Really smiled at him and pulled him in for a quick peck on the cheek.

"What was that for?" he asked.

"Do I need a reason?" I said, my eyes fluttering, distracted by the gargantuan digital billboard over our heads as it morphed from an ad for a luxury watch brand to the cover of a book. This week's number one on the *New York Times* Bestseller List.

I recognized the outline of a moon against a purple-black sky. No, no, no. *As long as we share a moon, we'll find each other again.* Will's words were like a song I couldn't forget on permanent repeat in my head. I stared at the billboard as the floodgates opened inside my imagination, revealing the pathway to a future paved with what ifs.

What if he still loved me? What if I still loved him? Did it even matter if we still loved each other? After all, I was marrying someone else.

I pulled back from Gavin, reeling with uncertainty, as the

sidewalk undulated beneath my feet like the deck of a rapidly sinking ship. I was simultaneously cold and hot. Desperate and calm. What if all my life choices had been made to avoid pain rather than to find joy?

I had forgiven the people who had hurt me most a long time ago. Will. Dad. Aunt Jackie. I had forgiven everyone except for the one person I held most responsible. Myself. And because of that, I hadn't thought I deserved to choose anything. To choose what made me happy.

I knew why I had stopped going home. Working through the holidays had kept the grief and guilt at bay. For years, I had basically held my breath until they were over and could flip my calendar to January.

Love and comfort and happiness—that was the steep price I had paid to avoid my grief. I didn't deserve the life I had dreamed of and now I had one I didn't necessarily want. So where did that leave me?

I had lied to my aunt. The realization struck me like a backhanded blow. I wasn't happy. I didn't want this. Not any of it.

I put a hand to my chest as a pressure grew behind my sternum. Building until I thought I might die from a vise that twisted tighter and tighter. Demanding an answer I wasn't ready to give.

"Quinn?" I heard my name amidst the fog of panic. "Quinn?" Gavin said and squeezed my hand. Had he asked me a question?

"I'm sorry," I said thickly.

Gavin tugged me out of the crowded street toward the nearest wall, his face pinched with worry. "What's wrong?"

I inhaled a steadying breath, closing my eyes then opening them again. Maybe this was a nightmare I could wake up from. "It's nothing," I said automatically to buy myself some time. Gavin looked at me skeptically. "You know this time of year is hard for me."

His face softened, his lips parting as his glasses slid down the bridge of his nose. "Your mom?"

I focused my attention on the shiny brass buckles of his loafers.

"You never talk about it."

I hated that awkward edge to his voice. I hated that he didn't really know what had happened to my mom. And I hated that I didn't want to tell him. Especially not right now. "I don't want to get married today."

"Oh." He stilled, his hands loosening their grip on my shoulders. "That's all right, Quinn."

I watched a tuft of his sandy hair flip upward with the wind. It made me sad in a twisting, frightful sort of way. "Gavin..." I bit down on my lip to curb a swell of words but they rushed out anyway. "I live with so much guilt and...it's suffocating me."

"Guilt?" He looked unsure as he slid his hands down the sleeves of my coat. "About the wedding?"

I shook my head and clenched my teeth together. "I feel guilty when I'm home. And guilty when I'm not home. Guilty for working too hard. Guilty for taking a holiday. Guilty for not wanting to get married today."

I threw my hands up at the glitter and grime framing us. I could have stopped right there with the soft expression on his face and the gentle scrutiny in his eyes. But I didn't.

"I feel guilty for loving too much and guilty for not..." I paused, blinking as the crowd continued to rush around us like we were two stationary rocks in a river of wool coats and hats. A man next to me held up his phone to snap a photograph of Broadway.

"For not what?"

I swallowed past the lump building in my throat as I

stood there, rooted to the street corner. Haunted. Shocked. Relieved. Cameras flashed around me. Billboards dissolved and reappeared.

I waited, a drizzle of light rain mixing with the dust and makeup on my face. I waited for something. A push. A tilt of gravity to send me in a direction. Any direction. I retreated to my most inner sanctuary of calm. My best memory of my mother. It was like a flower unfurling its petals.

In my mind she put her hand to my cheek. I touched my scar, running my fingers down its jagged path. She smiled. I smiled back.

"I'm sorry, Gavin. There's somewhere I need to be."

And then my legs begged me to start running. To run until my breath turned to ice in my lungs. To run all the way home if that was what I had to do. *Just get there*, a voice said. And I realized that voice was mine.

IT TOOK another thirteen hours for me to make it out of JFK. The flight was mostly empty except for a few weary suits and enlisted military making last-ditch efforts to arrive home for turkey.

I closed my eyes, breathing easily for the first time since I had landed in New York yesterday. The tightness in my chest remained, however, guilt pricking me between the ribs every time a new face flashed through my mind's eye. Gavin. Aunt Jackie. Dad. Mom. Even Will.

Life was easier when my choices narrowed down to which horse needed an operation or what movie I was going to fall asleep to. And despite my quest to find a world bigger than my small town—and a life to match it—my existence had shrunk just like my heart.

I had told myself I didn't go home because I didn't want

to be a burden, when in reality, the only person being burdened was me. Because every time I looked at my family, I only saw what we had lost. What I had made them lose. And I hadn't wanted the guilt anymore.

I had run from it. As fast and as far as I could. But it had found me anyway. I thought if I acknowledged it, I might be crushed by its weight. Maybe I deserved to be. Secluding myself from my past had insulated me from the guilt but also from the people I loved most.

It was late evening by the time I slipped inside the back door. The chandelier was on, illuminating a perfect circle in the center of our dining table. My aunt was there, head bowed as she flipped the plastic pages of a photo album.

In my tragic, clumsy, fatigued state I stubbed my toe on the threshold. Hissing an expletive, I dropped my bag to the floor. Jackie's shoulders jerked at the noise, but she didn't turn around.

"Aunt Jackie?"

"Hey there," she said, pressing the heel of her hand to one eye. "I wasn't expecting you 'til Friday."

"I decided to come home early." The word left my lips before I realized what I had said. *Home.*

Some of the pressure eased in my chest as Jackie's eyes, soft and welcoming, met mine. I licked my paper-dry lips and sat down next to her, the scrape of my chair filling up the void of silence between us. "What are you looking at?" My gaze wandered over the curled plastic pages. "Is that me?" I pointed to a faded snapshot of a child with bright yellow pigtails clutching an orange tabby to her chest.

Jackie pushed the album closer to me. "That's you and the poor cat you used to torture."

"Mrs. Whiskers was more than happy to undergo a daily evaluation with the tools from my medical kit."

Aunt Jackie snorted. "And you had the scratches to prove it."

I chuckled softly, pulling the album closer and flipping the page. A photo collage of me and Dad and Aunt Jackie at a summer barbecue. I was in a flowered two-piece bathing suit, proudly holding a slice of watermelon. Young enough that I didn't care who saw my soft abdomen or the pink juice running over my chin or the fact that I was missing my top two teeth.

My mouth watered, remembering the sweetness of the melon, the sun warming my back. My dad had thrown his head back in laughter as my aunt looked on, hands on her hips, a smile splitting her face in two. They looked happy. Not like two people who regretted their choices or had been too steeped in tragedy to stop living.

I chewed on my bottom lip. Had I imagined it then? Hearing them in the kitchen that night when they thought I wasn't there. The whispered conversation that had thrown a bucket of black paint over the rainbow of my childhood.

I turned the page, the cardstock and plastic crackling with age. More pictures acting as a two-dimensional narrative of my youth—spring birthday parties and summer road trips to Canyon Lake. Childhood me holding a giant bear I had won at the county fair. The baby raccoon I'd raised in a cardboard box. Teenage me, stringy and bony, in a pair of denim cutoffs posing on the hood of my dad's vintage Camaro the day I'd gotten my braces off.

I turned the page. College me. Freshman year. And the last time I had come home for any length of time. I remembered the delicate crispness to the air as I stood on the front porch in a red V-neck sweater on our way to the Linzberg Christmas parade.

My hair curling around my face in soft layers. My eyes sparkling as I paused on the steps to smile for my dad. I hadn't known then that it was a night I would never forget. The back of my neck erupted in gooseflesh as I slipped the picture out from under its plastic covering.

"You look a lot like her in that photo." My aunt studied me with watery blue eyes, the chandelier's light reflecting off unshed tears.

I held the photo gingerly. Like the fragility of this moment was palpable. As delicate as blown glass. I had the signature McClain steel gray eyes and stubbornness. But the honey color of my hair and the softness behind my smile. That was all her.

"I wish..." My voice caught in my throat, words and emotions tangled and lodged in the most painful way.

What did I wish? Too many things to name. That my mother hadn't died young. That my father hadn't needed to raise me alone. That my aunt hadn't given up a life and a husband and children...for me. That I hadn't worn the guilt of being the catalyst that had put our lives on this path. That I hadn't been too afraid to want more. To want to give more. To believe that I could really be enough for anyone.

A hand slipped over my cheek, a smooth thumb brushing away the wetness. "Welcome home, Quinn," Aunt Jackie whispered.

I slept later than I intended the next morning, waking to stare at the ceiling then drifting back into tumultuous dreams. Twisting around in my flowered sheets amid flashes of drizzling rain and hands cupping my face. Dreams I shouldn't be dreaming but couldn't stop.

When I awoke to a hint of sunrise and the smell of bacon frying, I flipped over and stared at the phone on my nightstand. No missed calls. No texts. I dreaded calling Gavin. But I would. After breakfast, I promised myself.

The next time I awoke, sunlight streamed through my window. I schlepped downstairs where my aunt was nursing a cup of coffee. I went over and put my arms around her, resting my chin on the top of her head.

A warm, solid hand gripped my forearm then patted it. "There's bacon," she said, "but it's probably cold."

I released her and slid into the seat next to her, snagging a piece of bacon from the plate in the center. "Warm...cold...bacon is bacon." I shoved it in my mouth. "What time is it?"

"Nearly noon," she said, flipping over the newspaper that had been splayed out across the table. "Any plans today?"

I cringed as I swallowed. Only conversations I didn't want to have. Apologies I didn't want to make. I had no idea how Gavin would react to my dramatic departure. I pictured his face from the last time I had seen him, unreadable and bathed in the glow of the digital glare of Times Square.

"You're welcome to join me," she added when I didn't answer. "I'll be driving over to the medical supply to pick up your father's crutches and stool softener."

I stifled a snort. "Thanks, but no."

She gave a wry smile and traced a finger along the rim of her coffee cup.

"I bet he's ready to come home," I said, my chest tightening. Between the clinic hours and dealing with my own personal drama, I hadn't visited him enough lately. I frowned as Will's face popped into my head instead of Gavin's.

My aunt's indignant snort pulled me out of my own head. "He's doing just fine," she remarked. "When I dropped some food off for him yesterday, one of the twenty-five-year-old blonde nurses was giving him a foot massage."

I emitted a low laugh. "He always was irresistible."

Closing the paper and pushing it toward me, she stood up, her chair legs scraping the wooden floor. Ruffling the top of my head, she said, "He'll be proud of how you managed the clinic. Later, gator." With a wink, she was out the backdoor and I was alone, feeling like I was five years old again.

I reached for the newspaper, tugging the velvety edge toward me, a headline in the right lower corner catching my eye. Twenty-six years since Linzberg's tragic flood.

Even as my blood chilled, I pressed trembling fingers to the typeset print.

Exactly twenty-six years ago today, the worst flood in a century struck Linzberg when Caney Creek swelled from unprecedented rainfall and washed out the Old Town Bridge. The traditional post-Thanksgiving holiday celebrations were brought to a standstill as the county focused on search and rescue missions. Although many in the community lost their homes and livestock, fortunately only one death resulted from a night of celebration turned tragedy.

Fortunately. A word I would never associate with my mother's death. I continued scanning the article my stomach clenched into knots.

At this year's annual tree lighting ceremony, we will be collecting donations for restructuring the bridge as we usher in Linzberg's festival of lights.

The article was only two inches long. It might as well have been a two-inch blade lodged in the delicate muscle of my heart.

I purposefully gave myself no time to think or to process or to weigh the decision that my body was already making. The next thing I knew I was behind the wheel of my dad's truck.

When I entered an intimidating iron gate, I wound through a trail overgrown with vegetation, solid granite markers guiding me to the northwest corner. I slowed to a stop, the truck lurching once before I killed the engine. Without its incessant rumble, the day was perfectly quiet.

A winter wren chirped. The wind rattled through the last leaves of autumn. I stuck my head through the window, closing my eyes against an effusive sun and inhaled. The air was crisp. Clean. Without judgment. I brushed my hands over my jeans then pulled the door handle, gravel crunching under my boots as I walked over to the heart-shaped arch of gray stone nearest the path.

"Hi, Mama," I whispered. I clasped my hands in front of me as a gust of wind blew strands of hair across my eyes. I knelt down to escape it. "I know it's been a while." I paused, waiting as if I were having an actual conversation and she might answer. It was like the world waited with me.

I reached out trembling fingers to rub the sediment from her name. Laurie McClain. Hearing her name inside my head put a dagger through an old wound. The last time I had been here, Will had found me clutching her headstone in the pouring rain.

There were flowers in a vase off to the side. I frowned and reached out to stroke the petals. Fresh ones. And Mom's favorite. I wondered where Aunt Jackie had found lilacs this time of year. I should have been making sure my mom's grave had flowers. I should have been doing all sorts of things. But I had tucked myself into a cocoon. Somewhere warm and comfortable. But also dark. And being back here was fracturing my chrysalis.

"What do I do now, Mama?" I mused. An intensity built in the stillness around me until my senses were hyperaware. Waiting.

I perched on the edge of a precipice of change, waiting for something to tip me over the edge. Would I fly, or would I plummet to the bottom of whatever existed below? I waited and, still, nothing.

A modicum of relief washed over me. Maybe the universe wasn't asking me for anything. And once I left here, my life would go exactly back to what it was.

I pulled the neckline of my shirt from under my jacket and ran it across my eyes as I heaved a sigh. My phone rang in my back pocket. The sound was shrill and out of place and I quickly pressed it to my ear.

"Hi, Gavin," I said, the natural timbre of my voice diluted into something meek and apologetic.

"Hi, Quinn." He cleared his throat, and I could picture the flush creeping up his neck past the rounded collar of his sweater. It unhinged something in me.

"Listen, I'm sorry about leaving. I just had some things here that I needed to do." Silence ensued. And I knew my apology was too little too late. I awkwardly stumbled over words amidst his broken sigh. "I'm sorry," I repeated. "For so many things. Gavin, I—"

"I'm sorry too, Quinn."

"What in the world are you sorry for?"

"For not..." He cleared his throat a few times. "For not being enough for you, Quinn."

"Of course, you're enough for me."

"I'm not," he said firmly. "Otherwise, I wouldn't feel like I'm always left trying to understand...trying to be worthy of having more of you."

You can't have more of me. There isn't anything left to give.

Letting out a whimper, I said, "You are worthy. I never expected anything more from you."

"You should have."

"Why?"

"Because I know I have more to give." His voice broke on the last word.

"And you can't give it to me?"

"You won't let me, Quinn."

I sucked in a breath. This was it. I teetered on my life's precipice, forward then backward, my feet grappling for a hold. "I'm so sorry, Gavin," I cried. "You know I'm not myself this time of year and the stress of my dad and being engaged...if we can just put this off until I get back..."

"I don't want to put it off."

"What are you saying?"

"I can't do this anymore, Quinn." He swallowed hard before continuing. "I deserve more. And so do you. Whatever that is."

"Gavin, I—"

"Unless you're going to tell me I'm wrong, I can't hear it, Quinn."

His words were like a slap across my face. I choked on my emotions. My shock. I grappled for words. I wanted to tell him he was wrong. But he wasn't. And I couldn't lie anymore. Not to him. Not to myself.

"I thought so," he said quietly. After clearing the phlegm from his throat, his next words were steady and unwavering. "Goodbye Quinn."

I stared at the phone in my hand. So much for my life going back to what it was. The chrysalis cracked wide open as I stood up and headed for the truck.

CHAPTER TWENTY-SIX

SPRING, THEN

"Quinn, I absolutely forbid you to stay in tonight." Sid side-eyed me in the sliver of the bathroom mirror that we shared. She pursed her lips to apply a second coat of lipstick. A deep crimson shade that she only wore on two occasions—when she was giving an important presentation in one of her many honors classes or when she was in the mood to be noticed by a certain suave sophomore who wore pants with perfect pleats and glasses with square frames.

I groaned and glanced at her over the pages of the textbook I wasn't actually reading. "I don't know if I can take Sky Lounge tonight."

"I wasn't necessarily headed there." She shifted her eyes to the pile of cosmetics strewn over our bathroom counter.

I arched a brow, giving her a pointed look. "Yes, you are." She was perfectly aware that I was aware that Derrik would be at Sky Lounge tonight. Playing saxophone in his preppy fratboy jazz ensemble.

"I don't know if he's even playing tonight."

"Yes, you do."

Sighing in defeat, she ran a curling iron through her recently cut bangs. "Come with me then. It's the Friday before spring break. You can't possibly have to study."

"I do if I want this internship at Penn this summer...and this"—I patted my biochemistry textbook—"makes my brain hurt less than jazz music."

Sid spun around and propped a hand on her hip. "Come on, Quinn. It's the least you can do for ditching me."

A pang of guilt rippled through me. Sid had invited me to drive up to her parents' lake house in New York for spring break, but I had decided to stay on campus and get started on my end-of-the-year required research project. I was so lame.

"I'm sorry, Sid."

"Don't be sorry. I just worry about you staying here all by yourself."

"The fruit flies in biology lab will keep me company," I joked.

She gave me a look that reminded me of a mother's glare, attentive yet disappointed. "What's Will up to this week?"

Will. I smiled at the sound of his name and how it filled up the room. "He's handling the winery while his grandparents attend some grape convention in Napa."

"He needs to be handling you," Sid remarked. "I don't think I can take much more unrequited love or the late-night glare of your laptop screen and your longing sighs as you read his emails."

I tossed a stuffed monkey that had been her Valentine's Day gift to me at her head. "There's no unrequited love."

"Mmhmm. Whatever. Why aren't you going home for spring break?"

Because it costs money that I don't have. "I'll be home soon enough. I'll have three weeks between finals and my internship at Penn. Assuming I get it."

The springs on my bed creaked as Sid plopped onto the

end, curling her legs underneath her. She removed the textbook from my hands and laid it face down on the comforter. "You'll get the internship, but is that how you really want to spend your summer?"

"Of course it is. I've heard the director will write me a rec letter that's practically a golden ticket for vet school."

"Just for a moment." Sid paused, a faraway look in her eyes before her lids drifted closed. "Let's picture an alternative."

"Am I being used as a psychology experiment?"

"Possibly." Her eyes popped open to reveal the rich earthy brown inside. Grabbing my hands, she scrutinized my face, her eyes lingering on my scar. Her hands were dry and cool and reminded me of the pages of a book.

"What's Will doing in the fall?"

"Starting college at Berkeley."

"And what's he doing this summer?"

"He'll be in Linzberg working for his grandparents."

"So why in the world would you want to be apart from each other this summer?"

"I don't know. We haven't even talked about it...and it's not like...I mean...I don't even know what this is yet."

"Yes, you do." Her grip tightened on my fingers. "Imagine, Quinn. One last epic summer before everything changes again."

And when she said it like that, with the passionate fervor worthy of a Jane Austen novel, I could imagine it too.

WHEN I LANDED in Texas for only the second time since I had left for college last fall, everything seemed bigger and brighter. The sun seemed closer to the earth somehow. The land a shade of spring green I only imagined existed in fairy tales. And the wildflowers lining the highways and coating the hills were a mix of vibrant blues and oranges and pinks. When my dad's truck ascended the last hill before our driveway, the sky was close enough to touch.

Aunt Jackie was waiting inside for us with a wide smile underneath painted letters on white butcher block paper that read 'welcome home.' When I finally made it to her outstretched arms, she squealed, nearly crushing me against her torso. I inhaled the liquid smoke in her hair from the brisket she had cooking in the oven mixed with a whiff of her floral perfume.

"Supper's almost ready," she said near my ear, rocking me back and forth in her arms. "I made barbecue."

"I can smell it," I teased and pulled away from her to collapse in the nearest kitchen chair.

The weeks of late nights and caffeine binges and adrenaline spikes from final exam week had left me with a permanent tremulousness. Now that I was in the comfort of my house, I realized how my heart skipped an occasional beat.

It was good to be home. I kicked my shoes off under the kitchen table with the ancient, flowered tablecloth where I had done my homework and where Aunt Jackie had given me a repertoire of coming-of-age talks. It was exactly as I remembered it, but I was seeing through new eyes. Different eyes. Eyes that had seen and experienced another place.

"Your hair looks good." Aunt Jackie reached in a cabinet for a stack of white plates.

"Thanks." My hand immediately began smoothing the layers around my face. I had let Sid convince me to cut off a few inches and add some bangs to celebrate the end of freshman year.

"And your dad tells me you have a fancy internship lined up in a few weeks?" She winked at me over her shoulder as she tossed cut up vegetables into a bed of pasta.

"I wouldn't call organizing bandage supplies and shoveling horse manure fancy." I wrinkled my nose hoping she and my dad didn't notice the nervous twinge to my voice. I hadn't said yes to the internship yet...and I wasn't going to. Not until I talked to Will, at least.

"When does it start?" my dad asked from where he was slouched in his recliner.

I cleared my throat. "The first of June...but I might decide to stay here this summer. Maybe work for you again, if you'll take me," I added jokingly.

He cut his eyes over to my aunt, whose serving spoon had paused above a bubbling dish of baked beans. It was the briefest falter in his expression, but it had happened. I had not imagined the tightening around his mouth.

"You're always welcome here, Quinnie," he said slowly, "but I don't know how much more I can teach you."

I smiled and nodded, masking the uncomfortable wringing in my gut. Truthfully, I was ready for the next step. But was it so bad if I didn't want to take it just yet?

A light knock sounded at the door as if the universe agreed with my silent ruminations, and I startled. Aunt Jackie frowned as she slid a plate in front of me. My dad grunted before saying, "Why don't you see who it is, Quinnie?"

I rose, my chair scraping against the tile, and wiped my hands on the back of my jeans. Through the rectangular side windows flanking the door, I could make out a tanned arm, long and sinewy, balanced on the porch railing. *Will.*

My heart exploded into a gallop, and I wrenched open the door. Shadows from the flickering porch light danced across his face. His hair was longer, shaggier, and a light row of stubble sprinkled the outline of his jaw. His eyes, the incandescent blue of a flame, drifted over my face, my neck, the V of my shirt, the curve of my hips.

I smirked. "Like what you see?"

His eyes flashed to mine, dimmed by a hint of embarrassment. I closed the distance between us and slid my arms along his sides, wrapping them around his torso.

"I missed you," he whispered, dipping his head so that he could nuzzle my hair. His warm exhale sent shivers down my spine.

"I missed you, too."

"Who's at the door, Quinnie?"

I jumped back from Will at the sound of my dad's booming voice. "Come say hi to my dad and aunt," I said, tugging him by the arm.

He stayed rooted to his spot on the porch. "I think your dad has seen enough of me lately, and I get the feeling he doesn't like me terribly much."

I cocked my head quizzically.

"My grandmother's terrier is high maintenance." His lips quirked into a grin.

"So, he's told me." I smirked back at him. "Why don't you think he likes you?"

"I don't know for sure." Will rubbed his neck with the back of his hand. "But it's possibly the death threats he sends me with a simple nod of his head."

"He's protective." I glanced back at the table at my dad who was trying and failing to focus on his plate. "I'll be back later," I called. "Will and I are—what are we doing?"

Will cleared his throat and peeked inside the doorway to wave an awkward hello. "Hi Dr. McClain, I was about to ask Quinn if she wanted to go for ice cream."

He stared at us, perception outweighing trust, then frowned. Jackie dissected Will over the rim of her reading glasses, her lips slightly parted like she wanted to say something.

"Don't stay out too late," my dad finally growled and dove back into his potato salad.

I rolled my eyes. "Dad, please, I'm in college now."

Grabbing my purse that hung from the hook by the door, I pushed Will back onto the front porch, closing the door on the shocked glare from my aunt and the resigned, weary one from my dad.

Two minutes later we were in Will's car, my knees vibrating with excitement. "Are we really going to get ice cream?" I asked.

"Not unless you really want to."

"I don't."

"What do you want to do?" His smile was breathtakingly beautiful.

I settled into the passenger seat of his car like an old friend. I loved the ease that we shared despite only seeing each other a handful of times since last summer. If Will was a planet then I was his moon.

"I want you to take me somewhere," I said, feeling wild and reckless with possibility.

Will slid his hand over to my knee and it immediately stilled under his touch. Tires crunched over the loose asphalt. The honeysuckle smell of an early summer rode on the wind. I watched him spin the steering wheel as we turned down a familiar stretch of country road. His hand crept up my thigh as we left the amber glow of the city lights for the dusk settling over the hills.

"You're really starting to know your way around," I teased.

"I suppose it's better than being lost all the time."

"I'll have to stop calling you lost boy."

"You never called me that."

"I did in my head." I smirked and the hand on my thigh tightened.

Will's cheek ticked up for the briefest smile before his face froze in thought. I waited anxiously for his mouth to catch up with his head.

"The truth is," he started slowly. "I was lost when I first arrived here. In more ways than one." His face broke with a wry smile. "When my mum died, I felt like the only person that ever really loved me was gone and I couldn't bear it. I thought I might never...feel close to anyone...for a while at least. I was searching for meaning. For something worth holding onto. For something..."

"More?" I finished.

"Yes, something more."

"And now?"

"I'm not lost anymore."

My heart lurched and twisted.

I had barely noticed that the car had rolled to a stop off the main road onto a dirt path dotted with sparse grass inside a ring of green mesquite trees. A not-quite-full moon blinked at us from the inky black sky.

"Where are we?" I asked, squinting to find a familiar landmark in the distance.

"You'll see," he said with an enigmatic smile.

He swung his long legs over the side of the car, skirting it quickly to open my door. I took his hand, which was imbued with the warmth of my own thigh.

"Seriously, where are we?" I asked, my intrigue nearly unbearable.

He clicked on a small flashlight and tugged me forward. The ground remained level for twenty yards or so before we began a swift descent past random chunks of pink granite glinting in the moonlight. I tripped over the jutting root of a tree, and Will's hand tightened around mine.

"It's just a bit farther."

When we cleared the last crop of mountain laurel, a

grassy embankment stretched out in front of us until it ended in a lip of granite, and beyond that, a body of water sparkled like a black jewel.

"Is that our swimming hole?"

"One and the same." His lips stretched into a grin.

"How did…" I started as realization dawned. "This is what it looks like from the top?"

"It's quite beautiful during the day. We'll have to come again when it's light out."

"Maybe every day." My cheeks began to burn from smiling. And I could picture it then. The summer we could have. The lazy afternoons talking and swimming. Waiting for a star to fall from the reclined seats of Will's convertible. The smell of summer rain and blooming sage.

"When did you find it?" I shook my head in disbelief.

"About a month ago."

"Too bad there's no way down to the water from here." I took a tentative look over the edge and the near vertical drop into nothingness.

"Actually, there is." He dipped his head sheepishly. My eyes nearly bugged out of my skull. "There's a path down to the water over there." He pointed to where the grass dwindled and transitioned into smooth granite. "It's steep but manageable."

"So no more squeezing my backside through that tiny crack of utter doom?" Last summer the slit-like entrance to our swimming hole had given me more than one panic attack.

"I don't know." He paused and rubbed his chin. "I quite like how you look when you writhe around inside that crevice."

"I do not writhe." I took my free hand and smacked him on the stony hardness of his chest.

He trapped my hand there with the flat of his palm and tugged me into his middle.

"You do and it's..." He ran his tongue across his bottom lip, eyes igniting with sparks.

"It's what?"

"Sexy."

My stomach dropped into my feet, and I bit my lip. Hard. "Sexy? I don't think I've ever heard you use such simple vocabulary before."

His face grew more and more amused. "Shall I try again? Let's see...suggestive? Provocative? Arousing?"

"Arousing, huh? Speaking of...." I ran a hand down his pectorals then continued to the defined ridges of his abdominals. "Wow."

He contracted them underneath my hand. "I've spent an entire year toting around crates of wine bottles. It was bound to happen." He smiled at me crookedly, the dimple in his left cheek deepening into an abyss.

I inhaled a sharp breath and let it out slowly. The night stilled around us, the air the exact right amount of warmth. The sky was cloudless, streaked with starlight and the cool glow of the moon. The only sound was the undulating rhythm of a brood of cicadas.

I curled my fingers into the waistband of his jeans and rose the remaining few inches to his parted mouth.

CHAPTER TWENTY-SEVEN

SPRING, THEN

Will melted into me, long arms snaking around my waist and banding my shoulder blades. And then his entire body shuddered. I felt it in my very bones. Felt him in my bones. I teased his lips open with my tongue and tasted the fresh sweet mint there.

"Do you like your surprise?" he whispered when we parted for breath.

"I love it," I whispered back. He smiled against my lips.

When my lids fluttered open, I was met with the glint of gold in his blue eyes, and my heart stuttered and stilled. I slid my hands under the soft cotton of his shirt to feel the warm cords of his back. I started massaging the knots, my fingers digging into his muscles until they began to relax under my fingers.

He stilled, completely inert as I rode the fabric of his shirt higher ... and higher. Will reached backward to tug his shirt over his head. Gooseflesh erupted over his chest tightening the pinkish beige of his nipples.

A breeze lifted the ends of my hair, and I shivered. Will's eyes were endless pools of midnight as they searched my face, asking a question that I had already decided the answer to.

"Yes," I whispered, so low that I didn't think he heard me, not until he reached over to tip up my chin with the pads of his fingers. He skated them along my jaw, and I began trembling despite his nearness. Maybe because of it.

"Yes what?" He reached up to brush the hair clinging to my scar.

"Yes to everything you're thinking right now."

He smiled until the moonlight glinted off his teeth. "I'm thinking quite a lot."

"I was hoping you were."

His breathing stilled, and his fingers splayed out to cup my cheek. "Are you sure?"

Was I? Underneath all the jittery excitement and nerves existed the calm reassurance that yes, I was. I had waited for a reason. For this moment. For this now. For Will. I reached for the top snap on my denim shirt. Its tiny pop served as my answer. I moved to the second one.

Will's eyes dilated with a desperate hunger until they appeared entirely black. A churning heat grew low in my abdomen, spreading in waves to my inner thighs, my chest, my throat.

I reached for the third snap, but long fingers were already there working it open. Delicious night air caressed the exposed skin of my torso. I shrugged off my shirt and it fell noiselessly onto the grass.

Will cradled me against his chest, dipping his head to plant a kiss on my bare shoulder. Soft tendrils of his hair tickled my neck, and I giggled softly. In between kisses, Will sent warm hands up my back and underneath my bra strap. I let the flimsy satin fall at our feet, sucking in a breath when my bare nipples grazed the surface of Will's chest.

"How do you feel?" he asked.

"Free," I said. And I did. It felt good.

"Not nervous?"

"Maybe a little."

"Don't be," he said, "I've got you."

"I guess you've done this before." I bit the inside of my cheek. I didn't want to think about who had come before me.

"Not exactly...but I think we can figure it out."

My eyes widened to saucers for the second time that night. "So, we're two virgins about to deflower each other under the moonlight? It sounds like something from a novel."

"That's what I was hoping for." He smiled shyly and ducked his head.

"What? That your epic fantasy has become your reality?"

"Of course," he said softly. "That's the entire point of living."

His lips found my mouth and I was lost. Lost inside Will's world of magic and fantasy. Epic love and heroism and happy endings. I would remember those next few minutes as sensations only. Sighs and soft groans. Flashes of skin and teeth. Will's hands on every inch of me and mine on every piece of him and an enveloping darkness around us. Hiding us from the world. From the past. From the future. There was only the now.

There was slicing pain before my world erupted in bliss. In an electricity that buzzed underneath my skin and heightened my senses. Growing and expanding until it became too much for me to contain. I couldn't hold it. It spilled over into the tremors of my thighs and the arch in my back and the flush spreading through my skin.

And Will. He had transformed into a panting, tremoring mess with sweat along his brow and bits of grass stuck in his hair. I relished seeing him come apart, emotion after emotion shimmering through the cracks in his protective layer.

We lay in the grass afterward, stunned into silence. Spent from laying waste to our emotional reserves. My ear rested on his chest listening to his heartbeat as it slowed from a gallop to a trot to a steady walk.

Will exhaled against the top of my head. "Best moment of your life?"

I didn't give him the practiced answer I always had. Instead, I turned my face into his neck, inhaling the scent of fresh wild grass. "This one," I whispered.

When Will dropped me off I had no idea what time it was. Only that we were deep enough into the night that my dad would be peeved. If he found out. Which he wouldn't. His early mornings always made for early nights where he slept like the dead.

I leaned over to give Will a lingering kiss goodbye and stopped just shy of his beautiful mouth. "I'm not taking the internship at Penn."

He tilted his head back and assessed me. "Are you certain? I know how much—"

I interrupted him with a press of my finger to his lips. "I would rather spend the summer with you...if that's what you want too."

"As exciting as emailing you has been, I think I want the real thing for a while."

"You'll get more sex that way too," I quipped, and he barked a laugh.

"My grandparents will be in Italy all summer which might make for some interesting adventures."

My eyes grew huge with possibility. "All summer?"

"Yes. All"—he ran his nose up the side of my neck, and I shivered—"summer."

"And they're leaving you to handle the vineyard while they're gone?"

"Among other things," he whispered and closed in on the sensitive skin behind my ear.

A delicate shiver skittered down my spine, and a purr rose in my chest like that of a cat in heat. What would it be like to...

The porch light flickered on, and we both froze in our seats. Will drew back from being on the cusp of kissing me and I nearly whimpered.

His face sobered. "I'm no good to you if your dad kills me first."

"Very funny," I said and couldn't resist pressing my lips to his once more before pushing open the car door. "See you...tomorrow?"

"Of course, you will." His eyes were clear and bright, throat bobbing as he waved goodnight.

My steps were light as I floated onto the porch but as soon as I was bathed in the golden glow of the overhead light, I thought better than to barge through the front door. I might have been an adult, but the teenager in me continued to live for my dad's approval. And I doubted he would have approved of me losing my virginity in the middle of a pasture with Will Deremer. No matter how magical it had been. Somehow with Will, everything always was.

I snuck around to the back door and eased it open. The kitchen light was still on, and I could smell the faint aroma of last night's dinner.

Voices, low and thick with emotion, rose and fell from around the corner. Were they waiting up for me? I nearly called out to tease my dad as I crouched to remove my shoes, but my nose chose that moment to tingle, and I paused to listen.

"She needs to take that internship this summer." Aunt Jackie sounded grim. Desperate even.

"I know. I'm still in shock that she's thinking about

turning it down," my father answered in a voice that was equally as grim.

"Everything is so different than it should have been, David," Aunt Jackie said, her voice strangled and raw. Like she had been crying. "I could have been married. With my own kids. You could have—"

"Don't say it, Jackie. A bad thing happened and there's no sense laying blame."

"That doesn't change the fact that it was *her* fault. *Her* fault that Laurie slid off the road that night—"

"We can't change the past," my dad interrupted sounding sterner than I'd ever heard him.

I heard a sniff then the scrape of chair legs. "No, I guess we can't. But that past doesn't also have to be in our face every day."

My chest seized and I couldn't breathe. I had to get out of there before I suffocated under the tense silence I could sense in the other room. Somehow, I willed my legs to move, to duckwalk backward step by agonizing step until I was through the door, my bare feet scraping across the pavement then sinking into the dew-drop-ridden grass.

The fluttering elation from a few minutes ago had dissolved in the sea of my own dread. My insides cracked open, the gnawing guilt inside me exploding to a mammoth proportion. I had always known it.

Somewhere deep inside, I knew I was to blame for everything. And now I knew that they believed it too.

Despite the warm night, I shook violently. Was everything a lie? Their love for me a lie? They couldn't hate me outright, so did they simply tolerate my existence?

I waited outside, twisting around in the tire swing that hung from a giant pecan tree in our back yard until I saw the kitchen lights flick off. And then I ran through the grass like a shadow, my hand on the back door one moment and on the doorknob of my bedroom the next.

I didn't bother to shower or even shuck off my clothes. Crawling onto my bed, I pulled a flowered quilt up to my chin and took a shaky breath. I could still smell the outdoors on my shirt collar—the wild grass and wisps of night. And Will. I inhaled his scent on my skin as hot tears rained over my cheeks.

When I woke the next day, I waited until the clattering sounds of breakfast were over. Waited until my dad's truck rumbled out of the driveway. Waited until Aunt Jackie had closed the front door and set off for a walk.

I languished in the warm buttery sunshine streaming through my window, my limbs refusing to become vertical until I forced them upright. I commanded myself to shower and change clothes. Then left a quick note.

Went for a run. Be back later.

When I crept through the sagging iron gate, only one other person was in the cemetery. Old man Solomon waved at me as I walked along the shale road then returned his attention to the hedges he was clipping into perfect cubes.

A thick cover of clouds blocked out every speck of sunshine. The air was thick with the promise of a coming rain. The fragrance of wildflowers and freshly mown grass in every inhale. I found the perfect arch of her headstone and ran my hand over it. It felt warm against the chill of my palm.

I knelt in the grass and wrapped my arms around it, pressing the scarred side of my face flat against the granite. Words and feelings and memories blended together, but I wasn't able to turn any of it into intelligible speech. So, I held on, squeezing my eyes closed and willing that night—that night I lost her—to have never happened.

I remained glued to my mother's headstone while the clouds swirled and darkened. While the first droplets of rain struck my face, streaming across my eyelids and down my cheeks like they were my own tears.

The rain changed from soft pattering droplets to splinters of cold that daggered me all the way to my heart. Burying themselves so deep that I would never be able to dig them out. I stayed there, frozen and shivering, until the stone lost all its heat, and still I didn't move. Maybe I never would again.

A hand clamped down on my shoulder, and arms swept under my legs then around my back. I was lifted off the ground as if I weighed nothing—as if the marrow of me had simply vanished and I was a husk.

"Quinn," Will said softly, urgently. "Open your eyes."

I debated disobeying, but if I had to return to reality, to stop pretending as if my life wasn't one cruel nightmare, I wanted the first face I saw to be his.

Slits in my eyelids appeared, wide enough to confirm that it was, in fact, Will who was carrying me through the cemetery. I wrapped my arms around his neck and nuzzled into his shoulder, letting his warmth seep into my skin.

"Quinn, can you stand? I need to put you down for a moment."

I nodded, my legs jiggling with the impact of the ground. I heard a car door open, and then I was being guided onto a worn leather seat. A moment passed before the driver's side door opened, rain hitting me sideways before Will settled into the other seat. The door closed with a resonant thud as a brilliant streak of lightning lit up the sky.

Will took my hands and began massaging them as I stared into the sky, waiting for the inevitable boom of thunder.

"Talk to me," he said gently.

I pressed my lips together and squeezed a fresh round of tears from my eyes. Or maybe it was leftover rain. I struggled to find words. How could I dive into the black abyss of my mind to explain how my worst fear had materialized? My mouth opened and closed like a fish gasping for oxygen on the riverbank.

"Did I do something wrong?"

The somber tilt to his head and the pleading look in his eyes snapped me out of my mutism.

"No," I croaked and shook my head for emphasis.

"Okay." The skin around his eyes pinched together as he looked me over. "After last night, are you missing your mum?"

A strangled laugh came out of my mouth. I hadn't even thought of him. Of what we had done last night. Of what it meant. And the cemetery was the last place I would have gone to relive the details.

My mother had never been there for any of the pivotal events of my life. Not my period or my first kiss or my graduation. And I didn't know what to miss. It had always been my aunt who shared those glorious moments of coming of age. Except now—after last night—the world I knew had crumbled and I was left standing on the rubble. Alone.

Or maybe not alone? Will pulled my hands to his chest where I could feel the pounding of his heart, the fervor behind it. The life.

"I miss mine too," he said. "All the time."

"It's not that."

"Oh," he said. "Are you regretting..."

"No...no," I said, my voice gaining strength. "Not at all. Are you?"

"Absolutely not." A shadow of a smile ghosted his face, and I gave him one in return. He tightened his grip on my hands. "Tell me what's bothering you, love."

Love. The term of endearment undid me. And in that moment, I knew I could trust him with my secrets. My truth...and my lies.

"Remember when you asked me about my scar?" I said slowly.

"I do."

"I told you I got it from a cat, but I didn't."

One corner of Will's mouth stretched into a wry grin. "I figured not."

"You knew I was lying?"

"It was either that or the possibility that the cats here grow gargantuan-sized claws." He eyed me curiously.

"If you knew I was lying"—I paused to bite my lower lip—"why didn't you ask me about it again?"

"I knew you would tell me when you were ready."

The ice in my chest thawed under his soft eyes and the tenderness there. I took another breath and took my time exhaling. "My scar is from a piece of shattered glass." Will watched me expectantly, all the while massaging the circulation back into my hands. I blew out another shaky breath. "A piece of glass from the window of my mom's car."

Will's face became one continuous furrow from his brows to his mouth. "You were in the car accident with your mum?"

I nodded tightly. "We had gone to the town Christmas tree lighting. It happens every year on the day after Thanksgiving. With carols from a real choir. And a Nativity scene. With real animals. Very exciting for a small town."

I paused for a wry smile. "That year it started raining so my mom scooped me up and we ran for the car. I remember her laughing in my ear." I cleared my throat. "I had this doll, and on the way home, I remembered that I had left her sitting on a park bench next to the hot chocolate stand. I must have cried enough that my mom finally turned around to go back for her."

I swallowed past an expanding lump in my throat. "We never made it back to town. I remember the rain hitting the car like gunfire and I'm guessing the roads were slick and that's why we slid through the guardrail of the Old Town bridge. They found the car halfway down the embankment."

"How old were you?"

"Nearly six." My throat burned in protest, but I continued anyway. "I don't remember anything else from that night. Only bright lights and white floors and running down a hallway toward where I thought my mom was. But I don't even know if that memory is real. After that my mind is like a void. I don't remember getting stitches or my mom's funeral or Christmas that year. It's just...blank."

I paused to run my finger across eyelids that were plastered down by sticky tears and forgotten memories. "My aunt moved in with us that year, and after that, my childhood was pretty much perfect. My dad and Aunt Jackie made sure of that. But inside...in here"—I extracted my hand from Will's and pressed it to my chest—"I always knew something was off. No, not just off...wrong. I mean I couldn't actually deserve a perfect life...because if I could remember everything that happened, I would remember that I had caused the accident. Deep down I think I know I did."

My voice tremored with emotion. "And when you dropped me off last night, I heard them talking in the kitchen...and they were talking about me and the accident and how it changed everything...and how it was my fault."

One last tear expanded from a speck to a fat engorged droplet and rolled down my face, gathering speed by the time it reached my jaw then free fell into my lap, where it splattered into a million glistening pieces.

Will's mouth tightened into a thin line. "How could you ever think the accident was your fault?"

"If I hadn't been crying...or made her turn around...I distracted her...I—"

Will sandwiched my face between his palms. "You were a child."

"I know, but if it wasn't for me, my mom would be here. My dad wouldn't have to be alone. My aunt"—my voice cracked like an egg, delicate and raw—"my aunt could have gotten married...had her own children."

"They made those choices on their own."

"But..." My lip quivered under the gentle pressure of his thumb.

"The accident was not your fault."

"How do you know?"

"I know." He looked so certain, his mouth opening like he wanted to say more. I watched him inhale and exhale. Chest rise and fall. His hands dropped from my face into my lap.

"I think I love you," I whispered hoarsely.

His face morphed into shock, eyes widening until they were the pool I was diving into. Into their cool middle where I was weightless. Free.

"I know that, too," he rasped and assessed me before placing his lips on mine.

CHAPTER TWENTY-EIGHT

AUTUMN, NOW

The aimlessness of grief sent me toward Main Street. I veered around the curve into town and meandered around one block and then another one. Something urged me back to the main drag with its kitschy storefronts and restaurants advertising live music.

I parked on a side street and began walking with no destination in mind. An evening wind ruffled the ends of my hair, and I shoved my hands farther into my coat pockets. Burning energy took the edge off my grief. Every click of my boots on pavement tamped it down into something containable.

The desire to forget sent me inside the doors of Crossroads, which was ironic since that's basically what my life had come to. One gigantic fork in the road. When I slunk in through the creaking wooden door, the sight of an empty bar reeled me in like a gravitational force.

I slid my knees under the wood grain top stained with generations of water rings. I held up two fingers, a distress signal intended for the lone bartender who was mopping up a spill with a ratty towel. She slid her eyes to me, tossing the towel over her shoulder.

"What'll it be, darlin'?" Her accent was nearly as thick as the pressure in my chest.

Wasn't that the question of the decade? What would it be, indeed? Did I even know?

I hedged and asked, "Do you have a menu?"

Snorting like a cranky broodmare, she rolled up the sleeves of her denim shirt. I watched as she smacked two glasses on the bar and poured something into them from a dingy bottle with no label. She slid one in front of me, and after sniffing it, I took a swig. It burned like the good kind of fire.

"What's in here?" I wheezed.

"Somethin' that kills the pain," she said curtly.

I took another sip, and it burned just as much as the first one. "Fire whiskey?" I inquired, my voice taking on a smoky quality.

She shrugged, a smile playing on her thin lips. "Don't matter as long as it does the job."

I offered a wry smile, clinking her glass with mine before she threw the contents into her throat.

"To killing the pain," she said, wiping her mouth with the back of a freckled hand.

"There's not enough fire whiskey in this place to make a dent in mine."

"We'll see 'bout that." She closed one heavily shadowed eye in a wink.

Two drinks later, the pain wasn't altogether gone, but it had dulled to the sharpness of a butter knife. It twisted periodically in my side, but it didn't quite hurt anymore.

Eileen. That was the name of the bartender. Fifty-three, divorced with two sons who were both serving overseas in the military. Their names were tattooed on her forearms.

"Life couldn't be that bad when you got a rock like that on your finger," she said, folding her arms across her chest.

"About that..." I tugged on the ring that fiercely gripped the skin of my knuckle. "I'm not engaged anymore so I should probably take it off." I tugged again, grunting when my efforts yielded nothing but an abrasion. I muttered a few curses under my breath.

"What happened?"

I shrugged and splayed my hands across the sticky-film-coated bar. "Nothing really happened." *He just finally saw through me.*

"You still love him?"

"Not like I should." I paused over the raw honesty leaking out of my mouth like it was a dripping faucet. I had always been a loquacious drunk.

Eileen nodded sympathetically. "Only a few reasons why that could be."

I flicked my eyes up at her and really studied her face. Her sharp cheekbones and streak of purple through a mop of otherwise lifeless hair. The look of a veritable sage if I had to imagine what one looked like.

My brain started mumbling without my mouth opening. Because I'd only ever given my heart to one person. And that person had stomped all over it. Shredded it into ribbons so thoroughly that I was doomed to love no one ever again. I was pathetic.

Eileen slid another drink in front of me. This one was clear with tiny bubbles collecting across the surface. "But I think it's probably 'cause you don't love yourself like you should neither." She eyed me critically before gliding down the bar to attend to a group of twenty-somethings all dressed in different shades of pink, one of them in a sparkly dime store crown.

I pondered over what she had said. Some food for thought to go with my beverage—something that looked deceptively like water and tasted everything like tequila.

A guitarist began strumming in the background. My blood hummed and the room swayed with his rhythm. With every riff, more people crowded into the bar. Couples dressed in denim and boots, laughing and smelling of Friday night's cologne. I was grateful for the way they took up the space in the room and in my head.

The music started. Twangy and upbeat. A few couples slipped out to the dance floor, and I watched their easy rhythms, a gnawing wonderment and jealousy blooming inside me. I didn't have many clear memories of my mom, but I knew she had loved to dance.

I remembered a kitchen floor bathed in sunlight and a lady spinning in the middle of it, the hem of her flowered sundress taking flight. Maybe she had picked me up and twirled me along with her to the fading notes of a George Strait song like we were both as light as air. At least that was what I thought she would have done.

Gavin and I had danced a grand total of once during the three years we had been together. At the upscale wedding of one of his college friends. He had gripped me with clammy palms, awkwardly shuffling his feet as we struggled to find a common rhythm.

I threw back the rest of my drink. I guess I should have known then how much I was lying to myself about seeing him as my future.

My eyes grazed the room, following the outlines of cowboy hats and puffed-up hair. The girl with the crown was touching the base of her neck as she giggled next to a tousled dark head.

I wondered if he would be taking her home later tonight for the mindless, blameless sex people had when life was uncomplicated. It didn't sound like such an awful idea. As long as she didn't fall in love with him, she could be a princess who never needed rescuing.

The man turned toward the bar as she tilted up her chin and laid a hand on his bicep. I watched, mesmerized by the wordless gestures. Though his face was hidden in shadow, I could tell by his profile that he was cute at the very least.

He was tall with just the right amount of lean muscle and deftly placed angles. He leaned closer to her, the light dancing over his full lips pulled back in a polite smile. Dime store cowgirl's posture sagged a notch as he looked right over her crown and directly at me.

I jerked my head the other direction and gulped the last dredges of my drink. Maybe he wouldn't walk over here. Would I be disappointed if he didn't? No, I wouldn't, I told myself. He was probably here with his leggy publicist cele- brating his dominance of the literary universe.

"Quinn?"

God, I hated that I loved how he said my name. My chest cracked open like an egg, all the messy runny emotions drip- ping down my face before I could turn around. I summoned as much sarcasm as I had left.

"Will," I said, forcing a brow up into an arch. "Fancy seeing you here."

"Well, it is *my* bar," he said, crystal blue eyes glinting in the suffused light.

I drew back in surprise. When had he...? It didn't matter and I didn't care. "Of course it is," I said petulantly, shaking the ice in my drink, then holding it up to request a refill. It was only then that I noticed the shelves upon shelves of Deremer wine staring back at me from behind the bar.

Will plucked my glass out of my hand and motioned over my head. Eileen appeared in front of us in less than a second, her face pliant with professionalism. Her hand moved to the towel over her shoulder and swiped the area in front of me clean. "What can I get for you, darlin'?"

"Refill," I mumbled, the word buzzing over my lips.

"How about water?" Will countered.

"The one with the tequila," I added as Eileen's eyes bounced back and forth between the two of us. And damn it if her last look didn't stop on Will.

"You're drunk," he said, and I couldn't tell if it was a statement or a question.

"And you"—I gave him my widest smile and poked him in the chest with my index finger— "are not drunk enough."

"Give her a break, boss," Eileen said. "She's had a shitty day."

Will looked right over my head at Eileen. "Really? Why is that?"

"I'm sitting right here." I glared at the two of them. "And it's none of your business." I was past caring that I sounded like a complete child.

Still ignoring me, Eileen spoke in a raspy stage whisper. "She got dumped."

"Dumped?" Will's quizzical expression struck a chord of humor inside me, and I smothered a giggle. "What?" he asked, he and Eileen regarding me as if I were an object of curiosity. And not the good kind.

I snorted. "I'm surprised a word as simple as *dumped* is in your vocabulary. You're more of a..."—I tapped the bar with my forefinger for emphasis—"forsaken, jilted, shunned, cast aside type of guy."

"I assure you I know what dumped means," he said dryly, and I swore hurt flashed through his eyes. He smoothed his face, his gaze catching on my ring. "He didn't want the ring back?"

My cheeks flooded with heat as Eileen answered for me. "She can't get it to come off," she cackled. "Which is why she deserves one more before I cut 'er off." A fresh glass with a lime floating in the effervescence appeared in front me.

"Thank you so much," I said with the hint of a slur.

I inhaled the vapors when I brought it to my mouth, closing my eyes and preparing for the burn that had become gentle and welcome over the last hour. Right before I put it to my lips, the glass was smoothly removed from my hand. My eyes flashed to Will as he threw his head back, throat bobbing as he drank deeply until ice clacked against his teeth.

"What the hell, Jacob William Deremer?" I focused every drop of residual emotion into a single glare.

Eileen startled and glanced between us, smoky eyelids raised in a multitude of questions. In my languid stupor, I thought I could read her thoughts. *She knows him? He knows her? How? And how well?*

Wouldn't you like to know, I snarked in my head.

"I needed that," he mumbled to no one in particular, and for the first time, I noticed a fraying edge to his ever-present smoothness, a slight tremor in his fingers as he placed the glass back on the bar, a shifting of his gaze as he looked for something the rest of us couldn't see.

Eileen's eyes nearly bugged out of her head as she swiped up the glass and put it under the bar.

"I needed it more," I grumbled.

"I'll make it up to you," he said, his face once again smooth, a smile cresting his lips. He held out a hand. A mellow acoustic piece started up in the background.

"How exactly?" My heart rate spiked as what he was offering became absolutely clear.

"A dance followed by a ride home."

I bit my lip as I searched for an ounce of resistance or anger or sarcasm. Something that would keep me from making another monumental life mistake. I couldn't find anything. My insides had heated then cooled until I was out of reasons to say no. I took his hand and let myself be led onto the dance floor.

The music was languid, slow, ethereal for a country song. Or maybe this was only what it sounded like after downing a few drinks. Most of the couples had peeled off to sit at the tables, which left us nearly alone.

Every guitar strum reverberated through my chest as we stepped together. I wobbled as I moved, shaky and clumsy as a newborn horse. Until halfway through the song when Will's hand drifted to my lower back and anchored me. I began to step with confidence. With grace. With easy rhythm.

In my peripheral vision, I noticed him studying my face. I refused to meet his eyes, instead focusing on snippets of his body here and there. *Thirteen years.* It wasn't fair that he had filled out in the most attractive way. The angles of his face had sharpened. His awkward parts had disappeared. My shy, beautiful boy had become a devastatingly handsome man. Not mine, I reminded myself. Never mine.

He twirled me around, the world in slow motion and me with it. My palm landed on his chest, steadied by the beat of his pounding heart. It matched my own. I made myself look at him, to study him studying me.

I wondered a million things in the final few chords of the song. Did he ever think of me? Did he feel guilty for promising me the world then leaving me? When he looked at me, what did he think now? I didn't know. And I wasn't about to conjure answers to questions that still haunted me.

"Thanks for the dance," I said, pulling my hands away to wipe them down my jeans. "I think I'm going to head home."

"Last time I checked the bustling metropolis of Linzberg didn't have a taxi service."

"It's not that far of a walk."

He crooked an arm and flashed a grin. "Then a walk it is."

I reared back. "I didn't mean you had to go with me."

"I'm not letting you go alone." He grinned wider, a

shallow dimple appearing in his left cheek. Suddenly he looked eighteen again. "I'd never forgive myself if some creature carried you off into the night."

I sighed and rolled my eyes, resigning myself to another hour of torture as we stepped outside into the night. A luminescent glow of a half-moon greeted us as soon as we crossed the bridge off the main road. With the town at our backs, the moon dominated an abyss of black. A perfect half circle cleaved down the middle, just like my heart.

"Which one is this?" Will asked, pointing skyward.

"Which one is what?" I squinted up where he was pointing.

"That constellation," he said softly.

I followed the outline of neatly visible stars, little punctuated dots that began to blur the longer I stared at them. "I don't remember."

"I doubt that," he scoffed. "I recall you knowing every single one of them."

"I used to know a lot of things that I don't know anymore." I quickened my pace so that I was a few strides ahead of him, the cool air slicing into the dull ache behind my eyes. Will's feet crunched under the roadside gravel behind me. It was easier to talk if I didn't have to see his face.

A tension stretched between us, tighter and tighter as I lengthened the distance between us. If I walked fast enough or far enough, it would snap. This thing between us. This ridiculous thing that had transcended time and distance and change. It would snap and I would be free.

"I'm sorry, Quinn."

I froze mid-step and turned around. Will was standing in the road, arms at his sides, silhouetted by starlight. A perfect inverse image of the first time I had seen him, a glaring sun above us on a country backroad. And at that moment, I didn't feel anything but resigned and exhausted.

As much as I had tried to run away, unbeknownst to me, I had been running in a circle instead of a straight line, because the cruelty of the universe had led me right back where I started. My nose tingled with the crispness of the night air. Or maybe it was the smell of regret and sweet relief.

"Are you okay?" he asked in a low voice.

I puffed out a breath, watching the heat form a cloud in front of my lips. "Surprisingly...yes."

"What happened?" he asked, running a hand through his hair.

The same question Eileen had asked me earlier.

"He finally saw me for who I was." This time I said the words out loud.

He paused a beat before asking, "And who are you?"

"Someone who doesn't know what she wants."

"Someone who doesn't know what she wants...or simply doesn't have it?"

I laughed nervously. "Why do you always ask the best questions at the worst time?"

"It's a gift."

He smiled. I smiled. And then a look crossed his face that I knew was mirrored on mine. The tequila had made me bold...or reckless. I didn't care which. But it was giving me perceptions that weren't there. Or maybe they were.

Maybe since everything in my life was changing, this could change too. Maybe I didn't have to carry a decade's worth of anger and resentment. Maybe if I was forgiving myself, I could forgive Will too.

"What about you?" I asked. "Do you have everything you want?"

He stared at me with unrelenting focus. "No."

There was so much meaning behind that monosyllabic response that it took everything I had to make my voice as light and airy as possible. "Yeah, because having a *New York Times* bestseller is a real bitch."

He barked a laugh. "I'll rephrase. I have most of what I want."

I wanted to ask more. What did he have that he wanted? What else could he want that he didn't have? But I didn't. Liquid courage only went so far, and I wasn't sure I wanted to know that he might be secretly in love with his publicist.

I turned to start back down the road, tripping over a rock in my haste. Will caught me by the arm. I hadn't even realized that he had moved closer over the last few minutes. The heat from his palm traveled all the way to my toes.

"Thanks," I whispered, my words caught by a sudden chilly gust of wind.

I pulled away before I could lean into his touch and began walking faster, head bent into the wind. We didn't talk again, our feet taking on a predictable, soothing rhythm.

By the time I recognized the dark outline of my house, my nose and fingertips had taken on a painful chill. I halted at the end of the driveway. "This is my house," I announced hoarsely.

"I know." The breath of his exhale filled the shell of my ear. I stiffened, fighting the urge to lean back the slimmest inch into the center of his chest.

The ground wavered beneath my feet, a reminder that I was still intoxicated and therefore couldn't be held responsible for my own actions. I needed a blameless, careless moment. Just one.

I turned around and lifted my chin until I met Will's eyes. In the dark, they were wide and black. Fathomless and endlessly curious. I exhaled. He inhaled.

"You," he murmured, "smell like a distillery."

I was expecting him to say something else. Something

poetic. Something epic and Will-like. I tittered to hide my disappointment.

"Seriously, I think I'm becoming intoxicated just from breathing your air."

I laughed harder, clutching my stomach.

"I hope no one lights a match in our vicinity."

And I laughed even harder until I was crying, messy emotions erupting from my throat and my eyes. I let them go.

"I fucking hate you," I said, lifting my head to a watery, shadowy version of Will trying to hold in his own laughter.

Because I was walking the tightrope of insanity, I flipped him off with my fourth finger, the one still wearing a useless hunk of rock.

With a sad smile he took my gesturing hand in both of his and stepped close enough that I could sense the heat and want rippling off him. "I know you do," he said then dipped his head to my fourth finger.

I froze, the entirety of my sensory input narrowed to where Will's lips now pressed to the pad of my finger. When a tingling sensation started at the base of my spine and zipped up my back, I welcomed it. His mouth parted and the wet heat of his tongue slid farther down my finger.

Blood rushed to places it shouldn't have as a part of me that had been lying dormant suddenly awoke. A part of me that I had buried and left to die. How had I ever expected to live a happy life knowing that I could never recreate what I had felt with him?

And here I was, despite everything he had done and everything he hadn't done, betrayed by the teenager inside me who wanted me to remember how it felt to be alive and in love with someone.

His teeth followed his tongue until my entire finger, ring and all, was inside his mouth. With a few short sucks, the ring popped over my knuckle, and I nearly collapsed from lack of blood flow to my brain.

My knees shook as he slowly, gently withdrew my empty finger from his mouth then turned over my palm. He plucked the ring from his lips and placed it in my hand.

"There you go."

I closed my fingers into a fist until the metal cut into my skin. There I went, indeed.

"Good night, Quinn," he said, before cutting a path through the moonlight back toward town, hands stuffed neatly in his pockets.

CHAPTER TWENTY-NINE

AUTUMN, NOW

I awoke to a pounding on my bedroom door that matched the pounding in my head. I tried to raise it from my pillow without success. A mournful groan escaped my lips.

"Why?" My voice was as gravelly as the driveway, my head splitting with the axe of my poor decisions from the night before. Little snippets of memory began floating to the surface as I scrunched my eyes closed against the sunlight streaming through the window.

Eileen and her heavy eye makeup and throaty laughter. The smell of limes and tequila. And Will. I rubbed the pad of my thumb over my bare fourth finger, which still tingled from the feel of his lips. I heard a creak as my door was pushed open.

"The phone's been ringing off the hook all mornin', Quinn."

I pried open one of my eyelids with my fingers and Aunt Jackie's hazy figure materialized through a layer of grime. "What for?"

"Third Saturday, kiddo."

"And?" Somewhere in the dregs of my memory that meant something.

My quilt was being tugged off my body. The body that I had not even bothered to undress prior to collapsing into bed last night.

"Free spay day at the clinic. Sonia called to let you know the waiting room is filling up." I twisted my neck to look at her. "Come on," she encouraged, patting my calf. I'll drop you off on my way to the store."

Once she headed downstairs, I made myself roll out of bed. My legs quivered like jelly when they were required to bear my full weight. The glint of sunlight on metal caught my eye and I picked up the ring on the nightstand, feeling no emotion whatsoever as I opened the drawer and tucked it inside amongst a pile of scarves and mismatched socks.

So many things were changing, forcing me out of the stagnancy of my adulthood. I wiggled my fingers in the motes of dust swirling through a sunbeam. I was out of the chrysalis and just beginning to test my wings.

The clinic buzzed with a yowling so chaotic and impatient that I cringed behind my sunglasses. The waiting room was a sea of claws and tails and teeth from pampered pets to strays to everything in between. I pushed my shoulders back and waded toward the hallway door. This day was going to suck.

Sonia shouted at me through the din, hand cupped around her mouth. "Where have you been, *mi hija?*" In her other hand, she had a carrier that rocked back and forth with the momentum of a frantic feline.

I didn't answer, my throat still coated with dust, and instead, stumbled past her, motioning her to follow. With every step, the floor sent a painful jolt all the way to the back of my head. I pushed open the swinging door to the sterile clinic hallway, the same door showcasing a massive poster board that read "spay day" in bright pink glitter. Sonia's work for sure.

Every third Saturday of the month for as long as I could remember, my dad's clinic opened its doors for any pet that required divestment of his or her reproductive organs. It was our service to the community, he said—to prevent unwanted litters of kittens or pups that would then either become feral, barely surviving, or be rounded up and sent to the county shelter where they had little hope of being adopted before they were euthanized.

As soon as I could see over the surgical table, he had let me scrub in to hand him shiny instruments and eventually taught me how to close the skin at the end of the procedure. I had performed so many spay operations that I could do them with my eyes closed. Which might be necessary today if my head didn't stop pounding.

While I prepped over the sink, Sonia anesthetized cat number one, who scrabbled and hissed in protest. I counted to ten in my head until his meows subsided into blissful quiet.

The overhead lights pieced my skull as I picked up the scalpel and made a neat incision into a soft, velvety scrotum. Ignoring Sonia's pinched expression, I settled into the familiar rhythm of cut, stitch. Cut, stitch.

We were on our third cat before Sonia spoke again.

"You smell like last night's tequila, *mi hija.*"

I snorted under my mask. "How could you possibly know? I'm wearing a surgical mask."

"It's coming out of your pores," she said primly, her accent thickening. "What happened? Your *papi?*"

"No, Dad's great. We're actually picking him up tomorrow from rehab."

"Your *mami?*"

I froze mid-incision. I hadn't realized she knew, or cared,

that yesterday was the anniversary of my mom's accident. "Oh. No. It's not my mom," I stuttered as a sharpness twisted through me. "I did visit her grave though." I finished sewing, clipped my last stitch and gave the cat a pat it wouldn't feel.

"Then what?"

I sighed and pulled the strings of my mask. Sonia was nosier than usual today. "Gavin and I broke up."

"I see." She dipped her chin solemnly, eyes boring into me above the etched glass of her bifocals. She didn't look the least bit surprised.

"What?" Another wave of guilt crested even though I couldn't tell anymore what it was from.

"Did you break up before or after leaving Crossroads with the *guapo* author?"

My hands gripped the steel of the surgical table. "How did you know that? Never mind." I flapped my fingers in her direction. "I don't know why it still shocks me when everyone knows everything in this town."

"We need things to talk about, *mi hija*. It gets boring around here. Don't worry, Eileen—" Sonia started.

"How do know Eileen?" I pictured the bartender with the gravelly voice and thick eyeliner.

"She's in my cancer survivor support group."

My eyebrows rose as she continued in a loud whisper, "Ovarian cancer." Her face remained serious for a split second before her lips curved up suggestively. "So, *mi hija*?"

"So?"

"What happened last night?"

"He walked me home."

"And?" She fluttered her eyelashes, gyrating her hips to a beat only she could hear.

I ground my molars together. "Nothing...happened. Nothing will ever happen."

"Never say never, *mi hija*."

I cringed, trying my best to look utterly disgusted when inside, I was anything but. My ring finger tingled with the memory of Will's lips like the traitor it was. Something like last night could never happen again. *Never again* would become my mantra. I would tattoo it on my ass if I had to.

"By the way, I need to know what size sweater to get you."

"What on earth for?" My face pinched in exasperation, reminding me that I still indeed had a hangover.

"For the Christmas parade, *mi hija.*"

I continued to stare at her in absolute bewilderment.

Sonia sighed dramatically. "The clinic makes its own float. Your dad wears a Santa outfit, and we dress Mildred as a reindeer."

How had I missed this the last few years? My dad dressed in a red velvet suit, his mostly bald head gleaming in the glare from a multi-colored strand of lights? Mildred the goat in antlers?

"My dad's out of commission, so what kind of float are you making this year?" I was almost too afraid to ask.

"We rented a snow machine." She grinned broadly. "And we're all wearing matching outfits."

Oh, brother. Sonia blinked at me expectantly, her hands clasped tightly at her waist. My resolve crumbled. My week had been filled with bad decisions. Why not add one more?

"Count me in," I groaned, already regretting the words I had just spoken.

As soon as I shucked my clothes off that night, preparing for the world's longest shower, or at least as long as the hot water lasted, my phone rang. I tensed as I flipped it over.

"Hey, Sid," I said, my voice thick with relief.

"Hold on," she whispered. I heard mumbling in the background, followed by the clicking of heels and the snicking shut of a heavy door.

"Are you pretending that *I* was the one who called *you?*" I chuckled to myself.

"Possibly. But my friend radar is going off and I wanted to check on you." Her tone had taken on a warm, maternal quality. "Are you okay?"

"I'm covered in cat fur and nothing else." I barked a laugh, catching the wild look on my face in the bathroom mirror. The flushed cheeks and frizz in my hair. The flash in my gray eyes. "Why wouldn't I be okay?"

"Gavin called me earlier."

Of course he had. Of course my ex-fiancée was that thoughtful. He probably thought he had left an emotionally wrecked shell in the wake of his epiphany. Except that our breakup hadn't shaken me the way I'd thought it would. I frowned at myself in the mirror, wondering if I should feel worse about the decimation of our relationship than I did.

"I'm fine," I said unconvincingly as I stared at myself in the bathroom mirror. I heard the rise and fall of voices in the background. "If you need to get back to whatever you're doing—"

"Girl, please. I'm at an open mic poetry night with Stacey and I'm two onomatopoeias away from gouging my eyes out."

I giggled, but the sound resembled more of a smoker's hacking.

"What happened to you?" Sid asked, a note of alarm in her voice.

My head hurt just thinking about last night. "I spayed about a thousand cats today...after I drank enough tequila last night to drown a horse. And I saw Will. Again. And I told him about Gavin and me breaking up. And I read his book, Sid, before I went to New York. And I think...I think the book is why..." I paused to scrunch my eyes closed so that my mirror self would stop judging me.

"Why you broke up Gavin?"

"No," I sighed. "Actually, he broke up with me."

"Wow. I didn't know he had it in him."

"Sid!"

"Sorry. I just assumed this all had something to do with Will." I pictured her rubbing her thumb and index finger together. A habit I had observed about a million times while we studied together in college. "So, what happened?"

"I don't know. No, I do know." I gave myself a hard stare in the mirror. "I think Gavin finally realized how much more he could give...and that I wasn't the right person to be on the receiving end."

"Oh, honey. I'm sorry."

I released a pent-up groan. "Don't be." I took the hem of my shirt and began wiping the fog from the bathroom mirror only for it to reappear moments later. "It was bound to happen. One way or the other."

"Can I be honest?"

"It's what you do best." I gave the phone a wry smile.

"I never saw you and Gavin ending happily."

"Why not?"

"Because I've seen you in love and you weren't...in love with Gavin."

"When have you ever seen me in love?" My voice trilled an octave higher than normal, and blood rushed to my cheeks.

"In college."

"Don't say it, Sid," I pleaded.

"I'm going to say it and you're going to listen." She paused for a breath, and I could picture her flipping back her short braids. "You were in love with Will."

Hearing his name out loud resonated a forgotten frequency inside of me.

"And I think"—Sid paused to suck on her teeth—"that he never got over you."

"Why would you think that?" I asked.

"Quinn," she replied in her school principal voice. The voice she reserved for ninth graders who repeatedly forgot their homework. "He dedicated the book to you."

"No, he didn't." I shook my head for emphasis despite the fact no one could see me.

"The title page clearly says 'to my something more.' That's what he used to call you, right?"

"Yeah, but that could be anyone now."

"No, it's not and you know it."

I let the unwanted thought sink in and anchor itself inside my chest. "So, what if he did? It was likely motivated by a decade of guilt." The words rushed out before I realized what I had said.

On the other end of the line, Sid sucked in a breath. "Guilt for what exactly?"

"For—" I halted mid-sentence. I had never told anyone what had happened between us. Out of shame? Embarrassment?

No. I knew it was because deep down, after the shock had worn off, I believed I had deserved to lose him. The universe had finally punished me for what I had done to my family...to my mom. I had accepted it and moved on.

"I thought you said things with you guys just fizzled out," Sid remarked. "That you decided to go to Penn for the internship and he left for summer semester at Berkeley."

"Not...exactly." My chest tightened. I was glad I could no longer see my face in the vanity mirror that had accumulated a sheen of condensation.

"What actually happened?" Sid pressed.

I told her everything. About my mom's accident. About

going to the swimming hole with Will that night. About the conversation I had overheard in the kitchen afterward between my dad and my aunt. About my entire world crumbling beneath my feet and about Will, who had kept me from spiraling.

"What did he say when you told him you loved him?" Sid asked gently. I hadn't even realized I had stopped talking.

"He said..." My voice cracked as I heard those words again in my head. "He said 'I know that too.'"

"He certainly has a way with words," Sid snarked then clucked her tongue. "What happened after that?"

"He dropped me off at home and that was the last time I saw him." I bit down on a papery lip. "Not until a month ago at least."

"Wait...what?"

I wrapped an arm around my middle as memories flooded me.

Those next few days after Will had found me in the rain next to my mother's grave had been torture. My chest had felt like it was splintering apart every time I tried to get out of bed.

And when I'd come down with a fever and bronchitis, I had blamed exhaustion from my last semester at school and used it as an excuse to remain in my room.

Will had called every evening, and we had talked late into the night until the pauses between our words filled up with even breathing as we both drifted off to sleep. I could remember every single word of our last conversation.

"Do you think you'll be well enough for an outing on Saturday night?" His voice had sounded muffled through the plastic rotary phone I kept on my nightstand.

"Depends on if by 'outing,' you mean I get to see you naked."

Will had barked a laugh, his mattress protesting as he

turned over. "I was going to take you somewhere special to see the Strawberry Moon."

"You remembered the name!"

"Of course I did. It's your favorite."

"You're my favorite." I had yawned into the receiver.

"And you're mine." A quiet settled between us. A quiet so comfortable that I began to drift off to sleep. "Quinn," Will had whispered through the phone.

"Mmm," I had mumbled.

"I need to tell you something."

"Okay," I had replied sleepily then waited, hanging on to the fringes of consciousness as I had listened to Will breathe.

Finally, he had said, "I'll see you on Saturday."

"Tell me what happened next, Quinn." Sid's insistence brought me out of my own head.

"After that day in the car," I began shakily, "we made plans to see each other that weekend."

When the night of the Strawberry Moon had come, I had skipped our traditional Saturday dinner at the Bluebird Café. I couldn't bear the thought of sitting across from my dad and Jackie through an entire meal after what I had heard in the kitchen. When they'd left, I had gone outside to the porch to wait for Will.

"He was supposed to pick me up that night and, when he didn't, I assumed something had come up, and he was running late. I kept waiting and he just never showed up."

Sid made an audible gasp, and my stomach twinged in response. "And he just ditched you?"

"I wasn't sure at first," I answered, my brow furrowing with the memory. "I thought maybe he had been held up with something at the vineyard. But then my dad got home from dinner and mentioned how he had stayed late at the clinic that afternoon to board Mrs. Deremer's terrier for her trip to Italy."

"Okay...then what?" Sid prompted.

My voice starting to shake. "My dad told me the Dere-mers would be gone all summer. That they were taking Will to Italy for one last trip before college started in the fall."

I swallowed hard as I relived the devastation of hearing those words and not believing them. Of enduring a sleepless night, of waiting until the first light of dawn to drive over to the Deremers' estate only to find the house empty. Of real-izing that Will was gone.

"There has to be some explanation," Sid offered.

"Trust me," I clipped, "I spent my entire twenties consid-ering the possibilities, and there is only one conclusion—Will was nothing more than a teenage fling that ended in disap-pointment."

"I don't believe that. He wrote that book for you, Quinn."

"Even still..." I blinked against the prick of tears. "He left me, Sid. Without a word. Without an explanation. And I never saw him again. Not until a month ago. You don't do that to people you...love." The word tasted foreign on my tongue.

"Maybe later on he realized he made a mistake."

"I doubt it." But as I said it, my mirror self passed judg-ment with her eyes.

The last few weeks he had seemed kind and genuine. Exactly like the Will I had known. Not the kind of selfish asshat that let a girl fall in love with him then disappeared into the Italian countryside.

"Maybe he deserves a second chance," Sid murmured.

"Why are you suddenly team Will?"

"Because I can't imagine someone who writes that passionately—that beautifully—could break your heart like that."

"Sometimes people aren't what they seem, and I'm obvi-ously a terrible judge of character."

"Quinn," Sid hesitated before continuing, "When we were in college, you never told me about the accident...about your mom...about what your family said about you."

I knew I was crying again, and I hated myself for it. I wiped my eyes angrily. "I've never told anyone. Anyone besides Will."

The emotions had become too real again. All my layers exfoliated deeper and deeper until I could remember exactly how I had felt packing up my bags to move to Philadelphia for my summer internship. Confused and betrayed. Wondering if everyone who had ever said they loved me was lying. Suffocating in a guilt that I believed I deserved.

When I'd stepped off the plane, instantly overwhelmed by relief, I had known it was within my power to be someone else. Someone who hadn't caused the unhappiness of everyone she had ever cared about. I had vowed to create a new life and bury the past. And for years I had told myself that I was there. I had done it. And I had never been more wrong.

"Did you ever try to talk to your family about it?" Sid asked.

"No, and I doubt I ever will." I released a breath. "Some things are better left unsaid." I thought of the fragile bond reforged between Aunt Jackie and me these last few weeks. It wasn't what it once had been...but it was something worth holding on to. I wouldn't jeopardize it by dredging up the past.

"Did you ever try to get in touch with him?"

"Who? Will?"

"No, Taylor Lautner," she said sarcastically. "Yes, of course, Will."

God, I had thought about it so many times. Especially before I had met Gavin and my career had taken off. Back when I was a struggling vet student who spent her weekends half tucked into a pizza and a bottle of wine. But what would I have written? *Hi, Will, it's Quinn McClain, the girl who fell madly in love with you right before you dumped her without a word.*

"No," I answered emphatically. "I never did. I know I'm hard on myself, Sid, but I'm not a complete masochist."

"Jury's still out on that one, Q," she said half-jokingly. "Didn't you ever want to find out why?"

"Why he left?"

"Yes."

"Only every day of my entire life since then."

And it was true. I had lain in bed at night staring at any sliver of the moon I could see through my bedroom window. Wondering. Dissecting every conversation. Every touch. Everything he had said. Everything he hadn't. Until I wasn't sure if the why even mattered.

Regardless, Will had left. He could have chosen me, and he hadn't. Nothing says *I don't actually want you* like jetting off to Italy for the summer.

"Why don't you ask him?"

I cut my eyes to the phone. "That's...that would be..." I struggled to find words.

"Too sensical?"

"Pointless," I said.

"I disagree," Sid countered. "What could it hurt?"

As much as I hated to admit it, she had a point. I was already laid bare and stripped down to emotional nudity. What could possibly hurt me at this point?

"Okay," I sighed. "Maybe I will."

CHAPTER THIRTY

WINTER, NOW

B ringing my dad home from the hospital was much less climactic than I had hoped. Not nearly intense enough to distract me from thinking of Will.

Jackie and I picked him up on a cold, gray Sunday afternoon, filling her trunk to the brim with flowers and balloons and an entire basket of homemade jam from one of the female physical therapists.

Dad said it was because of his work ethic, but I imagined it had more to do with his irresistible charm.

When I hooked my arm around his waist to transition him into the backseat, his form was noticeably less solid than what I remembered. I buckled his seatbelt, leaning over to hug his shoulders tightly before climbing into the front seat.

His skin was wrong against my cheek, too dry and papery and missing the signature spice from his aftershave. The only familiar thing about him was his eyes, the same color as the gray sky above our heads.

On the hour-long drive to Linzberg, he talked nonstop, his voice full but raspy as he described the people he had met over the last few weeks. More than once, I found myself bracing my midsection with my forearm to stifle the laughter.

He always had been the best storyteller. I had nearly forgotten that about him. Aunt Jackie nursed a silent smile as we bantered back and forth, not interrupting until we eased to a stop at the fringe of town.

"Anybody hungry?" she asked with an arched brow.

My stomach rumbled under my hand as my dad erupted with a "hell yes."

He clapped a hand on my shoulder from the backseat. "The hospital food was like eating stuff that had gone through the dishwasher first."

"That's disgusting." I wrinkled my nose and caught his eye over my shoulder. "What are you in the mood for?"

"I'll give you three guesses." He smiled mischievously.

It only took me one. As we pulled up to the squat orange and brown building, the smell of grease and freshly baked buns filled the the car.

My dad rolled the window down and belted into the loudspeaker. "Two number ones with cheese and a side of fries." I cleared my throat. "Make that two sides of fries," he said before tapping me on the shoulder. "Hey Quinnie, if Mr. and Mrs. Cheeseburger had a daughter, what would they name her?"

I rolled my eyes and groaned.

"Patty," Aunt Jackie offered from the driver's seat, as she eased the car to the pickup window.

I watched her fight a smile as my dad howled from the backseat. Once she handed him a brown paper bag splotched with grease, the sound of paper being discarded joined his chuckling as he tucked into the burger.

Something bloomed inside my chest at the sound of their laughter. Something hopeful and fragile. Something that remembered how good it felt to be loved by them...and how much I had missed it.

I hadn't thought things could ever be the same after that night in the kitchen. But maybe I was wrong about that too.

Once we arrived home, my dad had enough energy to use his crutches to reach the sofa, where he promptly settled into a horizontal position and began snoring. The rain picked up outside, a proper winter rain that made the sky a canvas of gray tones, the bare tree branches glistening with the promise of ice. I had been prepared to entertain my dad the entire day or, at the very least, fetch beverages and fluff cushions.

Instead, I stood awkwardly in the living room, arms folded in stagnant inertia. Aunt Jackie bustled off and I heard the dryer door closing and the familiar rumble as it started a cycle. My gaze flicked around the room, from the neat stack of wood next to the fireplace to the quilt thrown over a leather armchair. I reached for it, tugging it free and then tucking it over my dad's legs—the normal one and the one encased in an immobilization device.

I settled into the leather chair next to him, curling my legs underneath me. I watched his chest rise and fall. Up and down with beautiful regularity. A pressurized tension at the base of my shoulders that had been there since receiving the phone call about his accident suddenly began to unravel.

I took a deep breath. My first easy one in quite a while. I let my lids close, my head loll, and surrounded by the sound of rain pinging our roof, I slept without dreaming.

THE DAY of the annual Linzberg Christmas parade dawned the perfect combination of bright blue sky and bitter cold. So cold my finger bones ached when I dug them into the steering wheel of my dad's car. The black vintage Camaro that had left me stranded in the road a month ago had magically appeared in our driveway last week, along with a hefty mechanic bill.

The engine purred like a sleepy kitten as I guided it around the gentle curve into town where the storefronts had exploded with glittery decor overnight. Strands of white lights stretched between the lampposts like blinking neural networks. Doorways were outlined in brightly colored tinsel. The coffee shop had a gigantic inflatable Santa on its roof, complete with a team of reindeer.

Sonia had outdone herself with the clinic. A pair of giant wooden candy canes greeted me when I turned into the parking lot, along with a smattering of oversized ornaments hanging from any available tree limb.

The bite in the air teased my skin, as I meandered up the walkway, the sky a blushing pink behind me. I embraced the sweet silence of the morning punctuated only by the bellows of Mildred the goat from her pen.

I was simultaneously calm and invigorated. Deeply settled yet acutely aware. Caught in a moment where the present juxtaposes the past. And the bright tenor of my soul resonated with being where I belonged.

Maybe it was because I was starting to forgive myself. Maybe it was the sweet familiarity of being home again, my dad commenting from his favorite chair and my aunt bustling around the kitchen.

Maybe the universe was on the cusp of offering me a second chance at the life I'd thought I would have. And maybe all the loose ends of my past were tying themselves into neat knots.

When I saw Will again, which I inevitably would, I would finally get answers to the questions taking up space in my head. I needed them gone so I could make room for something else. Maybe for someone else. One day. A brilliant star blinked at me from where it hung inside the clinic door as I pushed it open.

A few hours later, my epiphany safely tucked away, I crouched on the floor of an exam room and clucked my tongue at the Jack Russell terrier trying his best to wriggle free.

"Not so fast," I scolded, kneading and palpating the undersurface of his paw until I exposed the edge of a cactus spike.

When I grasped it between my forceps, he reached around and sank his teeth into the back of my hand, leaving behind two beads of fresh blood. I jerked back as he leaped away, his legs scrabbling for purchase on the tile.

"Damn it," I cursed under my breath. Where was Sonia? Or Kody? I wrapped my bleeding hand in a surgical towel. "I could use a little help in here," I shouted through the cracked door. A full two minutes passed before Sonia poked her head inside, her hair freshly highlighted a warm ginger color.

"What do you need, *mi hija?*"

I held up my bloody hand and used the other one to gesture toward the brown and white trembling mass of fur in the corner.

"What I need is for you to do your job." Although my words sounded harsh, I couldn't keep a stupid grin from spreading when I noticed her outfit. A candy red T-shirt embroidered with the outline of a reindeer with the word "vixen" spelled out in rhinestones.

Sonia pursed the lips that matched her shirt and put her hands on her hips. "Finishing the parade float is my job. It's tradition."

I rolled my eyes. "You're lucky this one's up to date with his shots." I turned the water on in the sink and began rinsing off the back of my hand. "I prefer hooves to sharp teeth," I grumbled as my blood turned the water into rosé.

"I keep forgetting you have to go back to your real job, *mi hija*," Sonia sighed, reaching toward the cowering terrier with gentle hands.

"Yeah," I said thoughtfully, reaching for a stack of paper towels, "so do I."

"All the more reason you need to be at the parade tonight."

I audibly groaned. Wearing glittery garland while I froze my ass off on top of a parade float was not on my top ten list. "I don't know."

"Come on, *mi hija*. You promised me." Sonia blinked at me through her false lashes, her eyes as brown and steadfast as the dirt I was raised on.

My already flimsy resolve crumbled like it was made of gingerbread. Being in Linzberg had been forced upon me by necessity, but now that I was here, the experience had been more like a warm embrace than a punishment.

Apparently evolving as a person required traveling in reverse because my past had not stopped its relentless pursuit of me since I had arrived. My life had arced full circle so that I was moving forward from the past and returning to it at exactly the same moment.

I chewed my lip. I was running out of chances. Not just to see Will but to live this life a little longer before I returned to reality. Realization as warm and comfortable as cocoa settled in my stomach, and I found myself nodding. I quirked up the side of my mouth at Sonia. "Okay. Fine. As long as I don't have to wear anything garish on my head."

Unfortunately, that was exactly what I had signed up to wear. A Santa hat that glittered Barbie pink and a sweatshirt to match, the front fully blinged out with the outline of, what else, a cat. Sonia had made one for each of us. On her sweat-shirt, she had bedazzled a rabbit.

Roberto, our long-time clinic manager, would be driving his Ford, pulling us on a flatbed trailer strung with white twinkling lights and carrying a sign that read *McClain Veterinary Clinic*. Hay bales were stacked in a pyramid, in front of which stood a crotchety goat wearing reindeer antlers.

A precariously mounted speaker blared Christmas tunes, and Kody sat cross-legged on one of the bales wearing her sweatshirt, which glittered with the outline of a galloping horse.

I crossed my arms and glared at Sonia. "You couldn't have given me the shirt with the horse?"

"I thought you liked cats, *mi hija*."

"Yes, but I'm an equine vet, Sonia. As in horses."

Realization dawned over her face and then a flash of exasperation. "Aye, *dios mío*. I can't remember everything." She reached down and playfully patted my cheek with a hand that smelled like peppermint cream.

I climbed into the trailer without a word and claimed a haybale of my own next to the goat.

When the marching band started up with the first notes of "Jingle Bells," I became eighteen again, staring through the twinkling lights and glitter and fanfare for someone I hoped to see. The trailer lurched forward behind the truck, and the goat side-eyed me with rectangular pupils, her hoofs never budging.

Despite the swell of the crowd, the exclamations and oscillating lights, Mildred was unfazed. I wished I could contain my nervous energy that well. As we rounded the curve into the swell of Main Street, Sonia leaned over and thrust a paper bag into my lap.

"And what, pray tell, is in here?" I asked.

"Candies," she said, eyes swimming with delight. "For the *niños.*"

I peered in the bag. Tiny packages of multicolored gumdrops. Peppermints shaped like stars and chocolates wrapped in shiny silver and red foil.

I swallowed hard. I had once stood on the sidewalk in mittens, eyes shining as I darted into the street to scoop up candy, using my jacket as a makeshift basket. I sighed. I couldn't deny my childhood had been anything less than magical. If my family had ever resented me, they had never let it show.

I watched Sonia shimmy to the edge of the trailer and wave to a group of women wearing straw cowboy hats, her lips mouthing the words to "Santa Baby." Next to her, Kody squealed and waved to a group of friends.

It wasn't surprising. It was hard to move ten feet in this town without seeing someone you knew. My eyes drifted over the crowd, and I picked out the familiar faces. Mr. Weatherby from the bookstore. My sixth-grade biology teacher. Even Eileen the bartender wearing a hot pink leather jacket.

But not the face I was looking for. The face I always seemed to be looking for. Even when I didn't want to see it.

"Quinn! Over here!"

My aunt Jackie waved like a maniac next to a streetlight. Her other hand rested on the back of a wheelchair, which barely contained my dad's large frame. From the waist up, no one would ever have ever known he was recovering from major injuries. He whistled and waved, his face pink with cold, his eyes bright.

My chest swelled with love. I was sure that his did too. I snatched up a fistful of wrapped candies and lofted them in his direction, watching the kids wrench free from their parents to scoop them up. It wasn't my imagination that something between us healed in that moment.

His face, despite being thinner, was more alive than I had seen it in a long time. I was finding it increasingly harder to believe what I had heard in the kitchen that night. And even harder to believe that the last decade had even happened. I gave him a smile, bright and unabashed, as the parade inched forward.

Once we turned the corner, the frenetic noise of Main Street faded to a distant hum. Roberto's truck tires squealed as he coasted to a halt down a side street. My bag of candy was empty. I crumpled it between my palms and tossed it over to Mildred, who immediately began chewing it.

I swung my legs off the trailer, wobbling as I landed. Roberto offered a hand to Sonia, and she navigated over the bump of the back tire before ending up next to me.

"So, *mi hija*, did you have fun?"

"I did," I said, and I meant it.

"Kody and I are going for cider at the café." She glanced at something over my shoulder, her eyes widening a fraction. She reached over to squeeze my arm.

I was opening my mouth to ask if I could join them when I heard footsteps behind me. I knew it was him before I even turned around. A familiar flutter started deep inside me. Like a bird waking up from a winter slumber.

While I had trundled along behind this year's Christmas pageant queen as she waved to her court, I had been preparing myself, tamping down my emotions into something containable so that I could focus on what I needed to say. Only one question. Nothing more. Nothing less.

I set my jaw, determined to wrap this part of my life in a neat bow, and turned around. He looked devastating in the near dark, a kiss of moonlight on his raven black hair. My breath hitched and I forgot everything except the feel of his lips on my skin. The smell of leather and fresh paper and mint.

So much for evolving. I was completely screwed.

CHAPTER THIRTY-ONE

WINTER, NOW

"Kiss?" he said, the hint of a smirk forming on his face.

"What?" My voice was an octave higher than usual. A shockwave traveled down my spine all the way to my feet which remained rooted to the sidewalk.

"Kiss," he repeated and dipped his chin toward his hand that held a chocolate wrapped in shiny silver foil.

"Oh." My face heated to furnace level. "No, thank you."

"Too bad." He kept his hand out. "Lost your taste for sugar?"

"No." I bristled. How did he remember everything about me? "I just don't want any right now."

"Again, too bad." He took his time unwrapping the foil then popped the chocolate into his cheek.

My hands clenched into fists at my sides. "What are you doing here?"

"I came to find you."

Oh. My courage faltered, and I looked over my shoulder. "Well, that's too bad because I was actually about to get some cider with…"

No one was behind me. Even Roberto had disappeared with Mildred in tow.

We were utterly alone apart from a few parade cows bellowing in the distance. I turned back to Will who wore a celebratory smirk.

"Lead the way," he said, gesturing toward the glow of Main Street.

We settled into a corner table at the café, not far enough from the prying eyes of Sonia but at least out of earshot.

"Friends of yours?" Will asked the third time he caught Sonia winking at the back of my head.

I spared a look over my shoulder and gave her my best glare. "Yes." I turned back around and added, "Some real nosy ones."

"Is that Sonia?"

"The one and only. You remember her?"

"Only a little. Didn't she always wear the shirts with the...embellishments?" He pointed at my sweatshirt. "Nice cat by the way."

I snorted. "I bet she could make one in your size. I hope pink is your color." I pushed up my sleeves and rested my head on one hand. "Now that you have my attention, what do you want?" The words came out harsher than I expected and across from me, Will stiffened.

He parted his lips to speak—those beautifully full lips that felt like satin against my skin—but was interrupted by the arrival of the waitress.

"Hey there, I'm Holly," she chirped and laid down two menus made from cardstock. "What do you folks wanna order tonight?"

Will made an obligatory glance at the menu. "A cider please."

"And how 'bout you, Doc?"

I startled. I didn't imagine she would know who my dad

was, much less me. The shock must have shown on my face because she immediately began to clarify, "You saved my Brewster's life a few weeks back after he got into it with a wild hog."

The memory came flooding back: the scrappy fox terrier with the large gash right through his abdomen. "How's he doing?" I asked, worrying my bottom lip.

"Right as rain," she said with a smile that revealed a large gap between her front teeth.

I smiled back at her. "I'm glad. Female hogs can be relentless."

As she turned to go, I caught Will staring at me. "What?" I asked, a nervous twinge blooming in my chest.

His eyes cut to where my hands were splayed over the table. My hands with their wide knuckles and crisscrossing pattern of scars. My hands that were now missing a very sparkly piece of jewelry.

"Nothing," he said, running a hand through his hair. And he looked ...nervous. I was not imagining that the hand he laid on the table was trembling. "It's just ... well, I—"

"Trouble finding your words Mr. Bestselling Author?"

"Not usually." He flashed a wry grin before schooling his face into an annoying shade of neutral. "What did you think of the book?"

His question took me off guard. Why had he brought me here to ask about his novel? Surely, my literary opinion was inconsequential. Especially when the rest of the world seemed to be in love with his writing. I licked my lips before answering. "I liked it."

His brow arched but he remained silent, like he knew not talking would urge me to elaborate. He was right.

"I...more than liked it. It was great, Will. Really great. Outstanding even."

"I wrote it"—he swallowed hard—"hoping you would read it someday."

I could tell he wanted to say more by the absolute stillness of his body, like every cell was funneling energy into his next words. My ears were on high alert, waiting to scoop up everything he said so I could dissect it later.

Holly the waitress appeared out of nowhere, sliding two mugs of steaming cider onto our table from her precarious tray of confections. "On the house," she said with a wink, leaning between me and Will to set down a plate of cookies.

When she was gone, so was the moment. Once more, Will's face was unreadable as he took a mug and lifted it to his lips.

"Bloody hell, that's hot."

"Thanks for warning me," I said with a smirk. I swirled the amber liquid in my mug without drinking. Seconds passed and he said nothing. When I finally lifted my cider to take a tentative sip, he cleared his throat again.

"How's your father?" he asked, the same sincerity in his voice that I had once loved.

"Oh," I said, setting down my mug. "Surprisingly good after falling off the roof." I grimaced at the visual. "And he's almost completely healed. Which makes him restless...and cranky." The tension coiled through my middle loosened, and I smiled. "And ready to get back to work."

I had more mixed feelings about that than I'd realized. Not because he couldn't handle it, but maybe because I wasn't quite ready to leave him. To leave this fragile peace that had evaded me for most of my adult life.

"I'm sure you're ready to get back to your real life, as well," Will said softly, and I tempered my face against the conflict occurring there.

"Yes," I said. "Definitely. Mitch Jenkins will lose his shit if I'm not back soon." I thought of the last round of emails we had exchanged. Each one shorter than the last. Which meant Mitch was flirting with outright panic.

"Who is Mitch Jenkins? Your boss?"

I snorted. "Oh, God, no. He's one of the trainers that I work with. I've sort of become his personal vet. And he's extremely needy."

"And you don't mind?"

"Not really. He's harmless. And he's promised to take me to Paris next June for a horse show."

Will's body stilled next to me at the mention of Paris. He had lived there for a brief time as a kid, among other exotic places that I had only dreamed of visiting. For a second, I remembered how different we had been. How different we still were. He was the son of an art curator. Born into a family who made wine and traveled the world.

By the time he was thirty, he had written a bestselling novel, which was probably the first of many to come. It was becoming easier to understand how I had been no more than a summer fling. How I had been the country girl who wanted to see things as bigger and brighter than they were.

I was the little bit of reality in the exploding fantasy fiction of his mind. I was the tragic ending that had inspired him to write a love story. One that had ended differently.

"That sounds like an exciting adventure."

"I hope so. I've wanted to see Paris since I was a teenager." I paused to gauge his face and the intense, devouring look in the depths of those ocean eyes.

"I remember."

A shudder skated down my back, and I gripped my mug like my life depended on it. "What about you?" I trilled, anxious to change to subject. "Are you heading back to California or wherever it is you live these days?"

"I live here now," he admitted quietly, his eyes trained on me, studying my response.

I didn't disappoint him. My jaw nearly unhinged. "Since when?" I narrowed my eyes at him. "I thought you said you were in town for a book signing."

"I was," he proceeded cautiously, "but then I realized how much this place inspired me and I decided to stay. At least until I'm finished writing the sequel to *Lune*."

"There's going to be a sequel, huh?" I teased, trying to keep the mood light even as my heart rate sped up. "What happens in the end?"

"I'm not sure yet," he said, his eyes drifting down to my lips.

Under the table, I pressed my thighs together until they ached. "Well, I hope it's good. I can't stand bad endings."

"Me neither." He smiled. I smiled back. It was effortless. God, what was I doing? I kept forgetting to remember the last tortuous years of my life hating him. And hating that he wasn't mine.

Across from me, his brows knit together. My mind raced to consider the possibilities of what might come out of his mouth next. When he parted his lips, my stomach dropped into the soles of my sneakers.

"Can I ask you a question?" he said, drumming his fingers on the checkered tablecloth.

"As long as I can ask you one."

"Anything," he said, his eyes burning with intensity.

Here it was. My chance. An open door. All I had to do was walk...right...through it. "You first."

"Do you still hate me?" he asked, and his shoulders clenched to steel himself for the answer.

"Yes," I blurted before I could even think about changing my mind. "Thoroughly."

"I thought so." A look settled over his face that could only be described as...grief. His brows knit together even tighter.

"Even still...if I asked you to go somewhere with me tomorrow, would you say yes?"

"Maybe," I hedged, looking over his shoulder at the wall of photographs the café kept on display. I spied one of George Strait from 1986 holding a plate of chicken fried steak. What would George say? The chorus from a classic country song started up in my head. "Ok...sure."

Will's posture straightened as I scanned his face for any deceit or false pretense. I found nothing but relief. "I'll pick you up tomorrow night then. At eight."

"Okay," I said, running my tongue over my teeth. "But I swear to God, if you don't show up, I'm letting Sonia bedazzle your fancy Range Rover."

"Noted. Although it might distract from the dust."

We both laughed and the conversation turned light and comfortable—like we were old friends and had been for years. We talked until the café lights dimmed and my cider grew cold.

Will gave me a ride home, dropping me at the end of my driveway. I was all the way to the porch before I realized I'd never asked him the question I had promised myself that I would.

I WAS NERVOUS. Nervous to the point of twisting my hands in my lap, rubbing the spot where my ring used to grip the underside of my knuckle. What was I doing?

I stood up to go inside then sat back down in the porch swing. Then stood up again. The sky was overcast, dark gray clouds against deep violet. No stars out tonight. Only a biting cold as a reminder of why I should be indoors huddled under a blanket enjoying my last few weeks at home.

I glanced into the house through the large picture window next to the porch. The lights had been clicked off. My dad would likely already be snoring. He went to bed early these days, which did wonders for his energy level. Yesterday he'd even managed to walk across the house on his own with a cane that looked like it might buckle under his grip.

No doubt he would be ready to get back to the clinic—at least for the small animals—by the first of the year. I could see the signs already. The frequent glancing at the clock. The press of his hands on the table to steady himself from fidgeting.

Neither of us had ever managed to sit for the purpose of being still. We shared an inertia, he and I—one that maintained forward momentum. I supposed that was why we had survived every curve life had thrown our way.

Car lights sliced up the driveway. A familiar crunch of tires. I realized I was clutching the handrail of the porch for dear life to keep from scrambling back into the house. Or the woods. I glanced longingly at the trees that rimmed the west side of our front yard.

The headlights loomed closer until I was bathed in yellow spotlight like a stage performer. There was nowhere to go but forward into its beckoning glow. By the time my jiggling legs made it to the bottom of our concrete porch steps, Will was waiting next to the open passenger door of his sleek black SUV. His face betrayed nothing. A placid mask.

But I knew him better than that. He was nervous. I could see it in the way his fingers twitched at his sides. In the way he rubbed his thumb along the seam of his jeans. I climbed in smoothly, pushed forward by a restless, pent-up energy that no longer slumbered. My hands, numb from cold, fumbled with my seatbelt, and I drew a steadying breath.

One, two, three, four...I counted silently as Will eased his truck out of the driveway and onto the main road. I was doing this. And I hoped like hell I wouldn't regret it.

Will broke the silence first. "Are you warm enough?" Before I even answered, he was adjusting the vents so that warm air skated across my cheek.

I wasn't warm. Not in the slightest. All my blood flow was being shunted away from my extremities toward somewhere low in my abdomen. My heart skittered along, matching the uneven tempo of my words. "So, where are we going?"

"You'll see." His mouth flirted with a half-smile, and he turned up the volume on the music.

As I was surrounded by the caroling of bells and pre-pubescent voices, I scanned the road for clues. Only the undulations of shadowed hills, their smoothness disturbed by fence lines and the frozen shapes of trees, were visible. We headed west, leaving the last vestiges of town far behind us.

I shivered again, wondering if I would be warm enough in the flannel shirt I had dug out of the back of my closet. The snaps were smoothed with age, the pink and blue plaid material soft and pliant. Other than fitting a bit snugger than it used to, it still looked decent. Decent enough to do whatever this was.

I pressed my forehead against the passenger window glass, watching the twilight swallow the rolling hills in the distance. We continued driving, and I was lulled into a trance by the gentle curves of the road and the hint of blinking starlight behind the clouds.

All at once, in the most surreal way possible, the contours of the landscape became familiar. Something from a memory? Or from a dream? I rolled down the window to sample the wind rushing past. And there it was. The barest hint of cedar and sagebrush.

At first, I only remembered how I had felt that night. Terrified and thrilled. My heart beating so hard it had nearly burst out of my chest. The cool air dusting over my bare chest. The sweet smell of lavender and innocence. The tingling in the ends of my fingers as they raked down a heated strip of skin, tucking into the waistband of a pair of dark jeans...

Will braked so hard that I lurched forward, bracing my hands on the dashboard. "Sorry about that." He looked sheepish in the luminous glow of the speedometer. "It's still difficult for me to find this place in the dark."

Suddenly I knew exactly where we were. I knew there was a sloping stretch of earth along the lip of a canyon. I knew that if I peered over the edge, I would see a glistening, natural pool bathed in moonlight.

Ahead of us, the field of dry, slender grasses and patches of wildflowers had been empty the last time I was here. Now, a house stood there. A two-story stone structure with a peaked roof and oversized windows.

I gasped in bewilderment. "I can't believe someone built a house on our spot." I bit the inside of my cheek. *Our spot.* I hoped Will hadn't noticed my choice of words, but the dimple flirting with his left cheek indicated otherwise.

"You don't like it?" he asked casually, the Range Rover skidding to a halt in the freshly poured gravel driveway.

"Yes...no..." I fumbled with words and my seatbelt at the same time.

Will climbed out of the driver's side only to skirt the vehicle and open my door. The glow from the front windows backlit his exquisite profile as he held out a hand.

"Come on," he said, excitement lining every angle of his face. "I hear the view from the balcony is spectacular."

CHAPTER THIRTY-TWO

WINTER, NOW

"I can't believe this is your house." I glanced up at the exposed beams crisscrossing the cathedral ceiling.

The walls were freshly painted, a warm white outlined with trim of natural wood. Plush carpets were artfully placed underneath coordinating leather furniture centered around a giant stone fireplace. The decor was simple yet luxurious.

"Me neither," he said, tugging me up a set of wide stairs.

I followed like a docile pony, wondering when he would realize that he still held my hand.

"The entire thing turned out just as I hoped, but this"—he reached over to pull an iron handle that belonged to a set of double doors—"is my favorite room."

My nose immediately tingled with the smell of paper and leather. Two oversized armchairs sat opposite one another, a wooden coffee table with a natural edge in between. And the walls. Every available wall was lined with shelves that reached the ceiling. And on those shelves, books of every color and texture filled every square inch of space.

It was so...Will. The back of my throat burned with emotion.

"So, this is your version of paradise?" I managed to choke out.

"Pretty much," he said, eyes trained on me in a way that I knew he wasn't only talking about the house...or the books.

I ran my fingers over the woodgrain of the shelves, my eyes wandering over the spines. Some pristine, some cracked with age. I found a familiar one and wrenched it free from its neighbors. "Is this mine?" I held up the faded sky-blue cover, a rearing black horse pawing the torn edge.

Will's brows furrowed and he pressed his lips together to keep from smiling. "I don't think so."

I peeled back the cover and pointed to the name written in shaky cursive on the title page. "It most certainly is!"

Will closed the distance between us. His warm breath coated the back of my neck as he plucked the book out of my hand to examine it. "So it is," he said thoughtfully. "Or was."

"What do you mean 'was'?" I reclaimed the worn paperback and clutched it to my chest.

"To be fair, I found it in the used bin at Weatherby's about"—he ticked off an amount on his fingers—"four years ago."

"And you bought it?"

"For an entire dollar."

I tore my eyes from his face before I could be accused of ogling and looked down at the cover again. With my index finger, I traced the outline of the horse's back. "This was my favorite book as a kid."

Will took a step closer until the material of his sweater brushed the back of my hand. "I know," he said softly. "Consider it yours...again."

I glanced up and nearly drowned in his tender expression. I gulped. And clutched the book tighter to keep my hands from reaching for him. But before I had decided whether to act on that impulse, he took a step back, the shadows hiding whatever expression crossed his face.

"I thought you promised me a balcony," I said lightly, and his posture loosened, perhaps relieved by purpose.

"I most certainly did." He pushed back a set of deep blue velvet drapes to reveal a door made entirely of glass rimmed in black iron. Cold air blasted my face when he wrenched it open and disappeared into the night.

I followed him outside, the night's chill helping to soothe the hum of energy under my skin. I could see every star. Could even smell the traces of sage and lavender that hadn't been completely decimated by the winter. And when I closed my eyes, I heard the water gently lapping against the rocks below. Our magic swimming pool.

"This is...incredible," I breathed, knowing there weren't words to describe the delicate haze overtaking my senses.

"You should see the view during the day," Will said from where he had positioned himself on the cushioned outdoor sofa.

He reached for a wine bottle perched on the perfectly cylindrical end table and pulled out the stopper with a soft *pop*. "Would you like some?" he asked as I settled onto the other end of the sofa, where my thighs would the lowest chance of brushing against his.

I rubbed my damp palms along the seams of my jeans. "Definitely." I sniffed the inside of the glass he handed me. Cherries and something smoky. And decadent. I took my first sip followed by another. "Is this one of yours?"

He nodded, pouring a glass for himself. "It's old. At least twenty years or so." He closed his eyes, savoring his first sip. "My grandparents definitely knew what they were doing."

I swirled the faded red liquid around in my glass. "This might be the first Deremer wine I've ever had."

He raised a brow. "Oh? Really?"

Shit. That wasn't true. And he knew it. We had passed a bottle back and forth sitting on the hood of his car the night we'd had sex for the first, and only, time.

If I squinted, I could probably pick out the exact spot from this balcony. My mouth was suddenly bone dry. I took a giant swig and swallowed without even waiting for the aftertaste.

"I have a question for you," I blurted.

Will reclined into the cushions, irritatingly calm. "A question for a question."

"That game again?" I asked with an arched brow.

"It's timeless." The left half of his face quirked into a smile.

I stifled a laugh before draining the rest of my glass. I was stalling. He knew it too. I could tell by the way he sipped his wine in near absolute silence. As if one wrong move from him would send me scurrying back inside.

My throat burned with questions and the trace of alcohol. I started with the most obvious one. "Why did you build a house here?"

Will shifted in his seat. "I needed a quiet place to write, and the winery was a good excuse to make Linzberg a home base of sorts."

I nodded thoughtfully. "It must seem pretty boring compared to all the other places you've lived."

"Maybe at first, but it's gotten more interesting lately." Starlight glinted off his teeth when he smiled at me.

My stomach tightened in the worst and best way.

"My turn," he said then paused a beat before asking, "Are you really okay after your...disengagement?"

I frowned in thought. God, it had been so short-lived. By now, I had been unengaged almost as long I had been engaged. I barely even remembered the girl who had said yes two months ago and put a ring on her finger.

I tucked a thick strand of hair behind my ear. "I'm really okay," I said. "I knew I didn't want to marry him...and I think I would have eventually broken it off, but things happened that sort of sped up the process."

"What things?"

I shifted uncomfortably and tucked my hands into my lap. "It was my turn for a question."

"By all means," he said before taking a long draw of wine.

"Did you..." I shifted my gaze from his face to the slice of cream-colored moon overhead. "Did you dedicate your book to me?"

"Yes," he whispered, so low that I barely heard him over the pounding of my heart.

"Why?"

"It was my turn."

Damn this game of his. I bit the inside of my cheek and gestured for him to get on with it.

"Do you actually hate me?"

"No. But I wish I did." My entire body trembled with the adrenaline of honesty. I didn't hate him. I never had. Not really. Hence the crux of my problem. "Why did you dedicate the book to me?"

Will's throat bobbed. He took his time putting his wine glass on the table before answering. "Because you are...you have always been...something I didn't expect. Something I didn't know I needed and knew I didn't deserve." He ran a hand through his hair, leaving a row of tousled waves. "You were the something more that made me feel alive again. Made me want to be close to someone again after my mom died and my life changed. It was always...you."

I shook my head in disbelief, unexpected tears stinging the corners of my eyes. "That summer," I choked. "Even though you never said it, I thought you loved me. Did you?"

"Yes," he said. Plainly. Simply. As if it was the easiest question to answer in the universe. "And I've loved you every summer since."

"Then why? Why—"

"I regret every single thing about that day," he interrupted, his voice cracking like the surface of a frozen pond. "I should never have left you."

He knew what I was asking without me asking. He knew that day had broken me. It sounded like it had broken him too. Inside, part of me was screaming, *then why did you*, even as he shifted closer to me. Even as he took my hand into both of his.

"I was so angry. For years Will."

"I know. I'm so sorry, Quinn." His voice had dropped an octave as he started to massage my palm with his thumb. Slow, soothing circles.

A cloud drifted past the moon, exposing its sharp edge against the black sky. I sucked in a breath. "You used our moon in the book."

"I know," he said, and if there had been enough light, I knew I would have seen his cheeks deepen with color. "It's because I think of you every time I look into the night sky."

The air shimmered around us, the universe urging us together. Like two orbiting celestial bodies being sucked in by each other's gravity. I couldn't have stopped even if I had wanted to.

His exhaled breath warmed the chilled skin of my forehead, his face inches from mine. Without a curtain of darkness separating us, I could see every detail of his expression, and he looked completely shattered. His eyes a mixture of sadness and regret and the faintest glimmer of hope.

"That must be...inconvenient," I joked.

"You have no idea," he said with a smirk then tightened his fingers around my wrist. "I can't change what happened,

Quinn, no matter how many times I've lain in bed at night wishing I could."

The image of Will in bed silhouetted by shadows and moonlight made a thrill twirl upward from my lower abdomen. A sensation powerful enough to make me ignore the nagging sense that something didn't add up.

When his thumb brushed my throat, I forgot every word I ever knew. When his gaze fell to my mouth, a rush of want licked up my spine. The coiling tension was too much to bear.

I closed the narrow distance between us, pressing my lips to his in what I thought would be a simple kiss. A kiss that happened when something ended. Not when something began.

I should have known better.

Once they settled into place, my lips refused to separate from Will's. Like they had become magnetized by familiarity. The perfect fit of a key into a lock. Latching onto the intoxicating nostalgia of epic love.

Will's eyes flared in surprise and, before I regained my senses and backed away, his lips started moving. Encasing mine in pillowy softness. A groan vibrated into my mouth, and I nearly melted into a puddle.

My brain shorted out until there was only sensation. He grasped my bottom lip, skimming it with his teeth before begging entry with his tongue. I was powerless to stop him. And not one part of me wanted to.

Once I parted my lips, I was suddenly nineteen again. Desperate to find out how his skin felt under my hands. How much heat his mouth would add to mine. How it would feel when we established a rhythm together of lips and tongues and muffled exclamations.

I had imagined this moment. Fantasized about it in my drafty bedroom when I was alone. Not less than a thousand times had I wondered if kissing Will had been exaggerated in my mind. Romanticized in my memory past a reasonable level of expectation.

I had wondered if I ever kissed him again, would I realize that it wasn't as earth-shattering as I had once thought? Would it be something less than extraordinary? Would I realize that I had kissed better kissers and we had truly been nothing special? A passing chemistry between two lonely teenagers trying to grow up?

It took approximately ten seconds of making out with Will to discover it was definitely as good as I remembered. I angled my mouth so he could swipe his tongue along the roof of my mouth. No. It was better.

Heat churned in my middle. A dormant volcano brought to life again. I tasted the wine on his tongue like it was a drug —a drug that left my head spinning into orbit. And I wanted more.

For a beautiful moment I let it all fall away—the guilt, the pain, the constant clawing toward a life I no longer had. And I let myself want. Let myself hope and wish and dream.

I was flooded with sensations. Will's hand, warm and firm, underneath the hem of my shirt. The night air rich with the bite of sage that tingled inside my nose. My fingers diving into something feathery soft. Oh my God, were they in Will's hair?

How had I ever lived without being kissed this way? Without being thoroughly ravaged by someone's lips alone? Will tugged me into his lap without breaking the connection with his mouth. And now that I was on top of him, the friction between our lower halves was desperate and purposeful.

When my thighs gripped his waist, I could feel every bit of him through his jeans. He tore away from my mouth only to his run his lips along my jaw then down my neck, every kiss thoroughly wrecking me.

I wanted this. Wanted him. The fog of my own lust crowding out rationale or intuition. For a moment, I didn't care what had happened in the past or might happen in the future because for the first time in forever—I felt alive.

Will paused just shy of my shirt snaps, his head bent as if in prayer. His breath warm on the exposed V of my chest. I slipped my fingers farther into his thick mass of hair and tugged. He hesitated for the tiniest second before renewing his assault on my exposed skin.

Every few kisses he separated one of the snaps with his teeth. God, is this what it would have been like between us? Our chemistry was cosmic.

A molten heat spread through my thighs and up my back. My shirt hung around my shoulders as Will's fingers crested the lacy rim of my bra. When he eased it over the swell of my breasts and my nipples met the cashmere of his sweater, the beautiful agonizing friction nearly undid me.

"You have too many clothes on," I mumbled throatily, pushing his sweater then his undershirt over his head.

As soon as his face was free of clothing, I met him with an onslaught of kisses. I was a feral animal. Something that wanted to devour and be devoured at the same time. I leaned back to take in the vision of the gorgeous man in front of me.

His chest with its hollows and dips filled with shadows. The moonlight reflecting off the bronzed skin of his abdominals. I ran my palms over them, and he groaned, his head snapping forward, the tufts of his unruly hair brushing my chest.

Will's hands swept up my back as he settled me into the crux of his lap. I shivered as his fingers massaged gentle circles next to my spine.

"That feels amazing," I said, my eyelids fluttering closed.

Will pulled me even closer, his lips finding my ear. "You're beautiful."

Somehow when he said it, I believed it so thoroughly that it settled in my marrow.

"Are you sure you want this, Quinn?" He slipped a finger underneath my chin and tipped it up. "Are you sure you want me?"

I *was* sure. And I wasn't. Would it be that bad for me to take something I had wanted for...forever?

My lips lifted in a playful smile. "I've had over a decade to think about it, so yes, I'm sure."

His mouth quirked up, the asymmetric dimple appearing in his left cheek. "One last question," he drawled, his fingers already curling inside the waistband of my jeans.

I arched a brow. "What would that be?"

"Best moment of your life?"

The breath stalled in my chest, and I couldn't stop the vision filling my mind. An empty field above a rocky cliff. A velvet night studded with stars. Moonlight on bare skin. A bottle of golden starlight being passed back and forth on the hood of a car.

"That one, huh?" He grinned exactly like the Will I had loved when I was nineteen.

"Yes," I said, feeling my cheeks heat.

Will brushed a thumb over my lower lip. "Mine too."

I lifted my eyes to his face and the mask of calm, of tethered emotion, had disappeared. And what I beheld was a man with a radiant smile. A dazzling glint in his eyes.

My heart stuttered at the sight of it. My hand returned to his bare chest, to the spot where his heart pounded the underside of his sternum.

"Are you nervous?" he asked.

"It's not like we haven't done this once before," I said with feigned confidence.

"Once wasn't enough for me."

"Let's see if you learned anything," I said, my tone light.

Teasing even. It belied the swarm of butterflies taking flight inside my stomach.

I leaned over to nip at his bottom lip. He responded by pressing me into the most luxurious kiss, exploring me thoroughly like we had all the time in the world. When my impatience spiked, I reached for the button of his jeans. He released a soft groan when I popped it open.

"Quinn," he breathed, and I swallowed my name on his lips.

"Quinn," he repeated between kisses. Fingers gently encircled my wrist as Will's body quieted beneath me.

"Everything okay?" I blew back a strand of hair.

"Everything is perfect. You're perfect." Will reached his hand up to tuck my grown-out bangs behind my ear. "I've had a long time to imagine this and, trust me, it's even better than I ever thought it would be."

"But?"

"But before we do this, I need to know if what happened in the past—"

"You mean have I forgiven you?"

"Yes."

I chewed on my lip and rocked backward. "Yeah, I guess I have. Even though a part of me still wonders why. What we had when we were younger—it was real to me."

"It was real to me too."

"Then you can imagine how hard it was for me to understand why you would ditch me and go to Italy for the summer."

A blast of cool air whooshed between us when Will's torso jerked backward. "Italy?"

An uncomfortable weight settled into the pit of my stomach. I didn't want to ask again. Maybe I didn't even want to know. But I forced myself to say the words anyway.

"You remember," I started, "when we were nineteen, the summer after my freshman year of college."

"Yeah." He stared at me with a bewildered expression.

"I told you I loved you and then *boom* the next thing I knew you were gone. I always wanted to know why."

Will ran a frantic hand through his hair and I slipped off his lap onto the sofa cushion. "Oh bollocks."

"Come on, it's been a decade. I can take it. And I'll probably still have sex with you tonight."

"Quinn." He sounded like he was strangling on my name. "I never went to Italy."

CHAPTER THIRTY-THREE

WINTER, NOW

I *never went to Italy.* The words drifted around my head like some gibberish I couldn't decipher.

"Yes, you did." I reached down to the balcony floor and picked up the first soft thing I found, which happened to be Will's cashmere sweater, and pulled it over my head. It smelled exactly right. Like sandalwood and a hint of mint.

"You don't have to lie, Will," I said matter-of-factly. "The night we were supposed to see the Strawberry moon, I waited for you. And when you never showed up, my dad told me that you left with your grandparents for the summer. To Italy."

"I spent that summer at Berkeley taking classes."

"No." I shook my head violently. "No, you didn't."

Too many thoughts and questions and memories were vying for room in my consciousness all at once.

"I went to your house the next day and you were gone. You left Linzberg." A strangling sensation started in my throat. "You left—"

"I left because you said you couldn't stand to be around me."

"Are you delusional right now?" I pulled the sleeves of his sweater over my hands.

"I almost wish I were." He leaned over until his forehead nearly touched his knees, like he was trying to keep himself from retching.

"Will Deremer, tell me what you're thinking, or I swear to God I'm going to crack you open and figure it out for myself." I wrapped myself tighter in his sweater and scooted toward the edge of the couch.

Silence ensued. A tense fragile silence that was finally broken by the sound of Will blowing out a breath through his nose. When he sat upright, his fingers shook as they clutched the frame of the sofa, belying the unnerving mask of calm he now wore.

"Remember when I found you in the cemetery, in the rain, and you told me what you had overheard in your kitchen."

"Yes." I squirmed uncomfortably at the memory.

"And I told you the accident wasn't your fault."

"I remember, Will."

"I said that because I knew it wasn't your fault."

"But it was my fault."

"It wasn't."

"How could you possibly know?"

"Because I know who caused the accident."

"What are talking about, Will?" Every muscle in my body froze into absolute stillness.

"My mum," he choked out before his voice quit working entirely.

"That doesn't make any sense," I said between gritted teeth. My fingers dug into my thighs.

Will drew a breath, his bare chest heaving up then down. "When I was a child, we came to Linzberg every year to visit my grandparents. That particular year my mum volunteered to work the booth for the winery at the Christmas tree light-ing." His jaw ticked as he continued. "She had a bit too much to drink but decided to drive home anyway. And it was raining."

"I remember," I said, my voice nothing more than a whisper.

"And she got confused. We were living in London at the time and she—"

"Drove on the wrong side of the road." Blinding lights. Breaking glass. Screams. Then silence. Those were the only scraps of memory I had of the accident.

"Your mum swerved to miss her and went off the bridge."

My entire body stilled, all its functions seeming to cease at once. I swallowed past the painful lump in my throat. "How do you even know any of this?"

"She told me," Will said, raking a hand through his hair. "Right before she died. I suppose facing death makes the truth easier to tell."

"So, you knew? The whole time we were friends, you knew?" I spat.

"No." It was Will's turn to shake his head. "I didn't put it all together until that day in my car when you admitted where you got your scar."

I stared at him skeptically.

"And I wanted to tell you, Quinn," Will stammered, "but then the moment passed and you were so sad and I thought I would have another chance."

"Why didn't you?"

"I went to the clinic the next day—to see your father. I told him the truth about the accident, but he already knew." Will moved closer to me on the couch, his hands reaching out for mine but then resigning themselves to his knees. "Apparently, prior to her death, my mother had confessed

343

her crimes to him as well. And I told him that you should know. To be able to choose you had to know."

"To choose what?"

"Me." A muscle in his jaw ticked, and when he lifted his eyes to mine, they reflected the same sorrow and guilt that I had carried with me for years. "You probably don't want to hear this now, but, that summer, I knew I was in love with you."

My stomach tumbled into an abyss.

"And I needed you to know that it was my mother's fault that yours died. You deserved to know the truth. And I didn't want to wonder if you could have ever forgiven me. Ever could have truly loved me."

"What happened then?" I was no longer connected to my body. Half of me relived that day in Will's car. The other half wondered what could have been had I known the truth.

"Your father said that he should be the one to tell you, so I waited for him to do it. And the day I was supposed to pick you up for our date, he showed up at my house. He said that he told you everything and that you never wanted to see my face again. That I shouldn't call you or email or come by the house. That you would reach out when you were ready."

"That can't be true," I sputtered. "My dad wouldn't...he said you left for Italy with your grandparents."

"I didn't," he said, his body tremoring from emotion. "You thought I would fall in love with you in every way possible then abandon you?"

"Yes." Waves of wordless emotions crested and died and crested again. Excruciating sorrow and disappointment and anger. "You never told me you loved me," I shouted in Will's stricken face.

"I know," he shouted back, "but I did." He slid off the sofa to kneel in front of me, hands gripping my outer thighs, face turned up with eyes crackling with blue flame. "Didn't you ever wonder what happened to me, Quinn? Didn't you ever have the desire to call me or message me, for Christ's sake?"

In that instant, shame engulfed me like a tidal wave. I had let Will go without question. My cheeks burned with anger and disbelief. I had asked for this, hadn't I? And now I was left with more questions and a tumult of emotion that consumed me like wildfire. "You left me," I repeated weakly.

"Because I thought you hated me," he said.

Tears filled the bottom rims of my eyelids. "I do."

I PRESSED on the accelerator and the engine responded just like I knew it would. Fancy fucking foreign car. The wind whipped through the window, and I leaned into it. I was wild. Reckless. Unhinged.

I pictured Will's face as it had been moments ago. The flickering shadows softening the hard edges of his mouth. The wide-eyed gaze limned with fear and uncertainty as I had opened my hand and said, "I need your keys."

He had remained silent as he had reached into his coat pocket and handed them over. I'd curled my fingers around the sleek black rectangle and pounded out of his house without another look.

As I sped around an S curve and over the railroad tracks that marked the southern border of our county, I began listing the things I knew. The accident had never been my fault if Will was to be believed. My family had never resented me, and my lifetime of angst had been fucking pointless. Maybe my dad and Aunt Jackie didn't hate me, but now I had to contend with the fact that they were liars.

There was only one way to find out the truth.

I drove aimlessly until the first specks of dawn appeared on the horizon. I drove until I had unpacked a decade of sorrow. Until the cuffs of my flannel shirt were soggy. Until Will's car was nearly out of fuel.

I waited in the driveway inside the haven of the Range Rover's leather interior until the kitchen light flickered on. I saw the slim silhouette of my aunt and the lumbering frame of my dad taking turns at the coffee pot.

Like a wraith, I crept through the yard, cracking open the back door that announced my entrance with a ridiculous squeal.

My aunt's voice, still raspy from sleep, met me at the archway to the kitchen. "Quinn? Is that you?"

I didn't answer. Instead, I took my time quietly putting away my boots, slipping into the kitchen in stockinged feet.

There they were. Sitting at our round breakfast table. My aunt in a fluffy pink robe, her hair pinned to her scalp. My dad in green tartan flannel pajamas. They looked at me expectantly. Their eyes soft and warm if not a touch judgmental.

"Yeah," I said softly. "It's me."

"Just getting home?" My dad grunted in mild disapproval.

My face blanched with a last spike of adrenaline, and once it had drained away, fatigue the size of an ocean filled every crevice of my body.

"Don't worry, Quinnie." My dad chuckled. "You're way past the age where I could ground you." He paused to scan my face for a response. I didn't give him one.

I closed my eyes and gripped the wainscoting along the wall for strength. "I have a question," I said, my voice the quality of a rusty hinge. "And I want the truth. No matter what it is."

When I opened my eyes, I could feel the tension thickening the air like a summer fog. In the way my aunt gripped her coffee mug. In the clench of my dad's jaw and the angle of his hands against the table edge.

"What really happened to my mom?"

My aunt sucked in a breath. My dad exhaled so forcefully it gave him a coughing fit.

Jackie pressed her lips together then said, "Why don't you sit down Quinn."

Sitting down was the last thing I planned on doing so I made a point of crossing my arms over my chest like I was five and had just been told to clean my room. I took a breath and let it out slowly. "I want you to tell me the truth."

"Your mother died in an accident. A tragic terrible accident." Jackie's voice was on the verge of cracking.

"I know that part. Tell me the rest."

An interminable silence ensued before anyone spoke. "We didn't know what really happened...not for many years," my dad said thickly. "We knew she had turned around for some reason and was headed back toward town."

"My doll," I said flatly. "I had forgotten my doll."

"No." My aunt shook her head firmly. "The doll was in the car when they found you."

"She had lost her wedding ring," my dad choked out.

And suddenly a memory flared. A gleaming gold band speckled with a tiny square diamond. It was at eye level and sitting on a porcelain sink as my mom washed her hands.

"She left it at the cafe," I whispered, something caving inside my chest.

My dad nodded. "And on the way back to get it, the rain started. She didn't make it very far. There were skid marks on the bridge. We assumed the car had hydroplaned then slid off onto the embankment."

My chest tightened with recognition. I knew what part of the story was coming next. And I wasn't sure if I wanted to hear it.

"I got a call at the clinic one evening." My dad paused to sip from the steaming mug in his hand. "From a woman named Sofia. She said she had family in town. Wouldn't say who but she claimed she had been visiting them one winter many years ago. That she had too much to drink the night of the Christmas tree lighting and ran someone off the road."

I leaned on the wall for support, my legs nearly buckling with the weight of a confession that wasn't mine.

My dad had grown uncharacteristically pale. He stared at me, at a rare loss for words.

It was my aunt's husky voice that continued. "She said she was real sorry and there wasn't a day that went by that she didn't regret that night."

"She asked for our forgiveness," my dad added.

"And?" I glanced between the two of them.

"We took some time," Jackie said and I didn't miss the flick of her eyes over to my dad. "But we eventually gave her what she asked for. Except for one thing."

"What was that?"

"She wanted to talk to you," Jackie said, the skin straining against her taut knuckles as she gripped her coffee.

"But you said no?"

My dad nodded affirmation. "You were a teenager at the time. We didn't want that burden on you. On your life."

"What burden?" I spat out. "The truth?" My eye's bored into my father's. Mirror images of gray imbued with steel. "Did you know that she was Will Deremer's mother?"

My dad's shoulders slumped, and he suddenly looked every bit the hexagenarian he was. "We figured it out pretty quick when he showed up here to live with his grandparents after she died."

"Everyone in this town really does know everything," I mused, suddenly captivated by a section of the wall where the paint was peeling off. "What about when Will and I"—I blinked back the sting of tears—"when Will and I became friends?"

"We didn't think it would last past a summer," Jackie offered. "Both of you were headed off to college soon. We thought time and distance would—"

"Take care of it," interrupted my dad.

"Take care of it?" I retorted.

"We thought it would run its course."

"Run its course?" I repeated and pinched the bridge of my nose to keep from screaming. "What happened when he didn't go to college that year? Or when I decided to come home for the summer?"

"We thought you would take the internship at Penn," my dad said haltingly. "But then you seemed like you might decide to hang around here. For him."

"His name is Will," I said, my voice as cutting as a scythe.

"When you came home that summer, we talked and decided—"

"I know," I interrupted, cutting off the words I didn't want to remember. "I heard what you said that night about the accident being *her* fault." My dad and aunt exchanged a modicum of shock. "Except that at the time I thought *the her* you were talking about was me."

A beat of silence ensued before they both reacted at once. "What?" Jackie cried right as my dad barked, "How could you ever think that, Quinn?"

I stared at them both without blinking. "Maybe because no one ever told me the truth."

My aunt slumped back into her chair, the legs scraping against the hardwood floor. "Will wanted us to tell you the truth."

"But we didn't see how that would do anything except for give you more grief." The line of my dad's jaw tightened. The same one that tightened in my own.

"It happened anyway!" I seethed. "I thought you blamed me for Mom's accident. I thought you couldn't wait for me to be gone so that you could get on with your lives. For years, I thought everyone I had ever loved had never really loved me." *Not you. Not Will.* They both withered under my glare. "Didn't you wonder why I never bothered coming home anymore? Why I never called? I have been living in a hellscape of guilt and self-hatred for a decade."

I sucked in a breath like I had been plunged underwater for the last few minutes, and this was my first taste of oxygen. My chest heaved and I put my hand on my sternum. Who knew heartache could be this physically painful when it crawled out of the hole it had been living in for years?

"I just"—I panted—"have one more question." This was it. The final sliver of truth that might shift the kaleidoscope one more time. Into what I didn't know. "Did you tell Will that I knew the truth and that I never wanted to see him again?"

Jackie lowered her chin. "We did."

"Why?" My lip quivered with exhaustion.

"People talk..." she began.

"Don't I know."

"And we knew how close you were."

"We weren't just close. He was the goddamned love of my life."

"Quinn," my dad said sharply. Reproachfully. I didn't care.

My aunt stood up from the table and reached toward me as if to hug me. "We didn't want that for you," she pleaded. "You had everything—dreams and goals and a future. We couldn't stand the thought of you being stuck in the past. A past that *he* would constantly remind you of."

When I refused to meet her embrace, she plopped back in her chair and stared into the depths of her coffee mug. "Would you have wanted to be with him?" she murmured.

I bit my lip. *No. Yes. Maybe?* "I don't know," I finally said. "And I guess I never will."

CHAPTER THIRTY-FOUR

SPRING, NOW

I rolled my shoulders, feeling every snap and pop of my ligaments as they stretched then rebounded. The operating room lights burned holes in my retinas when I glanced upward periodically. Why did I still maintain this nervous tic after five years? Praying to the nonexistent god of equine surgery that my hands would know what to do next.

I admired my latest artwork—a neat row of transparent stitches that approximated the glistening edges of a ragged tendon. This mare's foreleg would heal. Eventually. And she would probably even compete again. The thought made me smile and refocus on my hands.

"Turn up the music," I said to no one in particular.

By the end of an angsty playlist of nineties hits, we were done. Outside the suite I pulled off my gown and gloves, high-fiving the various operating room staff that filed past.

The new anesthesiologist who had joined our group last month winked a caramel-brown eye at me before pulling down his mask. "Nice work in there."

"Thanks," I said, my lips stretching wider than they should have. I blamed it on the sharpness of his jaw and the mellow decadence of his Australian accent. Wiping my hands down the front of my scrub pants I stood to my full height and met him at eye level. "For a minute there, I wasn't sure how it was going to turn out."

He moved a step closer to me. Close enough that I could smell citrus and sweat.

"I never doubted you." He grinned as he loitered, two symmetric dimples appearing in his cheeks. I suddenly knew where this was headed. I stuck a hand between us, and, after a beat, he took it, arching a brow.

"It was nice working with you," I said before purposefully loosening my grip and reaching into my pocket for my phone.

"I hope we can do it again sometime."

I pressed my lips together then replied, "Maybe." I shimmied backward, turning on my heel in the opposite direction. Damn, I was bad at this. And the worst part was, I didn't want to be any better.

No sooner had I stepped a toe outside the operating suite than my phone began vibrating a hole inside my palm. I rolled my eyes at the name flashing on the screen.

"Hello, Mitch," I sang, grinning as I put him on speaker. "What can I do for you?"

"Don't be cute, McClain."

"You think I'm cute? I'm flattered. Truly." A laugh reverberated inside my chest.

"What you are is a pain in my ass."

"Likewise."

Patricia breezed past me in the hallway and pretended to gag herself with her index finger. She had never warmed to Mitch but, behind her cutting words and vulgar gestures, I knew she reveled in his sarcasm. His wit. His Mr. Darcy-esque qualities if this had been nineteenth century England.

I smirked and put the phone to my mouth. "Want to know about the tendon I just repaired?"

"No," he said flatly. "I'm calling to invite you to a tea party. What the hell else would I be calling about?"

I chuckled as I pushed open the door to my office and settled into the new chair that had been delivered last Tuesday and smelled suspiciously like the one in my father's office. I crossed my legs and closed my eyes, leaning back into the sumptuous cognac-colored leather. "The leg was a mess."

Mitch began cursing under his breath.

"But," I crowed, "I was able to repair it." I paused to let that statement settle in. " I think with some time and some excellent rehab, she'll compete again." Nothing but silence on the other end of the line. I waited, holding my breath.

Finally, after a short lifetime, Mitch spoke. "Good. I'm glad I don't have to fire you and find a new vet."

I bit the inside of my cheek to stifle a smile. "See you Monday at the case review." I hung up before the old bastard could respond.

Twenty seconds later, Patricia barged through my door without knocking and caught me shamelessly pumping a fist into the air. "Why all the theatrics today?" I parted my lips to answer but she held up a hand. "No let me guess. Mitch has intractable diarrhea?"

"That's disgusting." I leveled a gaze on her wistful smirk.

"Dr. Hauserman is canceling the staff meeting tonight?" she ventured.

"Unfortunately, no." I grimaced. I had completely forgotten the boss had put that on my calendar.

Patricia tapped her index finger on her chin before pointing it at me. "I got it. That new sex on a stick from anesthesiology asked you on a date?"

"What?" I sputtered. "No." I shifted my eyes to the wall then back to her knowing grin.

"I knew it. I saw the way you looked at his behind when he bent over to show you—"

"I did not," I growled. " Your mind is perpetually in the gutter."

"I have to put it somewhere."

"Sorry the clinic isn't entertaining enough for you."

"It would be"—she made a point of pursing her lips—"if someone around here would get back on the proverbial horse." Her stare made me wither.

Wouldn't she like to know that I already had. At least, I almost had. My treacherous mind flashed to the night at Will's. Starlight and winter's chill on bare skin as I moved in his lap like he was Secretariat winning the Belmont and I was Ronnie Turcotte.

My cheeks heated. I pointed to my open doorway. "Get out before I start screaming."

Her hand pumped the air. "That's exactly what I'm saying you need, Quinn. Scream. Let it out. Preferably while underneath—"

"Okay," I said. "I'm closing the door." I rose quickly, nearly catching the hem of her scrub top as I clicked it shut.

Breathing a sigh of relief, I settled back into my chair, the leather perfectly curving around my bottom. I stared out the window at the waning afternoon, the sun slipping into oblivion behind a violet swirl of dust.

For the first time in months, I had nothing to do. No charts to review. No calls to make. No notes to catch up on. I took a breath, unsure if I was ready for what the stillness would bring. Work had been my respite. My welcome home. My frenetic refuge.

Three months ago, when I had returned to New Jersey, my office desk had been piled high with referrals and covered in reminders from Patricia. Now it was nearly empty. Except for the framed photograph of my mother I had snagged when I had packed up after the holidays.

Despite...everything, I hadn't left right away. Christmas had come and gone quietly at my dad's house, each of us navigating the fragile edges of a newfound peace. Each of us afraid to grip it too tightly lest it shatter. And even more afraid to let it go.

But the day had come when Jackie had decided to extend her stay and look after the house and Dad had gleefully returned to a part-time schedule at the clinic. Somewhere inside my head, a timer had dinged.

I had expected leaving Linzberg to be easy. A relief at the very least. But once I was back on the East Coast, the more something tugged inside my chest. Something restless and persistent that even work couldn't assuage.

I studied the picture of my mom, my chest fracturing open. My remaining resolve crumbling like the sandcastles I had made on the Texas coast as a kid. One powerful wave of nostalgia destroyed it entirely. And now I couldn't help but think of *him*. Of the last time I had seen him.

"Need help with that?"

I dropped the packet of freshly sterilized surgical instruments that I was carrying. They clattered and rolled when they hit the cement floor. I had been lost in my own head. Looking for any task that would keep me at the clinic after hours.

"How did you get back here?" I asked, glancing at the clock above Will's head. The clinic had closed over an hour ago.

"Sonia let me in on her way out," he said, sheepishly rubbing the back of his neck.

"Figures," I said, curling my lip.

"She said you're leaving soon."

I nodded, bending down to pick up a pair of forceps that had landed near my left sneaker. "Next week actually. Dad's back on his feet and can handle most of the clinic schedule."

"I'm glad I caught you then," he said, a tentative smile gracing his lips.

Even in the dim hallway I noticed the brightness in his eyes, the set to his shoulders. I knew exactly what this was.

"Could we go somewhere and talk?" he asked, reaching out a hand to my crouching figure.

I hesitated a beat before taking it. Feeling the warmth of his skin had the exact effect I'd known it would. A flicker inside me sparked to life. "Sure," I said, knees cracking as I stood, purposefully slipping my hand out of Will's to clutch the roll of instruments to my chest. "I was just leaving."

"Lead the way," he said.

My stomach flipped once, a languid backward arc, when his left dimple appeared in his cheek. I turned around and headed for the back door, swallowing hard against the blooming heat in my chest. With every step, I let it leach out through the soles of my sneakers.

We settled into the front seat of the Camaro. The leather creaked and groaned when I shifted to tuck my ankle under my thigh. The air in the car chilly but not unbearable. I reached into the backseat for a sweatshirt and tugged it over my head. It made me feel less vulnerable somehow.

Will ran a hand over the dashboard. "Looks exactly the same."

"Dad's been driving it around more the last few years, which is probably why it broke down in the middle of the road." My lips twisted into a wry grin.

Had it only been a few months ago that I had reluctantly climbed into Will's truck on the way to deliver puppies, hell bent on making his life miserable?

"I never thanked you," I said quietly. "For getting her to the repair shop that time."

"It was the least I could do."

"The very least," I said with feigned sarcasm, and we exchanged soft laughter. After a beat, his eyes sobered as he focused on the caramel leather of the dash, his hand continuing to run back and forth.

"How are things? With your family, I mean?" he asked.

"Better than you would expect."

"Good. That's good," he said, his voice low and thoughtful. "You never told me what happened after you left that night."

"I know." I bit my lip as I relived the memory. "I confronted them about everything, and they didn't want to...but they finally told me the truth."

When he turned to look at me, I avoided confronting the crystalline blue pools that were his eyes. I told myself it wasn't because I was afraid of what I would see there. But I knew that I was a shade shy of terrified.

Instead, like the coward I was, I focused on the landscape framed by the front windshield. The tops of a few scrubby junipers. A bird circling inside the violet halo of the setting sun. I licked the day off my lips.

"I was angry at them for lying," I admitted, "but once that burned away, I realized I was mostly just tired. Tired of feeling guilty all the time. Tired of staying angry. Tired of being confused and lonely. It turned out that I wanted my family back more than I wanted to hold a grudge for something they couldn't change." My brows furrowed and I rolled my lips together. "What they did was wrong but it's not unforgivable. And I know they thought they were acting out of love."

I dared to look at him then. Letting him inside the sphere of my grief and wondering if I would survive it.

Will nodded in understanding, his eyes pliant with sincerity as they studied my face.

"I know it's more than I should ask, but...I hope that one day you can forgive my mum and forgive me."

I sighed long and hard, tearing my eyes from Will's face to study the geometric stitching in the seat cushion. "I don't think I have the energy to be angry at anyone anymore. It was all so long ago...and I don't want to live in the past."

Will ran a cursory hand through his hair. "I should never have left. I should have realized something wasn't right when you never called me. I just assumed—"

"That I hated you?"

"Yeah," he exhaled painfully.

"To be fair, I did. Just not for the reason you thought."

"Quinn, I wish I could go back and—"

"I know but we can't." I reached over to place my hand over his. I knew what he was going to say next.

"Quinn, I still...I still want...bloody hell, I'm having a hard time with words." He released a self-deprecating laugh that melted the resolve in my chest. His hands tightened over mine, eyes piercing with intent. "I love you, Quinn. And I was wrong—you weren't something more. You were every-thing. I feel you with every breath I've taken since the last time I saw you." His hands pulled mine up to his chest where his heart hammered away behind his sternum. "Right here."

I let my fingers absorb the truth of what he said. My lost boy and his way with words. His way of creating the perfect ending to a perfect fairytale where stars align and love triumphs. Will could easily play the part of the prince. But me? I was never meant to play the princess.

With the scrap of willpower I had left, I gently pulled my hands out of his grasp, tucking them under my thighs for safekeeping. "I don't hate you," I said quietly.

His face emptied as if my words had opened a spigot that drained his emotions. He looked away, probably focusing on hawk that continued to circle above the dropping ball of the sun. "But you don't want to be with me either."

I pivoted my body forward, unhooking my ankle from under my knee and dropping my forehead to the steering wheel. "I can't, Will."

Three words uttered in the span of three seconds that severed the invisible string tying us together for thirteen years. The invisible string known as what if.

~

THE PHONE JANGLED on my desk, jarring me out of the memory. My eyes fluttered open, and Sid's ears were met with my jaw-cracking yawn.

"Quinn?"

"Sorry about that." I scrubbed a hand down my face.

"Hard day?"

"Long day," I said, stretching my legs underneath my desk until they protruded under the front panel.

"Me too," she sighed. "Want to join me for a drink? Trilogy is doing half price wine. And I know you can't say no to a good Pinotage."

"I...can't," I said, the words creating an uncomfortable knot in my chest.

"Can't or won't? Come on, Quinn, I've barely seen you since you got back."

"I know. Work's been...well, you know how it is."

"All the more reason for you to take a break. Please."

There was a pleading quality to her voice that she rarely used. "My divorce became final today."

My resolve disappeared as readily as soap bubbles above the kitchen sink.

CHAPTER THIRTY-FIVE

SPRING, NOW

Trilogy was a quaint wine bar in the heart of Cherry Hill that served as a little slice of Parisian culture on a main thoroughfare that otherwise housed a nail salon, a yarn store, and a questionable tavern lit up by three screens of Premier League soccer.

Winter gripped the city in the form of biting winds and disparaging chill. My hands ached as I shoved them farther into the lined pockets of my field jacket. When I spotted Sid sitting outside at a bistro table on the sidewalk, my shoulders slumped in relief at the sight of the pulsing heat lamp next to her.

"No indoor seating?" I asked.

She bristled and ran a hand through the thickest section of her locks but grinned when she said, "You're a vet. Therefore built for the elements."

"Good point," I said and plopped into the chair across from her. The sight of her mended some of my fractured insides. "I missed you." The love I had for my friend at that moment was so sharp. So precious. I wondered how I continued to deserve it.

Sid reached around the minuscule table to wrap an arm around my shoulders. "I missed you too."

"How are you holding up?"

Sid pulled away to swirl her wine and take a long sip. "Strangely, not as devastated as I feel like I should be. I mean it hits me at times. Like when I walked into a coffee shop the other day and Charlie Parker was playing. But good news, I only cry at night now." She lifted her glass and clinked it with mine.

I frowned as I bit the inside of my bottom lip. "I'm sorry, Sid. That I haven't been here for all of that. I should have been here." A new piece of my chest caved in.

Sid flashed a hand toward me, her bracelets sliding and clinking. "Please. You've had more than enough to deal with."

"I know but—"

"Girl," she lectured. "You deal with your shit. I'll deal with mine. And we'll call it even this time." Winking, she reached over to grasp my wrist. "Speaking of..."

"Mine is basically water under the bridge."

Sid gave me a pointed look that bordered on a glare. "You flew off to Texas to take care of your dad, who had a life-threatening accident, you reconnected with the biggest blast from your past, you broke up with your fiancé—"

"Technically, he broke up with me."

"—found out that your mom died in an accident caused by Will's mom, which was the catalyst for the biggest misunderstanding of this century." Her expression softened, eyes becoming liquid and tender. "And where does that leave you?"

As I took my first sip of wine, a palpable spice slipping down my throat, the comfort of it sending a cashmere-like warmth through my insides, I took a quick tally of my life. No longer engaged to Gavin. No longer estranged from my family.

The pieces of the past finally made sense. The rubbing ache in my heart seemed less tender. Less acute. I had no one left to forgive. Including Will. Including myself.

I struggled to find one word that would encompass how the last few months had changed me. I had thought that absence was freedom. That staying angry and not allowing myself to hurt was freedom. I had thought I'd chosen a life that helped me escape, but it had only become another prison.

"I finally feel...free."

"Yes!" Sid exclaimed, in her rich, throaty alto. "Free. Free to choose something because it's right and not because it protects you from more pain. Free to choose someone because you're in love, and you can accept the 'something' that you can't imagine you deserve."

Her words settled inside me, like silt drifting to the bottom of a river. Words that were so beautiful that I wasn't yet ready to entertain what they meant. "Do you have someone in mind? For you, I mean?"

"Girl please. I'm in relationship purgatory. Technically available but I'm not ready to roam, you know."

I nodded, reaching over to my own wine glass, and drinking steadily until it was nearly empty. "I do."

"I ordered for us." Sid's face stretched to show her perfect row of white teeth as the waiter slid a wooden board of cheese in every size and shape between us. She snatched a formidable wedge of pecorino and popped it into her mouth. Her eyes closed and she sighed contentedly. "There's not much I enjoy more than good cheese."

"Except for your Bob," I teased, sliding my own wedge to the edge of the board.

The skin around her eyes crinkled and she laughed bawdily. "You know you want one."

"I think I might," I replied, my voice cracking with hysteria. "A battery-operated boyfriend might be the only one I ever need."

"All the benefits. No awkward conversations."

"And they don't take your favorite pan when they leave," I said, lips twisting up into a wry grin.

"God, Derrik is the worst. He took that just to spite me." Sid threw up a hand and made a fist.

"Do you ever miss him?" I asked tentatively.

Sid studied her wine thoughtfully before taking a loud sip. "Actually, I realized something while you were gone."

"What's that?"

"Sometimes I do miss him, but you know what I never miss? I don't miss the version of myself that was married to Derrik." She drained her wine glass and set it down. I immediately began pouring her another one. "I don't miss the words I wouldn't say so that he wouldn't feel like less of a man. I don't miss the way I shrank myself down, dimmed my light, let my colors fade. All to make sure that the world as I knew it—the world known as Derrik—didn't stop turning."

"Wow," I exclaimed. "You should write that down."

"Maybe I will." She laughed again, lighter, breathier. The laughter of first possibility.

"I'm serious, Sid. You are the most gifted writer I know. The world should know it too."

"I'll think about it." She pursed her lips into a perfect burgundy heart. "Most gifted, huh? More gifted than a certain *New York Times* bestselling author?"

I winced and slurped down the rest of my wine. "Second-most gifted I suppose."

"How *is* the most gifted writer we both know?"

"I wouldn't know. Good, I guess."

"You guess?" Sid was appropriately incredulous. "How did you leave it with him?"

I didn't want to replay that last conversation with him in my dad's car. Once today was enough. "I said goodbye." I pursed my lips, a silent dare to either ruffle me with her questioning or leave it at that. Of course, she chose the former.

"As in *see you later* goodbye or *never again* goodbye?"

"I think it was more like never again."

"Because you can't forgive him?"

"No."

"Because he doesn't love you?"

"No."

"Because you don't love him?"

"No!"

"Gotcha."

"Sid, it's more complicated than that."

"No, it's not, Quinn. It's really not."

MID-APRIL IN TEXAS was about as different from central New Jersey as weather could be. I left my drafty bungalow home dressed in a bulky sweater under a gray sky leaking icy rain and stepped into a dome of sun-kissed air that smelled like wildflowers. Every inhale was divine, welcome, brushing my soul with gentle healing fingers. I rolled down the window of Aunt Jackie's sleek white sedan to feel the wind rushing past my palm.

"I'm so glad you're here," she said, taking her eyes off the road for a second to glance over at me. As if to make sure I was real.

"Me too." I smiled broadly back at her, thinking how much I meant every word.

"He's going to be surprised," she said.

"You think?" I watched out the window, mesmerized by

the deep blue and fiery red blooms filling up the green space along the highway. "It's hard to catch him off guard."

Jackie's shoulders lifted up in a shrug, her earrings catching the sunlight as they dangled above her shoulders. "He's been busy."

"He's supposed to be taking it easy."

"He is taking it easy...for him."

I grunted in response. "Which means he's working nonstop every day at the clinic. He's supposed to be going to physical therapy twice a week."

"Work is therapy for your dad."

"I guess that's where I get it, then."

As the car slowed, exiting to the highway onto a two-lane road, I rolled the window down the rest of the way. I knew exactly when to tense my body to anticipate the turns. Knew exactly how the landscape would undulate and change as we traveled closer to Linzberg.

"What time is the party tonight?" I asked.

"Six. Don't forget. I'm dropping you off at home then heading over to the bakery to pick up the cake."

"I won't forget." I squinted against the mid-morning sun. "Do you need me to do anything?"

"No." Aunt Jackie shook her head and fluffed the back of her hair with one hand. "Just rest and stay out of sight until the party. We don't want to ruin your entrance."

"Don't worry." I yawned. "I was up all night. I'll probably spend the day in a coma."

"Doing anything exciting?" Her hand squeezed my knee.

"Definitely," I said. "I spent all night with a new tall, dark and handsome."

"Oh?"

"Yeah." I schooled my face into neutral. "He was a real stud."

"Do I want to hear the rest of this?" my aunt deadpanned, and I broke character with a naughty laugh.

"Too bad he had four legs rather than two."

She smacked my thigh with her palm. "You're worse than your father."

"Then I'm truly reaching my full potential." I grinned at her before closing my eyes.

I listened to her soft chuckle, and she patted the area on my leg she had just whacked. My heart throbbed, in a good way, at the comfortable silence that expanded between us. At the tension that no longer existed. I sighed, floating in between blissful dreams and reality.

When the car ground to a stop, I barely acknowledged it. I hobbled out of the car with my weekend bag, eyes matted nearly shut with sleep, and climbed the porch. The house smelled the same as when I'd last been here three months ago. Like vanilla candles and lemon wood polish. And home. One that centered and grounded me. And after a circuitous path of regret, one that I was finally coming back to.

My feet were light as I ascended the wooden stairs to my old bedroom. I stopped on the landing where the window always allowed the perfect square of sunshine to bathe the floor. Closing my eyes, I soaked it in, letting it imbue me with heat. Letting my soul flicker with it.

If only I could bottle this feeling—somehow contain it— so that I could save it for chasing away the shadows. Not that many remained. I sighed as I cracked open my bedroom door.

My body stretched out to its full length on the bed amidst the squawking of my mattress. The ragged tapestry of my past had been neatly hemmed. No more loose strings. No more unanswered questions. I closed my eyes and only the quiet remained.

I drifted on a sea of thoughts and dreams pushed along by

the breeze whispering through my open window. I must have slept deeper and longer than I realized because, when my eyes fluttered open, the tree outside my window cast a long shadow over my bed. The sunlight had waned, the outside air chilling my skin.

I had been dreaming. Vividly dreaming. And I couldn't recall the images. Only how I had felt. What I still felt on awakening—a depthless longing in my chest and the smell of leather and mint in my nose. It was enough to make me gasp and push myself upright. *Will.* His name was an unwanted whisper inside my head. *Will.* Like some sort of plea to the universe.

I heard noises downstairs, the hum of excited conversation and the clank of a pot as it was placed on the stove. I pulled the band off my wrist to tie back my hair. The chaos downstairs grew in intensity. More voices. More clanking. Footsteps on the stairs. My bedroom door cracked open slowly. The smell of a freshly baked cake wafted through, and I gulped the fresh air, if only to chase away the scent of Will in my nose.

"I'm just making sure you're awake." My aunt stood in the doorway with a wooden spoon in her hand, her chin-length bob perfectly straightened and shiny.

"I am," I croaked. "Give me a minute and I'll be down to help."

"Take your time. Your dad's held up with a dog that swallowed somebody's car keys." She rolled her eyes and turned to leave.

"Should I go to the clinic and give him a hand?" I asked, almost hoping she would say yes. My hands...and my mind...itched for a distraction.

Aunt Jackie groaned in frustration then whipped around. "Quinn McClain, if you go over there, don't you dare ruin my surprise party."

My lips twisted into a grin. "Wouldn't dream of it." I hopped off the bed and began tucking my shirt into my jeans.

She watched me from the doorway, her eyes softening as she tilted her head. "I found something when I was cleaning out your dad's office the other day."

"Oh?" I bent down to tug on my boots.

"I left it on top of the dresser. For when you're ready to read it."

My eyes flashed up to meet hers, but she had already clicked the door shut behind her. Interest piqued, I reached over and slipped a slim envelope, yellowed with age, off the edge of my rickety lavender dresser. There was no name on the outside. I frowned as I removed a single sheet of paper and unfolded it. My heart leaped into my throat at the sight of my name at the top in my mother's slanting cursive.

Dear Quinnie,

I hope this is the first of many letters I will write you, and I'm sad I didn't start before now. When you are a wife and a mom, the years click by and poof! I can't believe you are about to turn six. It's quiet tonight. You're already tucked in, and your dad's working late at the clinic. You might expect that I would be lonely, but I'm grateful for the moment to exhale. To just...be.

Today you asked me what I wanted to be when I grew up. Funny girl! When I told you I wanted to be your mom, you looked at me with the cutest expression and said, "No, Mom. What you really wanted to be." It's amazing that you already know the answer to this question, darling girl. You tell me every day how you can't wait to be a real horse doctor!

What I really wanted to be? That's a good question kiddo, and I'll tell you I wanted to be a lot of things. But what I wanted to do never mattered as much as how I wanted to live. I wanted to be free to dance in the rain and smile at the sun. I wanted to be content with whatever life threw my way, but mostly Quinn, I wanted to love with my whole heart.

That's my wish for you, sweet one. Not what you will do one day but how you will do it. I see passion in you—a fire. Find your happy and hold onto it. I have a secret for you. Love doesn't find you. You find love. You curate and grow it. Like a flower garden. First, love for yourself, and then, when your garden is big enough, when it is bright enough, you can choose someone to share it with. Your dad thinks he chose me, but I just let him think he did. I knew from the moment I saw him that he would be my one. And I went out on that pier in the moonlight every night knowing he was watching me.

Oh, that's him pulling up the drive, late as usual, but at the risk of mortifying you, I want you to know that I still get butterflies every time I know he's about to walk through the door.

I'll write again soon.

Love,

Mom

I LET OUT a shaky breath and read it again. And again. The letter was dated three weeks before she died. My entire life I had tried to imagine what she would have said to me. What wisdom she had curated just for me.

As a teenager then later an adult, I had tried without success to remember anything she ever told me. And now here it was. Everything I needed to hear on one simple, beautiful page. The only page I would ever get from her. It was more than enough.

I folded the letter with painstaking care and slipped it back into its envelope, which I tucked safely into my bag.

CHAPTER THIRTY-SIX

SPRING, NOW

I hustled down the stairs, breezing through the kitchen as I ignored the open stares and surprised greetings. It appeared Aunt Jackie had kept my visit a secret from not only Dad but everyone else as well.

The downstairs was filled with friends from town and everyone we had ever employed at the clinic. I spied Calvin in the corner trading stories with a group of men, most likely involving the latest escapades of his Irish wolfhounds. Mr. Weatherby waved from where he was helping my aunt string up a happy birthday banner. Distracted, he dropped his end, and she gave him a dramatic eye roll.

I stopped to absorb the evolution of the living room since earlier today. Bright blue and gold balloons floated on iridescent strings through any space that wasn't occupied by a person. Instead of odds and ends, the entryway table held a pile of gifts wrapped in shiny paper. When my dad walked through the door later, he would simultaneously hate and love this entire ordeal.

An album lay open on the coffee table and was being perused by two ladies in scrubs who I didn't recognize. I craned my neck enough to catch a glimpse of a photograph of my dad as a young man holding twin newborn lambs.

I had resumed striding through the kitchen toward the back door when I was caught off guard by a delighted shriek. "*Mi hija!* I didn't know you were coming."

I turned to watch Sonia squeeze her round hips between the kitchen table and the wall, her arms extending in an embrace.

I twisted around long enough to blow her a kiss as she struggled to free herself from behind a chair. "I'll be back later," I said quickly, "and we'll catch up."

Her lips, painted an obnoxiously bright shade of pink that matched her blouse, split into a smile. "Looking forward to it, *mi hija*. We've missed you."

The backs of my eyes began to burn. "I've missed you too," I said and meant it. Swallowing the hefty amount of tenderness I carried for my work mom, I grabbed my field jacket off the hook in the utility room and snatched up the keys that hung next to it.

Once I made it out the back door, I counted my steps to the garage. Something to keep my mind off what I was doing. Because if I tried to rationalize this idea, I would lose what little courage I had amassed over the last hour.

The Camaro was right where I had left it. Sleek and black and too attractive not to be driven. The engine purred like a kitten when I started it. No stalling. No sputtering. Thanks to Will and his connections with the automobile shop arranging to have it fixed last year. And I couldn't help but think that maybe karma was real and good, and Will was about to get everything he said he wanted. I just hoped like hell he still wanted it. Wanted me.

I sped out of the driveway, engine growling and tires churning, and headed toward town. When I passed the clinic, Dad's dusty truck was still in the parking lot in its usual spot.

I smirked, hoping the removal of a foreign body from some pet's intestines would keep him busy until I could get back to the house. I checked the clock on the dashboard. Forty-five minutes until I was supposed to be back for the surprise party. It wasn't much time, but it was long enough to change my life.

While I half-listened to the crooning from the radio in the background, my mind raced with the possibilities of where he would be today. Writing somewhere at a café? Perusing Weatherby's bookstore or checking in with Eileen at the bar before the Saturday night crowd? When I reached the stop sign at the end of Main Street, I hesitated, my fingers drumming an erratic rhythm on the steering wheel.

To the right was Deremer vineyards. To the left was the place I hoped beyond belief that he would be. What I would always think of as our place. A place that had made me believe that the love of fairytales could be real. I sucked in a breath and spun the wheel to the left.

Anxiety clawed me as I drove, every shift of the gears jolting through my spine. Even if I didn't acknowledge it, my body knew that this had to happen today. And if it didn't, it would never happen. If I didn't take this chance, it would evaporate and like all transitional states of matter become something else somewhere else. In that moment, I wasn't rational. I wasn't logical or analytical. I was desperate.

If my life was decanted into a series of moments that directed my path, I wanted this one to be *the one*. Because I wasn't sure I would have another moment. Another flash of the liquid clarity required to forge two lives together. I remembered every moment I had ever spent with Will. And instead of reliving those over and over again, I wanted new ones.

The drive took longer than I expected on an unpaved windy road full of dips and bumps. Long enough for me to imagine exactly what I would say when I saw him. What I would do.

The words bubbled on my tongue when I spied the two-story craftsman home perched on the hill above our magical pool. With the car windows down, I could smell the lavender and sage, the mineral hint of the water below. And just like in my dream, I could smell him—the leather and fresh paper of the journals he was always carrying around. The intoxicating mint of his breath...

I parked the car under a tree, one whose pink blossoms had barely begun to bloom. Those blooms were me. I was a newly opened bud of barest pink, knowing, for the first time, that my heart was worth giving to someone else. It had always been his.

My knees trembled as I carved a path through the uncut grass toward his front door, past the shiny black Range Rover. My fingers trailed along its hood, warm from soaking in the sun all day.

When I made it up the few steps to the front porch, I was overcome by the beauty of this place. How the wind whispered the secrets of the wildflowers. How, if I strained my ears, I could hear the water below lapping against the limestone. The hills behind the house created the perfect chalice to catch the colors of a sky brimming with shades of pink and lavender.

I knocked on the door, hesitantly at first, then after some internal chiding, gave it three quick raps. I waited, anticipation seeping from my pores. I knew at any moment his face would appear. When it didn't, I waited longer, listening for his light footsteps or the creak of a door. I was debating texting him when I realized I had forgotten my phone back at the house in my bedroom.

Walking to the edge of the porch, I stuffed my hands in my back pockets and squinted into the distance. A cat slunk around the side of the house then squeezed its furry body between my legs. I bent down to scratch it on the head. It was friendly. Sweet. Exactly the kind of cat Will would own. Though I'd never considered him a cat person. The cat meowed loudly, suddenly interested by something only he could detect in the tall grass, and scampered off after it.

I sighed without looking back at the house. I knew he wasn't coming to the door. It would have been too perfect for him to be home tonight. To enact what I knew would have been a truly magical moment. An epic ending to one story and the beginning of the next. But this wasn't a novel in book club. Our story did have an ending, and maybe this was it.

If I drove the Camaro like it deserved to be driven, I could still make the party in time to yell "surprise." With a sinking sun at my back, one to match my sinking heart, I set off toward home.

I didn't bother parking the Camaro in the garage. In fact, I was lucky to get a spot at the juncture of our driveway and the drainage ditch. Trudging down the loose shale, I navigated a maze of automobiles. Trucks mostly. Texans were more likely to lose their houses before giving up their pickups. A few nifty cars took up the space between them.

One off to the side, several rows deep, gave me pause. A pair of round headlights and a sky-blue hood. Similar to the one Will had driven when we were teenagers. I shook my head and picked up my pace. The universe was cruel.

Lost in my own melancholy, I didn't realize the house was pitch black inside until I walked through the front door. I began the arduous process of slipping off my boots. "Aunt Jackie?" I called as hulking dark shapes tittered and shifted around me.

The lights flicked on, momentarily blinding me. "We thought you were David," she said.

A collective sigh followed, and Jackie's arm wrapped

around my shoulders, her short layers tickling the underside of my jaw. I blinked a few times, spots clouding my vision.

"Sorry to disappoint y'all," I grumbled, and the entire room collectively chuckled.

"She's got her accent back!" I heard someone shout and the room erupted in laughter once more.

My heart squeezed with an unexpected fondness for these people. For what I had missed since I had left. For something I'd never known I would miss. I sifted through the crowd, noting the smiles and waves, putting my grief about Will away for later. So many faces of my past and now hopefully belonging to my present. People who cared about me. And I about them.

I pulled Aunt Jackie in for a closer hug, scanning the room over her shoulder. I stopped breathing.

Near the stairwell, one dark head towered above everyone else's. His blue eyes churned like an ocean before a storm as they raked over me. His throat bobbed. It couldn't be true. But it was. A small smile played at his lips, his singular dimple making a brief appearance in his left cheek.

"Will," I whispered, so softly that there was no way he heard me over the din in the room. My emotions were splattered all over my face like paint. My lips parted as Jackie squeezed my waist then stepped away. "Hi," I said weakly.

Will's face bloomed into something that bordered on radiance. "Hi," he mouthed back.

I took one step after another, weaving between people to get closer to him.

A pair of headlights illuminated the living room window, and Sonia hissed, "He's here!"

I was immediately jostled by several sets of shoulders and elbows. Aunt Jackie's voice rose above the excited conversations. "Everyone quiet down."

When the lights were cut and the room plunged into

darkness, a solid wall of party guests still separated me from Will. I groaned too loudly, earning a chorus of shushing. My entire body vibrated with tension. So close. I was so close. But all the streamers and balloons and party hats might as well have been a mountain range.

Fingers grazed the inside of my wrist then slipped around its circumference and tugged.

I knew those fingers. I let myself be led through the crowd, my stomach tight, my legs wobbly. Like a newborn horse.

Outside, a truck engine shuddered. I instinctively reached a hand into the dark and ran it along the solid wood of the banister, recognizing the corner nook of the stairwell, next to the framed picture of me in second grade holding an orphaned kitten. That was where Will had tucked us into.

His hair grazed my cheek as he stepped to me. Body heat radiating and the cool mint of his breath on my forehead.

I tipped up my chin to whisper in his ear. "What are you doing here?"

"I was invited." A muscle twitched in his cheek.

Invited? "Aunt Jackie?" I asked.

"Yes."

I wondered why she had done that. Especially when she and my dad had gone to extremes to create distance between us. Then a realization hit me. Inviting Will was her way to make up for the past. To ensure my forgiveness. She hadn't needed to...but I wasn't complaining.

Will's body was nearly flush with mine. I inhaled and ever so slightly grazed my lips along the hollow of his neck. He shuddered, his hand moving to grip my waist. As my eyes adjusted to the dark, I could make out his perfectly geometric jawline. His lips poised for something spectacular. And whatever that was, I wanted it. I wanted him.

A car door slammed, and the collective crowd shifted,

pushing us even farther into the corner. My heart pounded a steady gallop. I put my hand inside Will's brown leather jacket. Neither of us said a word. I could feel the whisper of his minted breath. There were no thoughts in my head. Only an undeniable, monumental gravity.

I let it own me as I skated my top lip across Will's bottom one. He froze, his lips belonging to a statue, as I pressed the full weight of my mouth onto his. He wasn't moving. Wasn't kissing me back. The lights flicked on, and I skittered backward, whipping my head toward the door.

"Surprise!" rang out from all corners of the room. A burst of confetti exploded near my burning face.

"Well, I'll be damned," my dad spewed, his guffawing laughter resounding through the room. He moved through the crowd like a king, shaking hands and clapping his friends on the back.

When he spied me in the corner, incriminatingly close to Will, he paused, a look of confusion that morphed into pure joy. The crowd parted like the Red Sea as he started toward me, a noticeable limp in his gait. I winced thinking he might walk awkwardly for the rest of his life.

"Quinnie!" he boomed. "I didn't realize you were coming this weekend for my party."

"I thought you didn't know about the party, Dad."

"Oh, yeah." He rubbed his chin thoughtfully. "Don't tell your aunt, but Sonia might have given it away."

"That sounds about right." I grinned as he wrapped a protective arm around my shoulders. .

"Hey there, Will," my dad said, suddenly riveting his full attention on Will's retreating form. "Where would an author never want to live?"

The strained expression on Will's face relaxed momentarily, his lips twisting into a wry grin. "I know I've heard this one."

"Quinnie?" My dad looked at me expectantly.

"No idea." I shrugged my shoulders.

"The writer's block," he deadpanned, a mischievous twinkle growing behind his gray eyes.

Will made a sound that landed between a sigh and breathy laughter. It made my toes curl. "I'll have to remember that one," he said, shoving his hands into the pockets of his jeans. "Happy birthday, Dr. McClain. If you'll excuse me, I think I'm being beckoned."

I looked over my shoulder to see Calvin Hyde pointing to Will then to the hefty glass of bourbon in his hand. Who knew when they had become friends? Probably sometime after the puppy delivery escapade we had all endured together last fall. I supposed that was good for Will. To deepen his roots if he was planning to stay.

Imagining him building a life here, writing on his porch in the evenings while listening to the water ripple below, sent a sharp pang through my chest.

Will blended into the crowd without giving me a backward glance. His departure made teeth marks on my confidence. Once vacant, his spot near my father was filled in almost immediately by others wanting a word with the guest of honor. And it became very clear that I was just as popular.

After an hour of chitchat and reassurance that yes—it was, in fact, normal for horses to need twice yearly hoof exams—my feet shifted underneath me, the wooden floor creaking my impatience.

While I attempted to pay attention to Mrs. Stewart describing the lineage of her prize stud horse, my eyes betrayed me, flicking around the room to find Will engaged in various activities. Throwing back a drink with Calvin. Then in conversation with Sonia, who was using any excuse to reach over and touch his forearm. I smiled and shook my head. Always a flirt.

Every time I looked away, I could feel his eyes shift to me. But by the time I found him again, he was focusing his attention elsewhere. Was he avoiding me? Had I gone about this all wrong?

I couldn't really blame him for acting this way. I had told him over and over that I couldn't...wouldn't...fall for him again. That not hating him didn't mean that I wanted to be with him. How wrong I had been.

My father's frame sagged next to me.

"Come on"—I wrapped an arm around his waist—"let's hold court from the kitchen table." For once he didn't argue, either because he was that exhausted or because a two-tier monstrosity of a birthday cake awaited him there. Jackie, bent over at the waist, was happily arranging a row of candles.

As I settled Dad into a wooden-backed chair, my phone buzzed in my pocket. Not tonight, I promised myself. Everything and everyone back on the East Coast could wait.

The cake blazed with dozens of candles. Next to me, Aunt Jackie swayed, her hands clasped across her chest. "Happy birthday, David," she said fondly.

The applause started with a few staccato claps, growing in intensity to a generous thunder, only stopping when the church ladies began belting "Happy Birthday."

By the end of the song, my phone had alerted three more times, and I kept ignoring it. By the fourth time, an unease spread through my stomach. I yanked it out of my pocket to find Mitch Jenkins, grizzled face and all, scowling at me from the screen.

Stuffing a finger into my ear to stifle the chaotic chatter around me, I answered. "What's going on, Mitch?" I almost didn't want to know.

"Check your damn messages," he said and abruptly hung up.

This wasn't good. My index finger trembled as I swiped the messages icon on my phone. There were four messages, all from him, each a single line of text.

Good work this year

Guess that means I'll have to take you to Paris in June

Since I can't find anyone else to go

Ha.

The "ha" was followed by a digital Mitch doing an evil laugh. I rolled my eyes and shook my head, catching my lip between my teeth.

"Everything okay, Quinnie?" my dad asked, a furrow of worry lining his brow.

Part me reeled with equal measures of shock and elation. And sweet, sweet vindication. "Yeah." I gave a quick laugh. "I'm going to the Salon du Cheval this summer as the vet for Brookwood farms."

When I looked down at him, pure pride washed over his face, his gray eyes dancing. He clapped his hands a few times, and the room's noise immediately diminished to a lull.

"I'd like to let you all know," he announced, "that my daughter, the more famous Dr. McClain, is headed to Paris this summer as the official veterinarian for the Cheval horse show."

Most folks nodded politely, some of them offering a hearty congratulations. They had no idea what this actually meant. And not even Dad knew what it meant to me. To be accompanying some of the world's best show horses to the world's most famous horse show. And in Paris no less.

It was what I'd always dreamed of. And I was seven-eighths of the way to being the happiest I had ever been. Surrounded by my family. No more secrets between us. Finally being recognized for my skill at my job.

Yet my eyes couldn't help but search for him. Wanting him to share in my moment. To say in that smooth accent, *"I told you all your dreams would come true, Quinn."*

Maybe I was becoming greedy, but I wanted one more dream to come true tonight.

CHAPTER THIRTY-SEVEN

SPRING, NOW

I cut the largest, most obnoxious slice of cake and plopped it on a paper plate. When the scent of sweet vanilla hit my nose, I jolted with a memory. A fuzzy one but real, nonetheless. A slice of cake, thick with white frosting and tiny rainbow-colored confetti. Someone singing happy birthday off-key as I was mesmerized by the single candle flickering in the middle of it. The scent of perfume and a whisper of hair on my face as she leaned in for a peck to my cheek. Her dangling earrings had caught the chandelier light much like they were right now as I looked across our kitchen.

My aunt Jackie, beautiful, as always, with her head tilted back, flashed a giant smile. I realized in some ways I hadn't lost my mother at all. Because Jackie had always been there, making the world a stage for the production of my happiness. And mistakes or not, every decision she had made had been borne of love. Of that, I was absolutely sure.

Even now, she had arranged that Will and I would be in enough proximity to have a second chance. And maybe it was too late. Maybe Will had altogether untethered the invisible string between us. Maybe I needed to be the one to finally let go.

Suddenly, the buzz in the room felt like it was coming from my own head, and I craved the peace that only one place would bring. I shoved a fork full of cake into my mouth and began to edge through the crowd toward the door. I slipped out without anyone noticing. Everyone was elbow deep in either cake or conversation or some kind of liquor.

Like a thief in the night, I crept around the side of the house, chewing as I slipped through shadows. The soft glow of the front porch beckoned, and my giant slice of cake and I settled onto the front steps.

When I looked up, the sky was disappointingly murky. Not near clear enough to see the full moon that I knew hid behind a swath of clouds. Too bad.

Grumbling into my cake, I barely noticed the door squeak open and closed behind me.

"Do you intend to eat all of that, or might you be willing to share?"

I froze, my mouth too full to speak, a ball of cake crumb and frosting lodging in my throat. It took some effort to swallow. "I wasn't planning on it," I said without looking over my shoulder.

"Eating it all or sharing?" Will teased, descending the three steps down to the grassy yard and pausing right in front of me.

"What do you think?" I narrowed my eyes and pulled my cake into my lap.

"Any reason you're out here instead of enjoying the festivities?" He tilted his head toward the raucous party scene unfolding inside the front picture window.

"Not really," I hedged.

He bit the edge of his lip thoughtfully then said, "Congratulations...about Paris."

"Thanks."

"All your dreams are coming true." He took another step away from the porch.

Not all of them. I forced my lips up in a smile even as my heart pummeled me from the inside. "I guess they are."

"You'll love it," he said quietly. "Paris, I mean."

"I'm sure I will." Maintaining a smile was becoming a vendetta. *And I'm sure I love you too,* my heart screamed.

"Have a good night, Quinn." I swore his shoulders slumped as he turned away from me.

My heart wailed in protest. "You're leaving already?" I blurted at his backside.

He looked back at me, his eyes steady. Resolved. "I have an early flight tomorrow."

"Oh," I said, toying with the bit of cake on the end of my fork. "I was hoping you would...not leave yet."

A muscle in his jaw tightened. "Is there a reason for me to stay?"

Ba-dump...ba-dump went my heart. It might as well have shouted *tell him...tell him!*

But apparently, I was playing the anti-hero of my own story. "I'll give you some of my cake," I said weakly, proffering the plate and the rat-bitten slice atop it.

"Tempting," he said slowly, his left dimple flashing in and out. He worked his jaw like he was considering something before saying, "Walk me to my car?"

"Sure." I stood up quickly, brushing the crumbs from my lap.

"You can bring the cake along," he added dryly.

My knees cracked as I descended the steps, one hand on the rail and one balancing the plate of emotional support cake. I traipsed half a step behind Will through the grass, the dampness seeping through my sneakers into my socks. I was safe here, studying him where he couldn't see the array of expressions cycling across my face.

As I watched his long legs stride across the yard, jeans hugging his backside, it was hard to argue with my choice.

"This is me." He patted the hood of a familiar sky-blue convertible, the headlights perfectly round. Like curious eyes.

"I can't believe you still have this thing."

Will placed a protective hand on the door, a horrified expression on his face. "Felicia is not a thing."

"Felicia?" I snorted. "Your car is a girl?"

"Yes," he said,

"She's kind of old for you." Will's car had been a classic the summer he had driven us around in it.

"I prefer timeless."

We looked at each other, our eyes sharing a laugh. And the edge faded from our tension. Enough that wistfulness crept in.

"Your car always smelled like"—I paused to bite my lip—"old leather and peppermint."

"You and your smell memories." Will shook his head, eyes trolling mine.

I cocked my head in surprise. "You remember that about me?"

He nodded cautiously like he was revealing too much. "I'm fairly sure she still smells like that."

"I think I might need to check for myself." I peered into the abyss of the convertible's interior.

The camel-colored seat leather was worn, the steering wheel patinaed in places where Will's hands had lovingly driven her all these years. The floor spotless as always. No signs that I had ever been there. No indication of the words and touches that had been exchanged inside.

Will gestured to where I was pondering the backseat. "Go right ahead."

Without considering further, I sat on the folded top and swung my legs over the door, landing in the backseat, cake and all, in one uncharacteristically smooth motion.

"That was both impressive and unnecessary." Will chuckled. "She might be old, but the doors still work."

"My way was more fun," I countered, closing my eyes and leaning my head back.

I inhaled deeply. The spice of old leather. A hint of mint. Yes, it was exactly the same. An unmistakable warmth filled my chest. I heard the car door clunk open, and a body settled onto the bench seat next to me. I shut my eyes tighter, allowing myself a moment to think. To inch forward and peer over the proverbial edge of something.

Will scooted close enough that the waves of his body heat warmed my bare arms. *Touch me*, I begged silently. This would be so much easier if I knew he still wanted me. But he stayed put, refusing to grant me that last precious inch. I supposed I deserved that.

When I cracked an eye open, Will was mimicking my position in the backseat—head reclined, eyes closed. Chest rising and falling evenly.

The fingers gripping my cake plate itched to reach over and smooth the lines on his forehead. To touch the soft-as-silk hair that rested there. Instead, I fiddled with my own hair as I watched him. My blonde layers that I had let grow out for some reason. My hair hadn't been this long since we were eighteen.

The night was preternaturally quiet. Like it too waited for me. Undoubtedly, the moment had arrived. The kaleidoscope poised for turning. I sucked in a breath and clutched the cake plate resting in my lap.

"Did you get a cat?"

Will's eyes snapped open, and he shifted his gaze to my face, which I hoped was undecipherable in the dark. "Maybe," he drawled. "What makes you ask?"

"I never pictured you as a cat person but there she was on your porch, and she seemed friendly. Not wild." I cringed into the night, hoping Will realized I was trying to babble my way somewhere with this.

"Was she cream with a brown tail?"

I nodded my head enthusiastically.

"That one has been a lot less skittish than the others."

"Others?" I choked on a laugh.

Will rubbed the back of his neck. "I might have told Sonia the clinic could send a few of the homeless spayed and neutered cats my way."

My eyes nearly bugged out of my head. I started giggling like a maniac. "You did not."

"I did." He ran a nervous hand through his hair. "I have no idea how many are actually out there on my property."

I laughed harder, the hand not welded to my cake plate covering my mouth.

"They're cute," he said defensively. "And they drop the occasional dead rodent on my doorstep. It's very heart-warming."

I was crying. Will was a watercolor next to me seen through a film of tears. "You're the new Mrs. Abbott," I giggled.

"The who?"

"Mrs. Abbott." I wiped underneath my eyes with my index finger. "She used to take the cats too. She had a big farm outside of town."

"Something about this sounds familiar."

I stopped laughing, my chest constricting against the

momentum of the moment. "That's where I was headed... that day we met on the road."

"I remember." Will paused, thoughtful, lips quivering with the beginnings of a smile. "You and your truck full of yowling cats."

"You remember that too?"

"I do." His features blended with the night's shadows. His face a million questions that only had one right answer. I internally cursed the darkness that had settled around us.

"You remember a lot of things I thought you would forget."

"I didn't forget."

I quietly chuckled, an attempt to release the winding coil of tension between us. The invisible tether that had kept us connected over changing seasons and lost dreams—it had always been there. And I knew it still was.

I also knew that Will wasn't going to give anything away. Not after last time when I'd basically told him that forgiving someone did not equate to love.

"When were you at my house?" he asked.

I gripped the porcelain edge of my plate until I thought it might shatter. "Earlier today."

"What were you doing there?"

"Stopping by to say hi." My voice sounded as weak as watered-down tea.

He stared straight at me dubiously.

"What? I never said I would ignore you forever."

Will's arm slid behind me on the seat back and he moved one inch closer, enough that our thighs brushed. He bent his head, and my next inhale was imbibed with the light notes of vanilla spiced with whiskey. After a few breaths, I was the giddy version of drunk from huffing Will's exhaled breath. My stomach erupted with a kaleidoscope of butterflies.

"Not ignoring me implies civility," he said, "but driving over to my house...and kissing me in your living room...implies something else."

My thoughts spun without landing on a singular direction before I succumbed to my inevitable gravitational force, otherwise known as the man sitting beside me. I shrugged. "Then I guess I meant something else."

He dipped his chin, and I watched his lips move. Everything I wanted so close yet still out of reach. "Then are we friends now?" he asked.

"No," I whispered hoarsely, latching onto the ghost of a memory. "We are something more."

Beside me, he tensed. Not moving. Not breathing. Not daring to hope. I knew because the same look was mirrored on my face. "How much more?"

"That depends." I swallowed, my entire body blissfully shaky. "How much more do you want to be?"

"I think I've been very clear about that."

"What if I want to be...everything?"

He clenched and unclenched the hand resting atop his thigh. "What about what you said before?"

I averted my eyes, choosing to lose myself in the distant hills cloaked in darkness. "I'm sorry. At the time I thought I meant what I said." I bit the inside of my cheek, my heart rate spiking as my vulnerability unfurled like a wildflower. "I never thought I deserved the fairytale. The happy ending. I thought it would always be a dream. Something I couldn't have but something I could think about from time to time and...wonder what if."

"What changed your mind?"

"A lot of things," I mused, thinking of the handwritten letter in my mother's elegant cursive. "But mostly understanding how to give myself permission to hope...and to think that the heart I was giving away was worth having."

"It's always been worth having."

I twisted in my seat, determined to decipher whatever narrative might happen next on Will's face. "It's always been yours."

Despite the darkness, I could see him let out a slow exhale. Watched his eyes churn with possibility. His lips part with expectation.

"You have cake frosting on your face," he said matter-of-factly.

"No, I don't," I sputtered as Will smeared a thick layer of buttercream across my bottom lip with his thumb. His mouth followed. With little darts of his tongue, he erased the evidence, pulling back too soon to satisfy the yearning catching fire inside me.

"All better," he teased, licking the end of his own traitorous thumb.

"You're torturing me."

"Just a little."

"I think I like it," I moaned, crawling on top of him and snaking my arms around his neck.

He shifted underneath me so I could settle further into his lap. "I think I like this," he rasped.

Will's hands walked themselves up my thighs and gripped me. I bent down and kissed him with every flammable instinct I possessed. Every midnight fantasy come to life. Every wild and reckless part of me suddenly had an outlet.

I started with his lips, teasing until he exhaled a groan, his hands tightening on my backside. Then taking advantage of his open mouth, cautiously at first until the heady taste of vanilla and whiskey sent me over the edge. My entire being narrowed down to where our lips met.

This kiss became a masterpiece of the unrequited.

At one point, I pulled back with an abrupt thought. "Why did you run away from me tonight?"

Will relaxed into an easy smile. Dazzling even. With a heavily lidded gaze, he said, "Because I knew if I got close enough to you, I would be tempted to do this"—he ran his tongue up the groove in my neck—"and this." His hand slid under my shirt, fingertips tracing the outline of my ribs. I shivered uncontrollably.

The door to the house opened, sending a rectangular beam over the parked cars, and a lively group stepped out onto the porch. Sonia's throaty laughter carried across the yard, and I plastered myself to Will, giggling into his neck, breathing in his scent.

Keeping one hand under my shirt, he buried the other one in my hair until it rested behind my neck. My giggling died in my throat.

"You're beautiful," he whispered in my ear.

"I've missed you," I sighed, tucking my head between his shoulder and the underside of his jaw.

He tightened his grip on me until my chest was flush with his. The pounding of his heartbeat matched my own. *I remember you*, my heart sang. *And you belong with me.*

We remained there for a while, listening to the night's songs, memorizing each other's angles and curves with lazy touches.

"Never again," Will whispered at one point. "I'm never leaving you again."

"I am absolutely okay living the rest of my days in the backseat of your car."

Will laughed softly underneath me, and the shift of his weight sent an electric current up my spine. I stilled, thoughts and feeling and memories flooding me with a warm, honey-infused sensation.

"Everything okay? You're quiet." Will kissed the top of my head.

I raised my head from its spot on Will's shoulder so that I

could look at him, really look at him. And I saw what I knew I would. The boy I had loved then. And the man I loved now. I swiped my thumb over the crest of his cheekbone and palmed his face.

"What are you thinking?" he asked, eyes holding a hint of worry. A worry that I was about to completely eradicate.

"I'm thinking"—I paused to lean down for a chaste kiss on his perfect lips—"that I love you." I kissed him again as his lips parted in a blissful smile. "And...I'm also thinking I need a new best moment of my life."

Will's grin faded, his expression suddenly serious. And feral. "I can absolutely help with that."

I leaned down to whisper in his ear, my body vibrating with need, my hands going to the waistband of his jeans. "I was hoping you would say that."

For a handful of seconds, he let me explore, kissing up his neck in fervent strokes of my tongue and popping the top button of his jeans with purposeful dexterity.

When I had turned him into a ragged, heaving mess of a man, he pinned my wrists to his chest. His blue eyes nearly burned through the darkness as he said, "We can't do this in your front yard."

"Yes, we can," I whined. "No one will even notice."

A corner of his mouth lifted up in amusement. "Yes, they will. Sonia, for instance, is a bloodhound. And"—he clicked his tongue against his teeth—"I know for a fact your dad keeps a shotgun in his garage."

"I'm a grown woman," I hissed. "I can do what I want."

Will studied me, left dimple appearing as he drank me in. I couldn't imagine how I looked. Wild eyes and tousled hair. He reached up and tucked a golden strand behind my ear. "What is it you want?"

"You," I said sweetly, "and to be on the cover of *Equine Vet Monthly*."

Will barked a laugh before brushing his lips along my scarred knuckles. "At least let me take you somewhere."

I looked skyward, considering for a moment. "Take me somewhere I can see the moon, Will Deremer."

THE END
(of one thing and the beginning of another)

ABOUT THE AUTHOR

HK Jacobs is a lover of books, horses, and small Texas towns like the one where she grew up. Her debut novels, the *Alex Wilde Series*, have won several awards including the Indie-Reader Discovery Award and Georgia Independent Author of the Year. When she is not writing, she can be found doing her day job as a pediatric critical care physician. Dream big. Live wilde.